After
I'm Gone

BOOKS BY CLARE BOYD ·

CLARE BOYD

After I'm Gone

bookouture

Published by Bookouture in 2024

An imprint of Storyfire Ltd.
Carmelite House
50 Victoria Embankment
London EC4Y 0DZ

www.bookouture.com

ISBN: 978-1-83525-563-6
eBook ISBN: 978-1-83525-562-9

PROLOGUE

There isn't a word for what it feels like inside before she flips. She doesn't feel or think anything much. She just acts. There's no build-up or in-between bit. She never sees it coming. She doesn't even have time to see red. One minute she's in control, looking on at life, and the next – *boom!* – she's ejected and hitting the roof, and it's too late to put it all back inside.

She looks down at the bright yellow screwdriver in her hand. It doesn't have the power to poke at the bad side of her. Only actual people can do that, and right now, she's alone outside. The real trouble is behind the door she stares at now, where her sister is.

As she turns the screw, she thinks of words with enormous power like *fury* and *wrath*. Cartoon images of bearded gods storming immortally about on clouds come to mind. Yet she is just a very pale and earthly girl living in a normal house on an average street.

With steely focus, she twists until the metal clunks at her feet. She thinks she's being clever, feels capable of containing her rage. The practical side of her is winning. This is who she is ninety-nine per cent of the time.

For now, the feeling that has no name is asleep. For her sister, she must keep a cool head. For her sister, she breathes.

ONE

I'm not a mother, but sometimes I feel like one when I'm trying to fix my husband.

'They're going to love it,' I say, straightening the pillows behind my head. In truth, how the hell would I know? I just want him to feel good, boost his confidence. Isn't that what mothers do? Make their children feel better, lie to them, hold their hands through the tough times? Tell them it's all going to be okay.

Olly shuts his Kindle and twists onto his side, propping his head up under the heel of his hand. 'But we've been waiting almost a month.'

'No news doesn't mean bad news!'

He flops back down, draping his arm across his forehead, blowing out. 'It's going to be turned down by everyone in London, just like my others.'

'It's not. Because you're brilliant.' Another maternal lie. It'll probably be turned down by most.

He side-eyes me a fraction. 'Okay, so what if you're right and it *is* picked up by someone?'

'But that's exactly what you want!'

The worry lines on his forehead bunch up. 'You're still okay about it?'

My heart speeds up. 'Yes. I've told you I am.'

Olly's book is about a woman who doesn't want to be a mother. His main character is called Ellie. Her name sounds a bit like mine. Ellie. Emily. Ellie. Emily.

Ellie isn't me. But she is. No bones about it. And I'm okay about it. More than okay.

'I'm just quadruple-checking,' he says. His skin has a worn-out colour to it, a bit like the weathered pages of a paperback. His sandy hair is flattened on one side and sticks out like straw on the other, but his eyes are blinking an open-water blue under his thatched eyebrows. 'It's not too late for Rach to pull the plug.'

'Don't be ridiculous.' I remain stubbornly upbeat. No lie, I want the book he's toiled over for two years and had big dreams about to be published. It's like *his* baby. 'I can totally picture it as a real book on the shelves. This one's different.'

'That's nice.' He grins. 'I tell you the one person who needs to read it.'

'Who?'

'Charlotte.'

'Sister Charlotte or friend Charlotte?'

'Your sister. I know you love her and everything, but maybe she'll finally understand why we don't want kids.'

'Yeah, totally,' I say, which sounds convincing, I think.

'It needs to be said.'

'I agree.' There's a sharp ringing in my ears. It goes before I can worry about it.

Olly slips a hand behind my neck and pulls me in for a kiss. My return kiss isn't too encouraging; I prefer the idea of reading to sex tonight. He returns to his book, allowing me to re-engage with the script I'm looking over for work. It's impossible to focus now. The brilliantly funny scenes swim about. I stare at the page until Olly switches his bedside light off and mumbles a contented goodnight.

Soon afterwards, I slip the pages back into the envelope, let my hair out from its permanent inch-thick ponytail and position my blackout eye mask onto my face. The night-time sounds of Kentish Town are drowned out by the blood rushing through my head.

To help me sleep, I plan what I'll cook for the dinner party we're having tomorrow. I'll go to Chinatown to get the ingredients for a noodle stir-fry and buy that set of wooden chopsticks I've had my eye on for a while. Our flat isn't big enough for a big sit-down dinner, but we don't need much space. It's one of the many advantages of not having children. Our friends will squeeze around the kitchen bar, drink too much wine and steam up the sash windows with their hot cheeks and punchy chatter, letting it all hang out about the trials of parenting. Not a word of which they'll dare utter at home while their wide-eyed little ones or impressionable bigger ones are upstairs.

After they go, Olly and I will drink more wine and express how much we love our friends and share our mutual relief that we don't have children. Then we'll have noisy sex followed by a cigarette to prove the point.

My lids feel heavier as I picture all of that happening. Happy times, I think, as I begin to drift off.

But my earlier conversation with Olly sneaks in.

It needs to be said.

Does it, though?

I turn on my side and put the pillow over my head to smother any more thoughts about it, but immediately begin fretting about suitable presents for my niece, Hayley, who's turning fifteen next month and is very particular about what she wants. It's always a toss-up between what I'd prefer to give her versus what she has put on her list – usually clothes vouchers. Weirdly,

I never overthink what I buy for her younger sister, Mia, in the same way.

Everything I think about is an overstimulation. Guilt pokes through my concerns like fingers clawing through soil. Feeling desperate, craving sleep, I toy with the idea of shaking Olly awake and asking him about Chapter Seventeen.

A less drastic solution lies in my side table. I rummage in the drawer for the cannabis oil and pipette some drops onto my tongue.

A couple of hours later, at gone two, I'm still awake. I get up, avoiding the creaking Victorian floorboards of our bedroom, and go through to the kitchen. There's one blackened banana left in the fruit bowl. Bananas apparently help you sleep.

As I chew on it, my eyes roam over the open-plan room. The three ceramic vases on the side table create long shadows on the wall. I found them in a coffee shop near the Tube station. They were made by a local artist who'd been in and out of a shelter for domestic violence victims. The two rattan chairs were designed by the daughter of a friend, who's studying furniture design at uni. The rug was hand-loomed by a ninety-six-year-old grandmother who charmed us at a textiles fair in Ireland. We're still paying that off, but I like to sink my toes deep into it and think of that lovely woman's face.

Everything we own has a story. It's never just about the object; it's what's behind the making of it that interests me.

I was living in this very flat when I first met Olly, six years ago at a cocktail party thrown by the TV company I work for. We got drunk and walked home together and I asked him in, unaware that he was living with a well-known, annoyingly beautiful soap producer at the time. He kept her from me, then shamefacedly admitted it a few weeks in. Devastated, I told him I couldn't see him again until he was single. I buried myself in work, repainted the flat a snotty-green colour, drank too much, went running too much, cried on my sister's shoulder too much, injured my knee, and pretended I could live without him.

Two months later, he called to tell me he'd moved out of his girlfriend's place, that he loved me and couldn't live without me. Olly is an all-or-nothing kind of guy. And I'd become his all. The following year we were married at the Marylebone registry office in front of a handful of family and friends. I wore a three-quarter-length dress, which my mother didn't like.

As I sit here in the dark, I enjoy knowing he's there in bed nearby.

I chuck the peel into the compost. Experience tells me the banana won't knock me out on its own, so I go into my special drawer. I cut one of the sleeping pills the GP gave me in half with the fruit knife and put the other half back into its blister pack.

By four in the morning, it has worn off. The bad thoughts gallop in. On nights like this, I'm gripped by fear. Sometimes it's manageable; tonight I'm mentally bent double.

I get up to take the other half.

There's an orange glow from the street lamp outside. The positivity I spouted at Olly earlier about his book rings hollow. I'm a walking, talking BS dispenser. Something terrible is coming tomorrow, none of it is going to be fine, there's everything to worry about.

To go extra on the tablets, I roll a joint and smoke it out the kitchen window before climbing back into bed. Soon the combination of Big Pharma, wacky baccy and self-deceit is enough to force my eyelids shut, but spreading through me is the fuzzy sense that I'm not the person Olly thinks I am. My mind turns with whispers that warn of the unravelling of secrets I promised to keep. The book will expose me. I'm going to be found out.

TWO

Daylight brings relief for a short while. I wash my face with a flannel, trying to sponge off the smudgy memories of last night's anxieties. In the bathroom mirror, my face reflects the bad night: a dog-tired combination of stodgy-looking cheeks and deep sockets. My eyes are brown and framed thickly by stubborn eyelashes that just won't curl. I've always wished my eyes were less intense. This morning, my hair is probably too severe, plastered back into a ponytail. It can't be fixed now.

To get rid of the brain fog, I decide on a coffee and a walk.

I grab my reusable cup, my phone and bank card, a twenty-pound note and a handful of pound coins and drop them loose into my cloth bag. To avoid all work calls before my meeting, I set it to 'do not disturb', then press play on my audiobook and set off on a long loop across the Heath.

Almost two hours later, I'm back at the entrance to the park and feeling better. Marty's on the bench he often sleeps on, still wearing the jacket Olly gave him last Christmas Eve. I think back to that freezing-cold night. We had been walking home from a mulled wine and mince pie event at our local. The tree above Marty's bench had been illuminated by snakes of lights, which had strobed over his huddled form. I remember the rattle of his chest and the shock on Olly's face when I'd suggested he gift Marty his down parka – honestly, more suitable for Alaska than north London and far warmer than my threadbare velvet shrug. Olly couldn't object, and Marty had zipped it up with shivery fingers, mumbled 'Thanks, mate' and gone back to sleep. On the way home, Olly had tried not to brood over the loss, knowing as well as I did that Marty might not have survived the winter without it.

Now, Marty's hangdog eyes are rheumy and his hands are shakier than ever. I fetch two coffees from Swain's Lane and chat to him about his Jack Russell, Cher, who died last year.

He says morosely, 'You never know what's around the corner, do you?'

I shiver. 'Keep the faith, Marty. Things'll get better.' My daytime persona is all sunshine and rainbows. I nudge him while nimbly slipping the twenty-pound note into his pocket.

It's time to get back and finish off my notes for the script meeting in Soho later. I switch my mobile back on. A series of missed calls from Mum pop up, which is strange. She and Dad are in Antigua on holiday. The most contact I expected from them this week was a WhatsApp photograph of a sandy beach. Before I get a chance to call her back, she calls again. I pick up, wave goodbye to Marty and lope off.

At first, my understanding of what Mum is saying is like the poor connection on a Zoom call. There's a lag between hearing and comprehending; a delay in my ability to piece together her words. The noise of the traffic on the mini roundabout doesn't help, neither does the scorching liquid through my glass cup. I'm annoyed that I left its sleeve on Marty's bench. I ask Mum to repeat what she said. When she stutters something about an accident, there's a ripping sensation where my heart is and I put down my drink before I drop it. Only when a car swerves and presses its horn do I realise I'm in the middle of the road.

The car crunches over my cup, but I make it to the pavement on the other side. The adrenaline of the near miss is overwhelmed by the drilling, driving horror of the unacceptable thing my mother is trying to tell me. I will not hear that.

Quite unfairly, I shout at her. 'I can't understand a word you're saying!'

She begins again with fearsome clarity, and I wish she wouldn't. 'Emily, listen to me. Charlotte had an accident. She fell and sustained a head injury.' Then she pauses, and I know what's coming but I won't let it be so.

I interrupt her. 'Sister Charlotte or friend Charlotte?' It has to be that other Charlotte we sort of know. It can't be my beloved sister. Anyone but her.

'Your sister, it's your sister. *Our* Charlotte's gone.'

A roil of pain halts halfway up my chest. 'But I saw her last week.' Like this is relevant, somehow proving she's got it wrong. I won't let it sink in. Mum has got it wrong.

'They found her this morning. On the bathroom floor.' She lets out a small, muffled gasp, as though pressing it back into her mouth.

My words come out like expulsions. 'Oh no, Mum. No, no, no, please no. Tell me it's not true, Mum, please tell me it's not true,' I beg her, gulping in air. I need my mum to make it go away and tell me it's all going to be okay.

'I'm sorry, darling,' she breathes.

I let go of a sob. 'Oh my God, I can't believe this is happening,' I cry, trying to grasp what she's telling me about my big sister, the dearest person in my life. 'This can't be real.' I can't breathe. I need help. I look around me but can only see frightening blurs of an unrecognisable world.

'I'm sorry, Emily, I just...' Mum breaks off with a gurgling splutter before saying firmly, 'I can't deal with... I can't deal with this... I can't...' And then there's another gap, and I check my phone screen for lost bars, but she comes back on. 'I'm going to have to go now, darling,' she says. 'I'll pass you to your father.'

Her coldness shocks me like a smack, and I'm reminded of what she expects from me. I wipe my nose and eyes, banking the agony, trawling for strength before I fall apart. Suppression is a dark art, but I'm great friends with it. There's a painful tingling sensation in my fingers, then in my toes and up my legs. My chest is heaving, but I hold my mobile away from my mouth so that I make no sound down the phone line. Mum never told us it was all going to be okay. She taught us brutal resilience for when it wasn't.

Dad's voice, usually so strong and certain, is hoarse in my ear. 'Hi, Emily.'

'Dad.' I clutch my cloth bag, feeling the nubs of pound coins in one corner.

'It looks like it was an accident,' he confirms, repeating the information. 'We think she slipped and hit her head on that iron bath.'

'We think?'

'The police have had a crime scene up for a few hours now.'

'A *crime scene?*'

'It's just procedure.'

'Who told you all this?' I need to hear it from Charlotte herself.

He exhales heavily. 'Aiden from next door. And then a police detective called us to formally inform us of Charlotte's...' He chokes, gathers himself, goes on. 'Aiden and Robin were the ones who called the ambulance. Hayley went to them for help when she couldn't get into the bathroom.' He breaks off. After a moment, he clears his throat and continues. 'The police had to break in. It seems she'd been there on the floor all night.'

'Where are the girls now?'

'They're with Aiden and Robin still. They've given an initial account to the police, and I think a social worker is there.

I'm not sure. The house will be cordoned off for a couple more hours apparently. We're trying to book flights home now, but there isn't much availability. We'll let you know. When do you think you'll be able to make it over?'

'It'll take more than two hours,' I say, panicked, checking the time. 'I probably won't get there before two.'

'That's fine. Robin's taking care of everything until you do,' he says.

'Oh good.' I exhale shakily. There's a plan. To get there as quickly as possible. Dad can rely on me. I'm strong. Stronger than them, even. I'm the one who can sort shit out. 'Tell Mum I'm sorry for upsetting her and that I'll scoop up Hayley and Mia – she doesn't need to worry. You two just get home safely.' I hang up before he hears the catch in my voice.

In the aftermath, I shuffle around in a three-sixty circle on the pavement, blindsided, unable yet to step forward into this new reality without my big sister. A memory comes to me of her on Halloween night last year dressed as an impossibly beautiful Dracula, dancing in her kitchen to 'Thriller', wearing a red dress and fake cobwebs in her blonde hair. She was singing the lyrics at the top of her lungs, throwing all her efforts into a terrible moon dance, leaving me, Hayley and Mia in fits of giggles. I wanted to be like her, fed off her energy. How could someone so powerfully alive be gone just like that?

Then again, she always said she'd die young. And I imagined shrivelling up and withering away, starved of her light.

The trees and the buildings and the other people spin around my head. They're the ones moving, not me. I stop, dizzy, feeling my legs turn to jelly. My nieces' faces come to me. They need me. I rally myself again, tunnelling deeper inside for those reserves I know I possess, and put one foot in front of the other towards home.

There in the middle of the road are the shattered remains of my coffee cup. The liquid is still steaming in the cold air on what started as a normal Thursday morning in March. Before the car mowed it down, I'd been annoyed about leaving its rubber sleeve on Marty's bench. Like that mattered.

Somehow I make it to the flat.

My bag slips from my shoulder and onto the floor. Fifteen pound coins clatter and roll out. I drop to my knees and scrabble to pick them up. My whole body judders with the furious effort of containing the unbearable.

Olly emerges from his study. 'Everything okay?'

'I forgot to leave them on the railings,' I say. Staring at the coins forlorn in my palm. I lick away a tear that has escaped. It'll be the only one of its kind.

'Why were you going to do that?'

I mutter quite madly at him, 'The kids from Dartmouth Secondary find them after school and buy sweets with them,' like it's damn obvious, even though I've never told anyone about the random presents I leave around the place.

Chortling, he says, 'Sweets? Or drugs?'

My mouth hangs open. 'How can you laugh?' I ask incredulous. 'They're just kids, and they love it and it makes everything a little bit better.' I shake my head, stricken by his casualness.

Olly rubs his hair. 'Em, are you okay? Has something happened?'

And before I speak, I remember an exchange between me and my sister.

'You'd take them, wouldn't you?' Charlotte said. 'If something happened to me? You're the only person I trust.'

'Nothing's going to happen to you!' I told her.

'But if it did? Promise?'

'Promise,' I promised.

A lie I didn't know I was telling.

THREE

Mia tumbles into my arms at the door. Over her head, I spot a ribbon of police tape fluttering across Aiden and Robin's driveway. A remnant of the dismantled crime scene. By only ten minutes, I've missed the black ambulance taking Charlotte away in a body bag, and I'm glad I didn't have to see that.

I kiss Mia's head, leaving my face in her short, soft hair. She's wearing a green sweatshirt over the animal-print pyjamas I bought her on a shopping trip recently. I guess they haven't yet had the chance to go home and change. As I breathe in her vanilla-scented hair, I'm taken back to a disagreement with Charlotte.

'You've got to tell her she can't cut it that short. She'll listen to you,' my sister said, bossing me around as usual. She had the same determinedly stubby dark eyelashes as me, but lighter brown eyes. Then this sickeningly luscious mane of straight blonde hair, broken up by wild wavy strands, like unravelled rope. Her mouth, when closed, which wasn't often, was shaped by a set of squared-off teeth, which gave her lips a fullness, as though she were hiding something behind them. But when she smiled, her teeth and big gums were on full display, and she lit up the world around her.

'She's never really been a long-haired kind of girl,' I replied.

'Jesus. Why do you always have to take their side?' She laughed through her irritation. That's how she expressed herself, always in high spirits.

'That's what aunties are for,' I said.

'You know what, you two win, as per bloody usual. I'm going to let her cut it all off and see how she likes it. Learn the hard way.'

She sounded like Mum, but then she joked that she was going to move to the Maldives and leave me to bring them up. How I wish she were in the Maldives now so that I could call her up and say sorry for interfering and ask her to come home. And she'd tell me she wasn't serious about any of it. About leaving me with them nor about dying young. I want to see her. I can't believe that I can't. It can't be true. When is she going to walk around the corner and throw her arms around me?

As Mia sobs into my middle, I look around for Hayley. She isn't in the kitchen.

'Hi, Aiden.' I hug him, even though we're not quite on hugging terms. Charlotte was the one who taught me how to hug, as though she'd been born with the instinct. Neither of us had learned it from Mum.

Aiden's aftershave is floral, more like perfume. He and Robin are an odd couple. I've known them since Charlotte moved in. Aiden has movie-star good looks and is young enough to be Robin's son. Robin has a jolly paunch and wild grey hair, always swept back. They are – or, sorry, were – friends with Charlotte.

Their 1930s pebble-dashed semi is adjoined to Charlotte's and is identical on the outside. Both houses sit behind iron gates that open onto a permanently congested suburban cut-through, and both have sloping drives with enough room for a small car.

On the inside, Aiden and Robin's walls are velvet and the furniture is cloaked in bohemian throws in mustard and black. There are strange oversized sculptures everywhere you turn. By contrast, the twinned configuration of Charlotte's interior is as magnolia and clutter-free as a hospital corridor. The only features she couldn't afford to neutralise were the sparkly black marble worktops in the kitchen and the aubergine carpet throughout, inherited from the previous owners.

A frightening image of her lying by the roll-top bath on the first floor sears onto my eyeballs. I mentally clench everything.

Finally I spot Hayley. She's in the corner, behind the huddle of Olly, Aiden and Robin. She is tearing leaves from the spider plant. Her pallor is shocking against the red wall behind her. The translucence of her skin gives her an insubstantial quality. Her waist-length strawberry-blonde hair is divided into two ironed curtains, allowing only a small crack in the middle for her face. She too is wearing her pyjamas. They're the pink satiny striped pair that she'd saved up for over many months. Charlotte thought they were tacky. But she looks painfully beautiful and vulnerable in them now.

Aiden catches my arm and whispers in my ear, 'Go with caution. She's a little snappish.'

'Hey, sweetheart.' I bend to touch her knee, hesitate before making contact.

Her eyes lock with mine for a second of such searing love and loss, I'm almost relieved when she drops her gaze to her lap, where her fingers twist. I try to hug her, but her waif-like arms don't encircle me like they usually would, and I understand. I'm delivering a poor version of her mother's embrace. 'I'll be over there if you need me,' I say inadequately.

While Aiden makes tea, Robin confirms that the forensics, police and social worker have been and gone, and that Charlotte has been taken to the morgue at Epsom General. 'The detective said they'd be carrying out a post-mortem,' he adds.

I'm panic-stricken by all of it, but especially by this. 'A post-mortem? Is that normal?' It's loud enough to catch Hayley's attention. She looks over. Her eyes are red-rimmed, as bright as paint. She shoots to her feet and charges out.

A few eyebrows are raised. Mia lets go of me and runs after her sister. When I hear the front door slam, I hurry after them. In the hallway, I spy them through the glass panel in the front door. Hayley has waited for Mia on the driveway, has thrown a protective arm around her shoulders. They are glued to each other as they walk around the little wall to their own house. It's a private moment and I leave them to it.

'I think they're popping home,' I say to Aiden. 'That's okay, isn't it? Everyone's gone, right?'

'All gone, yes. Let them. I'm not surprised they want to get back. I mean, it's almost three now, but they were knocking on our door at six thirty this morning. They'll be exhausted.'

'Yes.' I sigh, rub my forehead. 'What were we saying before?'

Robin moves closer to me. 'To answer your question, when the death is sudden or unexpected, they carry out a post-mortem.'

'Okay. And Dad said the girls didn't see anything. That's right, isn't it?'

'I was with them when they spoke to the detective.' He steps even closer. 'Both of them were asleep when it happened. Earlier in the evening, Hayley'd had a row with Char about going out to the boyf's for a party. Char said no because it was a school night, although Hayley went out anyway – of course she did.' He makes a face at this. 'When she came in again later, about ten-ish, Char was in the bathroom showering...' He takes a gulp of tea, a dramatic pause. 'So Hayley went straight to bed in a strop without knocking or saying goodnight or anything.' He makes a different sort of face, a more sympathetic one. 'Poor kid.'

'Oh God, so the last time they spoke they were arguing.'

'Right.' Robin pulls out a business card, which he hands to me. 'The detective at the scene said to call if there was anything you wanted to talk about, but that the coroner would be in touch later this afternoon. She said your parents wanted you to be the main point of contact. Is that right?'

'Yes. Dad's not well. He needs full-time care now.' I don't know why I'm explaining this to him. 'Thanks, Robin,' I say, dazed. The small print on the card blurs.

'I've already called the school to let them know why the girls aren't in today. And my handy mate Jase is coming later to make good the panel on the bathroom door and clean up in there, just so they don't have to be reminded of... you know.'

'You're an angel. Thank you.'

'Nonsense. The other thing is, nobody's been able to get hold of David yet. Although it's been over an hour since I tried last.'

'Oh God,' I say. My head is spinning. 'David.'

David walked out on Charlotte and the girls ten years ago. Charlotte, who never had a bad word to say about anyone, had many bad words to say about David. He made another family with an Irish journalist and moved to Dublin, and is *persona non grata*.

'I'm happy to try again if it's too much for you,' Robin says.

'No, I'll do it.'

Already my hands are sticky with sweat as I scroll for his name and make my way outside. The hum of traffic drowns out the birdsong in the woodland. I turn up the volume on my phone to hear the ringtone, hoping he won't pick up.

'Is that Emily?' He laughs. 'My long-lost sister-in-law?'

'Hi, David. Look, I'm calling about Charlotte,' I say straight away.

He becomes so quiet I ask if he's still there.

'Yes, I'm here,' he breathes.

'I'm so sorry, but she's had an accident. She was found dead at home this morning.' I deliver the explanation with more clarity than my mother did.

I wait for his reaction. Considering their past together, I'm not sure how upset he'll be. It's super strange to hear him let out a series of quiet sobs. I mentally pinch all heart valves that might pump out any empathy. While waiting for him to regain control, I hold the phone away from my ear like a stroppy teen on the phone to her mum. My eye catches something at Charlotte's bedroom window next door.

Through a cloud of vape smoke, a red-headed boy appears, and then ducks back inside, slamming the double-glazing.

I hear David's voice. 'Emily? Are you there?' he splutters.

'Sorry, yes.'

'She just slipped?'

'They think she slipped and hit her head.'

'Was she drunk?'

Rage blooms inside me, but I catch it in the centre of my chest. 'No, she was not,' I reply through clenched teeth, although I'm not certain this is the truth.

Tearfully, he repeats, 'Sorry, sorry,' before muttering, 'Mia and Hayley must be a mess. I can't even imagine.'

'She was everything to them, so, you know...' But he doesn't know, he would barely recognise his flesh-and-blood daughters in the street. His contact with them has dwindled over the years to texts and awkward FaceTiming. They haven't seen each other in person for three years. 'When can you get here?' I say.

He hesitates, then says in more measured tones, 'Beth is literally about to drop with our third. It's just... If I miss the birth...'

My heart becomes a stone. 'Your daughters have lost their mum,' I remind him.

'As soon as Beth's had the baby, I'll fly straight over. It'll only be a couple of days, I'm guessing. Hours maybe. Is there any way you can take them for me until then?'

'Of course. That goes without saying.'

My eyes dart to the window again. Hayley's face peers out through the pane. Our eyes meet. She gives me a sad little wave. More than anyone else's grief, hers pierces my heart most cruelly.

FOUR

'It's routine, apparently,' I say to Olly.

'A social worker? Even though you're their aunt?' He removes a pile of bric-a-brac and clothes from a small white bureau in the corner of the spare room, where we'll sleep tonight. The vibrations of a lorry passing by buzz in the soles of my feet. Only yesterday, my sister might have been standing here and felt this same sensation.

'Yup, she's coming to meet us tomorrow. They'll also run checks on me on their system.' I speak while I'm typing into my iCalendar: *Mel – social worker*, scrolling to 11 a.m., Friday 15 March, adding a reminder thirty minutes before. Like I'll need reminding.

'Tomorrow?'

'I think it's just to make sure I don't have three heads and a machete in my back pocket. Then, hey presto, they're ours until David gets here.'

'They have to talk to the girls too?'

'I think so. Not sure how Hayley's going to feel about that.' I hope I'm speaking loudly enough for Olly to hear me, but my voice sounds quiet inside my head, as though I have two selves. One that can function and one that is going under.

'Who was that red-headed kid who was here before?' He places his laptop on the cleared surface and sits down on the kitchen chair we brought up.

'I was hoping you knew.'

'I caught him sloping out of Hayley's room.'

'And I saw him vaping out of Charlotte's window earlier.'

'Boyfriend, maybe?' He opens his laptop and makes a big show of typing. I wonder what the hell he is doing. 'This'll work as a desk.' He pauses, and glances nervously up at me. 'For when I'm working on my manuscript for my editor.'

'What? You've heard back?'

'Yes, Rachel called about an hour ago.' He bites his lip. 'Hodgson Press want to publish it. I didn't know whether to tell you.'

'Oh Olly!' I press my fingers to my mouth, amazed that I'm able to appreciate this good news in the middle of this other horror. 'That is absolutely incredible. I can't believe it.'

'They're just a small outfit, but the advance is decent, and they're keen to turn it around super quickly.'

We lock gazes, clutch each other, our eyes reddening. We're both choking with conflicting emotions. It's a ghastly setting for a dream come true. Ten years of striving for it, six of which I've been around for. Having witnessed each soul-crushing rejection, I've often questioned whether it was worth it, and longed for him to get a proper job. His journalism gigs were sporadic, which meant I was often the only steady source of income. But I never gave up on him, and he never gave up, and here we are. I'm brimming with pride. The issues of Chapter Seventeen fall by the wayside.

'We'll find a lamp from one of the other rooms,' I suggest, opening the metal blinds with a clash and a clank. No light comes in, and I remember it is evening already. 'Now that you're a *real* writer.'

'Steady on,' he says, smiling shyly, wiping away his tears.

I picture his study at home, busy with thought, lying in wait for its newly successful author. The dusty columns of books would be stacked against the green wallpaper, one on top of another like an insulating wall. His empty chair would be facing out onto a peaceful row of London gardens. The neighbours' black cat might be on his windowsill, waiting for her saucer of milk.

My phone rings again, bringing us back to reality. I rally myself for another conversation about Charlotte. Only minutes after speaking to the social worker, I got a call from a coroner's officer, who offered her condolences and asked probing questions about Charlotte. She then apologised for the delay to the post-mortem, which won't be carried out until next Tuesday due to a backlog. A backlog of dead bodies. Nice.

ST MATTHEW'S flashes up on the screen.

'It's the school again.' I sigh and pick up, wondering why they're still there at 6.11 on a Thursday evening.

'Hello?'

'Hello, Mrs Taylor, this is Mr Hanrahan, Hayley's form tutor. I wanted to personally offer my condolences.' Here we go again. Already I'm weary of platitudes. But then the teacher pauses and says something else in a less mechanical way. 'Charlotte lit up the place when she came in.'

'She was good at that,' I say, gulping away tears, understanding suddenly why the stock phrases are useful.

'I dragged her into school a lot, I'm afraid,' he continues. 'Back when Hayley was struggling. But things have been a lot better recently and we saw less of her around here, which was great on the one hand. But it wasn't so great *not* seeing her, if you know what I mean. Not that it's going to be at all great for Hayley now either, but you know... Wow, what am I even saying? I'm probably not helping. Nor am I sounding very professional.'

He sounds young and kind and charmingly overfamiliar.

'Please, Mr Hanrahan, honestly, it's lovely to hear something real.'

His exhale is ragged. 'How are they? Hayley and Mia?'

'As you'd expect – heartbroken.'

'I'm here to support them in any way I can. My phone will be on, day and night.'

I suck in air and hold my breath, blinking up at the ceiling before I can speak. 'Thank you, Mr Hanra—'

He butts in. 'Please, call me Jamie.'

'I really appreciate that, Jamie.'

After I've hung up, Olly says, 'Who's Jamie?'

'Hayley's form tutor. I remember that Charlotte liked him. He said something about Hayley struggling.'

'I never knew that.'

'Me neither.' A wave of exhaustion hits me. I plonk myself down on the bed. I don't have a brain cell left to contemplate the reasons why Charlotte kept that from me.

I'm transported to a moment in our childhood when I discovered her secret stash of Saturday sweets under a pile of teddies on her bedroom windowsill. Over many months, she'd been sneakily stockpiling them. I was so cross with her for not telling me, but she just laughed her head off. She shared the whole lot with me after lights out and I was sick. The smell of pear drops still turns my stomach.

Olly sits next to me and wraps an arm around me. 'I'm so sorry all this is happening to you.'

'Me too,' I say. 'Thank you for being here.'

He raises his wild blond brows in surprise. 'Where else would I be?' Tears fill his eyes. I kiss away an escapee, holding in my own like a true champ.

'You do think David's going to come through for them, don't you?' I say.

'Absolutely, definitely.'

'He'll have to.' Shaking any doubts away, I return to a happy topic to put a smile back on our faces. 'Seriously, Olly, well done on the book. I'm so proud of you.'

'Oh, that,' he says, as though it was nothing. For now, it has to be, I guess. But I nurse the news quietly. Unease creeps in. Chapter Seventeen will be waiting there for me when we return home to our normal life.

I contemplate my own job and recall the meeting I missed today. I hope the writer will understand. A modern construction of white lilies arrived on Charlotte's doorstep half an hour ago. They were from my boss, Jaylani, who owns the TV company I work for. Typically, she is the first to send flowers, terrifyingly efficient as always. Either she paid the florist triple or she threatened to smash their shopfront to get them here this quickly. Jaylani has tyrannical tendencies. But when she's on your side, you're safe. And I am. She told me I could take as much paid leave as I needed.

'Do you think I should go check on the girls again?'

I tucked them both under a blanket in front of the telly, searched up an old black and white film and handed them a mug of hot Ribena each.

He checks his watch. 'You only went in ten minutes ago.'

'I've got to tell them about their dad.'

'Maybe leave it until we call them for tea?'

Then I remember something. 'Oh my God, the dinner party!' I imagine our friends pressing our buzzer in a couple of hours.

'Don't worry, when Rach called about the book, I told her what had happened and asked her to tell everyone for us.'

Now I know why there were missed calls from two friends earlier. I'm incapable of talking to them today. They'll be all about expressing their real feelings, but even on a good day I don't like to go too near those. 'What are we going to make for the girls? Have you checked in the fridge?'

'Let's go see.'

He fumbles for my hand as we pass the bathroom where Charlotte was found this morning, and I crush his fingers. My heart races. The door panel has been replaced already by Robin's kind friend, but it's a different shade of white. I never want to go in. None of us have used it today, preferring to use the en suite in the spare room.

Downstairs in the kitchen, the first thing I spot is the large Mexican peppermill adorned by figures of women with swirls in their bellies. I bought it for Charlotte last Christmas. It stops me in my tracks. I tug my ponytail, transforming nearby tears into a pleasant scalp ache, then peel the cellophane off Jaylani's flowers. Arranging them in a vase helps me to feel closer to Jaylani somehow, and therefore to work and to the life that only yesterday was ordered and arranged and manageable, and as perfectly formed as this bouquet.

But the peppermill is in the corner of my eye as I prepare supper. After I've laid the table and called everyone down, I grab it and hurriedly try to find a place to hide it. As I shove it on its side under some pots and pans, though, Mia catches me red-handed.

'What are you doing with that?' she demands.

FIVE

'It's too tall to fit into any of the cupboards!' I manage to laugh, holding a smile with all my might, channelling my mother's infamous stoicism. 'I can't believe she kept it out.'

It was a tacky gift I'd brought Charlotte from Mexico. She hated it. The random pretty stuff that I liked was a long-running joke between us. Charlotte went for the expensive, ergonomic aesthetics: fitted appliances, drawers that closed themselves and sleek wine fridges. I expected her to laugh at it, throw it out, but she traced her fingers over the patterns, informing me that the women were fertility symbols. 'I thought they were just dancers,' I said, wishing I'd never bought it.

'She used it as a pretend microphone when she danced,' Mia says, taking it from me, turning on the multicoloured flashing LEDs. For a second, she wiggles her hips and looks like her mum, brings her to life. It's the gummy smile and short teeth. The smile that could melt the hardest of hearts. But it's only a moment of her old self, before the grief falls like a curtain over her features and her tears spill.

'What the hell?' Hayley sneers, slouching in. Olly follows close behind her.

'Mia was just showing me your mum's kitchen disco, that's all,' I say, patting Mia's face dry with a tea towel, adding sadly, 'She was such a good dancer, right?'

Mia's urge to cling to fun times is understandable. It keeps her mum alive in our minds, allows a brief respite from the wrenching foreverness of her death, which hasn't yet had time to sink in.

The lights strobe over the girls' faces, colouring them with a lurid, garish glaze. I switch them off. Mia sits down, subdued again. The rest of us follow suit and settle around the circular white table.

'You looked just like her then, sweetheart.' Olly kisses Mia on the head and crushes her into a side hug. He has always been more demonstrative than I am, and I'm so grateful for it now, for Mia's sake.

We sit in miserable silence while we eat. The scraping of knives on china is like fingernails down a blackboard. Day one of life without her has felt like a hundred years. Total collapse beckons. To say something, to say *any*thing, I ask the girls practical questions, avoiding the only one I can't bear the answer to: *How are you?* Such a high-stakes question.

'Who was your friend, Hayley?' I'm referring to the redheaded boy.

'Ayton,' she murmurs. Her fingers move like lightning over her phone screen.

'That was kind of him to come over,' Olly says.

'He's her *boy*friend.' Mia forks her baked beans. 'And he drinks beer.'

'Shut up, Mia,' Hayley snaps.

'You shut up!' Mia retorts.

'Don't fight, girls.' I reach out for both their hands. Hayley's is clammy, and I'm livid with the world for doing this to her and Mia. She snatches it back and returns to her phone.

As we pick at our food, I think of ways to tackle the subject of the social worker's visit tomorrow. I don't want to freak them out, so I decide to build up to that one.

'Girls, just to let you know that Granny and Grampy have finally found a flight from Antigua. They'll be home by Saturday, which is only the day after tomorrow.'

Mia says weakly, 'That's good. I love them so much.'

Hayley doesn't react.

'And I spoke to your dad.'

This time Hayley engages. 'You mean the sperm donor?' she retorts.

Mia puts her fork down and begins tugging at a tuft of hair at the back of her head and sucking her thumb. A habit she gave up years ago.

'Don't say that,' I say.

Hayley's eyes flash red and her skin becomes almost see-through. 'It's what he basically is.'

Olly and I exchange a look. Neither of us can deny he was absent. 'It was complicated between him and your mum,' Olly says, 'but he loves you very much.'

'And as soon as Beth's had her baby, he'll be flying over,' I add.

'*What?*'

'Isn't that good?'

'But *why?*'

'Because he's your dad.'

She bursts out with 'If you make me go live with him in that house with those brats, I'll kill myself!'

My mouth drops open. 'Nobody's going to force you to do anything you don't want to do.'

'*He won't want us anyway!*' Hayley yells. Her outburst rattles me. I'm not used to shouting of any kind. I do irritable and sharp excellently, but I don't shout much, have sometimes been curious about what my voice would sound like if I yelled at the top of my lungs. I can never let anything out just in case *everything* comes out.

'Of course he'll want you,' Olly says, saving me again.

'What if he doesn't? Who'll take us then? You?' She snorts through her fury. Her veins are blue through the skin stretched over her temples.

My hands begin to shake. The life I love flashes before me. Past conversations that Olly and I have shared crackle in the air between us. I can't look at him, part my lips a few times, trying to word a reply to the girls. 'I will be here for you for as long as you need me,' I say eventually.

Olly says more cautiously, 'We'll talk about it when your dad gets here and work out the best plan.'

'The best plan for *us* or for *you*?' Hayley screeches, glaring at Olly and then me.

'For you,' I say.

'That's fucking *bullshit!*'

I gulp back my shock. Mia slides onto Olly's knee and buries her head in his neck. Wordlessly I get up to clear my plate and reach for hers, but Hayley tugs it out of my hand and throws it onto the stone floor at my feet. It cracks into three large pieces. Both of us stare at it for a second.

'Let's clean this up,' I say, bending towards the fragments.

But she remains where she is and hisses down at me, 'Mum always said you were too much of a control freak to have kids.'

I gape up at her, dumbstruck.

Terror crosses her expression before she leaps up and flees upstairs. Mia follows.

Olly comes over to help me clean up. 'Are you okay?' he whispers.

'She's just lashing out,' I say, avoiding his helpless eyes.

'Em.' He reaches for me. I whip my hand away from his sympathy.

'It's fine,' I snap under my breath.

SIX

'Okay, I give up,' I say through a crack in Hayley's bedroom door. Her chest of drawers is pushed up against the door and has been like that since the plate incident last night. I check my phone. The iCalendar alert message *Mel – social worker* is still on my home screen. But Mel is already here, and I've tried every trick in the book to persuade Hayley out of bed.

I trudge downstairs without her. The word *FAILURE* should be stamped on my forehead.

In the kitchen, Olly has his arm slung around Mia's shoulders and is chatting in his easy way to Mel. He likes new people, enjoys their stories, loves a nugget of insight he can weave into one of his characters' journeys. Mia has one half of her face smooshed into his sweater. Her visible eye is barely blinking, hypervigilant.

I rearrange my features into what I imagine is a responsible, nice person's face – I *am* a responsible, nice person! – and stand next to Olly, needing that proximity. 'I'm so sorry, Hayley's got a bit of a migraine.' I stick my hands into my jean pockets to hide the shakes. People in authority have always scared me.

They are trained to look beneath the surface, to detect lies, to root out hidden truths. And I have many of those.

Olly shoots me a sideways glance.

'I'm sorry to hear that,' Mel says. 'Does she get them a lot?' She takes out a pen and notepad. I note that she's young. There's fake-tan residue around her blonde hairline and a bracelet stack on one wrist resembling Hayley's.

'Uh-huh, yup,' I say, sounding grave, although I wouldn't know for sure.

'She was very close to Charlotte,' Olly says.

Mel nods slowly as she jots something down. 'If she gets them too often, it's worth booking an appointment with the GP. Do you know which health centre they're registered with?'

'I do. Here.' I search for the contact details on my phone, stored the last time we babysat for Charlotte, when she went to Berlin for the weekend with Robin and Aiden. I read out the address.

Mel turns her attention to Mia. 'Thank you very much for sharing your feelings with me earlier, Mia,' she says, and I'm annoyed about missing their chat.

'You're welcome,' Mia squeaks.

'You've been awesome,' Mel says. 'You can scoot off if you want. I might come up in a bit and see if your sister is feeling well enough for a chat.' Now I'm doubly alarmed, wondering how it will look to Mel when she finds that Hayley has barricaded herself in.

As we watch Mia go, she says, 'Poor love,' before sipping her milky tea. 'And how are you both coping?'

Olly shrugs. 'Pretty awful. Emily's been amazing, though. So strong. Too strong, almost.'

Irritation bubbles up. 'Everyone probably expects me to be falling about the place in floods of tears. I'm almost embarrassed when people see me acting normally.'

'Oh no.' Mel is matter-of-fact. 'I've seen grief every which way.'

She's not old enough to have seen anything in any way, I think unfairly, but I accept her job must be a learning curve steep enough to cancel out the age difference between us. And I must keep her on side. 'It catches me at weird times,' I concede. 'Mostly I'm focused on the girls.'

She flicks back a few pages in her notepad. 'You're caring for them until their dad gets here, is that right?'

'Yes. For as long as they need us.'

'And their grandparents?'

'We never got to know David's parents, but mine are around, yes.'

'That's debatable,' Olly mumbles, always as open as a bloody book.

I frown at him, and explain to Mel, 'They've been away. But they live in Shropshire, and Dad's in a wheelchair and can't do stairs, so staying here is a nightmare because he has to sleep on a fold-out bed in the telly room. And Mum can't leave him on his own at theirs for more than a couple of hours now.' All these facts are true, but they're also excuses. My parents were unavailable long before Dad's disability.

'Do you have anyone close by who could offer support if you need it?'

The answer to that one is easy. 'Aunt Jane. *My* aunt,' I clarify. 'She lives about half an hour away.' My eyes burn with love for my aunt when I think of the frozen cottage pie that magically appeared on the doorstep yesterday. No doubt Jane's handiwork; always pragmatic and unshowy.

When Charlotte and I were young, our staycations with Aunt Jane at her house beat all the fancier holidays our parents took us on. She showed us how to do origami; got us out of bed for dawn walks in the woods to listen to the nightingales; let us plop three squares of chocolate in her bubbling chilli rather than the recipe's suggestion of one.

'Great,' Mel says, smiling at me and then Olly. 'Do you have your own children?'

'No, thankfully we don't.'

'Thankfully?' she asks, raising her eyebrows.

I blush. 'I meant I'm thankful we're in the position to drop everything to be here for my nieces.'

She nods, holding my gaze. Is she pigeonholing me as the childless aunt who likes cats more than children? Who is clueless about child-rearing and unable to care for two adolescents for a few days?

'And their father is expected when?'

'We're not sure exactly. His wife is due to have a baby any minute now. But he'll definitely be here in the next week or so.'

'Okay.' She scribbles that down too. 'No date, then.'

'We're all right though, we're flexible,' I insist.

'What do you both do?' She asks this perkily, as though she's interested in us rather than just evaluating us.

'I'm a writer,' Olly says proudly.

'Oh wow! I love reading. Are you famous?' She grins.

'Noooo,' he demurs, as though he is famous but isn't saying. 'My first book'll be coming out early next year.'

'I'll look out for it.' She jots something down in her notepad that I assume isn't about his book, then asks a few more logistical questions about my work and about the girls' schooling. Everything I say in reply sounds inadequate.

Finally she says, 'Okay, good. Any questions for me?'

I do have questions, about post-mortems and how normal they are, and whether we should expect an investigation, but I say, 'I don't think so,' paranoid that the mere mention of it would raise suspicion.

'Would it be okay if I pop upstairs and knock on Hayley's door now?'

'Um, I'm not sure.' I hesitate, panicking. 'She wasn't feeling well at all.'

But Mel insists. 'Ideally, I'd like to meet her today if I could.'

'Oh. Sure. Of course.' I tug up the sleeves of my sweater, hot suddenly.

Olly brushes a hand down my back and says, 'I'll hide away here.'

And I wish that I could do the same. I picture Hayley's wrung-out face and her paper-thin skin and the fire in her eyes, and I'm afraid that Mel will hold me responsible for the damage.

SEVEN

Mel follows me up the stairs with silent footsteps. I look over my shoulder to check she's still there. She has stopped to peer at a collage of family mug shots in a clip frame on the wall.

'Is this your family?' she asks. I'm guessing her interest is not casual.

'Charlotte made that in her teens,' I explain, quite loudly, hoping Hayley will hear us and move the chest of drawers away from her door. 'She called it the Hall of Fame because we all look so awful in it. We were never able to look at it without cracking up.' A chuckle – historic, I guess – gets stuck in my gullet. Without Charlotte, I wonder if I'll ever laugh at it again.

'These are your parents?' Mel asks, pointing at them.

'They look like axe murderers there, but I promise they're very normal!' *Axe murderers?* Why the hell did I say that?

Mum and Dad are in bright paper hats at a table festooned with Christmas decorations, yet their smiles are comically joyless. I took the photograph myself with the Kodak wind-on I'd been given as my main present that year. The thought of that camera pressed to my face gives me a shiver, remembering what else it captured.

'It's this one.' I tap on Hayley's door with one knuckle, mentally crossing my fingers. 'Hayley? Mel would love to meet you, if you're feeling any better. Can we come in?' I turn the handle to peek inside, but the door hits the furniture again. 'Oh,' I say, wondering if Mel has seen all this before too.

'Let me have a go.' But she doesn't try to open it. Instead, she kneels, rests her ear to the door and speaks through it. 'Hi, Hayley, this is Mel. I understand totally why you'd be anxious about meeting me, but I'm here to check you're safe and well, that's all, nothing scary or anything.' She pauses. 'Would you consider maybe coming out to say a quick hi?'

She twists her bracelets while we wait, but there's no response from Hayley. After a minute or two, she tears a sheet from her notepad, writes her name in bubbly letters next to a telephone number, folds it into quarters and slips it under the door. 'I've written down my number, Hayley. So please do give me a call or drop me a text if you want, even if you think it's a silly or small concern. Okay?'

I dig my toes into the carpet. It's unyielding, nylon, the sort of dark purple that hides a multitude of sins. Still nothing from Hayley.

'Hmm. Sorry about this,' I say under my breath. 'She's a lovely, lovely girl, just so strong-willed, more so than Mia, I suppose. I'm sure she'll be fine later. She goes up and down, whereas Mia's more consistently sad...'

As I ramble on, probably sounding too defensive of Hayley's challenging behaviour, a folded note shoots out from under the door. It is addressed to Mel, who reads it before handing it to me with a small smile.

Dear Mel,

Sorry I'm feeling too poorly to talk to you. Auntie Emily and Uncle Olly are my favourite people in all the world (who are

*still alive). I would like them to care for me and my sister. We
don't need to go in a foster home, and if we did, we'd run away
back to them.*

Hayley

Tears clog my throat. I don't dare speak.

'Okay,' Mel says. 'It's fine, we'll leave it for now. I'll pop by
again next week.'

On the way downstairs, she hugs her notebook to her chest
like a schoolgirl protecting her secret diary, turning her head at
the collage again as we pass.

Olly jumps up from the kitchen stool when we come in.
'How was she?'

'She wouldn't come out, but she put this under the door.' I
hand him the note.

He reads it and croaks, 'That's made me well up.'

I nod, reach for his hand and grip it, swallowing down tears.

'I'll leave this here for you,' Mel says, breaking the spell
between us, placing a pack on the worktop. 'There are leaflets in
there explaining a bit about the law. And some information
about other services you might want to access. There's also a
complaints form.' She slips her notepad into her bag. 'You sure
you don't have any questions?' she adds.

The pack reminds me of the questions I have about the
post-mortem. My heart thuds as I say, 'Er, I do sort of have one.'

'Go ahead.'

'I spoke to a coroner's officer on the phone yesterday. He
said he'd be in touch on Tuesday with the results of the post-
mortem, but...' I glance at Olly, who crosses his arms. 'I wanted
to ask how likely a police investigation is in these situations.'

'Honestly, try not to worry too much. It's standard procedure for the coroner to request a post-mortem when there's
been an accident or injury.'

'If there *was* an investigation, it would be so awful for the girls. I mean, Hayley won't even talk to *you*, let alone the police.'

She tilts her head. 'It's only a very small possibility that they'll open one. And if they did, you'd be with your nieces throughout the interview process.'

'God. Let's hope they don't have to be put through that then, if just now's anything to go by...'

'She'll be fine, I'm sure.' Mel loops her bag across her body and takes out her car keys. 'Right. I'd better get on.'

As I follow her out, I wish she'd give me a hint of how we've done. I know it's my last chance to ask. 'D'you expect you'll... I mean... I know Hayley wouldn't come out of her room and everything, but... you know... we love them very much... and I was wondering when... I mean... Do you think we're all right?'

Mel smiles. 'From what I've seen today, I'll be recommending to my manager that this is the right place for Hayley and Mia to be. But if anything changes, I'll let you know right away. Do you want to put my number in your phone? Then you can call me if you have any concerns or questions.'

'Oh, that's great, thank you. That's really great.' Mel is officially my new best friend. I type in her number, say an eager goodbye and close the door with a massive exhale.

'Phew,' I say to Olly back in the kitchen.

'I think I saw her write down "one head and no machetes",' Olly jokes.

I chuckle, and it feels good that I still can. 'I'd better go reassure the girls. Mia was worried Mel would take them into care if she didn't like us.' I snort, as though that wasn't my own back-of-mind concern.

Then I think of Hayley and fear she might not let me in.

I knock on Mia's door first.

EIGHT

Mia is lying on top of her duvet and reading through cupcake recipes in a Mary Berry cookbook.

'Just wanted to let you know that Mel seemed happy for us to care for you until your dad gets here,' I tell her.

'Oh good! Phewie!' she cries. 'When do you think Dad'll be here?'

'Soon.'

'I hope he's not too sad.'

'Don't worry about your dad, sweetheart.' I swallow down the lump in my throat and pat the back of her hand.

'I'm going to show this one to Uncle Olly.' She points at a recipe, jumps off the bed and shoots past me.

I step out of her room and gather myself; breathe in and out as I stare at Hayley's closed bedroom door.

When I try it, it swings wide open. I'm amazed. I go in, full of hope.

'Hayley,' I whisper to the mound of duvet, daring to bend down and kiss her head. 'That was a lovely note.'

She doesn't stir. I shake her shoulder. Her squashy, sleepy face reminds me of when she was a toddler. I used to take her out in the pram sometimes to give Charlotte a breather. She'd nod off clutching the illegal chocolate croissant I'd buy her from Pret, then wake up red-cheeked and frowny and tearful, and totally edible. The sweetness hasn't left her face.

'I just wanted to say that Uncle Olly and I have been given the stamp of approval.' I open the curtains. 'Come on, time to get some clothes on and come down. I'll make brekky.'

'No.'

Downstairs, I can hear Olly and Mia mumbling in the kitchen.

'Come on, sweetheart. It's almost midday.'

A claw-like hand elongated by false nails emerges to pull the duvet away. Her eyes shoot open. 'Don't lie to me,' she says hotly. Her head lifts from the pillow.

'I'm not!'

She sits up. 'I heard you and her talking.' She's breathing fast and heavily, snapping the elastic of the bra she slept in. Her collarbone protrudes. At roughly five foot seven, she's a good height, but her body is straight up and down, thin and childlike.

'What did you hear?' I'm racking my brains.

She bunches the duvet around her knees, her face distorting. 'She said that we'd have to do an interview with the police!'

I'm taken aback. 'Oh no, you've got the wrong end of the stick. They'll only do that if they open an investigation. And even if they do, which is really, really unlikely, you're not suspects or anything. It's not like on TV.' I poke her teasingly.

Her eyes stretch wide as she sucks in her breath. 'Oh my God, oh my God, I'm going to have a panic attack.'

'Shh, shh, Hayley, don't be silly.' I close the window, worrying that her voice might carry. 'I'm so sorry, I didn't explain that properly before. You mustn't worry. Everyone's expecting the coroner to confirm it was an accident. There's really nothing to be concerned about,' I say, reaching out to her. She recoils, shuffles back against the wall.

'But what if they don't?'

'Why wouldn't they?' I ask, feeling a prickle of fear run down my back.

'I don't know! Why would I know?' she yells, scrambling past me and out of bed. She circles the room, patting her chest, pulling at the neck of her pyjama top. 'Oh my God. I can't cope. Oh my God.' She begins to cry and moan.

'Okay, okay, hush now, calm down. Keep it together. Come on, it's going to be okay.'

Her breathing becomes more erratic. She flaps her hands, puffs out her cheeks, the tears rolling. Time is ticking forward. I become paralysed watching her, unable to think what to do or how to stop it.

'You have to help me, oh my God, oh my God,' she begs desperately, beginning to hyperventilate, rapidly losing control, spiralling.

'Count to ten, Hayley,' I say.

She gets to two, then curls up on the floor and starts to writhe and flail about, knocking things, kicking at the skirting. I stand back to avoid being struck. She's fully grown, but she's having a tantrum like a toddler. I'm out of my depth, feeling myself shutting down. Before now, I've enjoyed only cuddles and smiles from her. She needs Charlotte. She'll never again have her, and I'm a useless stand-in.

'I'll go get you some water,' I say, charging next door into the bathroom. Seeing where Charlotte slipped, I'm brought up short, rooted to the spot for a second. I clench my back teeth, pull myself together for Hayley.

When I return with the glass, she is still lying on the floor, gasping and clamping her hand over her mouth to press away a series of high-pitched yelps, 'Oh my God, oh my God. I'm going to die. Help me, help me, please. I can't breathe!' Her eyes are glassy, inscrutable. It's like she's possessed by something other, gone elsewhere.

'Here you go, drink this.' I sound too firm. I put the water down near her, but she slaps it away and it spills. Her hysteria is like a sinkhole, sucking me in. I need to get away.

'I'll leave you to get ready,' I say.

She grabs my ankle and rasps through gritted teeth, 'Don't leave me! You can't leave me!' Her panting and crying become louder. She's frightening me, almost repelling me. The lack of containment is alien and inappropriate for her age. It crosses my mind that there's something deeply wrong if a child of almost fifteen can have a meltdown like this. I try to leave again, but she stands up and clings to me, digging her fingers into my arms, shaking me. 'Please, Auntie Emily, please promise me I don't have to do that interview. I can't do it! I can't ever do that!'

I bite down on the side of my mouth, think hard about what is going on here.

'Look, Hayley,' I urge, holding her shoulders forcefully, bringing my face right up to hers. 'I get it, I really do. More than you'll ever know. But you've got to pull yourself together, okay? Come on, sweetheart, get your clothes on and come downstairs.' Then I regret being too intense and balance it with 'Or Uncle Olly will start worrying about you. And you know what he's like when he gets going. He'll be whizzing you down to A & E!'

Everyone knows that Olly catastrophises. It's the family joke. Usually it's about illness – a slight temperature equals meningitis, a bruise points to leukaemia, a mosquito bite will lead to sepsis. Hayley's features slacken, and she nods. It seems to have done the trick.

'Good.' I squeeze her hand. 'Good girl,' I say again.

On the way downstairs, my teeth begin chattering. I rub at the red marks left by Hayley's fingernails, trying to wipe them off. I'm genuinely afraid that the police might decide to open an investigation.

NINE

I can't let go of the panic I saw in Hayley's eyes. It forms itself into a little ball of confusion and fear in my stomach. I'm downstairs, cleaning up a splash of tea that the social worker spilt on the kitchen table earlier, when Olly ambles in.

'Did you hear all that?' I ask.

'What?' He sits down and then quickly gets up again, takes his phone out of his back pocket, checks the screen.

'Hayley just went nuts. She overheard us talking to Mel,' I whisper, balling the cloth into one fist and then the other.

'What did she hear?'

'Something about the interview.'

'Oh, right.'

'She really doesn't want to do it.'

'I don't blame her.'

'You wouldn't believe how distressed she got, though. I'm surprised you didn't hear her.'

'Why, what did she do?'

'It's hard to describe, but it was basically like a sort of panic attack. Or a tantrum. I don't know... It was awful...' I stop, unable to pinpoint it. 'It's like she's hiding something.' A ringing like tinnitus distorts my hearing. It grows loud in my ears for no more than the few seconds it might take for a hushed memory of my own to emerge and disintegrate.

'About that night?'

'I honestly don't know.' I shake my head, confused that I'm even saying it. Perhaps I'm projecting, more fearful of what's hidden inside me. 'Probably not.'

But Olly is of course undeterred. 'About Charlotte?'

'Seriously, I'm sure it's nothing.'

He steps back from me to lean his hips into the kitchen units and starts biting his thumbnail. 'But something sparked the thought.'

I look away and out the window onto the square garden. 'I'm just going mad, that's all.' The outdoor furniture is covered. The recollection of sitting there with Charlotte and Hayley one summer's evening spreads into the empty bit of my chest. Charlotte and I were drinking rosé and laughing about a man she'd been on a date with. He'd had a high voice and scary politics. Hayley, aged about twelve, was snuggled up next to me, sipping Coca-Cola, eating olives and chuckling along, adding in grown-up observations about the boys in her class. It's impossible to fathom how different her life will be without her mum. And how different mine will be without my sister.

Olly says in a panicked whisper, 'You're really worried about something, I can tell.'

God knows why I thought it was a good idea to share it with the worst worrier in the world. His concern will stir up mine tenfold. So I lay out the facts – for myself more than Olly. 'It's totally normal for a kid to get stressed about having to be interviewed by the police. And it's clear what went on that night. Hayley was out at a party with Ayton, then in bed asleep when Charlotte died, and the bathroom door was locked, so they can't have seen anything.'

'Yeah, even I'd be freaked out by the thought of an interview. She might even feel a bit guilty, not that she should. Isn't that what kids feel when their parents die? They think it's their fault. I mean, when Mum and Dad divorced, I thought it was because I'd nicked a fiver from Dad's wallet the week before.'

I'm moved by the thought of him as a little boy. 'That's quite cute,' I say, grinning.

'*Cute?* I was a tough guy.' He crosses his arms over his chest. His muscles are pumped up. The sleeves of his sweater are too short, and his golden arm hair sprouts from his cuffs. He is thickset and strong, but vulnerability shimmies about in those eyes of his.

Sometimes I think he needs to be scooped up and kissed better. Charlotte once called him a 'man-boy', which annoyed me because it was a little bit true. I got back at her by accusing her of being critical, *just like Mum*, and she retaliated by pincer-pinching my thigh. Then we poured two large glasses of something very orange and alcoholic and laughed about it. That's usually how our sibling spats ended.

Another thing to miss.

'It's incredibly unlikely the police'll open an investigation, isn't it.' I'm not asking a question.

'Exactly.'

'And Hayley's a good kid.'

'Yeah, she's a great kid,' he agrees, tugging his ear lobe. 'When is the coroner calling with the post-mortem results again?'

TEN

Ruth Farrah from the coroner's office will be calling later this afternoon with news about the post-mortem. It has been five days since Charlotte's death. Either she'll confirm that it was accidental and release her body or she'll inform us that the police will be opening an investigation.

Head down, thick with thoughts, I trudge along the noisy road to the Sainsbury's Local to pick up a loaf of gluten-free bread for my father. He and Mum are due to arrive after lunch, having been delayed by a few days. The trauma of losing Charlotte set off an arthritic attack in my father's joints, leaving him bedbound since their return from Antigua. He's better now, but I worry that the sofa bed in the telly room is too wonky and unstable to comfortably hold him and Mum.

I check my phone for the umpteenth time. No text from David. Why, oh why hasn't Beth given birth yet? A thought crosses my mind that we might never hear from him again.

Feeling dizzy, I find a perch at the bus stop and hang my head between my knees. The need for sleep feels like life and death. My eyes are scratchy with exhaustion and worry.

The pill I took last night didn't knock me out. My unease

about Hayley has been too strong. The gut feeling that she's keeping a secret from us has its grip on me and isn't letting go. I can't gauge it, have never seen the behind-closed-doors version of her. It's important to think with my head and wait to hear the police conclusions.

The man I've landed next to on the bench huffs because I've jostled him. I want to shout right up into his face, *My sister's dead, you fuckwit!*

I crave a calm mind, am almost gurning with the stress of holding it all inside. I envy Hayley's ability to shout and scream whenever she likes. Would it be wrong to catch the overground, jump on the Tube, take a bus and a twenty-minute walk to the flat to fetch my pouch of weed? The promise of a fuzzy, happy brain would be worth it.

Grow the hell up.

As I stamp back home, I notice some railings like the ones around the perimeter of Hampstead Heath, near our flat. I dig around in my pockets for pound coins, finding only tissues damp with Mia's tears.

When I left Charlotte's house this morning, I didn't remember to bring any loose change out with me. It's become a habit at home. Since reading a script once about a woman who integrated small, anonymous acts of kindness into her daily life, I've started doing the same. The thought of people's joy fills the little hollow in my heart. They are mostly silly, inconsequential treats, like a topped-up Oyster card left on a bus seat, or a bunch of flowers on a carer's badged car, or a book through a letter box or a winter coat laid out on a homeless person's bedding. It's still only a drop in the ocean, easy to do when you aren't frazzled and frayed by the demands of kids.

Today, because of my two new temporary kids, I'm not able to place a flask of soup on the doorstep of my elderly neighbour, Frieda, as I do every Tuesday. Moreover, this coming Friday, rheumy-eyed old Marty will wonder where his coffee is and why his pockets are empty. I feel miserable about abandoning him, most of all. Though if he knew why, he would understand. Anyone would.

Seeing Mum and Dad will complicate everything further. I dread bearing witness to their grief. Mum will find some way of blaming me for it. It's what she does. Like when Charlotte vomited gin and juice on her fancy cushions, and Mum scolded only me for making a hash of cleaning it up. Or when Charlotte used a whole can of hairspray for one hairdo, yet Mum told me off for Dad's coughing fit. And whenever Charlotte thumped me on the arm, Mum would ask me what I'd done to provoke her.

Now I am their only surviving daughter. They'll wish I'd been the one to die. Mum will love me a little bit less for that. It's just a fact.

'Why does Grampy eat that weird bread?' Mia asks, getting under my feet as I prepare the chilli con carne to Aunt Jane's special recipe. We've already gobbled up the frozen meal she left us, and I wish we hadn't. My head is so full, I can barely remember how to cook this simple recipe. Jitters about Ruth Farrah's call are like bees in my skull.

'For his arthritis,' I explain to Mia. 'Gluten causes trouble in his gut and it makes the inflammation of his joints worse.'

'What's inflammation?'

'It's when something gets sore and swollen.'

'Poor Grampy.'

I give her a quick side hug. 'Yes, poor Grampy.'

Giving up on the idea of finding headspace while I cook, I ask Mia to choose some music. She puts on some nineties house music and turns it right up.

'This was Mum's favourite playlist.' Her little face clouds over and she sits down at the kitchen table.

'Granny and Grampy will cheer us up,' I say, and crouch next to her, brushing my hand over her crop of hair. Two teardrops plop out of her eyes. I pat her cheeks with the tea towel, which should be renamed a tears towel. Then we smell the onions burning.

She helps me chop another round. The onion fumes allow her to cry unchallenged. She knows when to add the spices and the mince. 'Daddy said the doctors are going to force Beth's baby to come out.'

'You've been talking to him?' I stir the pot.

'On text.'

'That's good.' My heart hiccups. 'How are they going to force it to come out?'

She abandons the knife to get her phone and points at the word 'inducing' on David's text. As she scrolls through, I get the measure of their message exchange. Mia sends long punctuation-free entries full of emojis, while David barely manages more than a couple of lines in reply. It angers me for a second, but I concede that men are generally businesslike about texts. It doesn't mean anything.

I say to Mia, 'Looks like you'll have another baby brother or sister sometime this week then.'

'And Dad will come over to get us and take us to Ireland to live.'

I put the lid on the pan. 'Mia, we don't know what's going to happen yet. We've got to work it all out. You've got school here.'

'I hate school. I wouldn't care if I never went there again.'

'Oh? Why's that?'

'I hate the teachers,' she mumbles.

'You do?' I'm surprised. Mia is such a conscientious, compliant child.

Footsteps thunder down the stairs. I tense up.

'What's all this?' Hayley asks. Her hair is clean. The scowl has gone. Her expression shows less anguish.

She lifts the pan lid, inhales deeply and then rests her head on my shoulder. I slip an arm around her waist. 'Hi,' I say.

'Chilli con carne's my favourite.'

'I know,' I say, adding, 'Mia was just telling me she hates the teachers at school.'

Hayley stiffens. 'No, you don't, Mia.'

'I do!' Mia whines, glaring at her sister.

'She doesn't,' Hayley says to me, sighing, sounding like a cross parent. She crunches down on a leftover stick of red pepper and narrows her eyes at her sister.

Mia slams a bread knife through a chocolate bar to break it into chunks. 'Only some of them,' she mumbles.

'Secondary school teachers can be a bit tougher on you, right? Maybe you're still getting used to it,' I suggest, though I remember how kind Mr Hanrahan sounded on the phone.

Mia frowns. 'Where's Uncle Olly?'

'On a run,' I reply.

Hayley asks, 'When are Grampy and Granny getting here?'

'In about an hour.' Mia's chopping is aggressive. 'Careful, Mia. If you slice your fingers off, you won't be able to throttle Hayley with them.'

Hayley retorts, 'Oh, thanks a bunch, Auntie Emily! Whose side are you on?' There's an edge to it.

'Ha! I'm neutral, like Switzerland.'

'School sucks, sis,' Hayley says, pulling Mia into a side hug.

Never one to hold a grudge, Mia hands Hayley and me a piece of chocolate each. All three of us plop it into the bubbling mince at the same time and share knowing smiles. I've been doing this with them since they had the motor skills to hold the chunks of chocolate. Hayley was on my hip when I first taught her how.

I continue stirring. 'I'm glad you're both here, actually. I wanted to remind you that the coroner will be calling this afternoon with news of your mum's post-mortem results.'

Mia steps back from the stove and tucks her T-shirt into her jeans.

'It's no big deal, though,' Hayley says, though how could it be anything other than a big deal? 'You said there was nothing to worry about.'

'Well, that is true,' I say slowly. 'But we have to prepare for the possibility of it not being as simple as that.'

Hayley's forehead crinkles slightly. 'But you said it would be.'

'I said it was *likely* to be. Yes.'

'D'you know something you're not telling us?'

'No, no, not at all. It's bound to be fine. We all know it was an accident.'

She juts her chin out and raises her voice. 'Why did you say it then?'

'I was just being overcautious, that's all.'

She bursts out with 'I don't believe you!'

'I do,' Mia says, sticking her thumb in her mouth.

'Shut up, Mia.' To me, she says, 'You think they're going to find something bad, don't you?'

'No. I really don't. I was just trying to manage your expectations. That's all.'

'You're saying you don't think it was an accident.' Her head is thrust forward, and her eyes are reddening lividly in her pale face.

'Of course it was an accident.' I move backwards, unnerved by her sudden mood swing.

'*Just say what you actually think for once,*' she hisses viciously.

'I am, Hayley, please. Let's calm down now.'

'You're all such fucking liars!' And she charges at me and shoves at my chest with both hands. The force of it knocks me backwards, and I fling out a hand to steady myself. It lands on the naked flame on the hob. I yelp in pain and thrust my hand under running cold water.

Mia whimpers. 'Are you okay, Auntie Emily? Are you okay?'

'Yes, I'm fine.' The burn on my palm sets off a fire of resentment that rips through my body.

Hayley's long hair flies behind her, almost catching in the door as she slams it behind her.

'Are you sure?' Mia asks.

'Yes, yes, I'm fine,' I snap, which isn't fair on her and I apologise straight away. 'Sorry, sorry, that just shook me up a bit. It's nothing, really.'

'You need Savlon. Mum used it for burns. She was always burning herself.'

'Good plan, sweetheart. I'll get it. Where do you keep it?'

A crease forms between her eyes. 'In the bathroom upstairs.'

'Oh.' I try to hold my features in a smile. 'Right, yes.' I went in that one time to get Hayley a glass of water and I don't want to go in again. Mia clocks my hesitation. Her hand goes to the crown of her head to twist a strand into a knot. She's scared too. It shames me.

'Let's go together so that you can show me exactly where it is,' I say, finding the courage for Mia.

Once we're in there, my forehead and underarms break into a sweat. The floor is dry as a bone, even though it's a wet room and tiled from corner to corner, floor to ceiling in smooth, sealed surfaces. Nobody uses it any more. Both girls use our shower.

Behind a long glass partition on the left-hand wall hangs the huge silver showerhead with its rain setting. The free-standing cast-iron bath sits at the far end, where Charlotte fell, perhaps after finishing her shower. The sight of its roll-top edge provokes a flash image of her head slamming into it before her naked body ragdolled to the floor.

I've had this vision before, but this time I imagine Hayley shoving her mum in a rage like she did me.

With my rational brain in gear, I know this can't have been possible. Charlotte was alone behind a locked door. Granted, we don't yet know what time she died, or whether she could have moved after she'd fallen. Nor do we know if there were any other hidden injuries, bruises or breaks. What we know so far is more assumption than fact, gleaned from snippets from the police and paramedics at the scene – the positioning of her body, the bleeding at the base of her skull, the way she landed on her back – and testimony from the girls. Ruth Farrah will shed more light on the details.

Would a shove leave a mark?

My chest feels normal, unmarked by Hayley's attack five minutes before, but it was enough to unbalance me.

Olly is calling us. Before I can answer, he bursts in, sweaty from his run. 'There you are! I was worried.' He sees my hand. 'Oh! What happened there?'

'I thought it would be a great idea to grab onto the hob!' I can't reveal what Hayley did. He'd be protective of me, judge her, perhaps love her less. And despite my own conflicted feelings, I can't have that.

'Ouch,' he says, cradling my hand.

'So stupid of me.' I pat on a layer of cream to cover the burn, avoiding Mia's eye. She too says nothing about Hayley.

'You've got a lot on your mind.' He rubs my back.

'We'd better see to that chilli,' I say. 'Mum and Dad'll be here soon.'

Mia and I descend the stairs in silence, making no reference to our shared little secret. I feel sick about the prospect of Ruth Farrah's call.

ELEVEN

I'm glad Hayley has hidden herself away in her room. It's best she avoids me until my parents arrive. The thought of another confrontation scares me, not because of the possibility of being shoved again, but because of what I might say back. It's taking some serious willpower to stop myself from storming into her room and accusing her outright of lying about the circumstances surrounding my sister's death.

Unconsciously, I check my phone, thinking first of the prospect of the coroner's call, and then of David's non-existent call.

On the dot of three, I hear my parents' car on the drive. Olly and Mia are in the kitchen smearing jam onto a Victoria sponge they baked together. I go out to help my mother manoeuvre my father's wheelchair over the shingle drive.

A rush of cold hits me when I open the front door. Light snow has fallen and yet none of us noticed. Snow in March? It adds to the unpredictability of my new world.

The burn on my hand smarts.

My parents are sitting motionless in the car, simply staring straight ahead. Their profiles are handsome, majestic, yet the absence of Charlotte is plain as day. They are shells, as though their souls left their bodies along with my sister's.

Over the last couple of days, we have been speaking on the phone regularly, but nothing could have prepared me for seeing them as changed as this. I yearn to be wrapped in their arms and taken care of like a child, but it would be asking too much. It has always been too much to ask.

Both car doors swing open at the same time. I go straight to the boot to lift out Dad's chair. Unfolding it, I place it at the correct angle and lug him in. Mum comes over. The three of us murmur some church-quiet hellos and offer up brusque kisses. Our hugs are long enough to show how much we love each other, but not lingering, leaving no room to feel too much.

'You heard from David yet?' Dad asks, gathering himself, putting forward practical concerns to chivvy us along.

'Not yet,' I say. 'I'm guessing Beth will be induced quite soon.'

'But you've been coping okay?' It is a rhetorical question. There is only one possible way of answering it.

'Yes, fine. They're being amazing.'

Snowflakes melt on top of Dad's square head. His hair is too short, styled in a crew cut like a sergeant major. I cover his lap with my jacket, but his long thighs get wet anyway. He catches my hand in his contorted, sinewy claw, which was once as flat and wide as a plate of meat. He holds me there. Our eyes meet. His deep brown-eyed gaze melts through me, leaving a well of desolation.

'Okay,' Mum says. 'You'll have to tip it up and drag it backwards.'

I know this routine well and take the handles. Forgetting my injury, I press down. But as Dad's feet pop up in the air, a searing pain shoots from my hand up my arm and I let go, bumping the front wheels down hard. 'God. Sorry, Dad. Are you okay?' My eyes water. I put on the brakes, cradle my hand, glancing at the red-raw burn striping diagonally across my palm, folding my fingers over it to hide it.

'For goodness' sake, Emily,' Mum hisses.

Dad flashes me a smile over his shoulder. 'I've suffered worse.' Over the years, we have shared many clumsy wheelchair moments in our attempts to navigate the able-bodied world. We've been known to descend into fits of giggles over the very unfunny conundrum of a broken-down lift, a narrow shop doorway or a cobbled street.

Mum sighs. 'Come on, you two.' She never finds our wheelchair antics amusing.

'Sorry,' I say again.

'Give it to me.' She takes over, preferring full control of Dad, and pulls him across the gravel to Charlotte's red front door, shooting me a sharp sideways glance. Just that one dirty look reminds me why we are not close. In a nutshell, it's probably why I don't have my own children. She has loved me as best she can but has never liked me very much; has always made it obvious that being my mother was a shit job. Yes, that's about right. A shit job.

As soon as Dad is parked up in the kitchen, he begins sneezing uncontrollably, making it difficult for the girls to greet him. We move the condolence bouquets into the dining room.

Mounds of red pollen from the lilies dot the worktop surfaces. I wipe them away while everyone settles with a cup of tea at the white table. The tension in the air could be sliced into chewy pieces of cake. My father's sniffs prompt my mother to irritably shove a tissue at him. Olly is being a trouper, but his conversation is a little too emotional and touchy-feely for my unsentimental, upright mother. Then there's Hayley, who is being engaging and helpful, fetching milk and pulling chairs out. This should thrill me, but instead, her ability to turn on the charm whenever she likes unsettles me.

In the middle of Mia's funny story about Charlotte wearing her fluffy pink bedroom slippers into the school playground, my phone rings. My mouth dries. I look straight at Mum and then Dad. 'It's the coroner.' I do not risk looking at Olly, whose restless eyes would drain the courage from me.

'Answer it then,' Mum says. The sinews of her long neck visibly ripple under her silver necklace. Her fine skin allows the colour of blood to seep through and gives her a feverish edge.

My voice is small when I speak. 'Hello?'

'Hello, this is Ruth Farrah...' As she introduces herself, I move away from the others to find privacy in the sitting room, barely registering her preamble, impatient for the headline.

She shares her conclusions. I try to take it all in. Outside the window, I see that a light dusting of snow now covers the ground. It's dazzling against the grey late-afternoon sky.

I'm shivering uncontrollably by the time I say goodbye and walk back into the kitchen. All faces are turned to mine as I share the main headlines.

'She confirmed accidental death. A subdural haemorrhage due to severe head trauma.' I stop, explain it to the girls. 'A brain injury from the fall. She died instantly. No suffering at all. They're releasing her body to the undertakers this afternoon.' I feel the relief drop inside me so suddenly I think it might bring me down to the ground like an emptied sack.

Mum clamps her hands to her thighs and exhales. 'Thank God.'

There is more to impart, which we have less to thank God for, but I decide to keep it to myself until I've had time to process it. I'm working on a need-to-know basis for now.

'Quite right,' Dad says, nodding, ruffling Mia's hair roughly. Mia forces a smile as though she knows she should be happy but doesn't quite understand why.

Olly rushes over to hug me, or prop me up, maybe sensing I might fall. I rest my head on his shoulder. Hayley stares at me with wide eyes. Her utter astonishment sends goosebumps over my skin. It's so different to everyone else's delight.

'We can start planning the funeral now,' my mother says, looking at me. Her blue eyes are sharp with agony, her skin stretched thinly over her bone structure. White dashes of shock have appeared, seemingly overnight, down the length of each dark grey strand of her hair.

Mia suddenly yelps. 'Awesome! Beth's had the baby! Look!' She brandishes her phone at me. When I see the photograph of the black-haired newborn, I sense a loosening in my shoulders. David will be here soon.

As though reading my mind, Hayley barbs at me, 'I bet *you're* happy about that.'

'Yes, I am happy, actually. And so should you be. A baby is always joyful news, Hayley,' I retort.

My mother raises a disapproving eyebrow at me. I turn my back on her and begin clattering about with cups. Charlotte's spectral presence hovers at my shoulder. My cheeks smart. Who the hell snaps at a girl who's just lost her mum? She hates me, and for good reason, and it has only taken five days.

I think back to the lines in Chapter Seventeen of Olly's novel. It was the point at which I put it down. The main character's internal dialogue about feeling defective for not having maternal instincts mirrored my own. Yet as a reader, I was suspicious of Ellie, questioned her underlying neuroses. There was a side to me that second-guessed her child-free choices, doubting her character and her rejection of the status quo. Feeling this way about her shocked me. How insanely hypocritical it made me. Or just insane. Anyhow, rightly or wrongly, I read it and I stewed and brooded, quietly livid with Olly for writing down words that I felt.

I guess I'll always feel marginalised. Wanting to be a mother is the norm, more natural, more likeable somehow. Admitting I haven't the urge is hard enough. Specifically rejecting Charlotte's wishes is even worse.

You'd take them, wouldn't you? If something happened to me? You're the only person I trust.

Putting names to the children I don't want to nurture characterises me as that much more monstrously selfish. But I remind myself that the girls have a father, two half-brothers and, as of today, a baby half-sister. They have their own family – they don't need me.

I press David's number on my phone and listen to it ringing. Everything hinges on David. He is the girls' best hope of joining a proper family with a real parent who won't resent them. There's no point in pretending that I can slot in as Charlotte's replacement, even temporarily.

But if it did? Promise? No, I don't promise. My job is to orchestrate a smooth and painless handover.

David picks up after only a couple of rings and whispers down the phone, 'She's in my arms. She's a beauty.' He sounds tearful. There's a mewling cry. 'Shh, shh, little Bridie.'

'That's a lovely name. Congratulations, David.'

We talk about the water birth and how brave Beth was, keeping up the pretence for longer than necessary. We both know I haven't called to coo. Finally I say, 'Now that she's arrived safely, when do you think you'll be able to come over?'

'Any time now. Beth's already totally obsessed by the little mite and has forgotten I exist, so I'll get some flights booked. Tomorrow hopefully.'

I exhale. 'Oh, fantastic. Great news.'

'How are the girls doing?'

'Mia is desperate to see you. Hayley is...' I pause. 'To be honest, she's not coping well at all.'

'Och, poor child. She needs her dad, maybe.'

The baby has made him sentimental. It's reassuring, reminding me of what a soft touch he was before the divorce. When he and Charlotte argued, he whisked her away for a city break, wowed her with the architecture that inspired his own designs. When she felt blue, he threw her a surprise party with all her friends. When she was bored, he blindfolded her and drove her down a bumpy Devon lane to a plot of land, where he described the house he dreamed of building her one day. It was a champagne-and-flowers kind of relationship. It was the same with the girls. He was big on bear hugs and kisses and cheesy grand gestures for his two little princesses: giant cuddly toys or holidays to Lapland or pretty dresses with silk sashes.

'Just before you go,' he says in a sing-song voice, 'anything the coroner said that gave you a clue about Charlotte's... state when she fell?'

Ruth Farrah's words swim in my head. I'm still unable to digest them, and have told nobody what she said about the pathologist's request for one more test.

'Nothing at all,' I reply shrilly.

I hear a voice in the background that I'm guessing is Beth's.

'Let us know when you'll be arriving,' I say. 'Goodbye, David.'

I hang up and fret. Why is he so keen on knowing what the coroner said about Charlotte's 'state'? Is he as unsettled as I am about what went on that night?

TWELVE

I'm irritated with David for having deepened my own unease about Charlotte's fall. And anyway, why am I listening to anything he has to say? He isn't here, has not stuck to his initial promise to hop on a plane hours after Bridie's birth. He has postponed his trip over and over again: Beth has the baby blues, Bridie's got colic, Beth needs to catch up on her sleep, Bridie's spiked a fever.

Day after day throughout the rest of March, the excuses mount up. I do my best to understand, keeping the hope alive, wondering if I would empathise more if I was a mother myself.

The point is, I am not a mother. I never want to be a mother. I hate pretending to be one. And the passing days put big clanging bells on that message.

Motherhood is thankless. Official. No wonder my own mother was so unhappy in the role. I'm a secretary, taxi service, therapist, chef, cleaner, cash machine and general punchbag, on a no-salary contract, working eighteen-hour shifts – with an interrupted lunch hour, no breaks and no overtime.

While Olly pisses about on his book and drinks tea, I'm too busy to piss or drink. He's no help to me; is hyper-focused on his writing, like a teenager in the thick of exams. Maybe I don't blame him. A big part of me feels guilty for dragging him into my family's tragedy, so I leave him be, work hard not to resent it. Sometimes I try to explain how challenging I'm finding everything, and then realise there are no words to describe how it feels inside when Hayley throws a hissy fit, swears blue murder at me and chucks her dirty laundry at my head. It sounds funny – after the event.

When I'm not being hit in the face by knickers, the funeral arrangements take up the rest of my time. I secure the first available slot at Long Ditton cemetery and set a date for 4 April, which is later than we hoped. Mum and I spend hours on the phone making decisions about coffins and eulogies and other death administration.

I recollect a recent walk with Mum and Charlotte. Mum declared she wanted 'a nice wicker coffin when I pop my clogs'. Like Uncle Jeremy's, whose funeral she'd been telling us about. And Charlotte said she wanted *her* coffin to be covered in Ferrero Rocher wrappers. It made me laugh. When I remind Mum of this, she snaps at me, 'That's totally inappropriate, Emily.' And I'm not sure whether she means me bringing it up or Charlotte saying it in the first place.

In truth, we have no idea what kind of funeral Charlotte might have wanted. We have discovered that she did not make a will of any kind and did not leave official instructions for guardianship of the girls. To top that, David still owns the house. He gave it to her, but the deeds are in his name.

Mum defends Charlotte's lack of future-proofing, which of course gets right up my nose. But I can't tell her about the false promise I made to take the kids in the event of my sister's death, back when I thought her dying was impossible.

Why the morbid vow, Charlotte? I want to ask her now. What was going on in her life to prompt her to say that? Trying to remember the conversation better is like squinting into the sun. If I mentioned it to Mum, she would probably accuse me of being inappropriate.

I've always tried my best to please Mum. Like now, when I'm working hard to keep it together, be a good daughter, a good aunt. A good mother. I get the feeling I'm falling short on all three. Charlotte used to say that my default position was to be hard on myself. I'm being extremely hard on myself now. For not being good enough for the girls. Letting them down feels like a destitution of the soul. But I refuse to ask Mum for help. It would be selfish of me to pull her away from Dad, who is suffering enough as it is. Moreover, it would show weakness and prove Mum's point about me. *Charlotte* never needed help with the girls.

Except from me, I guess. In more ways than Mum will ever know.

Mia comes into the kitchen while I'm having these depressing, pointless thoughts. I'm making tea. She clings to my side.

'When's Uncle Olly finishing writing?'

'Not sure. Do you need him for something?'

She opens her cookbook to show me a photograph of a tray-bake covered in sprinkles. 'I want to make this.'

Olly makes cakes with Mia in the afternoons sometimes – proof that he does more than write and drink tea. It's sweet of him, especially when it's obvious he's exhausted.

'Go in at five. He should be finishing up then.'

'What's Hayley up to?'

'She went to Ayton's.'

'Again?'

It echoes my own worry about how much time she and Ayton spend together. He lives with his mum close by, only a few streets away, in a block of flats we sometimes pass by on the way to the shops, but from what I gather, the mum sounds flaky...

I'll stop right there.

It isn't our place to judge, interfere or impose the rules. We're their temporary custodians. David will take on all that responsibility when he arrives.

When he arrives. Not if. The 'if' issue came up in bed with Olly the other night. Note, we were not in bed in a sexy way – that pleasure is a distant memory – we were lying next to each other like inanimate planks, flattened by one of Hayley's scream-fests over a lost crop top. It doesn't take much.

And Olly whispered, 'What if he never shows up?'

He didn't have to say David's name out loud. I guessed from the fear in his voice.

'For God's sake. He's their father,' I hissed.

It wasn't an answer.

It's the Monday night before Charlotte's funeral on Thursday. As ever, I put dinner on the table on the dot of seven and dread Hayley's mood. She shows up at least, despite selectively muting her responses. Most of the time she is sullen and uncommunicative. Except when she swings the other way and strains herself with sweetness and light – because she wants money or phone data. Literally, she's limitless. Or she wants Ayton to come over, or she wants to go to his place. Perversely, the fake-nice Hayley grates on me more than the unpleasant side of her. Her resting b-word face and sweary backchat is more honest.

Olly, Mia and I share anecdotes about Charlotte as though she is away for the weekend rather than gone. Gone. *Gone?* It's as unfathomable as it was three weeks ago, on the day she died.

At the end of the meal, the same thudding question comes from Mia. 'When's Daddy getting here?' Hayley groans and leaves.

My heart hurts for them.

'Soon. I think Bridie's almost better.'

'Poor Bridie,' Mia says, then, 'But what if she isn't better for Mummy's funeral? It's only three days away.'

'Don't worry, your dad wouldn't miss that.'

I ruffle her hair, realising that I do this when I feel uncomfortable.

Late, near midnight, I text David.

Hi David, I hope you're well and that Bridie's sniffle isn't keeping you up at night, even though your conscience should.

Okay, I delete that.

Hi David, I hope you're well and that little Bridie is recovering. Just double-checking that you're able to come to the funeral on Thursday. Quite frankly, you owe it to them to show up after all the shit you've put them through. And Charlotte will haunt you for the rest of your life if you don't.

Delete, delete. One last draft.

Hi David, I hope you're well and that little Bridie is recovering. Sorry to be neurotic, but I'm just triple-checking you're able to make it on Thursday for the funeral. I don't want to build the girls' hopes up if you're going to struggle to get here. They do love their dad! Holding your hand through the tough bits will mean the world to them. I'll see you then. Emily x

A reply pings straight back.

Hi Em, my flights are booked. Wouldn't miss it. I adored Charlotte and wish to pay my respects. And I love my girls. I won't let them down. You have my word. Dx

My blister packs are in the sock drawer, and I pop a sleeping pill before climbing into bed again, upping the dose as advised by my GP in a phone consultation. It's like a pharmaceutical version of crying wolf. Before, I needed them to stop worrying about shit happening; then some real shit happened, and now the wolf is legitimately out to get me.

THIRTEEN

Fog clings to the trees, leaving a film of gossamer on our black wool coats. I clutch Olly's hand. He's shaking as he cries. All I can think of when I stare down at Charlotte's tasteful wicker coffin, chosen by my mother, is that I wish I'd glued on Ferrero Rocher wrappers. I've let her down. In more ways than one.

I didn't think you'd actually die! I look around me, hoping I didn't say that out loud.

In between me and Olly, Mia is crying quietly and consistently, as though her state of distress is so natural she can't feel it any more.

Hayley flanks my father. Her expression is colourless. Her black dress is too short and her hoodie too flimsy. She refused to go near the smart coat and loafers I bought her from M&S. Admittedly, the look was more middle-aged undertaker than teen mourner.

Hayley's presence next to Dad highlights the absence of her own father.

I scan the gloom beyond our little huddle within the grounds of Long Ditton cemetery, hoping against hope I'll see David emerge. Letting the girls down like this is unthinkable.

There's still time. His plane from Dublin might have been delayed.

Hayley's words echo through me: *Who'll take us then?*

I glance at my parents. Dad looks heroic standing with his two canes. It's rare to see him on his feet these days. I forget how imposing he is. Even stooped, he is a head taller than everyone else at the graveside. The deep lines on his wide, thick forehead are set and still, beaded with sweat despite the cold. The tip of Mum's Roman nose and her pointy cheekbones are a stalwart purple. Every time Dad wobbles a little, she puts her arm out for him to hold.

The priest says some words about Charlotte's infectious laugh, and how she was the life and soul of the party and the most wonderful mother. The sentiments strike a false note coming from a complete stranger in a sombre cassock. Nervously I check Hayley again. I see the goosebumps prickling across her cheeks and wrists. She stares resolutely down at the ground.

The reality of today lives up to the gut-churning dread I attempted to smother with pills last night. Saying goodbye to my big sister as she's lowered into the ground is horrific.

Back at the house, Olly and I shake mourners' hands, serve them burned sausages and pour acid wine into their glasses. These are the routine motions of death and leave me emotionally disembowelled. After a while, I escape to the downstairs loo even though I don't need to go. I glance in the mirror. My eyes look like they've been punched in, brutalised by loss.

Towards the end of the day, a young couple approach me. Anyone who isn't David is a disappointment. The man holding out his hand to me sports a goatee and carries a ringleted child on his hip. The woman is holding the wrist of an older, dark-haired boy in a waistcoat. They are a soap advert for the family next door, but prettier than any of us next door.

I stop gnawing my lip and try extremely hard to smile. The muscles of my face are juddering with exhaustion. My eye is twitching. Let this be over, please, I think.

The man puts his hand confidently into mine. It feels hot and firm. His baby clamps her squidgy legs tighter around his middle. 'Emily, hi. Jamie. This is my wife, Kristin. And these two mischiefs are Tiger and Fleur.'

I rack my brains. Jamie and Kristin? Who is Jamie? Tiger and Fleur? Names like that aren't easily forgotten. But I can't place them. Kristin has similar ringlets to her daughter and is almost as baby-faced.

'Thank you so much for coming,' I say, on auto.

Jamie kindly prompts me. 'I'm Hayley's form teacher. Jamie Hanrahan.'

'Oh, Mr Hanrahan,' I say, surprised. His good looks are unexpected. 'Jamie. Course. Sorry. It has been a long day.'

'You've done an awesome job. Charlotte would have loved the party. She's the only one missing.'

For the first time in hours, my smile is real. 'Yes. It doesn't feel right without her.'

'And it's lovely that the sun is shining,' Kristin adds.

I want to say, 'Yup, shining on a turd!' and ask her why the hell the weather should make a blind bit of difference to the mind-bending misery of losing my sister. 'It's lovely, yes,' I say instead, squinting out at the chemical-blue sky.

Jamie steps closer. 'Hayley hasn't cried today, I noticed.' He scratches his clipped beard. His eyes are a dark, thoughtful brown, but they are swollen, as though he's been crying enough tears for all of us.

'Not everyone cries.' I track the room for my niece.

He drops his voice. 'I had a feeling she'd be like this.'

I spot Hayley squashed up next to Mia on the sofa. Her hair

is in a long plait and makes her look young again, innocent. My aunt Jane is in the armchair opposite them, dealing out playing cards. They love Great-Aunt Jane, and it flits across my mind that she, as an ex-head of an inner-city secondary modern, might make a better parent than David. A long time ago, she even fostered a boy who'd stabbed someone. Aunt Jane is a legend.

'She's furious with the world,' Jamie says.

I blow my lips out, rub at my temple and mumble, 'Furious with me, more like.'

Hayley is sitting too far away to hear us, but she glances up at that very moment. Jamie salutes her in a friendly manner. She pulls out a laughably fake smile and then looks down at her hand.

'Kids are always crossest with the people they feel safest with,' he says.

'That's a nice way of looking at it.'

His gaze intensifies. 'Come into school when they start back. I'll share some strategies. Charlotte and I had an arsenal of awesome anxiety-busters tailored to Hayley. I think we got to know most of her triggers. And this is a hell of a big 'un.' His lips stretch down. 'We don't want her falling to pieces on us or getting behind on her schoolwork. She's a bright kid.'

I swallow thickly. 'Thank you. But it might be their dad who comes in.'

'I'd be honoured to meet him finally,' he says flatly. His eyes dart across the packed-in faces around us in the kitchen.

'Sadly, he's not here yet.' *Yet.*

Something other than righteous anger flickers across his face. It could be intrigue. Or puzzlement. The cogs are whirring, certainly. 'That's great parenting,' he says wryly.

Kristin admonishes him – 'Jamie!' – which covers my own shock.

'Sorry, slapped wrist, not very profesh of me. Kristin tells me off for being too emotionally invested.'

'If it's directed at Mia and Hayley, I'm not complaining,' I say, trying to be gracious about him overstepping. At this point, any misgivings about David are not at all welcome.

Kristin's white teeth shine. 'You're obviously a brilliant auntie.'

I gather myself and say assuredly, 'Believe me, I'm definitely not that.'

Jamie steeples his fingers. 'Don't worry, Auntie Em. We'll break Hayley down and make her cry.' He hah-hahs like a comic-strip villain, and I laugh. Actually *laugh*.

'Thank you,' I repeat, shaking both their hands, rubbing the top of Fleur's head, patting Tiger's shoulder. 'I'll be in touch.'

As I say it, I'm not sure I mean it. Will I be in touch? Will Olly and I still be at Charlotte's taking care of Hayley by then? Shame throbs. I hope I'll not be here. But at the same time, I can't imagine not being.

FOURTEEN

The guests begin to say their goodbyes and filter out. I feel the emptiness of the room. Having been desperate for them to leave, I now have an urge to cling onto them, tug them back inside. Looming in front of us is the reality of David's no-show. His rejection of the girls is a stab to my chest. It is unbelievable that he could be this callous. I imagine Charlotte looking down on me, shrugging and saying, 'Doesn't surprise me at all.'

You're the only person I trust.

I reach for a random glass on the side, planning to pour the leftover wine down the sink, but instead I glug at it thirstily, hoping its previous owner doesn't have something catching. The liquid tingles in my throat, and I decide to forget clearing up and play cards with Aunt Jane and the girls. My parents have joined them too.

We play gin rummy as though our lives depend on it. I try not to think of the implications for the girls – for all of us – if David never pitches up.

The last few stragglers leave. The doorbell rings.

'Who's that?' my mother groans.

'Someone's probably forgotten their bloody scarf or something,' Aunt Jane croaks with her ex-smoker's lungs.

Mum says, 'Give me strength! If I hear one more I'm-so-sorry-for-your-loss, I'll throttle someone.'

But my heart beats a little faster. I've a good feeling about this latecomer.

'I bet it's Dad!' Mia cries, leaping up.

And we're right. It's David on the doorstep.

I've never been so pleased to see anyone in my life. He's dressed for the funeral he has missed, in a black polo neck, a black beanie and a black pea coat with leather epaulettes. It suggests he had the right intentions.

'I'm sorry,' he rasps. The reddish tinge around the rims of his eyes and the auburn strands that shoot through his light beard remind me of Hayley. He's the other half of her, the half we never see. He stoops and encircles Mia's elfin frame in a long hug. He rambles poetically about planes being cancelled due to fog, how his phone ran out of juice, a crash on the motorway leaving a ten-mile tailback... A litany of disasters, like fate itself has been against him arriving at all. I don't care why any more. He is here.

After a stilted supper, my parents go to bed early and my aunt Jane bustles home to Surbiton in an Uber. David is trying his best to keep the conversation going, but the rest of us are worn out. By nine o'clock I'm ready to turn in. The girls are too wired around him to be sleepy. The conversation flows between the three of them as though he has never been anywhere else but here in their lives.

Their personalities suit each other. He gives them his undivided attention, hangs on their every word. His habit of nodding a lot and repeating what they've said back to them with a 'bless' thrown in is effective. The spiritual quotes take it a little far sometimes, but, hey, whatever makes them smile is okay by me.

He shows them Beth's Instagram page, where she plays the piano, walks their two collies – Yeats and Joyce – goes to music festivals in short smocks and wellies and swaddles her children in Celtic blankets and kisses. She is ethereal and wholesome and maternal. It's hard not to admire their good life in Ireland.

It's curious how differently David and Charlotte's love lives panned out after their divorce. Charlotte was strangely disinterested in meeting a life partner. She'd go through long periods of abstinence, when she'd hate on men and talk openly about her vibrator. But when she was in the mood for sex with a real-life man, she would put her profile up on a dating site and the offers would flood in. Her unique smile and those untamed twirls in her hair were arresting in photographs. Helped by the fact that she was relaxed about one-night stands, rarely growing attached to the men she slept with. But after a spurt of this, she'd get bored, take her profile off the website and be fabulous and single again. It was all or nothing.

I watch David now and can see why Charlotte was once madly in love with him. He is charming, like a magician or hypnotist. In the space of a few hours, he has thawed Hayley out and has seemingly been forgiven for the missing years. Mia melts into his lap. If she could climb inside of him, I swear she would. The tragedy of losing their mum is in a small way eased by gaining a father. Just in the nick of time, he has stepped into the breach.

At one point, Olly and I share a knowing smile. This is how it's meant to be. These girls deserve to have their real father around. Olly and I are destined for a different sort of family life. A family of two, passionate about each other, our friendships and our careers, loving our nieces and giving them back at the end of the day.

Although we can barely afford the rent on our north

London flat, we don't mind, and know that we can move at the drop of a hat without disrupting any childhoods. I yearn to be back there, a stone's throw from good coffee and a village-like community and my circle of friends. It's where everything goes according to plan, where there are fewer curveballs; where antagonism comes in the form of a lovers' tiff followed by make-up sex; where sleep deprivation is cured by a guilt-free joint; where meals are peppered with chat about narrative drive versus character depth; where spontaneity is a last-minute dash to the Everyman to catch a film, chased by a bowl of spaghetti at an Italian in a tucked-away side street. It's not everyone's cup of tea, but it's ours. It is how we choose to spend our years on this planet, living life rather than enduring it.

'I actually quite like him,' Olly says now.

While the girls choose a movie with David, Olly and I are clearing up supper.

'He's all right,' I admit. 'He says "bless" too much.'

'If that's as bad as it gets...' He picks at the cellophane on the box of chocolates Aunt Jane gave us. 'It's funny, I'd got it into my head that he was this complete ogre.'

'Charlotte slagged him off so much, that's why.'

He lowers his voice. 'Would she hate the fact that he's taking them?'

'We're not handing them over yet. Not until we've scoped him out.'

'What's going to happen? I mean, he can't leave his other family behind for too long, can he?'

'He told me he can stay for a few weeks, as many as six, he thinks. His other kids are apparently used to him being away for long periods project-managing.'

'And after that?'

'We talked about maybe sharing it for a while. He could do the week and we could maybe step in at weekends sometimes?'

'When did you have this conversation?' he shoots back.

'Before, only briefly, when the girls were upstairs. Nothing's been decided. I was going to tell you, but I haven't had the chance. You wouldn't always have to come along too. I'd be happy to do it on my own.'

He settles at that. 'Oh great, it's just with the book and everything...' And I'm piqued, reminded that his writing makes him selfish. 'And then what?' he asks.

'By then we hope they'll have come around to the idea of moving to Ireland, and he'd sell this place.'

'And if they kick off about it?'

I bite my lip. 'It would be unfair of him to rush the move and completely ignore what they wanted at this point. He does have some making-up to do.'

'It doesn't tend to work like that.'

'But he walked out when Hayley was only five and Mia was two, just like that.' I click my fingers. 'Just because a pretty Galway girl batted her eyes at him.'

Olly muses thoughtfully, 'I wonder what went wrong between him and Charlotte.'

'Give that to me.' I gesture at the box, giving myself time to decide whether to share with him my latest theory on why Charlotte's relationship with David fell apart. The details of my conversation with Ruth Farrah prey on my mind. The indignation I've just expressed about David's abandonment of her wouldn't hold up to scrutiny. It was never that simple.

'Charlotte was no angel, Olly. Let's face it,' I say.

He looks down, picks lint off his suit trousers. 'Yeah. She was a tour de force. Quite a handful to live with, I imagine.'

I open the chocolate box, suddenly unable to stomach eating one, pushing them at Olly. 'I didn't tell you...' I drop my voice, 'but when the coroner called about Charlotte's post-mortem, she mentioned that the pathologist had requested a toxicology report.'

The chocolate he's chosen hovers at his lips. 'They think there was something in her bloodstream?'

'I guess so.'

'They're doubting the cause of death?'

'No, not at all. It wasn't that.'

'What then?'

'She assured me it was just a technicality. Box-ticking more than anything else. I'm meant to call for the results sometime next week.'

'Why didn't you say anything about this before?'

'There's absolutely no point thinking about it unless something comes up in the results, is there?'

'Fair enough.' Eyeing me, he places the chocolate in his mouth and chews slowly.

I look away and down at the chocolates, which seemed pretty enticing a few minutes ago. 'We'd better go next door,' I say.

In the telly room, the huge flatscreen fills the room with blue light. The image is paused on the opening titles of the film. It looks like a thriller. David sits between his two girls. Mia is tucked under his arm.

'Is this suitable?' I ask, sounding prim.

'I've seen it,' David says. 'It's quite funny. And it's better than Mia's suggestion of *Rosemary's Baby*.' He and Olly laugh.

'You haven't seen that, have you, Mia?' I cry.

'Sir said I looked like the main actress in it, and that she was called Mia something too. I really, really want to see it.'

'Which "sir" is this?' Olly asks.

'Mr Hanrahan.'

'Don't ever watch it,' Olly warns. 'Not until you're at least sixty-five.' He settles into the armchair and I sit on the cushion at his feet.

'Bless you,' David says, tweaking her ear. 'All you need to

know is that Mia Farrow was a beauty and had the same pixie cut as you.'

Mia grins. Hayley presses play.

The film starts out as a silly crime caper, and seems, at first, harmless. However, there is a hammy scene involving a young woman who is hit over the head in a park. The shot of her dead body lasts no more than a few seconds, but Mia screams out at the sight of her ghoulish blue face and bedraggled, rain-soaked blonde locks.

'How can you be scared of that? It's so unrealistic. Dead bodies don't even look like that,' Hayley blurts out.

My neck twinges as I turn my head too sharply to look at her. Our eyes meet. An unmistakable flash of terror crosses her fine features. This is all it takes for the cold, hard penny to drop deep inside of me. I begin shivering, reacting viscerally to the implications of what she has unwittingly let slip.

Mia buries her head in David's side, whimpering.

'I saw a YouTube about it,' Hayley explains coolly, turning the volume up over Mia's whimpering.

'Press pause a minute, Hayley.' David pets Mia's head, and I only vaguely listen as he continues. 'I have this film director mate who makes horror films, and he told me they have actual corpse actors on films who come on set just to play dead bodies. I'll take you on one of his sets one day if you like.'

'Yeah!' Mia says.

'For real?' Hayley asks.

'It's a deal. One hundred per cent,' he confirms. Clever David. He's exposed the film's fakery while promoting his cool lifestyle, luring them to Ireland without the need for a magic pipe.

The real forgery is Hayley. What she revealed, albeit by mistake, has hit me between the eyes: *Hayley saw her mother dead*.

FIFTEEN

I toss and turn until Olly groans and asks me to stop wriggling. I'm keeping him awake. I creep downstairs and watch re-runs of *Friends*, drink camomile tea, yogic-breathe, google 'meditation techniques', want to scream. My thoughts run at a hundred miles an hour.

In the end, I have to wake Olly up. I need help. I'm frightened. Of madness. Or myself perhaps. Of Hayley.

'What's up?' he murmurs, checking the clock. The digital numbers 02:03 shine into the dark.

'I need to tell you something.'

He sits up, rubs his eyes, yawns. 'What is it?'

'It's hard to say out loud.'

'Go on.'

I speak as though the words are stuck together. 'I think Hayley was there when Charlotte died.'

'How could she have been? The door was locked from the inside. All night.' He pulls his hair back, stretching his hairline.

'Yes, yes, I know that. It's just, when we were watching that film, the way Hayley looked at me freaked me out. After she'd said that thing about the dead body being unrealistic.'

'Em,' he says with a weary sigh. 'That's a bit of a leap, no?'

'You think I sound insane,' I shoot back, turning away from him, pulling the duvet around my ears.

His pause drags. 'Not insane, no. But I've been... I wonder if... Don't shoot me down, but d'you think it would be a good idea if you saw a grief counsellor? It might help with all this.'

I sit bolt upright and glare at him through the gloom. 'Did you actually just say that?'

'I'm worried you're bottling things up.'

I resist punching the duvet with my fist. 'Why does everyone want me to splurge my feelings all the time?'

Bottling things up is underrated, I want to explain. I have a secret I forget is there. I *feel* it there, always, but there's no need to think about it. It has sunk deep, become part of me, and I leave it well alone. Preserving its integrity while Olly is needling me about my feelings requires a surge of energy, a mental push-down, and I begrudge this, feel the anger rise in me.

Olly sighs. 'I haven't seen you cry once. Not even today, at the ceremony.'

'I have cried!'

'That was over some pound coins or something. But not about losing your sister. You loved her so much, Em.'

My windpipe closes. I try to breathe. I visualise that one errant tear rewinding up my cheek as though it was never there. 'Crying is a private bloody thing,' I fume. 'I'm not like you, I'm not happy vomiting everything up all the time, thinking the whole fucking world has to know all our fucking business.'

There is a ghastly silence. I want to put the words back in my mouth.

Olly speaks ever... so... slowly. 'Before this all happened, you were fine about the book. I've signed a contract. I'm working on my structural edits. Next year it'll be out on the shelves. And somehow you're going to have to find a way to get on board with it.'

'This isn't about your bloody book.'

He breathes in through his nose. 'Okay, so it's about Hayley. What are you saying exactly?'

'I don't really know.' I gulp and sit up cross-legged, bending forward, whispering urgently at him. 'All I know is that she's keeping something from us.'

His eyes glint pale in the dark and I hear a barely discernible exhale. 'What do you want to do about it? Talk to her?'

My fingers dig into the burn on my palm. 'I don't think she'll respond well to direct questions.'

'What about David? Maybe he could get through to her. Let's face it, he's going to be the one dealing with her every day soon enough.'

'I can't tell David!'

'Why not?'

I'm not sure. 'I mean, he'd probably tell Beth or something. And then what?'

'You need to start trusting him.'

'I want to. But what if he's... what if Charlotte was hiding something about him? Domestic abuse or something?'

The fragment of my conversation with Charlotte slips into my mind again like a brain-worm eating away at my sanity. *You're the only person I trust.* Why didn't I dig deeper, when it was plainly such an odd thing to say? Why didn't I ask her why she wouldn't want David to take the girls? Why did I skim over it, make it into a joke?

Olly snorts. 'Are you joking? You really think Charlotte would've kept something like that from us? Come on, if he'd been a wife-beater, she would've been announcing it on Facebook or something.'

'Maybe.'

'Look. You're always telling me to stop catastrophising, so take your own advice. David isn't Jeffrey Dahmer. And Hayley isn't Chucky. Okay?'

I can't help chortling. 'Okay. Fine. But, you know, I'll be keeping a close eye on them. And believe me, I'll find out if anyone is keeping secrets from me.'

'Okay, whatever, Agatha Christie.' He yawns, kisses me and lies down, turning his back on me this time, mumbling, 'I need sleep. I can't write if I'm tired.'

'Sorry, Mr Hemingway.'

'Ha ha,' he murmurs, and I can hear the smile in his voice, which makes me smile too.

Ugh. What the hell is wrong with me? He's right, I'm over-tired and overthinking. Taking on everyone else's sadness at the funeral today seems to have ratcheted up my general anxiety levels. I long for Saturday, when we will be returning home to the flat and David will be in charge of the girls. For a couple of weeks at least, he said he won't need any help at the weekends, which should allow me to get back on track and put everything into perspective.

Sadly, my self-soothing doesn't run deep. As I fall into some sort of half-baked slumber, I'm jerked awake by a plague of unanswered questions and a desire to nail down the truth before Olly and I head home. Perhaps Charlotte's house is like the Hotel California: you can check out, but you can never leave.

The next morning, I wake up with a compulsion to snoop through Hayley's things, and seize the moment when David takes Hayley and Mia out for lunch in Kingston.

Exactly what I'm searching for is unclear. Just something, anything that might offer closure, shed some light on the mystery of what really happened that night.

SIXTEEN

I pull out Hayley's dirty clothes from the laundry basket, making a pile of whites. The story goes that I'm organising the house in preparation for our departure tomorrow.

Before getting stuck in, I hesitate, listen out for Olly, who has been working since 6 a.m. and probably wouldn't notice if the house collapsed around him.

There don't seem to be many hiding places for secrets of any kind. She is untypically tidy for a teenager. The surface of her white chest of drawers is clear except for some incense sticks on a tray and three artfully bent candles that have never been lit. There's an oversized pen pot stuffed with brightly coloured markers on her desk. And a stack of exercise books, which I flick through. Her handwriting is crazy-messy, illegible. She doesn't have a wardrobe, which figures when I consider she wears only tracksuits.

I stand in the middle of the room, swing 360 degrees to look for possible nooks and then kneel to peer underneath the wooden slats of her bed. A trainer, a chocolate bar wrapper, a fleecy sock, a Tupperware tub without its lid.

Next are her drawers. It's sneaky going into them without her permission. On the one hand, I don't care, eager to unearth a secret she might be keeping from us, but equally I am nervous of it. My stomach is churning as I press my hands into the layers, feeling the softness, smelling Hayley's sweet body spray. Amongst the cotton fibres of her leisure wear, I feel something woolly. I bring it out and instantly recognise the fuchsia-pink cashmere turtleneck as Charlotte's. My chest caves in. I clutch it, press it to my nose, inhale her scent of musky cocktail-party perfume. It brings her back to me for a vivid, piercing second. Wow, I miss her. I want her back so much it hurts. I need one of her hugs.

Those tears that Olly is desperate for me to shed threaten to come, but how can I cry for myself when I think of Hayley's loss? I imagine her sleeping with this sweater, maybe waking up to its comforting smell in her head, as though her mum were again kissing her forehead and telling her to get up for school. It's like the insides of my bones are on fire at the unfairness of it.

What have Hayley or Mia done to warrant this? Nothing, that's what. Absolutely bloody nothing. They are the victims of the arbitrariness of life. My guts cramp angrily, tightening inside me. Why am I here prying into her private world? Why am I actively seeking out reasons to distrust her? It's totally unnecessary.

Am I imagining scenarios that mask my grief? That's what Olly thinks. That's what *I* must think. Hayley didn't see Charlotte's dead body. That's mad.

Having shoved the drawer closed, I scoop up the dirty whites and storm downstairs to the utility room. The room contains a large American top-opening washing machine and a drying tub, colourful plastic laundry baskets, Charlotte's natty sock clips in a bowl, wooden pegs in the front pocket of a frilly apron, and supersized boxes of washing powder with measuring scoops inside. Charlotte loved this room, not because she was a good housewife, but because she wasn't. She was always joking that a laundry room made the hell of domestic chores easier.

By tomorrow afternoon, I'll be back home, at the flat, where I'll be doing it my way and tricking myself into housework, pretending I'm not really doing it, fitting it around my life: shove in a few pants and sheets on the way to the coffee machine and take them out again if I remember at the end of the day. If I don't, I just press the cycle on again, thinking they might need an extra wash anyway. And without kids to think about, I get away with it. Nobody will be flipping out at me for forgetting to wash a velour tracksuit in time for a party. (Tick. Guilty of that.)

I spot the vacuum cleaner and decide to get it out one last time before I go. Leave it nice for them.

Hoovering makes me aggressive. As I bash the machine around the place, turning it off briefly to say hello to Olly, who's having a cup of tea – of course he is – all I can think about is how boring housework is, how much I hate domesticity and yet how much I love Hayley and Mia. And how these things clash.

Shortly, I hear them come in. There's a buzz of chatter and laughter, which is encouraging.

'Look!' Mia cries, showing off clusters of shopping bags.

'You've been spoiled!' I grin at David.

'They needed spoiling,' he replies.

'That's very true,' I say, ashamed of my suspicions.

'We brought these back for you.' Hayley presents me with a big box of Krispy Kreme doughnuts.

'Oh wow, my favourite. Thanks, sweetheart.' Now I feel even worse.

'Let's make a brew.' David fills the kettle.

As we sink our teeth into the pastries, I hold onto the feeling that things might be okay, that David will bring them joy.

Moments like these will get us through the worst bits. It's clear he loves them very much, which is why I suppose I should be happy when he comes out with an off-the-cuff idea.

'I've been thinking.' He turns his attention to his daughters. 'Why don't you two come over to Ireland this weekend? If I can get last-minute flights. It might be fun for a couple of days. Beth would love to have you. She's dying for you to meet baby Bridie.'

'You mean tomorrow?' I ask.

'Why not? They're not back at school until the week after next, are they?'

'They're back on the fifteenth,' I say sternly.

There is a beat. Hayley and Mia look at each other. Their pale, delicate faces are so alike in that moment, despite the difference in hair length. I don't know which way it will go, which way I want it to go. This wasn't the plan. It's too soon, too impulsive. Charlotte's funeral was only yesterday. He hasn't discussed it with me or Olly.

Hayley says shyly to Mia, 'Want to go?'

I hold my breath.

'Is that okay, Auntie Emily?' Mia asks me, twisting a short strand of hair at her crown.

'If you'd like to, then of course it is,' I reply cautiously. I remember Hayley's outburst on the night of Charlotte's death, only three weeks ago. *If you make me go live with him in that house with those brats, I'll kill myself.*

'I'm up for it,' Hayley confirms.

David claps his hands and exclaims, 'That's marvellous!'

'As long as you're sure?' I ask them uncertainly. Olly is also looking surprisingly unnerved as he takes a quick sip of his tea.

'Yeah,' they say in unison, nodding, glancing at their father, as though checking he was serious.

'I'll give Beth a bell now,' he says, taking out his phone and disappearing into the garden.

The four of us share nervous smiles. I want to be a fly on the wall of David's conversation with Beth. She might shut the whole dumb idea down.

SEVENTEEN

It's early Saturday morning, and I'm in the downstairs loo when I hear faint calls from Hayley upstairs. 'Auntie Emily!'

'I'm just in the toilet!' I call back.

She can't hear me. She ramps it up, sounding frantic. 'Auntie Emily! *Auntie Emily!* AUNTIE EMILY!'

'I'm having a wee!' I shout louder.

'*AUNTIE EMILY!*' she wails.

I flush and hurry up the stairs two at a time, doing up my flies as I go. 'Hayley? What's happened?' I ask, pulse racing.

'Why didn't you answer me?' she screeches.

'I was on the loo!'

'I can't find my blue hoodie! Where have you put it? I need to take it!'

'Calm down,' I say, flustered already. 'It must be somewhere.' I open her drawers, avoiding the corner where Charlotte's sweater is tucked.

'I've obviously looked there already, you idiot!' she screams at me.

I bristle, hyperaware of her proximity, glancing about for

potential hazards should her temper rocket further. 'Have you tried Mia's room?'

Mia is squeezing shampoo into the little bottle she bought in Boots along with a travel toothbrush and a mini mascara, even though she doesn't wear make-up.

'I haven't seen it,' she says without taking her eyes off the oozing liquid.

Her favourite pink Polaroid camera is on her lap and in the direct firing line of the shampoo. 'Mia,' I warn, 'Watch you don't spill that on your camera.'

Hayley yells again. 'What are you doing? Why aren't you looking for it?'

'I am, Hayley. Calm down. I'll go ask Olly,' I say.

When I storm in on Olly, he jumps, seemingly oblivious to the commotion playing out beyond his noise-cancelling head-phones. I explain the situation in an angry-calm voice. He denies all knowledge of the hoodie.

'But you're always putting things away in the wrong place. Can you please just think. They're leaving in an hour.' I want him to engage on some level with the hell of this child-rearing business. 'And you promised me you wouldn't work this week-end.' At any given opportunity he escapes into his fiction, while I'm left carrying all of our reality on my shoulders. The other day, I asked him why he couldn't at least share the supermarket runs with me, and he replied, 'I have to ring-fence my writing time, Em.' Why can't he bloody well ring-fence *us* at the weekends?

In this instant, I want to rip out his ring fence and stamp on it.

He doesn't respond. My eyes are drawn to a highlighted section in red type on his Word document: *We were free to do as we pleased that afternoon and wandered aimlessly, talking about this and that, finding ourselves on the crest of Parliament Hill. Here, I had the sense I was breathing in too much fresh air, too much freedom, too much happiness, yet still couldn't help craving more than my fair share, until I...* He closes the laptop before I can read on.

How I crave breathing in too much bloody fresh air on Parliament Hill, I think grumpily.

'Have you checked the laundry room?' he says.

Annoyingly, I haven't.

I go downstairs. He is right. It's in the dryer. Panic over.

Everything settles down after that. It never fails to amaze me how quickly a situation can escalate and how it de-escalates equally fast. Hayley and I even manage to laugh about it.

By mid-morning, they are gathering their bags and coats, ready to head to the airport with David.

Saying goodbye to them is harder than I expected. Hayley loiters at the door for longer than Mia. Her hands fidget. She asks me accusingly if I've put her anti-sickness pills in her ruck-sack for all the winding roads. When I tell her I have, she launches herself at me for one last clumsy hug. 'Thanks. Sorry.'

I melt. 'You silly sausage.' I pat her on the back, have a sudden longing to possess her, experience a pang of mind-bending regret about agreeing to the trip. 'Now, you stop worrying this instant and have a lovely time, okay?'

David is not Jeffrey Dahmer and Hayley is not Chucky.

'We'll miss you both,' Olly says sentimentally, and wraps his arms around the two of them.

'It's only for a weekend,' I say, which could've sounded unsentimental. But it's my way of confirming the shortness of this trip and pressing down on a panicky tugging sensation in my chest. One weekend. That's all it is.

'Okay. Bye then.' Hayley is first out the door, and my stomach seizes up. I hated her a few hours ago and now I can't bear to let her go.

EIGHTEEN

While tidying the house before Olly and I leave, I find Mia's wash bag lying on her bed. For a second, it equals calamity. I text David, letting him know she might be upset. He doesn't reply, probably thinks I'm fussing.

I return to the task of making Mia's bed, wanting it to be nice for her when she comes back on Monday night. I can't believe I'm not going to be here when they get back. I want to carry on caring for them for a little longer, unable to let go quite yet. I've still got the weekends at some point soon, I console myself.

While hiding a Creme Egg underneath her pillow as a treat for her return, I stumble on a Polaroid of Charlotte that Mia has tucked there. I sit on the bed staring at it. The quality of the photograph is poor. The colours of Charlotte's smile are fading. I strain to form a vivid picture of her face in my head, wishing the details were sharper.

My eyes are drawn to the snaps in the frames on the bedside table. One is of Charlotte and Mia, another of Hayley in a huddle with five friends, and a third of Charlotte and me standing outside Hamleys on Regent Street. It was a happy day to celebrate the completion of Mia's Year 6 SATs.

The silent house has an eerie hum to it. Without the girls, it's too quiet around here, and I startle when Olly speaks. 'Come on then, ready?'

I put the Polaroid of Charlotte back where I found it and regulate my breathing. 'Definitely, let's get out of here.'

It takes us three hours to get home on three buses, thanks to train strikes on the overground.

Our flat smells neglected. There is a whiff of mildew, which we trace to Olly's study, where he left the window open a crack allowing some books on the sill to get wet. We potter in and out of the rooms, feasting on all our things, expressing our relief. 'Oh my God, it's so good to be home,' I say.

We end up lounging about in Olly's study. I smoke a joint with my feet up on his desk, ankles crossed. I admire the Chinese embroidered slippers I'm wearing, which I forgot to take to Charlotte's. Olly pulls up the sash window and I join him, elbows on the sill, to look out onto our neighbours' gardens.

'Ishmael's been neglecting his lawn,' he says.

I laugh, realise I'm not feeling cross or guilty about anything. A less complicated sadness engulfs me.

Olly inhales and exhales. 'I've missed this view,' he says.

Over the rooftops lies Parliament Hill. It has been waiting for us.

My fingers curl over my right palm.

We now have the freedom to roam as much as we like. I'm not sure how to feel about that. I'm unfocused. I'll have to think about going back to work on Monday. Maybe not straight away. I'll give myself a day or two. With no work, and in the girls' absence, what will I do with myself? The whirlwind of them this morning seems like a lifetime ago. I can't even remember why it was so stressful.

I click my phone on to see if they've texted. Nothing.

We go for a walk. Marty isn't there on the bench and I worry he's unwell. Or worse. Like he can't survive without me. How arrogant of me. There are others who'll help. My paltry contributions are not missed. Before I left for Charlotte's, all this was central to my very identity, and now I see that it carries on without me quite well. Now I see that perhaps I did it for me rather than them. It made me feel like a good person, papered over why I'm not.

Are the girls carrying on without me quite well too?

Olly holds my hand and kisses the back of it. We talk a lot about his book. He's frustrated by his editor's notes. 'She wants me to soften the main character,' he explains, alongside other concerns.

I'm a little affronted by this. 'She wants you to soften *me*, you mean?'

'Ha. No chance of that.' He pauses, adds quickly, 'Anyway, Ellie's not you.'

'I know.' Although I don't know that. As far as I can see, she is definitely me. Or at least her thoughts are mine. Is that the same thing?

When we get to the roundabout at the bottom of Swain's Lane, I peel off to buy us some supper.

'Let's have fish!' Olly calls after me gleefully. I can tell he is enjoying our liberation more than I am.

'Good plan.' Neither Hayley nor Mia would countenance anything fishy. Not even a fish finger. The smell of chilli con carne floods my senses followed by the memory of Hayley shoving me. It feels shocking, more shocking than it did back then.

I buy some wild salmon. Later I cook it with buttery fennel. It's delicious. I keep checking my phone. I smoke a cigarette, even though I don't tend to smoke tobacco on its own. We drink more wine and joke about rekindling our sex life, which became non-existent at Charlotte's because we worried the girls would hear.

'Do you think I should call them?' I ask. 'Or is it too soon?'

'Maybe text.'

'Good idea.' I grab my phone and bash out a quick group WhatsApp to both girls headed *Hello!* with a waving emoji.

Just checking in! Hope your flight was okay. How were the winding roads? Olly sends a big squeeze. And a big one from me too. Love, Auntie Emily xxx

'I hope they're having a good time and that Hayley's behaving herself,' I say.

Do I mean this? If Hayley's behaving herself, does it suggest that I'm the problem? It is a ridiculously self-centred way of looking at it, but I can't help it. I remind myself of what Jamie Hanrahan said to me at the funeral about kids taking it out on the people they're closest to. That's me, right?

'It'll be quite full-on for her, I imagine,' Olly says, chewing his thumbnail. His clear blue eyes search mine for the positive spin.

I always oblige. 'But it'll be so much fun meeting little Bridie. They probably won't even have time to be sad. And Beth looked nice in the photos. I mean, they're just going to have to find a way to get along.'

He agrees wholeheartedly. 'That's the point. They have to make it work. None of them have a choice in the matter.'

In a while, after some TV, we go to bed. We do actually have sex, even though we're exhausted. Maybe we're just proving a point. It's nice, though. Worth the effort.

'I've missed this.' Olly flops next to me.

'Me too.'

But as soon as he's asleep, I get up and pad through to the

kitchen – wantonly naked! – to find my phone. I'm sure I heard a text come through.

It's from Hayley.

I want to come home i hate them they're horrible plse call me.

NINETEEN

I text Hayley back, but there's no reply. It turns out the farmhouse is stuck in the middle of a bloody field, and there's only intermittent signal. I know this because I searched it on Google Maps in the middle of the night when neither the girls nor David replied to any of my texts or calls. What if Beth's being cruel and locking them in cupboards? What if David is a child-beater? What if they're part of a cult?

By Sunday morning, I'm frantic.

Finally, David rings me back.

'What's up?' he asks, sounding harassed. Admittedly, it's only 7 a.m.

'Sorry it's so early. I just wanted to check on the girls.'

'They're grand, why?' He sing-songs it like a true Irishman, even though he isn't Irish.

I can't land Hayley in it and tell him she hates him, so I say, 'I texted them and didn't hear back. You know me, I like to know what's what.'

'The signal's terrible here.'

'So they're having fun?'

'A few challenges, but nothing Beth can't handle.' He yawns.

'Hayley's being okay then?' I let out a light laugh.

He pauses long enough for me to catch birdsong in the background and then what sounds like a car door slamming. 'A few issues...' he begins.

I can't find my voice for a second. 'Oh yeah?'

A throaty engine fires up. 'It's just, Beth can be intuitive. A bit witchy, you know?'

'Ooh, spooky. What's the Ouija board spelt out?'

An exhaust bangs. It's hard to hear him over the rattling of metal and the whistling of wind. The vehicle is probably some hippy-dippy death-trap. I hope the girls aren't being driven about in it. He shouts over the noise. 'She finds Hayley's aggressive energy difficult to be around.' His voice judders as though he's going over potholes. 'But she takes other people's wounds right into her heart. To a fault, probably. Helping others is a higher purpose for her, a calling. It's hard to have this gift, though. She feels other people's anger deeply. It's why she's such a good healer. Her meditation classes—'

He lost me at 'higher purpose'. I break in. 'Back to Hayley. Sorry, but grief causes anger. It's one of the stages. You must know that.'

'What's that? I can't hear!'

I repeat it, grittier this time.

'Yes, bless her, but when Beth tried working a little deeper with her on it, Hayley flipped.'

I feel sick. 'What did she do?'

'What?'

I shout way louder than I need to. 'WHAT DID HAYLEY DO?'

'She told Beth to fuck off. Beth was really hurt.'

A handbrake screeches. There's quiet suddenly. A relief. 'Saying fuck off to a stepmother is a rite of passage, no? Even for a teenager who hasn't lost their mum,' I say. I haven't even met Beth and I feel the urge to tell her to fuck off. Not sure why. Definitely not fair.

'Hmm. It's just I was hoping... Well... it hasn't been great for their bonding process, you know?'

I stifle a frustrated groan. 'That's the whole point of bonding, David. You're meant to take the rough with the smooth. They've been there less than twenty-four hours.' I'm a fine one to talk, but I plough on self-righteously. 'And there's quite a lot of history between you guys that wasn't any of Hayley's doing.'

There's a rustle-like interference, which might be a plastic bag. 'Well, I thought it was worth pointing out.'

'Brilliant. Thanks. Note to self: Hayley's a moody teenager. Got it.'

'Okay, I'm at the farm now. They leave eggs out in a box. I thought I'd make pancakes with Mia.'

'She'll love that.' I feel sheepish for snapping. 'It'll get easier. It's a lot for you guys to take on. I do appreciate that.'

'It's a lot for all of us to take on,' he says, which I hope isn't loaded.

'She'll probably settle down when it's just the three of you back at Charlotte's,' I say, which is loaded as hell.

'It'll be grand,' he says again, keeping up the sing-song.

The next time I speak to him, his tone is very different.

TWENTY

'I'm afraid there's been a serious incident involving Hayley,' Jamie Hanrahan says down the phone to me.

'Oh God, what's happened?' I slam my computer closed, ready to grab my things and bolt to Charlotte's, heart in my mouth. 'Is she okay?'

'Sorry, I didn't mean to scare you,' Jamie rushes on. 'Hayley's fine. But the girl she punched, not so much.'

'Oh *shit*.' My back teeth clench. I stay glued to my seat.

I haven't seen her or Mia since they returned home from their weekend in Ireland. I called them on FaceTime on the Monday evening, and we shared lots of giggles, and I hoped my role as their auntie could continue in this vein for ever more.

Now it's the following Tuesday, and I'm supposed to be reading a script. The idea was to enjoy the atmosphere of a quiet café in Highgate. It seems Hayley won't allow me that peace of mind.

'It was a gory scene,' Jamie continues. 'Jen's braces cut into the inside of her cheek, and she bled so much we thought she had a head injury.'

He breaks off, perhaps waiting for me to say something. I'm

so shocked, I can't even express it. 'Why did Hayley do it?' It's all I feel capable of asking.

'She won't tell us, but from what some of the others said, I gather it's something to do with rivalry over Ayton.'

I remember girls like Hayley at school who threw their weight around when things didn't go their way. The class bullies. Does it surprise me that Hayley is that girl? I feel again her shove in the kitchen, and try to distract myself from it, fixate on a man's jiggling foot under the adjacent table.

Jamie goes on. 'I'm afraid she's being suspended for a week with immediate effect, so you'll need to come in to collect her as soon as possible.'

'You'll have to call David. He's living with them now,' I say.

'Oh really?' he exclaims.

'He *is* their dad. He should be on the contact list.'

'Of course, sorry. From what Charlotte told me, I assumed she wouldn't want... I just thought... I didn't check.' He gathers himself. 'Because you and your partner were living there, I presumed you were their legal guardians.'

To coin my mother's phrase, he's being inappropriate. 'Shall I text you his mobile number?' I reply formally.

'Okay, yeah,' he says, but he sounds defeated. 'That would be great.'

Then he sighs heavily, and it flips a switch in me. 'On second thoughts, it's maybe best he hears it from me, and that I come down to the school with him this time. Is that okay?' It's a second thought I haven't thought through a first time. I have no idea if David will view this as interfering. I check my watch.

'Awesome,' Jamie says. He doesn't hide the relief in his voice. 'I'll see you then.'

'They've taken into consideration the tragic circumstances of your mum's passing, Hayley. But you have to realise how serious this is,' Jamie says, one leg crossed over the other. Hayley continues to pick at the ends of her hair. David, dressed all in black, shifts about in his plastic chair, making it creak under his weight. 'You'll face a reintegration meeting with the head on your return.'

The already hot classroom becomes stifling. I glimpse David's strawberry-blond stubbled jaw slackening. He rubs one temple while raising an eyebrow. It's lost on Hayley; her eyes are fixed on her shoe, which she taps repeatedly into the flimsy back panel of Jamie's desk.

'Do you understand what I've said, Hayley?' Jamie asks her.

'Yeah,' she mumbles. Then she shoots up and flies out of the room.

'Oh God,' Jamie says.

'I'll go after her,' I say, heaving myself to my feet and peering out into the corridor at a sea of kids. 'Which way has she gone?'

Jamie gets up. 'I can hazard a guess.' He grabs his phone from his desk. 'Follow me.'

He weaves through the throng like a pro. David and I trail behind, stop-starting, jostled by teenagers.

In my ear, David says, 'I'll google therapists.'

'You reckon she'll go to one?'

'It's up to us to make her go.'

Having lost sight of Jamie, we end up by the school gates. I try Hayley's mobile.

Eventually Jamie reappears from around the corner. 'It's okay, I saw her with Ayton. Come this way.'

He strides with his hands in his khaki trousers. I trot after him. 'What's this boy Ayton like?' I ask him. 'They're together a lot.'

He straightens his lanyard to the centre of his white shirt. 'He's a nice kid, but he has some challenges at home.'

David mumbles, 'Figures.'

Jamie walks on a few paces before he says, 'I guess you know, but he was only twelve when his dad died. Fell off scaffolding. And his mum goes AWOL for days on end, leaving him alone. Once, he had to rescue her from a motorway bridge because she was drunk and threatening to jump.'

I struggle with a mix of emotions. It's impossible to communicate how guilty I feel about not knowing all that already, so I say nothing.

David pulls out a tight smile for Jamie. There is a bristling quality to his charm now, and I sense his smile would drop off his face the second our backs are turned. 'I feel sorry for the fella, but he isn't our problem now, is he?'

Jamie twists his whole body to peer across me to David. 'No, I guess he's mine,' he says.

We get to the corner of the street. Jamie points at a cloud of vape smoke billowing over some lock-ups. 'Follow that cloud.'

'Jesus, really?' David says under his breath, and scowls, rubbing his brow. His hail-fellow-well-met act is well and truly worn out.

I suggest he gets the car and parks it up on the corner. He doesn't argue and strides off.

'He's already had enough of her,' I joke to Jamie, embarrassed.

Jamie swivels slowly on his heel to watch him go, shaking his head. 'Sometimes you wonder why people have...'

He stops, bends his knees with a little bounce and scratches his goatee. I silently finish his sentence in my head. *Sometimes you wonder why people have kids at all.* It's a sentiment I'm overfamiliar with. I guess I'm glad people have children, to keep the human race going and all that. But I can't help believing that fewer of us need to have them, considering how hard it is to bring them up and what a burden we are to the planet. For this last reason alone, it seems odd that not having them isn't as valued as it should be.

'He's going to get her a therapist,' I say to Jamie.

'It's worth a try.'

'She won't go though, will she?'

He sighs. 'Nope. Not a chance in hell.'

'He's hoping to take them over to live in Ireland at some stage. Might be just what she needs.'

'Might be.' He sounds non-committal.

My heart pinches when I picture Hayley's troubled, washed-out features, tortured by grief and confusion. Jamie must see it in my eyes. He steps forward to touch my forearm. I'm not sure his proximity feels quite right. He says sincerely, 'She'll be fine. She's very loved. Give her time.'

It is such a comforting thing to hear, I forgive him his transgression. He's more connected to Hayley's well-being than Olly has been, but then I immediately want to take that thought back.

'Thanks. I'll go fetch her and give her a lecture on popcorn lung and punching girls in the face.'

'Good luck with that.' He ambles off, coolly waving goodbye behind him.

All the teenage girls must be madly in love with him at school, I think nostalgically. Then I recall the fake smile Hayley pulled for him at the funeral, and I wonder about it.

TWENTY-ONE

The closer I get to Hayley and Ayton, the more nervous I become. I haven't a clue how to handle her. Wading in with another telling-off doesn't feel right. Letting it go for the sake of avoiding a blow-up doesn't sit well either. As I weigh up the best approach, arranging my features into the right combo of stern and compassionate, I overhear her yelling something.

'I didn't fucking say nothing!' Ayton bellows back.

She guffaws. 'You didn't say nothing? That means you said something, you idiot!'

'I never would've told her!'

'So why did she say that, then?'

'I swear it, babe,' he replies. He has a mannered tone, charming, lilting and as hard as the street. 'Jen's always talking trash about you. She's got major beef with you. You know it. But I said fuck all to her. It's the truth, I swear it on my life.'

'But she said she knew what really happened to Mum, like you told her you were there that night!'

Something clatters on the ground. Perhaps my heart.

'She's just winding you up. She doesn't know shit, babe. Nobody knows I was there, I swear. I didn't say anything to her about it. She's just making shit up to piss you off. You've got to believe me. Look at me.' There's a lull. 'Don't cry, beautiful. Come 'ere. Shh, shh, don't cry.'

I feel blown backwards. There's a klaxon ringing in my ears. Hayley's previous account of the evening Charlotte died plays out in my head: she and her mum had argued about her going out on a school night. Against Charlotte's wishes, Hayley went out anyway with Ayton and four other friends. She came home alone at around ten, heard her mum in the shower and went straight to bed without seeing her.

Now it appears that she *and* Ayton came back to the house. Why lie?

A car passes in front of me and turns into the side road where they're standing. It's my cue to make my presence known, have it out with Hayley, unlock the truth. My mind is racing.

Although it's hard to piece together the full picture from snippets of their row, was Ayton somehow involved in Charlotte's death? Or did he see something between her and her mum that he shouldn't have? Either scenario is like a firebomb going off in my mind, and I have no idea what to do next. A rushing sound makes me feel dizzy, and I steady myself by leaning on the brick wall just as David pulls up in his rented Audi.

'You okay?' he calls through the wound-down window.

He parks up on the yellow lines and helps me into the passenger seat. As he hands me a bottle of water, Hayley and Ayton appear around the corner.

TWENTY-TWO

As soon as Ayton sees David's car, his arm slinks off Hayley's shoulder. He pops his hood over his rusty red curls and lopes away in the opposite direction, leaving Hayley standing pale and alone on the pavement a few feet away.

'Look at her,' David seethes. His hand is clutching the gear-stick. 'All sheepish now, isn't she? She's going to hear it from me, I can tell you.'

Little does he know that a punch-up at school is trifling compared to the revelation of a few moments before.

'Go easy on her,' I warn.

He grunts, winds down the window and shouts, 'Get in, young lady!'

Hayley shoves both fists into her blazer pockets and glares at us. I can't help admiring her for a second. Her fine fair hair blows across her mouth in the wind. Despite the fire of red encircling her eyes, her features are delicate, elegant, defenceless.

'Come on, Hayley,' I coax. 'I've heard the other side of it. Jen sounds like a proper cow.'

Her face relaxes. 'How do you know?'

'Let's not talk about it here on the street. Come on, get in. We can stop off at Starbucks if you like.' I need to keep her on side and also ingest some caffeine myself, stay alert, think strategically about how to broach things with her.

David mumbles, 'Right, so we're rewarding her for punching some poor girl in the face now, are we?'

I ignore him. The Starbucks incentive works and she gets in.

As we crawl along in traffic, David starts giving her a lecture on how to manage anger. Hayley remains unmoved and stares blankly out of the window. Because she doesn't say sorry or show any remorse, David's own anger builds. Soon he's banging on the steering wheel and yelling at her. Her head presses backwards into her seat, as though she's scared, but her eyes suggest she's dead inside.

Or is she thinking about consequences far worse than a suspension?

In an adjacent car, a woman frowns at David. Even from afar, a stranger can tell that his shouting is disproportionate, an unleashing of something else.

My hands begin to shake. 'Calm down, David,' I urge in a low voice, fearing Hayley might snap if he carries on much longer. His eruption feels especially unsafe given that he's driving. I remember Charlotte telling me that he was the most chilled man on the planet until he was pushed too far, when he had the capacity to flip. And Hayley is pushing.

In the end, he runs out of steam, starts brooding. The animosity between the two of them makes the air sickly thick. When we find a space near Starbucks, David says he'll wait for us.

Hayley and I don't talk until we're in the queue. I'm pent up with a million questions, realise this isn't the right time.

'He went too far,' I say, touching her shoulder.

'I hate him,' she says casually. Her neck cranes as she stares up at the menu board.

'No, you don't.'

She looks me square in the face. 'I *hate* him,' she hisses, 'and so did Mum.'

I feel a tightness in my chest. 'How about I pop back to yours so we can have a little chat?'

Her eyes flick up to the menu again. One shoulder gives a small, unconvincing shrug. 'I thought you only had time at the weekends?' she says archly.

I get the message. 'I'll come back for a bit,' I say, and study her profile. The inscrutability of her face suggests she's holding herself together with all her might.

'I'll have the double-shot caramel latte with extra cream, please,' she says, pulling out her phone and moving away to the napkins and sugar.

I order our drinks and decide to buy some chocolate for David as an apology gift from Hayley. A sop. A cheap way into reconciliation.

My phone reads 14:35. Olly will be at the flat, typing away in his study, perhaps, or making himself a cup of tea. He'll assume I'm around the corner, working at the café in Highgate or meeting a friend at the ponds or picking up some supper for later. It's not unusual for us to spend whole days apart, unaware of each other's movements. Freelance life. Happy lives.

So far today, I've resisted texting him the headline about her suspension, even though I've had plenty of opportunities. Like with the burn on my hand, I have a strong instinct to protect him from all of this, especially from what I've just overheard, for as long as possible. However, the other, less generous part of me wants to say, 'Told you so, didn't I?' After accusing me of over-thinking and reading too much into her antagonism, it seems he was underthinking it and I was spot on.

I'm eager to get more out of her and make sense of what I heard.

By the time Hayley and I get back to the car, everyone is in a better mood. We've all had time to compose ourselves. Hayley gives her dad the chocolate bar and says sorry. It took a lot to do that, and I'm proud of her. David beams and clicks his tongue, and says, 'You little terror, you've always known how to wrap me around your little finger. Just like your mum did. Hop in.'

Thankfully he doesn't catch her smirk, which gives me a little shiver, and I wonder what we're in for later. She is volatile. A small poke at this could unleash all sorts of hell.

TWENTY-THREE

David slumps at the kitchen table with a beer. He hands me one, and I pace and sip, then text Olly to say I'll be home late. It's too early to drink beer, but it feels as necessary as medicine. He taps the tip of his bottle onto mine before draining half of it in one go. He is round-shouldered, breathing heavily like an older man who has run up a flight of stairs. His eruption in the car appears to have taken everything out of him. A dome of red skin shines through his stubbly hair. He rubs at it.

'I'm going to take them back to Ireland sooner than planned.'

I stop in front of him, alert. 'What? When were you thinking?'

'Probably by the end of the week,' he says.

My heart starts galloping. The timing couldn't be worse. Just when I'm getting close to finding out what happened that night. I slam my beer down. 'What? Hold on a bloody second. You can't do that. It's too soon.'

He replies matter-of-factly. 'We need to rip the plaster off. It's no good dragging it out like this.' He sighs, picking at the damp label of his drink. 'It'll be easier over there.'

'Slow down. You've got to think this through. No offence, but they didn't have the best weekend when they were over there.'

'They'll get used to it. And judging by Hayley's behaviour today, she could do with a fresh start.' He rolls the bottle between his palms. It's almost as if he's talking to himself, not too bothered whether he wins me around or not. He doesn't need my blessing.

'But what about school?'

'There's a great school in the nearby town.'

'And my parents? They're their only grandchildren. You'd take them away from them?'

'Something tells me they wouldn't fight it.'

Sometimes I forget how well he knows us. 'They're better grandparents than they were parents. They adore the girls.'

'And they're welcome to stay any time they like. As are you. The boys can double up. Beth and I have talked about it already.'

'And Beth? She's got a newborn to care for.' *Suddenly I care about Beth?*

'She's always dreamed of having a busload of kids. She's a natural mother.'

Good for bloody Beth! I shake my head, riled, scrabbling for the cons of his plan, finding none that will sound logical or sensible. 'You have to give them a say in this. It's too soon to uproot them. They've only just lost their mum. Come on, have some—'

Then something catches my eye. Or some*one*.

Hayley steps into the light. Her eyes are slits of fury. 'I won't go,' she breathes, and her breath might as well be fire.

I'm horror-struck. 'Oh Hayley. Nothing is decided.'

'Sounds like Dad's decided,' she says.

'No, no, not just yet,' I bluster. 'We've—'

David interrupts me. 'Yes, I have decided, young lady.' He

goes to the fridge for another beer. The metal lid clatters on the side. 'I know what's best for you.'

'You can't make me!' she yells.

'Watch me.'

She stuffs her feet into her trainers. 'I'm going out.'

'Suit yourself,' he says, angling his beer at the door.

I hear her zipping up her puffer jacket in the hallway. 'We can't just let her go like that.'

I follow her, put my back against the front door to stop her. She tries to shoulder me out of the way, then starts kicking me in the shins. I wince in pain, but I'm determined she shouldn't go.

'Kick me all you like. We need to work this out,' I say calmly.

'Get out of the way!' She reaches out and pulls at the latch, determined and powerful. I clench my back teeth, go deep inside myself. It takes every ounce of self-control I possess to stop myself from losing it.

'I WILL NEVER MOVE TO IRELAND. EVER!' she screeches.

She kicks harder. Ouch. Ouch. My shins burn.

I can't believe I'm in this tussle with a teenager. What is going on? How easily a shouting match can spiral into a physical fight. It could have played out like this between her and Charlotte on that fateful night. What if Hayley didn't go straight to bed when she came in that night, as she previously told us? What if she or Ayton somehow managed to get into the bathroom while Charlotte was showering? What if Hayley had a physical scuffle with her mum? What if Ayton did something to her?

What if...? What if...?

I'm losing the fight, losing patience. She is trying to escape, prising open the front door. As I push against it, I see her fingers are about to get trapped. I'm forced to let go, and she slips outside.

But I'm as stubborn as her. We've got unfinished business.

I kick my slippers off and put my boots on and go after her, chase her down the street. Passers-by stare. I'm losing her, and run faster. I'm gasping for breath by the time I reach the green opposite Ayton's block of flats. She's already stabbing at the button on the intercom. A car whooshes in front of me before I can cross the road.

'Hayley!' I pant, and press angrily at a stitch in my side as I run. 'We need to talk!' 'Please,' I say louder. She pretends not to hear. 'HAYLEY!' I yell, with more authority.

She turns to me, hand poised on the door ready for Ayton to buzz her in, leg jiggling.

I beg her, 'Please wait. Just for a minute.'

The door pops open. She slips in and it slams in my face before I can edge through the gap.

My rage erupts. I slam a hand onto the fortified glass and bellow at her, 'I OVERHEARD YOU AND AYTON TALKING!'

Finally I've discovered what shouting at the top of my lungs sounds like. It sounds like I mean business. It sounds like I won't take any more of her shit. It sounds like I've got her.

Her head snaps round, and for a second I can see the shock and confusion. Immediately she comprehends the stakes, which are way higher than a tussle over a move to Ireland.

She puts two fingers up at me through the glass and legs it up the stairs, her hair swishing side to side across her back.

What if...? what if...?

What if that child and her boyfriend killed my sister?

TWENTY-FOUR

I text Olly to let him know I'm staying overnight at Charlotte's and that I'll call him later to explain. And I tell David that I want to be here when Hayley gets in. He doesn't argue with the plan. He sinks three more beers before crashing out.

A flash of Hayley's terrified face at the door of Ayton's block of flats comes back to me. A chill runs up my spine. She knows I overheard them, but what's she going to do about it? Run away?

Mia pads into the kitchen a few minutes later. I'm still clutching my phone and in the same position, with my elbows leaning on the island.

'I can't sleep. Can we watch a movie together?' Her voice is babyish, as though she's trying too hard to be a very good girl in the face of Hayley's bad.

'Course. Come on, my love,' I say.

We get cosy in the telly room. This is where I'll sleep tonight, on the fold-out bed. David is in the spare room, which has become his bedroom.

Every time there's a noise outside, Mia and I glance at each other hopefully. Both of us, it seems, are waiting for Hayley to come home – for very different reasons. While I'm chomping at the bit to grill her about that night, I allay Mia's fears and tell her not to worry, that her sister will be safe and sound at Ayton's and will be back when she's calmer. I put her to bed and stroke her forehead until she's asleep.

Back in the telly room, I get into bed too, and call Olly. I tell him that Hayley punched someone and that she's suspended. I tell him that David's taking them to Ireland as soon as possible. I tell him that Hayley legged it to Ayton's in protest. I don't tell him what I heard behind the garages.

'All quiet on the Western Front now, though?' he says.

'Aside from the fact she'd rather die than live in Ireland and might never come home, yeah.'

'Of course she will.' He sounds irritable, maybe tired.

'You don't know that,' I snap. He doesn't understand how close I am to uncovering new information about the night my sister died.

'I wasn't judging you for worrying. I'm just saying she'll come home.'

I exhale. 'Sorry, I didn't mean to have a go at you. It's been a stressful day, that's all.'

There's the tap-tap sound of a keyboard in the background. I imagine him propped up on his pillows, fiddling about on his manuscript. 'No worries.'

'I mean, if she doesn't want to go live with David, how is he going to make her? Drag her by the hair?' I say.

There's some more tapping.

The silence is long enough for me to ask, 'You still there?'

'Sorry. Yup... He could cut off her pocket money and phone?'

'Even that wouldn't work on Hayley. She'd just move in with Ayton. Get a pay-as-you-go or something. She's so stubborn.'

Charlotte's presence moves inside my chest. I think about the toxicology report. With everything going on, I forgot to call the coroner's office for the results. I wonder now whether I even want them. Does it matter what state she was in?

'Ha, yeah,' Olly murmurs. Tap-tap. 'It'll be interesting to see how he'll physically get her to Ireland.' But I can tell by his tone that his mind is elsewhere.

'How did your writing go today?' I ask, just to keep him on the phone. Hearing his voice is comforting.

The tapping stops. His voice is less muffled suddenly, more engaged. 'Yeah. Great. Structural edits are going well.'

I put my phone on speaker, turn on my side and pull the duvet right up around my chin. 'Do you know yet when it'll be out?'

'They still haven't finalised the publication date, but it should be sometime early next year. Sarah's excited, though.'

Sarah this and Sarah that. I hear a lot about his editor these days.

'Annoying that we don't know,' I say. How good it would feel to know that something, *anything*, can be relied upon as a dead cert in this world.

I stay awake long after Olly and I have said goodnight to each other.

As the minutes tick by, my feverish desire to get the truth out of Hayley is gradually replaced by worry. What if she and Ayton went out somewhere and something happened? What if they had a fight and she's roaming the streets alone, thinking she can't come home? What if I've put her in harm's way?

This last fear sends a shooting white light across my brain. I send her a text.

Hi, sweetheart. Sorry for shouting. I'm not cross. Let me know when you're home so that I don't worry. Emily x

For the first time in my life, I'm grateful for my wakefulness so I can listen out for her. I'm without my pills, having not expected to stay over, but the absence of them doesn't send me into a tailspin. I'm keen to stay alert.

An hour and a half goes by. Blinking in the dark, I make a prayer-like pact with the powers-that-be in the universe by swearing I'll never again quiz Hayley about what happened that night so long as they deliver her home safely.

Childish, yes, but I'm desperate, feeling out of control and responsible.

When I hear her stamp in at gone 2 a.m., I'm giddy with relief and hold back the tears.

I remember a villa holiday in France one year when she was six. It was their first family holiday without David, a year after the divorce. Every day Hayley and I played volleyball in the pool together while Mia toddled about with Charlotte. Hayley wore a pink swimsuit with a yellow tie around her belly. We were both terrible at the game and giggled more than we hit the ball. By the end of the week, we'd achieved a whopping rally of fifteen, and her little face, with its sunburned nose and pale eyelashes, was full of delight. Then later, while eating a watermelon slice bigger than her head, she said to me, 'You're the bestest auntie in the whole wide world.' And I wanted to freeze time and hold the precious moment for ever.

Knowing that she's safe now, I park my worries about the fight we have ahead of us regarding Ireland. Do I even want her to go?

I remember my vow to the universe. But can I keep it?

TWENTY-FIVE

I wake up to the clatter of plates and cutlery in the kitchen and remember I'm sleeping in the telly room. I check the clock. It's 7 a.m. When we lived here, I was the one to wake them for school and make breakfast.

Has David missed the alarm?

Although Hayley won't need to get ready for school for one whole week, Mia will. I race into her room, rubbing my eyes.

The curtains are open and the bed is made.

I follow the smell of bacon downstairs, expecting to see her tufty little head of hair at the stove making blueberry pancakes or something. She tends to cook us brekky when she knows there's tension in the air. When I see Hayley frying bacon in Mia's place, I'm flabbergasted. Her long ponytail is static from being brushed.

At the island, David is sitting with a cup of coffee and Mia is sipping from a glass of orange juice, which is poured a little too full. The three of them are chatting animatedly.

'What's going on here?' I ask.

'Morning, Auntie Emily!' Mia sings.

Hayley turns down the hob, puts down the greasy utensil

and comes over to me for a hug. 'I'm sorry I ran off like that. And I'm sorry for... you know... the two fingers. You know you're still the best auntie in the whole world, right?'

I stutter. 'It was very late when you came in. Was everything okay? Did Ayton walk you home?'

'Yes, of course he did.' She grins at me and then at her father. 'And Dad and I have had a really good talk.'

David beams at her. 'Bless your heart, poppet.'

It seems the universe delivered some other miracles last night.

'Wait...' I run a hand through my bed-hair. 'When did all this happen?'

'After I came in, I couldn't sleep,' Hayley explains. 'So I went into Dad's room and we talked about Ireland and I've decided I'm okay about going to live there. He's going to do our rooms up like that photo I showed you – you know the one with all the spider plants? – and he's going to teach me to drive on the farm! And apparently the school has a DJing course I can do. And I can give up French!'

I'm lost for words, blindsided. My thoughts gallop ahead. I'm burning to unpick this mega-super-sized extreme U-turn of Hayley's. Trying to think like her, I put myself in her shoes. Last night, she knew I was onto her and Ayton. And she was scared.

Maybe she made a calculation that the move to Ireland would be a way to escape my scrutiny. The lesser evil maybe? Crummy stepmum? Bratty little brothers? Tumbledown farmhouse? New friends? Easy-peasy! Nothing compares to the risk of her secrets being exposed by Auntie Emily. Maybe it points to the magnitude of what she is hiding.

Mia pitches in. 'And it has an amazing skate park! And I can help birth lambs in the spring!'

I find an elastic on my wrist and tie my hair back, trying to play catch-up, stalling for time. 'Mia, you're not in your uniform.'

She giggles. 'Dad says I don't have to go in.'

'There's no point,' David says. 'I'll talk to the school today.'

'But what about this house?' I ask stupidly. It's no obstacle and we all know it.

'I wondered if you could take care of it. Sell the old place for me,' David says hopefully, glancing around the kitchen.

Like yesterday, I dig for some rational arguments and draw blanks. There are no reasons to keep them here other than self-ishness and nostalgia and, more than anything, a hunch I can't air. What can I say? I can't stop them without sounding obstructive.

I eye Hayley. She blinks innocently. She's smart. Too smart. For now, it's a dance between the two of us.

'I'm happy that you're happy,' I say neutrally.

For the rest of the morning, she continues to outsmart me. She makes sure we are never alone. She follows David around like his shadow. I suggest we go to the park for a walk, but she opens a board game with Mia, playing it for ages. At midday, David actually says, 'You can go home, Em. We're fine.'

I am a spare part, a nuisance even, lurking about for no good reason and getting in the way of their bonding time.

I step out of the house, down the little alleyway off the back garden, to call my parents, hoping they'll share my outrage about David's decision to take the girls to Ireland so soon, perhaps stall it.

'Oh. This week. Right,' Mum says to the news. 'Right. Okay. We suspected as much.'

'You did?'

'Let me get your father.' She relays the facts to Dad. His reply is too muffled for me to make out. She comes back on. 'He thinks it's for the best, darling. And we can visit them.'

I hang up, feeling beaten. There is nothing I can do. Nothing.

Before I leave them at Charlotte's, I make sure they promise to give me and my parents the chance to come over and say a final goodbye.

David promises. Mia promises. And Hayley promises.

Hayley's promise burrows inside me as I stride past Aiden and Robin's house on the way to the station. From the street, I hear Aiden's laugh. Their house and Charlotte's are joined. When I'm in Mia's bedroom, I sometimes hear the low murmur of them talking. The police have already interviewed them, but I have less trust in the process now. They failed to identify Ayton's presence in the house, which means they might not have asked Aiden and Robin the right questions.

I loop back on myself and ring their doorbell.

TWENTY-SIX

Aiden is in a neat black button-down with his hair slicked back. He asks me in for a cup of tea. Their house reeks of cigarettes, and I wonder idly if Robin has taken up smoking again. Weirdly, I know he'd given up, because Charlotte was annoyed she couldn't bum them off him any more. I was pleased about it, thinking she was less likely to die from lung cancer.

When we enter the kitchen, I see they have guests, one of whom is outside smoking.

'Oh God, I'm so sorry. I'll come back another time.'

'What? No! Please. We've even got a jug of Bloody Mary on the go, if you fancy. Hair of the dog. Charlotte used to love one.'

It's before lunch on a weekday, but still I'm tempted. 'Oh, no thanks, just tea would be great.'

He introduces me to their friends, and Robin leaps up to hug me. I feel awkward, knowing what I want to ask them, which isn't your run-of-the mill chit-chat.

While Aiden is making the tea, I hover. He asks me how I'm doing in that pointed way people do when you've just lost some-one. I could tell him that there's a skin of nightfall that covers all my daylight hours and that the waves of grief can leave me itching to escape my own body, but I say, 'I'm fine. You know. Getting on. But actually I wanted to ask you both something specific.'

'Fire away, you gorgeous woman,' Robin says in his exuberant way, tugging at a straining button on his shirt. Aiden hands me the tea, grinning handsomely.

'The night Charlotte died, did you see anyone come or go?'

'Oh hon. Lord, no,' Robin cries. 'The police asked us all this already. We were out until about four a.m., I'm afraid. It's a miracle we were even vaguely conscious when the girls rang the doorbell in the morning.' He makes a sad face. 'You know, the irony of it, we actually asked her out to Heaven with us that night.'

'Did you?' I gape at the two men.

'She loved it there.' Aiden nods. 'She was such a laugh. Oh sweetie, I wish now I'd dragged her out kicking and screaming. But I kind of got the impression she was excited about something, like she had a date. She swore she didn't, though.'

He glances at Robin, who booms, 'I left her a couple of my mate's More Slims and a can of G and T and off we went!' He flings his hand into the air, and then drops it. 'God, I regret leaving that fucking G and T.'

I shoot back, 'Why's that?'

'Because gin was not her drink, darling. If I'd known, I would've left her a cocktail shaker of margarita! Now that's the better way out.' He takes a dramatically sad sip of his Bloody Mary and mutters, 'For the love of God, a bloody can of G and T.'

This insight into Charlotte's love of gay clubs and More Slims and margaritas leaves me reeling. More big stuff I wasn't party to. The nugget Aiden shared about her excitable mood has added another sketchy layer to my thinking, muddying the waters further.

To be polite, I stay for half an hour or so before saying my goodbyes and promising to drop in again soon.

I march towards the overground station, now finding it impossible to retrieve the exact wording of the exchange between Hayley and Ayton behind the garages. It was only yesterday, yet all I can recall is the general gist of what they said, and I wonder if Robin added brandy to my tea.

To focus my mind, I go over what I know so far:

1. Ayton was there that night and he and Hayley lied about it. Fact.
2. Charlotte was being secretive about a date? Almost a fact.
3. Hayley's surprising knowledge of what a real dead body looks like led me to believe she'd seen her mother dead. Not a fact. A hunch.

With fact number one in mind, I veer off course, propelled towards St Matthew's Secondary School.

It's time for a frank discussion about Ayton with Mr Jamie Hanrahan. The teacher who cares.

TWENTY-SEVEN

It's coming to the end of lunch break at school. The receptionist is distracted by a teenage girl in an altercation with a teacher about the length of her skirt. I nip past.

After taking a few wrong turns against the flow of green-blazered kids, I spot Jamie through the Plexiglas panel of a classroom. He's eating a sandwich and marking what look like test papers.

I poke my head around the door, already regretting how rash I've been in coming here. 'Hi, Jamie,' I say uncertainly.

He's startled by my appearance, and chokes on his mouthful before beckoning to me. 'Emily! Come in. Come in.' He grabs a chair from behind one of the white desks and places it opposite his. 'Is everything okay? Mia's not in today, is she?'

'She's fine. Having a duvet day.'

'Oh. Right. Hayley all right after yesterday?'

'She's why I'm here. I wanted to ask you something.'

'Fire away.'

'You helped Charlotte loads with Hayley.' I pause to inspect his face. I'm still deciding how much I can confide in him. It'll be a risk, but I continue. 'And I know you've always had Hayley's best interests at heart.'

'Always.' He puts his sandwich down and wipes his mouth with a napkin.

For a minute, I am torn. I'm stepping over a line. While my loyalty towards my sister burns inside me, I realise that talking to Jamie opens a line of enquiry about Ayton that could in turn lead to trouble for Hayley. But I will be careful not to implicate her. Some cards I'll keep clamped to my chest.

'Are you able to talk completely off the record?'

'Yes. Sure. Off the record.'

I inhale before beginning. 'Yesterday, I overheard something between Ayton and Hayley that worried me.'

'Go on.'

'I might have misunderstood. I was only picking up fag ends, and I have no intention of involving the police. And if I share this, you're going to have to pretend you're hearing it not as a teacher but as Charlotte's friend. And if you don't feel comfortable about that, please say now.'

'I'm okay with it,' he says, wiping his fingers with the napkin.

I brace myself. 'So, Hayley and Ayton were arguing, and I got the impression that Ayton was over at my sister's house on the night she died.' I experience an unpleasant flutter in my stomach.

Jamie's olive skin turns grey as he leans forward, elbows on his knees. He is almost inaudible when he asks, 'You heard him say that?'

'Basically, Jennifer Conway made out she knew something secret about the night Charlotte died, which is, I think, why Hayley punched her in the face. But Ayton promised Hayley that Jen was just being a wind-up merchant and talking a load of shit. And he insisted Jen hadn't known he was'– I pause – 'there. That night.'

'He actually said he was there?'

'Yup.'

'Hmm.' Jamie smooths his hands down his trouser legs. 'I was under the impression that Charlotte's death was confirmed as accidental and that there'll be no inquest. Have I got that wrong?'

'No, that's right. The coroner confirmed accidental death.' I'm reminded of my outstanding call to the coroner's office about the toxicology results. I've been putting it off.

He sounds gentle when he says, 'Did you want it investigated further?'

'No, no, God no. I just want to understand why Ayton kept quiet about being there. If he was.'

He crosses one leg over the other. 'Maybe he was scared? He doesn't have the best rep with the police.'

'Doesn't he?'

'No serious offences, though. Only stuff like nicking sandwiches from Sainsbury's. Or mildly antisocial behaviour. As you know, he's a bit of a rogue and likes to bowl about the place full of cheeky backchat. He's quite popular amongst his peer group.'

'But if, for whatever reason, he coerced Hayley into staying quiet, it'll be burning a hole in her, you know?' I feel my cheeks heat up and begin twisting my fingers into knots.

He scratches his eyebrow thoughtfully. 'But she's such a strong personality. More a leader than a follower. It's unlikely she'll have done anything under duress.'

'When they started going out, did she change at all?'

'It was the other way around. Ayton's attendance dropped off massively after they got together. Whereas Hayley's truancy has always been quite bad. If you want my opinion, I think she gravitated towards him because she liked pushing her mum's buttons.'

'My sister didn't like him?'

'Not at all. They fought about him a fair bit.' He tilts his head and rubs his goatee. 'I'm surprised you didn't know any of this. She always said you two were so close.'

'We were,' I shoot back. Then I try to soften my defensive response. 'Maybe she didn't share stuff like that because I'm not a mum myself.' I pause. 'Probably thought I'd be bored by it or something. And she hated boring people. You know what she was like, wanting to entertain everyone all the time!' I laugh weakly.

'Huh. True.' He nods slowly and holds my gaze.

Determinedly I say, 'You plainly understood her. And I want to know what happened. Can you help me?'

'I would like to,' he says with a questioning rise at the end.

'D'you think you'd be able to get us together? Me and Ayton, I mean – something low-key over a cuppa. With you there too, of course, so he feels safe. I'd never accuse him of anything. I just want to find out if he knows more than he's letting on.' Even as I say it out loud, I know I'm clutching at straws.

Jamie clears his throat. 'Look, I really want to help.' His eyes seem to melt in sympathy for me. 'But even if Ayton did miraculously agree to it, I don't think it's a good idea. Not only would I be risking my job here, you could also get in trouble for harassment of a minor. And if he denies being there that night, which he almost certainly will, there's nothing much you'll have gained.'

The stark reality of it overwhelms me. I sigh. 'I just want to know what happened to my sister, that's all.' There's a crack in my voice. I gulp down what feels like a rock stuck in my throat.

Jamie comes around his desk, crouches on his haunches and places a hand on my knee. 'Emily,' he says ever so quietly, looking up at me, tears in his brown eyes, 'the whole thing was such a shock for all of us. I can't bear to think about what you and the girls are going through. You're such a lovely family. But this is not going to bring her back.'

I hold in the loss like I'm deep under the sea and unable to breathe for fear of drowning. I flap my hands at my eyes. 'Sorry.'

'You don't have to be.'

I look up to the ceiling. 'Sorry. Look. I'm fine. Honestly.' The emotional storm subsides. 'I need to drop it.'

'I think that's best.'

'At least it'll be a clean break when they leave for Ireland.'

'They're definitely moving?'

'Oh,' I say glumly. 'That's the other thing. David will be officially withdrawing them from school here today. They'll be setting off later this week.'

Jamie sits straight down on the floor on his bottom, cross-legged, back straight, wide-eyed. 'Wow, okay. That soon.'

'It's quite sudden, I know. Too soon probably, but he thinks they might as well get on with it. He wants me to sort out the sale of the house this end.'

'I'll miss them. But I think it's an awesome idea.'

'Really?'

'Honestly I do. Sticking around here is only putting off the inevitable. And I think Hayley could do with a fresh start.'

'That's what David said.'

'For once, I agree with him.'

'For once?'

He blinks repeatedly. 'Charlotte told me they rowed all the time about who took the girls and when, and for how long. I was always disgusted by how he tried to wriggle out of seeing them. He made no effort. It was as though he'd moved on to a shiny new family and couldn't give a crap about his daughters. But this... I don't know, this shows he really cares about them. They deserve that.'

I feel something release inside me. 'Yes, that's true.'

'Don't feel guilty,' Jamie says. 'Caring for them is one thing. Becoming a parent is on another level altogether.'

'I don't feel guilty!'

'Good.' He grins. He probably knows I do feel guilty. For not wanting to be their mother.

'Anyway, David never suggested he didn't want them. So it was never on the cards for us to take them long-term.' I smile and blow out my cheeks. 'Thank God I talked to you before I started rampaging around accusing Ayton of perverting the course of justice. Or worse.'

He laughs. 'In the event of any other similar urges, my door is always open.'

I gather my bag, stand up and hold out my hand to shake his. He surprises me by enveloping me in a hug. Without knowing why, I stiffen.

'Bye, Emily,' he says, releasing me. 'I wish you and the girls all the best. Please call if you need any help with the house. We're only around the corner. Kristin's at home with Fleur most days, so just say the word.'

'Thank you, that's really kind.'

'And tell Hayley to keep in touch. I want to hear all about how it's going over there.'

I picture Hayley's sneer at this.

As I'm leaving, I hear a mobile phone go. The ringtone is a snippet from the soundtrack to the movie *Love Story*. The distinctive melody catapults me back to the very last time I saw Charlotte, a week before she died. We were tucking into large dishes of curry at an Indian restaurant in north London when the exact same music rang out from her phone. She was flustered by it, mentioned rewatching the film with Hayley and Mia and switched her handset to silent. Then she stuffed a big piece of naan into her gob and carried on talking.

Now, I swivel around, as though she might be here, brought

back to me. My heart is in my mouth. I catch Jamie fumbling to turn his phone off.

'Sorry. Tiger was messing about with it. I've been meaning to change it.' I wonder how likely this is, remembering how young his son looked at the funeral. No older than four, at a guess.

I'm so quick to hurry out of the classroom, I forget to say a final goodbye. I tell myself a four-year-old boy could programme a phone better than any forty-year-old. I tell myself it's a coincidence.

TWENTY-EIGHT

Olly juts his head closer to me and whispers, 'You told a *teacher* that you suspect Hayley of lying about that night?'

'Oh for God's sake. It wasn't like that.' I dip my pitta bread into the taramasalata dip. The old wooden table wobbles. I'm wishing we weren't here, crammed into the corner of this busy Greek restaurant. Having suggested the place to cheer myself up after today, I realise it was a mistake. There are too many noisy feelings inside my head to cope with all the people around me.

'Jesus, Emily.' He knocks back a quick swig of red wine. 'I'm not sure that was a very good idea.'

'It's too late now.'

'But you realise this Mr Hanrahan guy could go straight to social services or the police?' He glances sideways at the couple next to us, so near I could comfortably reach over to grab an olive.

'He won't. I didn't give him enough information for him to be able to do that. And I trust him.' Then I remember the ring-tone and take a gulp of my own wine.

'However wacky and cool he pretends to be, he's still a

teacher, and all teachers have safeguarding responsibilities. Their jobs depend on it.'

'Well, if he talks to anyone, I can always deny it. Or say he misunderstood. It'll be his word against mine.'

'Let's hope it doesn't come to that.'

The move to Ireland goes ahead at pace. Even Hayley's fifteenth birthday gets lost in the mix. I'm over at Charlotte's again to help them pack. It's surreal that it's happening so fast, only two weeks after Charlotte's funeral, and it feels very much like the nasty business of ripping a plaster off, to coin David's phrase.

The logistics have been overwhelming. No surprise that I'm on my own with it. Olly has made it clear that his book is his priority. 'It's impossible to work in that house,' he says. 'And I've got this deadline. I've got to get it in to Sarah before she goes away in May.' I don't point out that I also have a job that I've put on hold, and that happens to pay most of our rent.

David has bought the girls expensive new suitcases with wheels. This is where his practical help ends. He has spent most of his time on work calls or talking Beth down from a baby meltdown. *What happened to the natural mother who wants a busload of kids?* I think with a childish eye-roll.

No matter, I get on with everything quietly. Every hour that goes by without hearing from Jamie or the police is a relief. I'm increasingly confident that my instincts are right about him, that he's as good as his word. The loose ends of the night Charlotte died continue to tie knots inside me. I can't help trying to unravel them. New scenarios and theories ping about in my mind still. It's hard to leave things unresolved, even though I'm having to embrace the uncertainty, which doesn't come naturally.

With every item I fold into Hayley and Mia's new suitcases,

another piece of my denial falls away. They are leaving me.
Ireland isn't down the road. David and Beth are not my family.
Visiting them will be fraught, both emotionally and logistically.
Once they have moved in, the farmhouse will not have a spare
room. The caravan Beth renovated into a so-called guest annexe
doesn't have a toilet, and apparently – according to the girls –
there's a rat nesting in the cupboard. Already I'm dreading
spending time with Beth. For so long, she has been Public
Enemy No. 1. A husband-stealer who ruined my sister's life.

Thinking ahead, as I like to do, I check online for decent
hotels or Airbnbs nearby and find a B & B six miles away with
simple guest bedrooms. It might be a solution. Perhaps Olly and
I can book a weekend trip to look forward to in the summer.
And then at Christmas with Mum and Dad. And on the girls'
birthdays. I hope they might want to stay with us sometimes, on
camp beds in the front room or at my parents', but David or
Beth would have to accompany them over to England. The
effort and expense probably mean it's unlikely to happen often.

A long-distance relationship is different in every way, and I
feel that keenly now. I won't be able to suggest a last-minute
movie night or a trip to a museum. I'll not bother booking a
pantomime at Christmas this year. How sad that Olly won't
have to fake-laugh his way through the 'HE'S BEHIND YOU!'
routine. It'll be a hole in the diary. A hole in our lives.

Will I become that distant aunt figure they'll fondly recall
from childhood but remember little about?

'Auntie Emily, I'm worried I've left something I need in the
bathroom,' Mia says, breaking my train of thought.

'Okay, let's go see.'

I hold her hand, which under normal circumstances isn't
necessary for a trip to the bathroom. But everything is far from
normal.

The room seems colder than ever. It would do. Nobody has
used it for many weeks. The heated towel rail has been

switched off. But there are still two shampoo bottles in the shower and a razor on the side.

Mia lets go of my hand and bends into the cabinet under the sink. I look inside the mirrored cabinet above it.

'Nurofen and plasters might be a good idea,' I say, taking some down from the shelf.

'Good plan,' she agrees. 'Beth probably makes herb potions for headaches.'

I chortle. Mia is very astute for a twelve-year-old. I say, 'Any time you need some real drugs, just text me and I'll send them straight over.'

'Auntie Emily!' she exclaims, scandalised not at all. She takes out a jumble of half-full boxes of sanitary towels. 'I'll need these, but they'll take up so much room in my suitcase.' There's a catch in her voice.

'Let me have a go.' I kneel next to her, manage to squeeze a good supply into one box and hand them to her. 'Remember, they have chemists in Ireland.'

She doesn't smile and hugs the box, staring down at it. A tear plops onto the cardboard flap. The wet splodge expands. 'I don't want to go,' she whispers.

'Come here.' I enclose her in a hug and rock her back and forth in my arms like I did when she was little, feeling a lump in my throat, wondering if I should have fought harder to keep them. Had there been anything more sinister about David than a bog-standard inability to keep it in his pants, I would have stopped him from taking them. Wouldn't I? 'It's going to be okay. You'll see.'

Over her shoulder, I catch sight of the place where Charlotte fell, and I feel a surge of rage at her for dying. Look at the mess you've left behind! I want to shout at that ghostly space.

When Mia pulls away, she seems better. I fold up the empty boxes for recycling and then sweep my hand inside the sink cabinet to check for anything else. I'm going to have to clear the whole house out soon anyway, so I might as well do bits and bobs as I go along.

There's a clatter. Something drops from the U-bend. 'What's this?' I pull out a bottle. 'Oh.' For some reason, I blush. It's an empty vodka bottle.

Mia laughs and slaps her hand over her mouth. 'Oh my God. Hayley used to steal vodka from Mum and pour it into her hip flask and take it to parties when she was like twelve, and Mum went mental when she found the bottle empty!' She giggles.

'Hayley kept a stash of vodka here?' I ask.

'No! Mum did!'

I'm finding it hard to hide my shock. 'But why did your mum keep vodka under the sink?'

'Daddy didn't like it,' she says casually, as though it were totally normal.

'You remember that?'

She cocks her head to the side and twists her hair. 'I guess Hayley told me.'

'And she carried on hiding it here?'

'It must have been there ages!' Mia says, frowning thoughtfully, possibly working a few things out.

I try to laugh, then stuff the bottle into the bin along with the folded cardboard and get up from my knees. 'Silly Mummy,' I say, trying to make light of it.

If Mia knows what she has revealed, she doesn't show it. But something has clicked inside me.

'Okay, Mia. Next task,' I say, rallying myself. 'You need to whittle down that massive mound of teddies on your bed and pick out two of your favourites.'

'Only two?' she whines.

'Yes, two. I'll ship the rest over. Promise,' I say, tweaking her nose.

I'm focusing on the practical, thinking with my head and

not my heart. My head is telling me that whatever problems existed when Charlotte was alive do not matter now that she is dead. Logic tells me that Jamie's ringtone was a coincidence. Good sense reminds me not to jump to the conclusion that Hayley and Ayton were involved in Charlotte's death.

But my heart is telling me that I must address the hidden vodka bottle. I expect the toxicology results will give me the answers I need.

The next day, I call the coroner's office and speak to Ruth Farrah. She first re-establishes the cause of Charlotte's death, then shares figures that shed light on a life less perfect.

TWENTY-NINE

Outside, it's a fresh, breezy day. But I'm sitting on a blue plastic chair in a stiflingly hot room in the health centre. Following my phone call to the coroner a couple of weeks ago, I requested a hard copy of the toxicology report and booked an appointment with the GP for a layman's interpretation of the figures.

A young, mousy doctor wearing a clear plastic face guard, reminiscent of the pandemic, is sitting on the opposite side of the room delivering facts about my sister. Facts I want to brush aside. She is holding the pages of the report in her pale hands. The information is dense and technical.

'This figure here' – she indicates the A4 sheet in front of her, straining her small voice mechanically through her mask – 'shows a blood alcohol content of 0.39 per cent, which is extremely high. In fact, it's potentially fatal. Life-threatening levels would normally range between 0.40 and 0.50 per cent, but 0.39 is still dangerous.'

'But the coroner didn't say that's why she died,' I bleat.

Dr Rundell scratches under the strap of her visor. 'As I say, it wasn't high enough to be the cause of death, but due to the clinical signs of fatty liver and the severity of the head trauma, the pathologist suspected high alcohol intake as a contributory factor in her death, which was why they requested this report.' She flaps the pages at me.

'I see,' I say, in a very grown-up manner, chewing the inside of my cheek, feeling my eyes watering.

The doctor rests the papers on her desk. 'Does that help at all?'

I'm aware of the seven-minute slot, but I say, 'Can I ask one more thing?'

Her eyes dart to the corner of her screen, where the digital clock ticks away. 'Yes, of course.'

'Did she ever come to you asking for... I don't know... any advice or help along those lines?'

Her out-breath leaves a circle of steam on the plastic, reminding me she's human. 'You mean advice for an alcohol addiction?'

'I guess that's what I mean,' I say, unnerved by her directness.

Her hand darts to her visor, as though about to take it off. 'There were times when I became aware she might've been struggling on that front, yes, and I provided her with information that I thought might offer support.'

She tilts her head sympathetically, perhaps expecting me to ask her what the signs were, but I can't face it. Having spent a lifetime skirting around my sister's problem, making light of it, underplaying the seriousness of her drinking habit, I now have the stark facts I need.

'Okay, thanks,' is all I manage to say before hurrying out, feeling sweaty and nauseous and slightly ashamed.

It was never any secret that Charlotte was a good-time-girl, didn't know how to stop once she'd started, was too sociable, liked to party hard, thought Prosecco and rosé were soft drinks. She wasn't an *alcoholic*, though. I reassured myself that she reined it in enough to function well for the girls in those crucial parenting hours.

I'll never forget one dinner party about a year before her divorce when I caught David's expression during one of her aggressive, slurry monologues at the end of the meal. While the rest of us were embarrassed for her, his grey eyes, rimmed red by his strawberry-blond lashes, were filled with rage and disgust. And I guessed then that the rot in their marriage had set in.

There are more stories like that. Many of them. Isolated incidents that we excused. Oh, she's stressed! She's coping with a lot at work! She's just letting her hair down! She's going through a divorce! The kids are driving her mad! It's a lovely summery evening! They've brought the shots out! Oh, she's so funny! Oh, oh, oh dear.

When gathered together, and in the context of her death, they're enough to paint a picture of a problem none of us wanted to acknowledge. Least of all me. Only I knew why she might have wanted to drink away her thoughts. The memories hover like shadows.

The toxicology report has scraped the scales from my eyes. It causes me pain to acknowledge that it's too late to help her. What hits me again now is that image of David's disgust. Had Hayley come to feel that way about her too?

THIRTY

Staying busy helps me to block out all the things I can't do anything about. Charlotte's drinking. All the secrets surrounding her death. The girls putting down roots in Ireland.

The things I can do something about include clearing out Charlotte's house and putting it on the market, with help from Jamie's wife, Kristin. If I'm tied up at meetings, she nips in before the estate agent's viewings to dust and put freshly cut flowers on the kitchen island. It's hard to express how grateful I am for this. Selling a house that has been the setting for a tragic death 'has its challenges', as the nice estate agent put it, and needs all the help it can get.

Work has been manic. Jaylani saved up the scripts that she didn't trust the 'new girl' with – the 'new girl' is fifty-five, with twenty years' experience at the BBC – but I don't mind the workload. I enjoy the decision-making process. After finishing a script, I know whether to throw development money at it or not. Mostly, scripts are agreeable and pliable and within my control. Unlike mothering Hayley and Mia, I'm told I'm good at my job. Jaylani often says I have a gift for sniffing out hit series. Like those mathematicians who stand at blackboards with a jumble of equations, I have found a role that suits my sort of brain. I enjoy the order of a good narrative.

The relief of going back to something I'm actually capable of is epic. My self-esteem has shot right back up to just below normal.

There's time for others again too. I set up a WhatsApp group for a supper club to get back into the swing of our social life. Tomorrow night, we've got some friends coming over. I can't wait to see them.

Returned to the fold of dysfunctional London, I pick up where I left off, secreting treats for friends and strangers along the way. Marty is back on his bench in Olly's parka, come rain or shine, waiting for his chinwag. Down the road, Frieda has again started taking the flask of soup from her doorstep every Tuesday. The first time she left it there for three days, and I wonder if it was a protest, which suggests she missed the soup. I leave a bunch of flowers for a bus driver under the back seat on the upper deck of the number 393, with a note telling her that her cackling laughter brightens up my day.

Who knows how any of them respond to these anonymous missives, but that's the point: it's the giving that's rewarding. I do it for myself, which I guess makes it all about me. And that's just fine. I like it being all about me. And about Olly. We're back to normal, and it feels good to be us again.

Olly's soon-to-be-published novel is the only fly in the ointment. He wants me to run through it again 'before it's too late to change anything'. It's now alarmingly titled *A Severed Womb*, and he's still in the thick of the structural edits, while also working up a proposal for book two of his contract for the lovely Sarah.

I have it open on my Kindle now. My thumb leaves a sweaty print where I've tapped the screen to the beginning of Chapter Seventeen.

Either I make peace with this chapter or I have it out with Olly. I haven't decided which yet. Sadly, the story is proving even more arduous and button-pushing the second time around. To make matters worse, I now find it impossible not to interpret it through the prism of Hayley and Mia's feelings as well as my own. The thought of them knowing why Olly and I are not parents is niggling away at me in a way it didn't before Charlotte died.

I dive in.

–You're not happy.

    –Did you expect me to be?

    –Because I am. Unexpectedly. Happy.

    –So you thought that I would be too?

    –Yes.

Jim rotated the band on his wedding finger. He said, – You knew how I felt when I married you.

    –Things change.

    –The world is changing, yes.

    –People are imperfect. We change.

    –You married me hoping I would change?

    –Stop twisting my words.

    –I'm not. It's simple. I said I didn't want to burden this fucked-up planet with more children, and you said you felt the same.

    –I do. But now it exists, yes. I changed. People change.

Ellie had said that twice. People change. Jim then said it out loud too.

    –People change. Huh.

Ellie put both hands on her knees. One knee jumped up and down. It was a nervous habit of hers. He found it endearing and bit his lip to stop a smile. She misinterpreted it, saying, –Tell me you're not just that little bit happy?

In Jim's pause, she chewed at her thumbnail. He imagined her chomping into her thumb until it was bleeding. The fantasy had a horror-movie edge to it. He contemplated what the surgeon was going to do to her body. The procedure would be gory. She would not see the blood or feel the pain.

–We still have a few weeks to decide, he said.

Her knee fell still.

–I'm glad you're still deciding.

He watched her reach into her bag for her headache pills. She read the back before taking one. She'd never read the back before. It meant she was already taking care of her baby. He knew she would hate him for making her have an abortion as much as he would hate her for having a baby. And it was then that Jim knew that if she had the baby, he would leave her.

I close my Kindle and shudder, reminded of when I first read those crushing words.

I'm irked by Olly's proximity. His feet are up on the coffee table as he scrolls through his phone.

'Can you take your feet off my books?' I ask. Wanting to say, *What's wrong with bloody speech marks?*

He lifts his crossed ankles and glances at the stack of photography books as though seeing them for the first time, then rests his feet down on the rug. 'I'm just booking that new production of *Hamlet*. It looks good.'

'For us?'

He raises an eyebrow. 'No, for me and my secret lover.'

'When, though? You haven't asked me if I'm free on whatever date you're booking it.'

'You said you weren't busy this Friday, didn't you?'

'But I might not fancy a three-hour tragedy in iambic pentameter.'

'Do you not?'

'I do, but could you ask next time?'

He grins at me. 'Phew, I thought I was going to have to ask my lover. And I much prefer you.'

'Ha ha.' I try not to smile, just like Jim tried not to smile in the book. In real life, Olly doesn't catch my attempt to conceal it, nor does he have a chance to misinterpret it in the way that Ellie did in his story. Because misreading me right now is guaranteed. Nobody would guess at the rage I feel towards the creator of Ellie and Jim.

I remember the reality differently. Back in 2019, Olly and I shared a less restrained dialogue about my unplanned pregnancy. It went something like this:

'I was fine about not having children, and now I don't know how I feel. But I don't want to put any pressure on you.' Emily snivelled through some hiccupy tears. The hormones were making her cry.

'Just saying that puts pressure on me!'

'I know, I'm sorry. I don't know what the hell to do about it!'

Olly took her hand. 'I love you.'

'I love you too.'

They hugged, and he said, 'Let's not argue. It's your body. I want you to be happy. I don't want to force you into anything you don't want to do.'

'Okay, I'll try to believe you.' She wiped snot away with the back of her hand.

'You're beautiful even with snot in your hair,' he said, grinning, handing her a tissue. 'I think you'll know what's right.'

Okay, it's not elegant, but it's how I remember it, how I felt it. There was always part of me that believed Olly would put his beliefs aside for me if I chose to have the baby.

It was then that Jim knew that if she had the baby, he would leave her.

When I read Jim's thoughts, I only hear Olly's voice.

'I'm going to bed,' I say, getting up, folding away a tea towel and putting a knife in the dishwasher.

'It's only nine thirty!' He cranes his neck, catching me dipping my hand in my special drawer. Undeterred, I take out the blister pack and make a big show of popping two pills onto my tongue and knocking them back without water. I've got that technique down.

'I'm going to read.'

'Okay,' he says with a frown. 'Night then.' He returns to his phone.

My emotions are more raw, less obedient when I try to shove them into the caverns of my unconscious. When I hear his footsteps creaking over the floorboards towards our bedroom, I brace myself for a conversation about my sudden mood, or maybe my sleeping pill habit. We've had those chats before, I can handle that, but anything more rigorous might topple me.

He pushes open the door, waving my phone at me. 'You left it on the side. It's Mia, I thought you might want to talk to her.'

'Oh.' In an instant, I forget my own unhappiness and engage with my phone, knowing that a call from Mia at this time of night does not bode well. It means an hour or more of her whispered tales about the grimness of life in Ireland, and specifically Hayley's rows with Beth. For me, listening to her becomes a guilt-fest.

Apparently, Beth and Hayley argue about everything. About the vegan cheese Hayley spits in the bin, the nettle tea she says tastes like piss and the yogic breathing sessions she laughs her way through. And screen time – by all accounts the most repetitive flashpoint between them – which Beth controls with an iron fist, allowing only a half-hour slot of Snapchat each night. In Hayley's mind, this equals social death. Arguably true. If I was only allowed half an hour on WhatsApp, I'd have no friends left.

I don't hear directly from Hayley about any of this. The odd one-liner in response to a text or maybe a photograph of some scenery is all I get. Mia has become the truth-teller. She calls me from the rat-infested caravan – it has its uses – where she says nobody can hear her, to give me the lowdown on what's really going on.

'Everything okay?' I ask, steeling myself for what's to come.

'No, nothing's okay.' She sounds edgier than usual.

I climb into bed and puff up my pillows, prepared to listen for as long as it takes and hand out my solid practical advice, to which she'll no doubt give small yesses and then ignore. If I ever criticise Hayley's behaviour – which she herself is complaining about – she leaps to her defence. They're a unit, have a bond that I relate to when I think about Charlotte and me. Sometimes siblings are the only ones who understand.

The pharmaceutical drowsiness weighs me down tonight. I try hard to push through the soupy feeling to listen to her carefully. 'How are little Bridie, Padhraic and Luke?'

'They're fine,' she replies briefly, and then hurries on, 'But Hayley didn't help sterilise Bridie's bottles tonight—'

I interrupt. 'Beth doesn't breastfeed?' Earth Mother uses formula? STOP PRESS.

'She uses this pump thing on her boobs. But Auntie Emily, that's not the point. Listen!'

'Sorry, sweetheart. Go on.'

'Beth asked us both to wash them up, and I did it, because what's the point in not? But Hayley didn't. And then Beth saw it was just me doing it and said how disappointed she was in Hayley and that she was grounding her for two weeks. And now Hayley's run away.'

Fully alert, I swing my legs out of bed and plant my feet on the floor. 'What? Back up there a sec, Mia. Did I hear that right? Hayley's *run away*?'

THIRTY-ONE

Olly comes in and stares at me as I throw clothes into a holdall.

'What's going on? What are you doing?'

'Hayley's run away. I'm going to the airport.' Briefly it occurs to me to ask him to come with me, but then I remember his book and decide I'm okay about not suggesting it.

He is silent for a second. 'How long has she been missing for?'

'I just called David.'

'How long has she been gone?' he repeats.

'Just over an hour.' Even as I say it, I know it won't sound as urgent as my packing suggests.

He stands in the bedroom doorway. 'An hour? That's nothing. She's done far worse than that before. Whole nights at Ayton's spring to mind.'

'Mia said she was really upset.'

'You can't go. For one, you're still in your PJs – and those are the ones with a hole in the bum.'

I twist to check, tugging at the seat of my trousers. 'Something's not right over there. I can feel it in my bones.'

'Em, it's only been a few weeks since they got there. It might take many more months for them to settle down with each other. But they absolutely will. I have every faith.' It strikes me he's trying to be the family optimist. It was a decent attempt, but I'm better at it. I'm the queen of building big fat walls of false positivity and convincing everyone that it's all going to be okay. When I say it, I make it come true. When Olly says it, it sounds stupid. You can't kid a kidder.

'I wouldn't be so sure of that if I were you,' I say.

He sighs. 'Remember, we also only have Hayley's stories to go on.'

'It's Mia who tells me everything, not Hayley! I haven't even spoken to Hayley yet. Not once since she got there a month ago.' This comes out more heatedly than I meant it to, but the fact he didn't know is annoying. It highlights how disengaged he has been recently. All he cares about are his edits on 'ASW' – as he sometimes abbreviates it in texts – for Sarah. Ugh. His bloody book for bloody Sarah.

'But Mia likes Beth, right?'

I pause. 'That's the impression I get.'

'And Mia's a sensitive soul and would've picked up on any evil stepmother Cinderella shit. Yes?'

'Bloody hell, if we're talking fairy tales, Beth's the wolf in sheep's bloody clothing!'

'In Toast clothing, you mean.' He chuckles at his own joke.

'God, no. Toast? She probably weaves her own bloody smocks.' I pause. The oomph to fly to Ireland has left me. I sit down next to my bag. There's a small smile between us. 'I'm being dead serious here, though.'

'And remember, Hayley behaves like this no matter where she is or who she lives with. She hides her pain by being a royal pain in the arse.'

'Yes,' I groan. 'I s'pose.'

'Em, she is David's daughter. You have to let them work it out between themselves.'

I squeeze my head. 'Oh, I know you're right! I just hate that they're so far away. I feel so powerless to help them!'

'I know you do.'

I check the time on my phone. 'Where the hell d'you think Hayley's got to, though?'

'She's probably skulking in the chicken coop and smashing hen's eggs, or something farmy like that.'

The funny and innocent image takes more of the edge off my worry, and I feel the twitch of a grin. 'Jeez. Your imagination.'

'You've tried calling her, I guess?'

'Yes, a few times.'

'And David said he'd call you when he has news?'

'Yup. And Mia.'

'Then the only thing we can do now is have a glass of wine and wait.'

'I need to stay clear-headed.'

'Half, then.'

I shrug.

'Done,' he says, padding down the corridor in his socks.

I watch him go, feeling affection at the way he walks. It's clear he is genuinely not worried at all. I worry for a second that he should be more worried, that we both should, then I conclude that the lack of worry is because the situation isn't very worrying.

Only an hour ago, I was hating on him enough to question the foundations of our marriage. Now, I love him enough to thank every star in the sky for sending him to me. I don't know what I would do without him.

I nestle into the crook of his arm while we watch a film together and wait for news. I'm too distracted to follow the plot, but the characters and the soundtrack are colourful and high-energy.

My phone lies on my thigh. Every time it lights up, I grab it to see. So far nothing more than a message from his agent, Rachel, about bringing the ingredients for mimosa cocktails tomorrow. I can't wait. I'll need one. Then I get a BBC news flash about the Foreign Secretary and the Minister for Education shagging each other in the broom closet. Nothing newsworthy there then. The only news I care about is Hayley. It's a pain how much I care. It angers me. *She* angers me. I wish I had an off switch for Hayley-induced anxiety, or at least a volume button to turn down the noise she makes in my head. I chuck my phone on the table.

'No news?' Olly asks.

'Just some cabinet ministers working hard for the hard-working people of this country.'

I show him the headline and he chuckles.

When the film finishes, I pick up my Kindle, deciding that reading the PDF of *A Severed Womb* – perhaps more appropriately titled *My Severed Womb* – is the only distraction powerful enough to occupy me.

But as I read past Chapter Seventeen and into the next chapter, the image of a seven-week ultrasound flickers in my mind. It morphs from Ellie's into mine. The embryo inside me was the size of a grain of rice. I used to picture the bouncing baby it would grow into. A dark girl like me, with my too-close brown eyes. My imagination ran like this often in those early weeks. I guess I loved it, was attached already, even then. Strange that I have never recognised it as love before now. A mother's love.

A text from David arrives just before midnight.

'Oh my God.' I chew the side of my mouth to stop the onrush of tears. 'They've found her.' I breathe in and out to slow the racing of my heart as I reread it, double-checking.

She came home. Sleep well. Dx

'Is that all I get?' I cry angrily.

'Where was she?' Olly asks, using the remote to turn off the television.

'Not sure. I'll text him back.'

Where was she???

There are three dots to suggest he's typing. It stops, then starts again. Then a text pings through.

It doesn't matter now. We're blessed she came home to us. Dx

'Is he having a laugh? *It doesn't matter*? Of course it bloody matters.'

'At least she's safe.'

'I bet Beth wrote that text for him. It's so smug. They're making a point of saying she *came home* to them, like she came to her senses and realised how wonderful Beth was after all. Bloody hell.'

'Reading too much into it, maybe?'

'Well, she's annoying.'

'Sounds like Hayley's met her match.'

'I'm going to find out exactly what went on, and if I don't like the sound of it, I'm going out to see them.'

'Let's talk about it in the morning,' Olly says. His jaw clicks with a yawn. 'It's time to go to bed.'

To bed. But not to sleep. Rather, to read and read and then to think and think and think and think until I go quietly mad with it. As is the pattern, I succumb to another sleeping pill, which knocks me out for a few hours. When I wake up from the chemical oblivion, I reach for my phone by my bedside and see a missed call and voicemail from David left at 00:47. I sit bolt upright and press play.

THIRTY-TWO

The following morning, I stuff my feet into my walking shoes, tie my hair back, plug in my AirPods and head out the door before Olly wakes up. I don't want him to hear my conversation with David.

As I jog down the stairs, I replay David's voicemail from last night, just to make sure I didn't dream it.

'Hi, Emily, sorry it's so late, but we need to talk. Could you call me as soon as you wake up? Beth and I have been thinking. We've been... well... Yeah. Just call me. Thanks. Bye. Oh. It's David, by the way. Thanks. Look forward to chatting.'

There's nothing about being 'blessed' in that message, I think churlishly, and I press his name to call him back. It rings out. I exhale.

The message marks a shift.

I wonder if the hyperactivity of my brain last night made something big happen somehow. Like black magic.

As I stride up Parliament Hill, I feel nervous and agitated, and grateful to be surrounded by peace and quiet. Very few people are up at this early hour. There's a chill in the air. The sky is cobalt. The leaves are acid green. I think of Charlotte.

The opportunity to experience more of this world was ripped from her. The injustice of it never fails to sting. I transport myself into her arms, sink into one of her perfumy, overenthusiastic bear hugs. They were a Charlotte speciality. Nobody else did hugs like her. I long for one now.

I jump at the noise of my phone and answer it. 'David, hi.'

'Hi, Emily. Thanks for calling back. Sorry, I was making breakfast. And double-checking Hayley had ketchup in her bacon sandwich to avoid a strop.' He laughs, but it's strained. I know how he feels.

'Everyone's up already?'

'We're early risers here.'

Is there anything they do that isn't annoying?

'Such a relief she's back,' I say. 'What happened?'

He coughs. 'Excuse me. Sorry about that.' He clears his throat. 'She hitchhiked to the local B & B.'

'*Hitchhiked?*' I exclaim. 'Who was the driver?'

'Luckily it was one of the local lads, who was coming home from his girlfriend's place.'

'That could've been a very different story.'

David blows air out. 'Tell me about it.'

A male jogger in black comes out of nowhere and pounds past me up the steep bit. I stop to catch my breath. 'Was it the Three Bells Inn she went to, by any chance?'

'How do you know that?'

'It's where Olly and I were going to stay when we visited.'

'Okay. Right. Yup, that's where she went all right. She tried to check herself in under a false name. Luckily Claire, the owner, recognised her and called us to let us know.'

'How was she?'

'I think she was sorry. And embarrassed.'

'She's a bloody hothead.'

'I wonder where she gets that from.'

'Ha. Yes.' I bite my lip too hard. It throbs. Again I imagine

Charlotte's arms around me. 'So, tell me what you wanted to talk to me about.' I reach the brow of the hill, spot a bench and sit down. The wind is strong and goes right through my cotton sweater.

'Beth and I are at the end of our tether. We don't know how to help her through this.'

'I got that impression from Mia.'

'Mia, my little angel. She's such easy company. I think she likes being here. She's trying to fit in and make the best of it. Bless her.' I forgive his use of 'bless' this time, because I can hear the smile in his voice.

'And Hayley is doing the opposite, I take it.'

'Worse than that. Last night, before she ran away, she slapped Beth when Beth docked her pocket money.'

I hold back a gasp. Mia didn't tell me that little detail. 'Oh. My God.'

'I think it's why she took off, because she felt guilty.'

'Beth must've been very upset.' A snatch of Hayley pushing me lights up in my mind.

'She feels hurt. Emotionally. She's doing her best.'

'Without a doubt.'

'I think it'll be better when Hayley starts school and makes some friends. I'm hoping so anyway. But the school won't let them start until after half-term, which isn't for three weeks. And we're racking our brains for ways to entertain her and get her to that point safely.'

I beam like a child. 'And you want me to come over for a bit?'

'Yes.' He breathes out. 'I know you're busy with work at the minute. And with the house. But I really think she needs you.'

'You know, I haven't spoken to her since she moved to Ireland. I'm not sure if she wants to see me.'

'That's not true. She told me last night how much she

misses you. It's the only time she stopped shouting and actually cried. She adores you.'

My heart swells to ten million times its size. Already my mind is hurtling forward to the logistics of visiting them: booking flights, packing cagoules, telling Jaylani I'm taking a few days off to catch up on my TBR pile – like that's going to happen. I'll need to ask Olly, who won't mind a bit. He'll love the space to get on with his edits.

'Okay. I could come out for a few days next weekend? Or is that too soon?'

'Not too soon. Not at all.'

THIRTY-THREE

I drive along roads so narrow the wing mirrors catch the hedgerows. A grey film of rain flattens the colours of the landscape. I've only seen one house in about five miles. If someone else had been sitting next to me in the passenger seat of my rental, I might have said, 'Wow, it's beautiful here, isn't it?' like you're supposed to. Blatantly untrue. I find it bleak and hostile.

Already I hate it almost as much as I hate David and Beth and myself for forcing the girls to live in such a remote spot. I even feel sorry for all the sheep having to plod around these soggy, soulless fields.

The track to the house is straight and bumpy. It's a decent enough house when it comes into view. Long and low against the green backdrop. The walls are whitewashed and the window frames painted an up-to-date navy blue.

My eagerness to see the girls is bouncing about inside me. Getting hugs from them is second only to receiving one from Charlotte. I am beside myself, desperate to make sure we've done the right thing by them and by Charlotte. And to see for myself that Beth isn't a wolf in anything hand-made or woolly.

In my head there's a little red notebook for flagging up anything I don't like the look of.

Beth is standing at the front door as I pull up. Her baby is a small lump swaddled in a lilac sling across her chest. The hem of her cotton skirt almost brushes the floor and shimmers with mirrored embroidery. Her features are less beautiful and more sturdy than in the photographs. She wears dark lipstick, which I wasn't expecting. I thought women like her frowned at make-up. I'm trying not to judge her.

'Welcome,' she says, opening her arms, enveloping me in a long hug. She smells of cooking spices and baby wipes, and perhaps baby poo, but I might be making that up. 'How was your journey? Come in!'

David appears behind her, followed by two skinny olive-skinned, dark-haired boys, who scamper out to cling at Beth's legs and stare up at this stranger they might have heard about. The family greeting is warm. I look about for the girls, which David picks up on. 'Sorry, you're a bit early. They went down to the meadow to get something for you.'

I blush for some stupid reason. 'Oh. They didn't need to get me anything.'

Beth smiles. She has a crooked smile that I'm trying not to like. 'It wasn't our idea. It was theirs.' I will not be charmed by her.

Inside, the ceilings are low. The rooms have a clean, simple feel to them. I imagine it warm and cosy in the winter. There are beams across the fireplaces. They're the only nod to the past. It's more modern than I expected. No Aga or varnished pine in sight. The surfaces are uncluttered. An elegantly placed wooden bowl on a deep-set sill here; a navy linen throw strewn on the wibbly oak bench there. The sliding doors in the kitchen look out onto a sloping walled garden, which is well stocked with flowery bushes that I can't name. Everything is impossibly lovely.

I will not be fooled by it. My little red notebook might be empty so far, but give me time.

Halfway through a floral cup of tea with curdled oat milk, I spot the girls striding up the garden in their wellies. Goose-bumps run along my arms. I'm eager to leap up and run towards them. Politeness holds me in place. I'm listening to Beth tell me about Bridie's colic, which she's teary about. Bridie sleeps soundly now. It's hard not to be sympathetic to someone who is being so open. I have no idea what to say.

I steal glimpses of the girls approaching. Mia is in dungarees and her hair is growing out, tufty and sweet, like her whole being. Hayley seems rangier already. Her pale hair is still long, but closer to shoulder length than waist, and it looks bleached out by the sun. It flies about her head, lifting in gusts of wind, frizzed from the rain. Back home, she wore so many layers of hair products the rain wouldn't have dared touch it. She looks beautiful – and of course scowling. They are each holding a posy of wild flowers.

When Beth spots them, her cheek twitches and she starts moving about the room, swaying her hips rhythmically, patting the curve of Bridie's bottom through the sling. It's as though she's soothing a fractious baby, which at present Bridie is anything but.

David jumps up to open the door for them, and they both – and I do mean Hayley too – bundle into me for a hug. I kiss the tops of their heads, close my eyes and gulp down my emotions.

'We brought you these,' Hayley says, proffering their gifts, which still smell of meadow.

'Thank you. How beautiful,' I rasp, and stuff my nose into them and inhale.

The girls stand in front of me, and we stare gormlessly at each other for a prolonged minute. 'I've missed you,' I say. It sounds matter-of-fact and yet feels the opposite. I'm overcome with the certain knowledge that it was right to allow them a new life here. And to let the circumstances around Charlotte's death rest in peace with her.

As the weekend passes in rural bliss, my little red book remains closed. All I do is marvel at how they run their lives. We go to pubs where people sing and play the fiddle; we walk along the Donegal coastline for hours and eat cake; we chat over hearty home-made stews. I almost say 'bless' a few times. It's apparent that Mia's skills in the kitchen are becoming chef standard. And Hayley is painting watercolours. Overall, she presents as the child I remember before Charlotte died. Sharp around the edges, but charming and creative and analytical.

They don't seem to need me, which is hard to admit. I wonder what I'm doing here.

Then, on day three, on Sunday evening, something happens at supper.

THIRTY-FOUR

'Hayley,' Beth says, in her softly spoken tones. 'Have you forgotten something, my love?'

Hayley is standing at the open fridge holding two antique glass dishes filled with Mia's home-made chocolate mousse. She crinkles her brow, seemingly perplexed about what she has forgotten.

'Don't look at me like that,' Beth says. 'You know exactly what the rules are.'

'It's okay,' David says.

'No, it's not okay, David.'

Mia trills, 'I'll do it,' and picks up Hayley's dinner plate.

In my head, my little red book is open for some mental note-taking.

'Put that down, Mia,' Beth says. 'It's Hayley's job.'

Hayley's mouth purses. Her eyes take on that familiar steeliness, which I'd almost forgotten about. All the dark memories of those weeks after Charlotte's death come flooding back. My suspicions, my dread, my fear of her.

'I was just getting these out to put them on the table,' Hayley says.

Beth nods slowly. 'Yes, I see that, Hayley, but first we clear the table as a family, don't we?'

There is a deathly pause, time for hatred to engulf Hayley's features.

'Oh gosh,' she says lightly. 'So sorry, Beth. I forgot. I'm such a lazy, ungrateful brat.' She then very casually lets go of both glass dishes. They smash and splatter over the floor. Beth's jaw drops, words failing her as she stutters out her dismay. Hayley steps through the slippery goop, picks up her dinner plate and slots it into the dishwasher. 'There you go, *Beth*.' And walks out.

Padhraic and Luke giggle nervously.

Beth slumps into the high-back wooden armchair at the table. She shakes her head back and forth and then puts her hands over her face and begins to cry. 'Sorry. I just... Sorry,' she sniffs.

Mia is about to burst into tears herself. I can't figure out who to turn my attention towards first. Do I cuddle Mia? Run after Hayley? Say something nice to Beth? Lead the boys out to the garden? Part of me wants to say to Hayley and Mia, 'Come on, let's go home now and stop all this mucking about.' But I can't, of course. They're not mine to take.

David rescues us. 'Mia, my angel, could you take the boys to the telly room and put on some cartoons?'

Once they've gone, Beth says, 'I don't know why I was such a bitch about clearing up. It was so petty of me. But it's the cumulative effect of her. You know?' She drops her hands. Her strong cheekbones are mottled with a faint imprint of fingers.

'If it's any consolation, she was like this with me and Olly too. It can be hard going.'

'I think I store up all this resentment inside me. Like, before you came, she was vile. Chucking her weight around, answering back, ordering everyone about, being argumentative with the boys and generally unhelpful. Then you arrive and she switches on the sweetness. Just like that.' She snaps her fingers. 'She's picked you flowers and been an absolute delight these last few days, while all I've got is a slap in the face. I've tried so hard to get her to like me. But that will never happen.'

'She will, honestly,' I say.

'But wow, her behaviour is so *calculated*. I don't stand a chance.'

David jumps in. 'She's not calculated, Beth.'

'Isn't she?' She looks to him and then me as though she genuinely wants an answer.

'She's been through a lot,' I say.

'No. It's not that.'

'We're thinking it might be ADHD,' David says, looking hopeful.

'We'll have her tested, of course,' Beth adds dismissively. 'But in my opinion, it's definitely not the cause of all this.'

'Beth. Not now,' he warns.

'Then when?'

'They're next door.'

Beth gets up and kicks away the iron doorstop. The door slams shut. The candle on the table flickers out. She relights it with a lighter from the large front pocket of her linen apron.

'They won't hear us.' She sits down again and begins. 'The other week, I made her some of my special herbal tea. My grandmother used to make it for me when I was bottling things up or lying about something.' She folds her lips inside her mouth, eyeing David before returning to lock gazes with me. 'It's meant to be a truth serum. It's a silly old wives' tale, of course. But I used it on Hayley because I thought it might be a way of getting her to open up to me a little, to see if we could talk about her feelings.'

I groan internally. Here we go again.

'And although she took the piss out of the tea, amazingly she ended up talking about her mum for the first time ever. It was just a silly insight really, about why she loves cheese, because apparently her mum loved it and made her experiment with all sorts of mouldy cheeses and goat and sheep cheese. It's why she refuses to eat the vegan cheese we buy, and why she likes the farm-shop counter in the local town. It was very sweet to hear that. I promised not to feed her "fake" cheese any more, as she put it, and she promised to explain things more. It felt like a big step forward for us.'

I smile at a memory. 'It's true. Charlotte didn't have cheese brakes.'

'Cheese brakes?' Beth asks.

'You know, she couldn't stop eating it when a cheeseboard came out.' I chuckle. 'Moderation didn't come into my sister's vocab.'

'It's maybe why Hayley has issues around impulse control.'

I set my back teeth. 'All teenagers have that problem,' I say.

'Anyway, after what I thought was a breakthrough, that night we were woken up by her screams, and I ran through to her room and saw she was having a nightmare. She was tossing and turning and crying out. The whole works. I listened from the end of her bed for a bit, holding her feet, monitoring her, worried about her. And then I heard her murmur, "I didn't mean it, Mum. I didn't mean it." She must have said it four or five times. And it gave me the chills. Because I've thought for a long time that she has been keeping something to herself about that night.' She crosses her arms in front of her as she concludes, 'I've told David I think something bad happened between her and her mum before she died, and I think it's why she's so angry all the time. She's acting as awfully as she feels inside.'

Her theory is so frighteningly in line with my own, I'm reeling from it. My fingers press into my wrist, absently monitoring my pulse, which is leaping about and skipping beats. I ply my mouth into the smile position. 'That's jumping to conclusions, isn't it? I've said all sorts of weird stuff in my sleep, according to Olly.' Beth doesn't know that I don't sleep at all.

She continues. 'Hmm. I wouldn't have thought twice about it normally. But as I've said already, there's guilt in her aura, a darkness there in her soul, and I worry for her. For all of us, to be frank.'

More powerful than my sense of vindication is an instinct to protect Hayley from this woman's spiritual judgement. 'I think it's grief,' I say.

Beth almost shouts her reply. 'No, Emily. I'm sorry. It's not just grief. I lost my dad at sixteen, so I know how it feels to lose a parent. This is *not* grief. It is *guilt*.'

Coming over me in an atavistic wave is the need to fight to the death to defend Hayley. I'm in sackcloth on an ancient battlefield facing this woman, armed with a shield and sword. Before slashing wildly at her, I crouch in the long grass and think strategically.

She is adamant that there is something awry, something wrong with Hayley. She may be right. I understand where she's coming from and have also believed that seeking the truth is important, that talking to Hayley about Ayton's presence there that night would release her of a burden. But that's my job, not hers.

'Okay. I admit I felt the same once,' I say, looking down at my hands. I'll offer her a crumb of truth, then present a more palatable alternative to her shadowy theories. 'I think I know what you're picking up on.'

'Do you?' Beth leans forward, elbows on the table now. Her billowy sleeves bunch up, revealing a series of tattoos on both forearms. Her 'listening ears' are in full flap mode, multiple piercings and all.

I nod. 'You're spot on. Hayley has been hiding something from us.'

'She has?' David cuts in.

'Basically, Ayton, her boyfriend, was there the night my sister died. But they never told the police.'

Beth leans back, turning her palms to the ceiling. 'Right.' She arches an eyebrow at David, who shuffles his bum about on the bench.

I add a white lie quickly. 'It's also clear that he had nothing to do with Charlotte's death. It's just he's been in trouble with the police before, for minor stuff, which is why I think they kept it quiet.'

'Have you talked to Hayley about all this?' Beth asks me.

'Not yet. I found out just before they left, but I haven't wanted to stir it up again.'

'But she's already stirred up inside, Emily.' She thumps her stomach with her fist. 'She needs to rid herself of it.' Her eyes flutter closed. She makes a gesture with her hands that mimes shooing something away. I want to laugh at her pretensions. I don't, because I'm in battle.

'I know what you're saying, but I'd like to do it in my own time, in my own way, if that's okay.'

'Would you like me to be with you?'

'I'd prefer it to be just us.'

'I understand.'

But she doesn't. I realise now that it's crucial I help Hayley to live with her secret and protect her from Beth, so that she can function without the fight-or-flight response kicking in at the slightest provocation. I don't want her to go through years of trying to manage such a thing alone.

In my own childhood, if my sister and I had had even one person to tell our secret to, it might have been easier, less isolating. One trusted adult might have equalled less suffering. I want to give that to Hayley.

'She's a good kid underneath,' I say.

'I know she is.' Beth reaches out to put her hand on top of David's. I picture Charlotte's smile: *Well done, sis.*

I don't care whether Hayley's a good kid or not. It won't change how much I love her. But Beth does care. Very much. And that's why she'll never be able to help Hayley.

It's imperative I speak to my niece before I leave tomorrow.

THIRTY-FIVE

The following day, I take the risk of disturbing Hayley first thing, cajoling her out of bed and persuading her to join me on a walk.

We march along the miraculous Donegal coastline, with the clouds like a shelf over the sun and the sea as grey as can be. The wind blows at our side.

There's nowhere for Hayley to escape except over a cliff or up a scramble of rocks and heather. It's why I picked out this route from the guidebook. But her strides are flat-footed and haphazard, and I worry about the drop.

Navigating the conversation is going to be no less precarious.

'Beth was being petty last night,' I say.

Lashings of pale hair cover Hayley's mouth. She disentangles them in order to speak. 'She always picks on me. It's so unfair.'

'I noticed.'

'At least Dad sticks up for me.'

'I think Beth will grow on you. She's aware of her shortcomings.'

'Shit-comings, you mean.'

'If you give her a chance, I have a feeling it'll pay off. She has a good heart. But you have to work at it too.'

Hayley grunts, looks resolutely ahead and says nothing more.

A block of sunlight hits the path, then fades.

'I want to tell you something before I leave. And I promise you I'm not angling to get anything out of you if you're not ready.'

'Oh my God,' she growls, and digs her hands in her pockets and shakes her hair over her face.

I fall in step with her, shielding her from the steep fall to our right, and plough on. My voice comes out gravelly and grave, unused to speaking deeper truths out loud. 'Hayley. If what happened that night is too much to carry alone, I can carry it with you. I can share the load. There'll be no consequences. It'll be as safe as screaming it into the wind. And I might be able to help you live with it. You are not alone.'

I hear her sharp in-breath. She jogs forward. I can almost smell the panic, her need to escape me. Escape this. She'll feel trapped, ambushed. But there isn't anywhere for her to run.

I raise my voice as I continue. 'Keeping it inside can eat away at you. But if you share it with me, you can trust me with it. I promise you that.'

Her step falters. It's clear she's listening. On some level.

If she wants to pretend the words were never uttered, or needs time, that's okay. I understand that more than most and decide it's enough for the time being. What I hope is that I haven't overstepped, that she will not hold a grudge, push me away and punish me for ever.

I test the waters, prove to her that we can move through this and function normally too. I bellow after her, 'I think those are the Slieve League Cliffs over there!' I point to them, trotting behind her, almost tripping on her heels. 'Did you know they're some of the highest cliffs in Europe?'

She shoots me a wary look with those big sharp eyes of hers. The blue seems to catch the grey hues of the sea. The apparent strain of holding everything inside has brought out the pink around her eyelashes. She stops abruptly. I bump into her, and we front up to each other.

'Did you know that?' I repeat.

I can hardly breathe, waiting to see what she'll do. A few weeks ago, she would have exploded, hit out or even pushed me. Over the edge? Have I been naïve bringing her here? I can see she's brewing with it, pent up with what she thinks are unmanageable feelings. Is her soul as dark as Beth suggested? I stand firm. Ready for any outcome.

She turns slowly towards the cliffs and whispers, 'Wow. Cool fact.' With her back still to me, she swipes something away from her cheek, and I notice the back of her hand is damp.

Feeling both sad and triumphant, I approach her, link arms and squeeze her close to me. The point is, while she's not ready to talk yet, she has accepted my attempt peacefully, which feels like a win.

We walk clamped to each other for a while before I break the silence.

'It's kind of special here, isn't it? Not such a bad place to grow up.'

'Yeah, not gonna lie, it's okay.'

'Okay's a good enough start.'

'And I've got my dad back. You know?' she says shyly, shrugging. My heart soars into that big sky above us. I feel Charlotte all around me.

It rests on Beth's shoulders now.

Accept her, Beth, please accept her into your heart, I whisper on the wind. *She has been through something we don't yet understand. And might never comprehend. She's a trouper. Give her time. She's a good kid.*

THIRTY-SIX

I'm watching Olly swim while I stretch my legs out on the concrete side of the lido. It's first thing on a June Saturday morning. A month has gone by since I left the girls in Ireland. The sun is out. My skin is drinking up the rays like a thirsty child. It's moments like these that I appreciate more than ever now. In Charlotte's memory, I never take them for granted.

Driving away from Hayley and Mia and their idyllic new life was a wrench, much harder than I had imagined it would be. I expected to feel better in the knowledge I'd scoped the place out, made sure they were in safe hands. True, Beth had turned out to be every bit as passive-aggressive and self-righteous and touchy-feely as I had expected her to be, but she was also tough and kind and had taken Hayley on with admirable determination. As I left their house in the rental car, I gripped the steering wheel like it was a buoy in a churning ocean, holding on for dear life, focusing on the route to the airport as though that were the shore. I breathed easier once I was on the plane.

Since then, the girls have started at their new school, and I've heard very little from either of them. A few days ago,

Hayley sent some photographs of her and her dad on a hillside, windswept and grinning. They look so alike, with their Celtic colouring. His arm is thrown protectively over her shoulders, and her head is snuggled into his shoulder.

Mia sends me lots of cute photographs of her little brothers. She seems obsessed. There are fewer phone calls from the rat-infested caravan, and it seems there are fewer quarrels between Beth and Hayley.

Putting my missing of them aside, I am profoundly content for them. I admit that occasionally the banner *It's too good to be true* sails in and out of my mind. I don't take it seriously. And then there are my night-time terrors, which when reflected upon in the day seem less powerful than they did only a few hours before. But I've always had those.

The pool filter sucks water back and forth. This is the life, I think. Not one ungrateful teen in sight. Nobody else to take responsibility for. I might go in for a dip later, if the day warms up. Or I might not. Olly and I have different ideas about swimming. He pounds out lengths in a powerful front crawl, up and down until he's completed 2,500 metres, whereas I might enjoy some leisurely breaststroke with my face as far out of the water as possible.

Parliament Hill lido is one of the reasons we chose this area of London to live. Every Tuesday and Friday throughout winter, Olly leaves home at 6 a.m. with his wetsuit and goggles in a gauze backpack, walks across the Heath to the pool, swims for half an hour and brings me back a coffee. His lips might be blue, but the exhilaration still dances in his eyes. He missed this at Charlotte's.

Idly, I watch him now. I have a book on my lap, which I'm not reading. Thoughts of Hayley and Mia keep cutting sentences in half and breaking my flow.

It's okay just to sit in these peaceful surroundings, listening to the gulp of the filter and the sploshing of the swimmers, and simply observe. There's a group of older women chatting in the slow lane as they swim. Two men fighting for supremacy in the fast lane. A teenage girl gliding past all of them at twice the speed.

When Olly pulls himself out of the water and heads over, I emerge from what feels like a dream and reach for our flask of coffee. 'Nice swim?'

'Amazing,' he says, dripping, unzipping his summer wetsuit. His taut skin is goosebumped. He looks tanned and fit. My physique is the opposite. I haven't had the energy for a run in weeks. He sits down next to me and crosses his ankles. His chest heaves gently. We drink our coffee from tin mugs and tuck into slabs of home-made flapjack.

'Bliss,' he sighs, and then he kisses me. He tastes of chlorine. He's quenching. I want more of his kisses. For as long as it lasts, I feel comforted. He nods at the paperback balancing on my bare thighs. 'Any good?'

'I haven't read a word of it.' I stab my temple and make my eyes go wibbly.

'What's up?' he asks seriously, putting his flapjack down. The question sounds genuine, like he might have the headspace for an actual answer. A few of my night-time fears pop into my mind. No. I can't share those.

'Nothing. Just thinking about the girls too much probably.'

'I'm going to quote you now... "If they can't be happy there, they can't be happy anywhere."'

I said that? Slightly over-egging it, I think now. 'Yeah.'

'And you had that good talk with Hayley at the end, didn't you?' He sounds unsure. I eye him, checking he's not fishing for information. For obvious reasons, I have withheld the details of what was communicated on that cliff.

'Totally.'

'Looking back, I can't believe we got through it. I love her and everything, but living with her long-term would have made us ill. Seriously.'

'I know,' I say. A flicker of yearning for those days, minus the loss of my sister, surprises me. Then an odd and inappropriate churn of envy for Beth moves through me. 'The distance between us is much healthier,' I agree mechanically.

'Speaking of distance, want to book a last-minute holiday?' he says, bringing out his phone. 'Remember I said we'd go somewhere amazing if I got a book deal?'

'It wasn't the biggest advance, Olly.'

'It's enough for a holiday. We need one. *You* need one. And tickets are dirt cheap right now.'

'Where to?'

'Costa Rica? Or...' He scrolls. 'Oh wow, check out this place in Goa.' He shows me a photograph of paradise with a reasonable price tag.

'Maybe that's exactly what we need,' I murmur.

'Let's go crazy and book it now!'

'Wait, I've already used up so much leave at work. I don't want to take the piss.'

'You've got some left, though, yeah?'

'Yup.'

'Well then...'

'I don't know. Let me talk to Jaylani first.'

'Okay,' he sighs, turning on his front.

Nearby, there is a mother with her two daughters. They're a peaceful unit at first, chatting and smiling, reminding me of Hayley and Mia when they were little. Then the younger one pushes the older one, almost into the pool, and the mum tells the older girl off. The younger one makes a face at her sister. Unexpectedly, it gets right under my skin. This little exchange is all it takes.

'You know what?' I say, slightly too loudly, then adjust my volume. 'Jaylani will be cool about it. As long as I get my work done, she doesn't care where I am. I guess I could say I need the space to catch up.'

Olly lifts his head, squints one eye. 'Right. Work remotely from a Goan beach? Why the hell not?'

My stomach flutters. I imagine being able to snooze in the afternoon under a palm tree. This is exactly what poor Beth, who is now saddled with five kids, cannot do. Not until she's ancient. 'Okay, let's go for it.'

His grey eyes glint at me. 'I'm clicking "book now",' he says. His eyebrows have dried tufty blond, while the rest of his hair is still slick.

'Do it! Before I change my mind!'

After only ten minutes of online form-filling, he says, 'Done! We leave in two weeks!'

'Bloody hell! I'm going to have to buy a decent bikini now!'

'You look hot in that one.' He grabs me and wrestles me onto my back, and we snog like teenagers.

And for a few days – only a few, sadly – it becomes all about that. Not snogs. But the holiday that we never go on.

THIRTY-SEVEN

I wangle some time away from the office to work remotely, buy suncream and sandals and visit Mum and Dad in Shropshire to check on them. While I'm there, I fight off glum thoughts about the rapid progression of Dad's arthritis. It's worsening by the day in the damp British climate. Before we go, I persuade them to book a package holiday. I remind them that the sunshine will improve his symptoms and hasten their visit to Donegal to see the girls. They have been waiting for him to feel up to it. They choose Croatia at an all-inclusive resort.

My final duty before leaving for Goa is the weekly clean of Charlotte's house. I could have paid someone to do it, but I feel closer to her when I'm here. Unlike visiting her grave at Long Ditton, which was a soulless, creepy experience and not to be repeated. Nothing about her headstone amongst all those hundreds of others brought her closer to me. This afternoon, in her home, where she stamped about, where she laughed and loved, I talk to her. It's like therapy without an annoying professional analysing every word I utter. I tell her I plan to pop some sleeping pills for the long flight, admit I'm nervous about it, and find some funny stories for her about Jaylani's highly strung antics in the office.

I find new tasks to do in the house. Last week, I dusted the architraves and hoovered under the sofa cushions. The estate agent advised we keep the furniture to give it a homelier feel – and obliterate the death?

This week I decide the rooms smell musty and resolve to change the sheets on all the beds. As I rip off Mia's sheet, I hear something fall onto the carpet. It's a stack of Polaroids, face-down. My heart thuds. They must have been tucked under the mattress. Remembering the one I found of Charlotte beneath her pillow, I steel myself for that familiar rush of love and agony. I kneel to gather them, turning them over. The quality of instants is never great, and at first, I'm not sure what I'm looking at. However, as my vision adjusts, the images become clear to me, and I have a head-rush and feel the need to sit down on the stripped mattress before I fall. Why does Mia have photographs of such horrible things?

I've broken out into cold shivers, and the photos judder in my hands. I can't deal with them. I shoot up from the bed, shove them into the bin and finish making the bed. I'm sweating now. Panicked rather than exerted. The photographs lie scattered in the empty wicker basket.

After the initial shock has worn off, I accept I can't leave them there. What would prospective buyers think if they spotted them? I pick them out and slide them into the back pocket of my jeans, try to put them out of my mind, gather myself, go downstairs.

I put the sheets in the laundry room, wipe down the surfaces, replace the now dying pink roses Kristin left with fresh yellow ones.

I've grown fond of Kristin, have an urge to see her now. If I'm in the neighbourhood, she always insists I pop by for a cuppa. On the rare occasions I haven't had the time, she never takes offence. No complaints here. Her sunny outlook is a shot in the arm, a booster jab of optimism, and I come away with a more robust mental attitude all round. I understand why Charlotte became good friends with her and Jamie.

If I showed her the photographs, she'd probably tell me the girls had been playing make-believe, that there's nothing to worry about.

I bury them deep in my handbag.

Hands on hips, I remain obstinately positive, surveying the bright, spacious kitchen. The house isn't unfriendly. Neither Kristin nor I understand why it hasn't sold already. According to the estate agent, the question 'Why are they selling?' comes up regularly from prospective buyers. Second viewings are rare. There has been talk of dropping the price.

Before I leave, I call Kristin to see if she's in.

'Got time for a quick cuppa?' I ask her, wondering if I dare ask her opinion about the Polaroids. 'I can drop off the key for the guy who's coming to do the damp-proofing while we're away.'

'Come on over! Fleur and I are having lots of fun finger-painting.'

On the way out, I dump the full hoover bag in the wheelie bin out the back, then notice that the gate to the garden has been left open. I close it, deciding to take the side passage to the street. It turns out to be quite a nifty shortcut to Kristin's, circumventing the main road.

It's four-ish by the time I get there, and I bump into Jamie coming home from St Matthew's.

He looks pleased to see me and kisses me on the cheek. 'Funny I should see you today of all days.'

'Oh yeah?' I say, interest piqued.

'Ayton's been in trouble. Stay for a glass of something?'

'I'll text Olly to say I'll be late in.' As I search for my mobile, my fingers catch the sticky photographic paper of the Polaroids sweating in my bag. Maybe later I'll bring them out. After I've heard about Ayton.

Fleur grizzles on Kristin's lap and Tiger watches cartoons on Jamie's iPhone. I admire their flawless skin and guileless faces and think of the girls, and then the Polaroid images flash up and I'm gripped by a wave of nausea. I hold my knees under the table until it passes. The others don't notice.

'High as a kite, he was,' Jamie continues, taking a sip from his glass of alcohol-free beer. 'In biology, first period. He then pulled a whitey and they had to call an ambulance.'

'Is he okay now?' I ask.

'He's fine. Just embarrassed for being a lightweight.'

I take a gulp of wine. 'Will he be excluded?'

Jamie winds the blue nylon cord around and around his St Matthew's lanyard and exhales. 'I persuaded the head to give him another chance and told Ayton he needs to sort his shit out. But he's on thin ice.'

'He's lovesick, the poor boy,' Kristin says, brushing her daughter's ringlets out of her eyes.

'He's not still in touch with Hayley, is he?' I hadn't thought to ask Hayley, stupidly presuming their relationship had ended.

'Apparently they're messaging a lot.'

I sigh internally, not wanting to show my disappointment, and ask, 'Why do you think he's acting up again?' I wonder if Jamie will pick up on the subtext of my question. *Is guilt causing this? Is there a secret that is eating him alive?*

'He's got a lot going on at home.'

'Oh God. His mum again?'

He smooths his beard and says cagily, 'Something along those lines.'

Absently, my eye catches the photo on his lanyard, and I notice how sinister he looks in his mug shot. More like a criminal than a kindly teacher. I recall the sound of his ringtone, which I'd forgotten about, and scrutinise his features again. On the surface, there is nothing to see except the young, handsome face of a dedicated dad and teacher.

Shortly, Jamie goes upstairs to get ready for his evening run and Kristin moves the subject on from Ayton. She tells me how much they loved Goa when they went in their twenties. Chatting light-heartedly is a welcome reprieve. For a short time, it allows me to forget about the horrible photos in my handbag. I hug a cup of mint tea, wishing I never had to leave their cosy kitchen. The bubble bursts when my mobile rings. As I scrabble for it in my handbag, it stops and then starts again. A sharp corner of a Polaroid scratches the back of my hand.

'You need a smaller bag,' Kristin says.

I laugh, finally locating my phone. 'It's Olly.' I answer it. Absently, I register Jamie appearing again in his red running shorts. He kisses Kristin on the mouth, then disappears out the back door.

Down the phone, Olly tells me not to worry, that everyone is safe but that I need to come home as soon as possible, point-blank refusing to tell me why.

THIRTY-EIGHT

When I see David sitting in my living room, I freeze. He's CGI, surely. He's my imagination working overtime. He's meant to be in Ireland with the girls. He cannot be here.

But he is. Flesh and blood, leaning forward, elbows screwed into his knees. His face is blotchy and his eyes wretched.

'What's happened?' I rasp.

'The girls are absolutely fine. They're with Beth at home,' Olly answers, while David only stares at me, almost through me. Then drops his head in his hands.

'Want some wine?' Olly asks me as he tops up David's glass.

I nod and mouth, 'What's going on?' He shrugs and shakes his head, plainly as baffled as I am.

The Polaroids come to mind. Shivers run down my back. 'Why are you here, David?' I ask coldly.

He mumbles into his hands. 'We can't do it. We just can't do it.'

'Who can't do what?'

He looks up. 'It's not fair on Padhraic and Luke.'

'What's not fair?'

'Hayley. She's... It's... The whole thing has been a living hell.'

I think of her eyes, deep-set and stubborn, like my own. 'What are you saying?'

He won't answer me. He growls, 'Beth's getting depressed. I can't do this to her.'

'Can't do what?' I repeat.

'Living with Hayley is impossible.'

'She's your daughter.'

'Yeah,' he says, eyeing me, pausing, sending an electric chill through my heart. 'And Charlotte really screwed her up.'

I breathe again. 'To be fair, you're the one who left them.'

He throws his hands in the air. 'Jesus, Emily! Stop blaming me for everything that went wrong! Charlotte was a fucking drunk!'

I blink back my shock, return calmly, 'She had a problem. I understand that now.'

'But somehow I was labelled the bad guy?'

'It takes two to tango.' The images in the snapshots lying in my handbag develop in my mind more virulently, and I look down at his hands. Are they capable of harm?

'I couldn't live like that! Nobody should have to live like that,' he says. 'I get it, she hid most of it from the girls. They were young, went to bed early, slept through it. The worst of it was at night, when I'd get it in the neck. Her anger and vitriol. The lying. The cheating. Especially when she got stuck into the whisky.' He laughs snidely. 'She used to hide bottles behind the DVDs and under the sink, like I didn't know. Then there were the strangers – you know, other men she'd bring back from the pub and flirt with, blatantly, in front of me. Or the evenings she'd drink alone, blunder about the place, knocking into things or falling over. Then the hangovers. Jesus. They were almost worse. She could lose her temper like this.' He snapped his fingers.

I can't speak. I knew some of it, for sure. Hearing the rest of it is appalling. Cheating? Men from the pub?

He adds, 'And don't tell me she was sober the night she died. I bet any money the toxicology report was an eye-opener.'

'Everyone gets smashed occasionally,' I say, point-blank refusing to open Charlotte up to his judgement.

'*And* some, right?' he sneers, knocking back a glug of his wine.

I cross my arms over my chest. 'What has any of this got to do with Hayley now?'

'Hayley's just like her! She's so angry. So hard to live with. So hard to *love*.' His teeth are gritted.

My hackles rise. I remember Hayley's heart-rending admission on our walk: *I've got my dad back.*

'Don't say that,' I seethe. This man is weak. So bloody weak.

'I'm sorry, but it's the truth. I mean, when it comes to Charlotte's boozing, it's kind of chicken and egg. The second she gave birth to Hayley, before they'd even had that first skin-on-skin cuddle, Hayley started screaming the hospital down. And she's given us trouble ever since. Maybe she's the one who drove Charlotte to drink.' He holds my gaze, then Olly's. The pause says too much.

'Hayley loves you,' I breathe, both agreeing with him and unable to fathom how she would feel if she heard him say this about her.

'Funny way of showing it,' he retorts. Then, 'I can't be the dad she needs. She makes me feel this terrible rage. I don't trust myself around her. Worse than that, I hate myself. She pushes and pushes and pushes. It's relentless. If it keeps up, I'm going to blow. I'm serious. Beth has taken on the role of buffer, and she's so calm with her, but she's got Bridie as well, and all this is taking its toll on her. It's making her ill – her colitis has flared up again and she's losing her hair in great clumps. And it's only been a couple of months. What could it do to her over years?'

He's imploring me to understand. But he doesn't have the guts to spell out what he wants from me.

'What about Mia?'

He shakes his head, ravaged by my question. 'She's the last person I want to hurt in all this.'

'Can't you give it more time?'

'I wanted to, honestly I did. But everything changed for Beth the other day.' He stares at his hands, wringing them. 'She didn't want me to mention it, but I have to.'

'What happened?'

'Hayley pushed wee Padhraic, and he had to have stitches in his forehead. Understandably, Beth was freaked. She says it's not safe to have Hayley in the house, thinks something's wrong with her – the way she flips, loses control. It's dangerous, like she has a split personality. And I agree. But she point-blank refuses to see a therapist or a psychiatrist, and none of the tests we took her to in Dublin flagged up anything like Asperger's or autism or anything like that.' He brushes a hand over his brow. The Polaroids strobe across my vision. 'We've tried everything. Beth's had enough. At one point, she was going to call social services.'

'She mustn't do that,' I say.

'I stopped her, obviously.' David locks his eyes on mine, then hurries on. 'I talked her down. We've been considering other options. There's this special Catholic boarding school. It's state-funded, but it's for kids who are... for kids who are troubled. Like Hayley. I went on their website, but it's—'

I interrupt. 'No.'

Olly cuts in here to tell me off. 'Emily...'

'It really is somewhere I think—' David starts.

I interrupt again. 'I'll take them,' I say. 'We'll take them back.'

Olly glares at me. I look away, can't deal with the utter horror in his eyes and what this means for us.

David begins to splutter through his tears. 'Do you mean that?'

The fury in my heart is a fireball. I want to kill him. 'Yes, I mean it,' I say, digging my nails into my palms. 'I'll move back to Charlotte's, take it off the market. St Matthew's will have them back.' Unspooling inside me are mixed threads of fear, regret, alarm. Disbelief that I am saying it out loud.

'Emily,' Olly says, 'We haven't even discussed this.' His voice is uncharacteristically low and thundery.

'I'm sorry. I know. But I can't let her go to some horrible state institution for problem kids and separate her from Mia. I can't let that happen.' I bite my lip, think of my big sister, hope I'm not doing this to spite David. Know that if I don't do this, we'll all lose Hayley for good. If she's feeling as isolated and frightened as I think she is, as I know I once felt with my own shameful secret, pushing her away will be the final nail in the coffin.

'We leave for Goa on the seventeenth,' Olly says, apropos nothing. Our holiday is irrelevant.

'I have to do this for them, Olly.' I shake my head at him; I'm lost for words to comfort him with. We could discuss it until we're blue in the face, yet my decision will be the same. I've never been more certain of anything in my life.

David garbles, 'I was hoping you'd... I think it would be the best...' I can see the guilt planting itself in the centre of each pupil.

'It's best,' I confirm.

'My God, this is insane.' Olly shoots up, storms out. His footsteps pound down the communal stairs.

David and I stare at the door. 'Are you sure about this, Emily?' he whispers, barely audible.

What's loud and clear is the sound of his terror. If I changed my mind, I wonder what he would do. I break eye contact, clear the half-full glasses away.

I pour red wine down the sink, then turn to look him in the eye. 'So how are you going to tell them?' I ask him. *How do you tell your two beautiful daughters that you don't want them any more?*

THIRTY-NINE

David and I decide it's best I go over to Ireland to be there when he tells the girls, after which I'm to bring them straight home. Olly stays behind to set up Charlotte's house for their arrival. As I sit on the plane, I picture him, resentful and cross, moving our stuff into Charlotte's and wishing he was on a flight to Goa.

My unilateral decision to take Hayley and Mia has put a wedge between us; locked him away, locked us away. The ease of our marriage is under house arrest. I told him there was nothing to talk about, so he is not talking about it. And now we're not talking about anything.

The night before I left, I read out a list of promises, trying to clear the air. Writing them down was Kristin's idea. Apparently, when she and Jamie argue – always impossible to imagine – she bullet-points her side of it so that she doesn't get in a muddle.

Mine went as follows:

- I'll be the girls' main carer, take full responsibility for the practicalities, give you the freedom to do as you please. You won't be tied down as a traditional father might be.

- If we move into Charlotte's, we'll be rent-free and you'll be able to afford to work as a full-time writer, regardless of book sales or publishing deals.
- We'll spend the girls' school holidays travelling with them to destinations on your bucket list, see the world ourselves while broadening their horizons.
- Caring for them is not a lifetime commitment. Another three years until Hayley is eighteen, another six for Mia. After that, they will be adults, will be heading off to university, leaving home. We'll have the rest of our lives to do as we please. Then we'll move back to north London. It isn't for ever, it's just for a few years. We still have us.

That's how I sold it. That's how I see it. Olly thawed out enough to make a joke about signing the list in blood at the bottom. We have always been able to laugh together. I'm a master at making him feel better.

We'll make it work. For better or for worse. He'll come round.

On the plane now, I sip sparkling water from a plastic cup. The bubbles give me indigestion. The cabin is cold at 35,000 feet. Every muscle in my body is tensed up. I have a strange cramp in my leg. It goes without saying that I haven't slept a wink.

David picks me up from the airport. On the way, we discuss practicalities. He confirms that social services don't involve themselves in private arrangements such as ours. A letter will be drawn up by his solicitor, but that's about it. Then he tells me how he and Beth want today to go. It has been decided that Beth will do most of the talking. I contested this, but was slammed down. He thinks they'll blame him less if she's the one to explain. She's willing to be the fall guy. He paraphrases what she plans to say, and my ribcage compresses my lungs until I'm shallow-breathing and heady.

The lovely photograph of David and Hayley on the hillside together fades to black. I've never dreaded anything this much in my life.

As soon as we enter their low-ceilinged white house – how did I not notice the oppressiveness before? – Beth says her hellos, and informs me that Bridie's taking her nap upstairs, while Padhraic and Luke have been shipped off to a friend's house down the road.

'Yes, David told me,' I say icily.

'Okay, let's get this over and done with,' she says. 'We'll do it around the kitchen table.'

She rings a bell and calls up the stairs. The girls thunder down. When they see me, their faces break into amazed smiles. Their excitement and delight are achingly awful. They chit-chat lightly as we head to the kitchen, telling me snippets of news. Hayley asks Beth in passing if it's okay if a friend comes over next week, and Mia requests a beanbag from Amazon for her bedroom.

Hayley groans, 'Oh my God, Mia!' and I jump. 'Beth's said no about a thousand times!' She explains to me, 'The poly-styrene balls inside aren't environmentally friendly.'

'Oh, I see,' I croak. My heart is thrumming in my ears.

'Sit down, please, girls,' David says gravely.

The chairs scrape. We settle into a grim circle.

Now Mia's leg is jiggling. She twirls at a tuft of hair at her crown and fiddles with the biscuits she and Beth made earlier. I wonder how Beth got through the process of baking with her – judging by her puffy face, not easily.

The adult tension changes the girls' sweet moods. Hayley has her arms crossed, her jaw set, her eyes glued on the fields outside the window. It appears both girls have gleaned that my visit isn't just for fun, that it's not going to be a good chat, but their young minds won't get close to how bad it's going to be.

Beth starts with her opening gambit.

'This is the hardest decision I've ever made. And I want to be clear, it's me who has made it, *not* your dad.' Her voice is already wobbling. David's head is hanging down. She shakes her hair off her cheekbones, gathers herself. 'You guys living here is not working out for anyone, is it?'

I wince at the casual use of 'guys'.

Both girls' faces slacken. Mia's hand drops from her head. Hayley sits back in her seat. Neither of them utters a word. Hayley glances at me and I hold eye contact, wanting to communicate that it's going to be okay, that she needs to stay strong.

Beth continues. 'Maybe you'll understand this one day, when you become mothers too, but I have to put my boys first. They don't deserve to grow up in a battleground. Padhraic has developed a nervous tic, I'm sure you've noticed. And Luke is clingy and withdrawn.' She turns to Hayley. 'Hayley, everyone is being caught in the crossfire of our fighting. Maybe it's neither of our faults. Maybe you're just being you and I'm just being me. But together we can't be under the same roof. I'm so sorry, but I can't put my family through it. It's not fair on them.'

Hayley's chin begins to crumple. 'I didn't push Padhraic. He tripped, I swear it.'

Despite agreeing not to say a word until after Beth had finished, I can't help myself. 'You didn't see it happen?' I ask her directly, sitting forward, flabbergasted.

'No, but Padhraic told me, and that's all I need to know.'

I suck back my anger, realise that arguing this point isn't going to change anything now. 'You never made that clear,' I grumble.

'I'll be better,' Hayley whimpers, and grabs David's arm.

'Dad, please, I promise I won't be horrible any more. I promise I'll try harder.'

David is hangdog, his eyes red like his daughter's. 'You've said that too many times before, sweetheart. You've pushed Beth too far.'

Mia's little face is frozen.

'But I swear on my life this time. I really do,' Hayley implores, swiping away the tears that keep coming.

My heart shatters. I reach out to hold her hand, but she whips it away. I try Mia's under the table and find a fist, stiff and cold. She doesn't unfurl her fingers to hold mine. Neither of them will want me. What did I expect? I'm sloppy seconds, the backup plan, the boring, strait-laced aunt who should have fought harder for them in the first place.

Beth's voice sounds strained but full of conviction. 'This is *my* home, Hayley, and my decision is final. I'm so sorry.'

'But where will we go?' Hayley's sobs are quiet as her shoulders heave.

This is my cue, and I'm frightened. 'I want you both back,' I say steadily. I won't cry like everyone else. I will be a rock for them. 'I should never have let you out of my sight. I hope you can forgive me for that. I love you both so much, and want to bring you home with me. If that's okay by you.' I'm all they've got.

I wait for Hayley to shout and scream, push me away, reject me. I'm able to withstand it. Not only for them, but for Charlotte. I can be the scapegoat, the punchbag for their pain. There's going to be a lot of that. Having just lost their mum, they are losing their dad into the bargain. He's cast them off. They'll feel faulty. There is no going back from this. My palms face upwards on my thighs, and I curl my fingers into them. I'm braced. I'm embarrassed. I'm inadequate.

Then Mia folds herself into my arms and grinds her forehead into my collarbone. I feel her wet eyelashes flutter on my skin. Hayley joins her. The three of us slot together in a desperate embrace and I tell them that everything is going to be okay.

Over their shoulders, I catch sight of Beth. There's a crease of concern between her eyes. Out of nowhere, Mia's Polaroids sift through my mind. The onus is on me to get to the bottom of them. I'm in charge now. I'm accountable. I'm overcome by the great responsibility of taking care of these two damaged young girls, who are clinging to me for dear life. My God, I'm not enough.

FORTY

Last night, Hayley and Mia were too tired after the drama of the day to do anything but flop into their old beds and sleep. This morning, they are euphoric. They are gallivanting around the house hugging sofa cushions they spent most of their young lives lounging about on; opening and closing cupboards they played hide-and-seek in as younger kids; yelping in the garden they weed on as naked toddlers.

'We're back home, suckers! Wahoo!' they shout into the neighbours' backyards.

I'm happy for them. The only blip is the issue of Mia's Polaroids, which I have not yet told a soul about. The least I can do is give the girls the space to put down roots at home again before I broach it.

Mia lets out a high-pitched squeal. Hayley has turned the garden hose on her. Olly and I laugh at their goofing about.

He raises an eyebrow at me and says quietly, 'If ever there has been any doubt...'

I exhale, dropping my arms by my sides. 'It's a good start.'

'Not bad.' He shoots me a mischievous glance. 'I'm glad I forced you into doing the right thing.'

'Oh yeah, okay, that's your story!' I shove him playfully.

He hugs and kisses me and looks into my eyes, murmuring, 'You're amazing. Sorry for being an arse.'

'Don't be daft.'

I rest my head on his shoulder as we watch them. We're sprayed lightly by cool droplets, occasionally jumping back if the hose gets too close.

The girls bound around, damp hair flicking in the air, eyes bright. Ireland has been good to them in one way. On the surface, they are healthier-looking, less spoiled. There's something to be said for the simplicity of rural life. I'm hoping it's a reset. They have learned a tough lesson about the shortcomings of adults, the weakness in their father. Twice now he has chosen Beth over them. They won't be approaching a third time. It's a sad truth, but one that will arm them in the future against more hurt.

'Can Ayton come round?' Hayley asks, pushing her hair back.

I'm not prepared for her question. The old suspicions rush in. 'Umm, I don't know. Maybe...' But at the same time Olly comes out with 'Yeah, sure.'

'Cool.' Hayley drops the hose and goes inside. The coils of the pipe are like a serpent around Mia's feet. Water spills from its mouth.

'We should've talked about it first,' I mumble to Olly, stamping over to the side return to turn off the outdoor tap.

'Oh. Sorry.' He looks sheepish.

The bubbling of fear about Ayton surprises me. It seems to have been sleeping inside me all this time. I consider putting my foot down, overruling Olly, refusing permission.

'It's okay,' I say, distracted by the fact that the gate onto the alleyway is open again. I close the latch, make a mental note to fix it, along with some other snagging issues I've noticed: there's a broken hinge on one of the kitchen units, the fridge needs cleaning, and the flagstone on the front doorstep wobbles. I need to get this house into good working order, create a functional foundation for our new family life. Start as I mean to go on.

Cutting into my list-making, Mia asks, 'Can we make some chocolate chip cookies, Uncle Olly?'

'That's a brilliant idea,' Olly says, throwing an arm over her shoulders.

As they saunter inside, I overhear Mia asking him, 'Uncle Olly?'

'Hmm?'

'Do I definitely have to go back to St Matthew's?'

'Don't you want to see all your friends?'

'Uh huh. Yeah,' she says quietly. I think of the Polaroids. My brain squeezes. Is now the moment to ask her about them? My thoughts are teeming with competing bullet points on my mental to-do list, yet I do nothing.

I'm left alone in the garden with slightly damp toes. Pulling those photographs out to show her after the twenty-four hours she's had might tip her over the edge. Even as I resolve to put it off until tomorrow, I think of a million counter-arguments to that decision. Same with Ayton. What do I do? Confront him now? Wait? Until when? When is a good time to bring it all up again?

Keeping the girls safe – my one and only job – feels impossible while there are so many variables and potential threats everywhere I turn. I've barely been their carer for a full day and already I'm second-guessing myself, feeling utterly lost and unworthy of the mission ahead of us.

Later, when I hear Ayton arriving, every fibre of me itches to get the facts straight about that night. As I go about our evening, I obsess over finding a moment to talk to him.

FORTY-ONE

From the television room, where I'm sitting with Olly and Mia, I can hear Hayley and Ayton murmuring in the kitchen. I guess they're heating up the pizza Ayton brought round for her. This is my chance to corner him. No more skirting around it. If he is to spend time here, I need to feel comfortable around him and clear the air. If I'm to help Hayley, the more I know the better; and the more she knows I know, the better. If I'm to build trust, she needs to know that I can take anything she throws at me. Even the truth.

'Either of you want anything to nibble on?' I ask Olly and Mia, who are snuggled up together on the sofa.

'No thanks,' Mia says.

'Want me to pause it?' Olly asks.

'Nah, you're all right. Go ahead. I'll only be a minute.'

I enter the kitchen.

'Hi, guys. Just making some tea,' I say. 'I'll be out of your hair in a jiffy.' *A jiffy?* Who says that? It isn't even true. It's the opposite of what's going to happen. Plainly embarrassed, Hayley winces through a smile. Ayton, who is placing the slab of frozen pizza on the baking tray, chortles, but not unkindly.

I click the kettle on. One pink daisy from the flowers Kristin and Jamie dropped round earlier this evening has a broken stem. I pick it out and put it in the bin. They also brought champagne. Jamie wrote in a card, *Welcome to the 'hood! Modern Family eat your heart out! We're so happy for you guys!*

As I get a mug down from the cupboard, Hayley hovers, ready to shoo me out. I wonder if Charlotte felt as awkward as I do around them, or if her status as Mum gave her more of a sense of entitlement in her own kitchen.

The peppermill from Mexico, adorned with its paintings of fertile women, catches my eye. It sticks out around here – a kindred spirit suddenly. How I'll fit in, how any of us will work this out, is at this point an unknown. I feel like an interloper, don't yet know how to play at being a parent.

'How's it going, you two?' I'm too jaunty.

'Good, thanks. How are *you*, Auntie Em?' Ayton asks, confident and overfamiliar. He pushes up the front of his hair, which is a thicket of red curls on top but freshly shaved to the skin around the sides. This style further narrows his already thin head. Because of his height, he looks older than fifteen. I picture his home life. Although Jamie was discreet about why Ayton was in trouble at school, I know that his dad is dead and that his mother leaves him alone for days while she disappears on drinking binges. All that would leave any kid looking older.

I adjust the temperature on the oven dial, knowing that for this particular brand of pizza it needs to be at 220 degrees. Trying to centre myself, I say, 'I'm not too bad, thanks, Ayton. There's been a lot going on, obviously.'

'Yeah. You rescued my Hayley.' He looks to Hayley, who rolls her eyes at him, bites her bottom lip through a smile, picks at a split end.

'It was just meant to be,' I say bashfully, heartened to have been labelled as the rescuer.

What I have in mind to ask them will ruin this flash of affection. I'm torn between keeping the peace and starting as I mean to go on. I need a parenting handbook with an answer in Chapter Three, or something. Oddly, I think of Chapter Seventeen in Olly's book. I guess I don't want to get to Chapter Seventeen of my relationship with Hayley and wish I'd been more open and honest. And there's Ayton, who deserves one adult in his life who is steady and straightforward with him at all times.

Steeling myself, I take the reins. 'Actually, I wanted to confess something.'

Instantly, their energy changes. They're wary, but Ayton quips, 'You've eaten the cookie dough, yeah?' His attention darts to the freezer, then straight to his phone, which he fidgets with like it's a stress toy.

I throw my arms up. 'Not guilty, your honour!' Oh God. Of all references to make!

'I'll call the Feds on you, Auntie Em. For real.' He leans next to Hayley, who rests the heels of her hands behind her on the countertop, ready to push off, arms angled sharply like wings.

'Ha!' I laugh, but I'm shaking. I close my eyes for a second to gather my courage. The memory of my sister's smile fills me with warmth. Then I deliver it quickly. 'I don't know whether Hayley mentioned, but I heard you arguing behind the garages. The day Hayley was suspended.'

'Aw, man, that's private business.'

Hayley glazes over. 'So you did earwig.'

'I gotta go,' Ayton says, snapping up his hood.

'No!' I go around the kitchen island that divides us and put my hand on his arm. He flinches. 'Ayton, please don't. I'm not here to get anyone in trouble. I just want to know what happened.'

To my amazement, he slopes back to Hayley's side. Closer to her this time.

'Hayley?' I ask her.

'I don't know what you're saying. What are you even saying?' she says, shooting what looks like a warning glance at Ayton.

He shuffles next to her. 'Yeah, dunno what you're on about.'

'It appears that you were here in the house that night, Ayton.'

His eyes widen. 'Huh?' He straightens.

Hayley jumps in, a steeliness in her voice. 'Well, it looks like you know that already, so?'

Her admission came so easily, I'm taken aback. 'Why did you lie?' I'm addressing Hayley more than Ayton.

'Why d'you think?'

'Babe,' Ayton hisses, twisting to face her. 'What the actual fuck?'

I reassure him. 'I'm not going to get you in any trouble. Please just tell me what went on.'

Hayley answers for him. 'He came back with me after the party. That's all. He didn't see any more than I did. We were in *bed*.' She emphasises the word, waiting for a rise from me. Four-teen-year-olds in bed together is icky, but it's the sideshow. I don't react.

Ayton moves away from her, paces forward two steps and back two, then stops in front of her and talks to her as though I'm not there. 'Nah, babe. Nah.'

She says, 'It's what happened.' But her voice isn't right, sounds too forced.

'I dunno. I dunno about this,' he mutters. He puts a hand on the crown of his head through his hoodie. I can't see his eyes, but I don't need to. I can smell his fear.

'Ayton,' I urge. 'Is there something you want to tell me?'

Hayley speaks for him again. 'No, there's nothing. We just didn't want the police to know he was here because they'd think he had something to do with it. And he didn't, I swear it.'

Having wanted this very outcome, this clear admission from her, I'm dissatisfied with it. Ayton is unsettling me. 'You have to understand, this is really hard for me to get my head around,' I say, trying to absorb it as the truth. 'All this time you've been holding something this big back, and to be honest, it's confusing. You can see why I'm struggling here, right?' It's true that I'm upset, but not because they've been lying all this time. It's that I still don't trust what I'm hearing.

Then Ayton blurts angrily, 'I can't. I just can't right now.' He's heading towards the door.

I jog after him, my heart in my mouth. 'What's going on, Ayton? I promise you, you can trust me,' I urge him.

He glances over my shoulder towards Hayley. He looks nervous, scared, but his response is aggressive. 'Why don't you ask that Mr Hanra-wanker if he was here?' he hisses, right up in my face.

I'm winded. The next few seconds unfold in a blur. I hear the door slam. Ayton is gone. I'm dumbfounded. I don't know what he could possibly have meant by it. It can't be true that Jamie was here that night, that he had anything to do with Charlotte's death.

I swivel around to find Hayley behind me. I wait for her to contradict him, to deny it, to laugh. But she doesn't. Her stricken face says it all.

FORTY-TWO

She begins to explain, but I stop her, put my finger to my lips, *shh*, and usher her through the kitchen and into the laundry room.

'We don't want the other two getting wind of this,' I explain, closing the door behind us.

Her bottom lip is quivering and blue. 'I'm so sorry,' she whispers.

'Oh love.' I touch her shoulder. 'I take it you're going to tell me now, though,' I say, jumping up to sit on the dryer. 'Take a pew.' I'm perhaps trying too hard to act casual.

She hefts herself onto the washing machine next to me. Our legs dangle. Shoulder to shoulder in the small space, it's like being in a confession box. I wait patiently like a priest for her admission. She bangs her heels on the metal tub, folds her hair into a knot on top of her head. The tips of her ears are bright red. My fingers find their way into the bowl of clothes pegs by my thigh. I take one and worry at it.

'When Ayton and I got back from the party,' she begins, unravelling her hair again – her gossamer, angel-like hair, which I have an urge to touch, 'I heard Mum in the shower, but I was too mad at her to call hello through the door or anything, which I would normally. Me and Ayton went straight to my room and, you know, like, started fooling around.' She drums her heels. 'But then we heard something through the wall. Some*one*. A man's voice. And Mum was giggling and saying some loud embarrassing stuff... like... what they'd done together before... and she was trying to persuade him into... you know.' She winces at me.

I try to hold my face steady. 'That must have been mega awkward.'

'It was so cringey, I can't even... with Ayton there and everything. But we had no clue who was in there with her. To be honest, I was worried about Mia overhearing them at this point, so I went to bang on the door and tell them to shut the... to shut up.'

'I wouldn't blame you for telling them to shut the F up.'

She shrugs. 'Anyway, that's when I caught sir coming out.' She makes a face. 'He was in his running gear, you know, and he was doing up the cord on his shorts. It was so gross.'

The image of him doing this in his kitchen before his run freeze-frames in my mind, and my guts churn.

'It was definitely Mr Hanrahan?' I croak.

'One hundred per cent. I swear it.'

'Oh my God.' I pinch the skin at my wrist with the peg, lean into the sharpness of the sensation, which is more pleasant than how this revelation is making me feel. 'Did he see you?'

'Oh yeah, he saw me. But I just ran back into my room and slammed the door and that was it. Everything I told the police after that is true. Ayton went home and I went to sleep, didn't see Mum or speak to her, and woke up the next morning to find the door still locked... you know.'

'Hayley, sweetheart... Sorry to have to ask.' I swallow. My mouth is dry as a bone. 'Do you know for sure that she was alive after Mr Hanrahan left? If you never went in there, how would you know?'

'Oh, she definitely was. She was singing and crashing about with all her lotions and potions. When she drank, she was so clumsy and stupid.' Both of us let that hang in the air between us. Clumsy and stupid. And unsteady on a wet floor?

'And did Mia know anything about any of this?'

'No. Thank goodness. She was asleep.'

'Has she ever shown you any of her Polaroids?'

She looks confused. 'What Polaroids?'

'Nothing, nothing. I don't think they've got anything to do with all this. But is Jamie – Mr Hanrahan – the reason she doesn't like St Matthew's any more?'

'Oh, right.' She thinks for a second. 'I don't think so. I think that's just more to do with all the weird looks we got. Because of Mum and everything.'

'I can only imagine.' I sigh. 'Made ten times harder for you because you had to see Mr Hanrahan every day.'

'It sucked.'

'And now you've got to go back to that same school with him.' I'm thinking aloud, my mind racing forward. What are we going to do? We've re-enrolled them at St Matthew's, thanks to Jamie. Kristin has become a friend. *Jamie* has become a friend. It's mind-bending. I don't even know where to start. 'Do you want to go back if he's still there?'

'Whatever. I did it before. He's irrelevant. Anything's better than that weirdo school in Ireland.'

I lean towards her. 'Hayley, why didn't you tell anyone about him being there that night?'

'He didn't say anything, so I didn't say anything. He didn't hurt Mum... And he's got little kids.'

'That was kind.' I pause. 'But the point is, he was there, and the police should have questioned him.'

'And then everyone at school would've known that my dead

mum shagged my teacher!' Then, less explosively, 'And Jamie's kids would feel like I did when Dad was shagging Beth. All for nothing. Because he didn't have anything to do with Mum dying. Yeah, great. Really worth it.' She begins to cry.

I say, 'As long as he didn't coerce you into keeping quiet?'

'No! No way!'

'Okay, okay. And we certainly know why he didn't fess up himself,' I mutter. I rest my head on the wall behind me and blow out. 'Jesus, what a mess.' I raise my eyes to the ceiling. 'Great job, sis. Thanks for that.'

But Hayley jumps to her defence. 'Sometimes when she drank she did really dumb stuff that she regretted. I mean, I don't know, maybe she was in love with him or something?'

'I didn't mean to sound judgy. Especially when she's not here to give me a good ear-bashing.'

Hayley doesn't smile. She seethes. 'Hanrahan's the frigging idiot here. Like, I mean he's the one married with littlies and everything. And he acts all caring to his students and so dedicated, like he'd do anything for us and everything, and he's just shagging all the MILFs at the school gates. It makes me sick.'

'You think he was having affairs with other mums... other women, I mean?'

'Maybe.'

'Do you know how long it had been going on for? Between him and your mum?'

'Only that she had come off Bumble, I knew that. She hadn't had a date with any of those guys for ages.'

'Although her dating always went in fits and starts,' I recall. Charlotte grew tired of Bumble after a fling with a marine biologist. She seemed breezy and happy and didn't mention meeting anyone else she liked, not even cryptically. But then she wouldn't have admitted that she was dating Hayley's married teacher. The syrupy, sad notes of that ringtone fill my ears. I'm learning that there was a lot my sister kept from me.

Kristin's face comes to mind: her pretty ringlets and her baby-blue eyes and the uncomplicated way she loves Jamie. Perhaps there's no such thing as uncomplicated when it comes to love.

I steal a sneaky glance at Hayley's profile, absorb every twitch of her delicate features. Her face stills my heart.

'What?' she says, catching me out.

I smile at her. 'Nothing.'

She sticks the tip of her tongue out of her mouth, then says, 'You do believe me, though, don't you?'

'Of course I do,' I say.

I wonder how certain I'll be of that when I'm banging on Jamie's door tonight, demanding answers.

FORTY-THREE

I didn't go banging on Jamie's door, even though I felt like it. I couldn't do that to Kristin. Instead, I mulled it over for twenty-four hours and thought of a better plan. Then I talked it through with Olly, who was as outraged as I wanted him to be.

Now I'm parked up a little further down the street from Jamie and Kristin's house, waiting for Jamie there. Because we all know he likes to run every evening.

Irately, I wonder if he plans a quick shag on his local loop tonight. Maybe with that woman going into her semi now? Or another woman at the 3.2-mile point on Strava? When I think of him returning home to Kristin, perhaps making love to her after visiting my sister, a hot flash rises in my cheeks. Through association, I'm ashamed of Charlotte and furious with Jamie.

It's why I'm lurking in the fading light under a plane tree, waiting for him in Charlotte's hot, smelly car, which I have inherited. Although I believed Hayley, and still do – admittedly with every passing hour it is harder to believe – I need to hear it from his lips.

When I see the muscular unit of him pounding along the pavements, I put my hand on the door handle like it's a trigger.

The timing has to be right. I can't let him swerve away before we're close.

He's brought to an abrupt halt by the obstacle of the open door in his path.

'What the...?' he exclaims, not seeing me yet.

I step out of the car.

'Emily?' He looks confused. As he absorbs my features, his expression changes from pleased to wary. 'What's up?' he says, resting his hands on his narrow hips, panting. Panting! Jesus. That's all it takes for me to imagine him having sex with my sister.

I don't reckon it's a good opener.

'I think we should talk,' I say.

'Now?' He looks around him. 'Here?'

'Believe me, you don't want Kristin to be around for this.'

He crosses his arms high over his chest and widens his stance, cocking his head to the side. 'Why's that?'

I slam the car door closed. 'I know about you and Charlotte.'

He shakes his head and frowns at me. I can almost see the cogs of panic whirring behind his eyes. 'What do you "know"?' He acts out speech marks and laughs.

His bluffing makes me cringe. 'You want me to spell it out?'

He opens his mouth, perhaps intent on keeping up the bravado, but his jaw remains hanging. No words form except the murmur of 'Shit'. He holds his head, paces in a circle, then goes to sit on the bird-shit-covered wall under the tree. When he looks up at me, his cheeks are wet with tears.

'Okay, okay. It's true. Kristin and I have been having problems for years.' He looks like a child ready to be told off by his teacher.

'Sorry, no, I can't wrap my head around this.'

'I was in love with Charlotte,' he says simply.

This statement knocks me sideways. I guffaw. 'Don't give me that—'

He interrupts. 'I think I fell in love with her the moment she walked into my classroom three years ago. It was Hayley's Year 7 parent–teachers evening. Charlotte was wearing her red jacket with the big white buttons.'

I splutter. 'It's been going on that long?'

'No, no. We were just friends until recently.' He sniffs, wipes his eyes. He's forlorn, like he might need a hug that I won't give him.

'What changed?'

'It was a simple thing really.' A smile spreads across his whole being. 'We went to this school quiz night last September. We were on the same team, and I don't know, I've never belly-laughed with someone like that, ever. We both had tears rolling down our cheeks for most of the evening. And when I walked her home, we meandered around the streets, detouring all over the place and talking about everything and anything. I would have kissed her that night if she'd let me, but she said she couldn't do that to another woman, because of what David did to her. She joked about being too old for me, but I just fell in love with her even more deeply. It was like I was awakened. We were soulmates. I don't expect you to understand. I know it was wrong.'

My mind scrolls back. 'But it doesn't make sense. Charlotte dated quite a few guys since September last year, so if you two were, you know...'

He straightens up, clicks his tongue. 'It was agony hearing about them, but I had no right to tell her she couldn't see other men, not only because I was married, but also because there was nothing physical going on between us.'

'Nothing? Over all those months? Come on!'

'I'm serious. The first time was only a few weeks before she died. After I'd told Kristin about her, which was—'

I break in. 'Kristin *knew*?'

'She did, because I told her, but to be honest, I'm not sure she actually absorbed it. She said my feelings for Charlotte would pass and she refused to talk about the logistics of a separation. And this is really at the heart of why she and I have problems. Her feelings are always so shut down. I can never get anything real out of her. She has this mega barrier up. Everything has to be so perfect. And if it isn't perfect, she gets at me. It's suffocating.'

'She should've kicked you out.'

'I know. Really, I think a small part of me wanted that. But it was so weird. After I told her, we just kind of carried on as if it had never been said. And then... then...' He lets out a low moan. 'And then only a few weeks later, Charlotte died. When I heard... Jesus, it was like all the lights in the world had been switched off. I was groping around in the dark, pretending to be fine. I can't even... I can't believe it still... I've had to hold it all inside.' He grinds a fist into his heart.

Stupid arse, I think, falling for my sister like that.

I say sternly, 'You failed to tell anyone about being there that night, though.'

'Every hour of every day I waited for the call from the police, but it never came, and I didn't have the balls to come forward because I knew it would blow my whole life apart. I wasn't thinking straight either, like I was living in another reality. Honestly, Emily, I didn't know whether I was coming or going. Kristin was the one who kept my head above water. Her and her beta-blockers.' He shoots me a sideways glance. 'And you.'

'Me?'

'With you, I was able to talk about Charlotte, stay closer to her somehow. And keep an eye on the girls.' He hangs his head.

'It was Hayley who told me about you.' I sigh. I'm deflated by his story. Depressed for him. I sit down next to him, probably in some bird poo, but I'm beyond caring at this point. 'And she's pretty angry about it.'

Who could blame him for falling in love with my sister? Who could blame him for keeping the truth quiet? Who could blame him for any of it? They would have been good together. Jamie would've made a good stepdad, a fun brother-in-law.

'Hayley's always bloody angry. She made Charlotte's life a misery. Charlotte was at the end of her tether.' When I don't immediately respond, he adds, 'Sorry, but she was.'

'Do I know everything, Jamie?' I breathe, scared even to ask.

'I promised Charlotte I'd never get Hayley in trouble.'

'Please. I need to go into this with my eyes open.'

He pauses. 'I'm only going to tell you because I want you and Mia to be safe.'

'Just spit it out.' A flash of irritation covers my fear.

'Okay.' He blows his cheeks out. 'When Hayley didn't get her way, or when she was anxious about something, she'd totally lose it. Charlotte described it as out of control, scary. She would try to hide from her – in closets, in locked bathrooms, in her bedroom – but she wouldn't always be able to keep the door closed or get away in time. Hayley's fully grown now, and strong, and the hitting started to really hurt and sometimes cause proper injuries. Charlotte was always bruised – I'm sure you know that. She'd tell people she'd fallen or she'd been clumsy, didn't she?' I want to nod, but I'm stiff with shock. He goes on. 'But it wasn't true. She'd show me the fresh marks on her body after Hayley's tantrums. I begged her to get help.' He lets out a long exhale. 'She wouldn't because she didn't want Hayley getting in trouble. And then suddenly she "slips" getting out of the shower—'

'No. Don't,' I rasp. I shoot to my feet.

The images captured in Mia's Polaroids hit me one after the other: bruises and marks on various limbs of an unidentified person. A black and blue splodge on a shin. A series of oval black marks on an upper arm. Angry scratches on a shoulder. Red marks on a thigh. And many other variations of the same.

My head is swimming.

'Emily. She hasn't done anything to you, has she?'

'No! God, no.' My fingers dig into the healed burn on my palm.

He stands up, too close to me. 'If anything happens, anything, even if it's a small thing, you must tell me, okay?'

'I won't need to do that.'

He eyes me, then says, 'I'll regret not going to social services about Hayley for the rest of my life. It was a terrible error of judgement. I should've known better, but when abuse comes from a child, it's harder to act on.'

'*Abuse?*'

'Yes, Emily. Hayley was abusive towards Charlotte.'

'That's going too far. I'm sorry. She's just a kid. Sorry, but I can't hear any more of this.' I back up towards the car, fumbling for my keys. 'Don't ever say anything like this to me again or I'll go to the police about that night.'

As I shut myself into the car and turn the key, the radio blasts out. Through the window, I can see Jamie trying to say something else, but I can't hear it. I won't hear it. I drive off, shaking so much I'm barely able to keep the steering wheel straight.

FORTY-FOUR

Olly talks to my reflection in the mirror as I brush my teeth. 'He actually used that word?'

'*Abuse*, yes.' I spit the toothpaste.

He holds out Mia's Polaroids and whispers hoarsely, 'Wow, Emily. Who are we living with?'

'Don't say that!'

'You've just told me she shoved you so hard you ended up burning yourself, and then there's these.' He waggles the Polaroids in my face. Earlier, he caught me with them in the kitchen, having heard me come home after ambushing Jamie.

'We don't know they're of Charlotte yet,' I say.

'It's the most likely scenario, though.'

'They could be of Mia.'

'You think Hayley's hurting her too?' His voice trembles. The harsh glare of the strip lighting brings out the deep bags under his eyes.

'She wouldn't lay a finger on Mia. No, I mean maybe they're not of anything serious at all. Mia could've just been mucking about, taking photos of everyday little knocks and scrapes on her own body. We don't know yet. Kids do weird things.'

Over the past few weeks, I've had many different theories about the origins of the photos. Maybe they're of Hayley, and Ayton is responsible; or David was violent to them all; or Mia was being bullied at school; or Hayley was cat-fighting with her frenemies. None of the theories has stuck for long. None of them Olly need consider. None of them I really believe.

'You need to talk to Mia about them,' Olly says.

I tug the photographs back and tuck them into my dressing gown pocket. 'I've been waiting for the right time. The girls have barely been here two days. Ironically, the one person I wanted to talk to about them is Jamie. He'll have dealt with countless cases of unexplained bruises on children at school.'

'You definitely can't now.'

'I do know that. I just can't believe Hayley would've done this to Charlotte. When she pushed me that time, she didn't mean to actually hurt me. She just lost her cool. She was horrified that I burned myself. It was my own fault really.'

He laughs without smiling. 'You sound like a domestic abuse cliché.'

'That's how it happened,' I snap.

He shakes his head, pulls his thatch of hair tight to his head. 'Was all this... us coming back here... a mistake?' We hold eye contact through the glass, separated by it perhaps.

The water runs warm under my fingertips for a minute. 'Olly, I know I can help her.'

'She needs professional help.'

I splash my face. 'No.'

'Why not?'

I glance up, and a whispered fear comes out. 'What if she says too much?'

'What are you scared of her saying?' A glassy window of light is carved into his irises. I can't tell what he's thinking.

Water drips from my chin into the sink. Now *I've* said too much. 'Nothing.' I dry my face, hold the towel there, press it into my eye sockets and breathe before speaking. The unwritten rule is that we can't mention it. Or even think of it.

'You're worried she'll talk about that night?'

My mind drifts away from his question. 'It's funny,' I say. 'When we were growing up, Charlotte was hard work, but Mum could never admit it. They were too alike. If she admitted it, it'd be like *she* had faults. And Mum's way too proud for that. She put out this idea of the perfect family all the time. It was always such a thing for her, how we presented ourselves. Good manners and nice clothes and good figures were all that seemed to matter, while we squashed so much emotional stuff down. Which is maybe why Charlotte drank.'

His voice is muffled as he takes off his T-shirt. 'D'you think Charlotte ever felt guilty about the drinking?'

I think carefully about how to answer his question. There was one emotion Charlotte didn't do, and that was guilt. Her tendencies were more towards righteousness. Self-reproach and overthinking were not her specialities, they were mine. Even when she was obviously in the wrong, she would stand by her story, stick two fingers up at anyone who dared suggest otherwise, have another drink, fuck everyone.

'I'm not sure about guilt. Pride is more likely. Like, she made out that she and Hayley were so close, the perfect mum and daughter, but she was hiding the rows they were having – even from me. Maybe because it didn't fit in with what Mum expected of us. But in effect, she was concealing the real Hayley, I guess.'

'We're certainly getting to know the real Hayley now.' Olly leaves the bathroom and I follow. He climbs into bed, turns his side light off.

The real Hayley. The vision of the tacky Mexican peppermill on the worktop flickers against my rapidly blinking eyelids. The reason Charlotte didn't share the real Hayley with me is suddenly so blindingly obvious that my blood turns ice cold.

FORTY-FIVE

The following day, after breakfast, I sit them down, hand Mia the photographs and wait for her explanation.

'I found them under your mattress when I was changing the sheets,' I say neutrally, leaning forward on the armchair. Mia's cheeks drain to the colour of the oatmeal sofa she's sitting on.

Hayley, next to her, tries to peer over her shoulder. There's something about the pair of them, two sisters with frightened little expressions on their faces, that triggers a deep-seated memory of Charlotte and me at similar ages.

Mia clutches the photos in a stack on her lap, doesn't flick through them. She knows exactly what she has in her hands. When Hayley tries to take them, she presses them to her chest and shoots a sideways glance at her sister.

'I want to see,' Hayley says.

'Mia, show Hayley,' I say firmly.

Hayley prises them out of Mia's grip and looks through them. Her raised eyebrows suggest she's more perplexed than guilty. 'When did you take these?' she asks, like she recognises what's in them.

I wait for Mia to explain, desperate to understand. When I

think back to what Charlotte and I hid from the grown-ups, I struggle to recall whether there was anyone who got anywhere near to noticing that we harboured such a nasty knot of secrets. Our parents were so wrapped up in themselves, I think they sometimes forgot we were there. It suited us, though, considering what we carried inside. Being discovered was a heavy, sweat-inducing sack on my little shoulders.

Mia twists the short hair at her crown. Elbow shooting out, eyes filling. A rivulet runs down each cheek. She sniffs. 'A while ago. I don't remember.'

'But I don't remember either.' Hayley's genuine bafflement doesn't fit with Jamie's theory of her abusive nature. On the other hand, I guess she's already proved what a brilliant liar she is. Lie upon lie upon lie.

I refocus on Mia. 'Go on, Mia.'

She nods. 'After Mum got back from the pub, she'd fall asleep here.' She slams a little fist into the sofa, then points to the carpet at their feet. 'Or there, and sometimes we'd have to get her undressed and put her to bed, wouldn't we?' She looks to Hayley.

Hayley's mood turns. '*Mia,*' she warns through clenched teeth, then puts the photos down and pushes them towards me as though suddenly understanding them.

'Go on, Mia,' I coax.

'Hayley didn't like the undressing bit, because she was embarrassed, so I did it.'

'Mia, don't,' Hayley says again.

'That's when I saw the bruises on Mum's tummy and legs.'

Hayley's head snaps round to gape at her sister, as though stunned by what she's just said. '*Mum's?*'

'Why did you take photographs of them, sweetheart?' I ask softly.

'I thought someone had done it to her. We didn't like all her boyfriends, did we, Hayley?'

Hayley looks down. 'They weren't that bad,' she mumbles, gnawing at her nails, one finger to the next in quick succession.

'They were!' Mia cries. 'They were all drunk and horrible and creepy. And I thought that if the police ever needed evidence to put one of them in prison, I'd be able to show them those.'

'You're so dumb,' Hayley says under her breath.

'Did your mum know you'd taken them?' I ask.

'Yes, Mia, did *Mum* know you took them of *her*?' Hayley asks archly, a little strangely.

Mia looks resolutely at me when she answers. 'She was too sleepy to notice.'

'She was drunk?' I ask, plucking up the courage to talk frankly about it.

At first, neither of them confirms it.

'If she was drunk, that's okay. It's not your fault.'

'Sometimes,' Mia says.

Then Hayley speaks quite matter-of-factly. 'She was an alcoholic.'

I control my expression, keen to show them I can handle this. 'Yes, it seems she had a serious problem. And you've been trying to protect her by not telling anyone, haven't you?'

Hayley nods, holds my gaze. Her chin dimples. I can see she's trying to keep it together.

'It's okay. I understand.'

She dissolves into tears. Hiccuping through them, she says, 'She didn't mean to be that way. She was just sad.' Her shoulders judder silently. There's no trace of anger at all.

I put my hand on her knee, gently squeezing it while squeezing away my need to cry. My voice comes out hoarse. 'I know, I know, sweetheart. We all loved her so much. So, so much.'

Mia slips her arm around her, and Hayley puts her head on her little sister's shoulder. Her chest heaves. I wonder how often they have comforted one another like this in the face of Charlotte's addiction. I don't want to disturb this moment between them. I wait, giving them space. I remember Charlotte and me clinging to each other like this once. It isn't a good memory. It's filled with shame and guilt. But I hope that Hayley's crying is a breakthrough. For me, it allows in a chink of optimism. Her intention to protect her mother, at great personal cost, appears to have stemmed from love. Nothing more sinister than that.

While watching them, I transport myself back in time, not to a specific moment but to the strong overriding feeling in my childhood that I needed to protect Charlotte, and how dishonest it made me. Even when I wasn't lying, I felt that I was. It's hard to think about that right now, but now that I have, I know that I will not be able to unthink it. The memory grows big in my head, unmanageable, and I take it out on Olly later on.

'Jesus, Olly! How hard is it to put them in the sink?' I bark when I find he's left two squeezed-out tea bags on the worktop.

'I was just about to.' He hands me a mug of tea.

'Why would you just leave them there? Who did you expect would clear them up?'

'Nobody.'

'I'm nobody, am I?' I seethe.

He offers me the milk carton. 'Are you okay?'

I take the black tea, turn my back and pour the milk in, trying to breathe, but I have a crazy, panicky feeling that I'll go insane if I keep it bottled inside me for one day... no, one minute longer. 'The girls reminded me of something,' I begin. 'Well, it's not that I'd forgotten. It's all this. All this fucking shit.'

I must be mumbling, because he leans into me, cradling his mug. 'What's that? Sorry, I couldn't hear.'

I sigh. 'Let's go outside.'

We slip out into the humid summer air and sit on damp garden chairs facing one another, knee to knee. In a splurge of honesty, a sentence comes out of my mouth rapidly, and without warning.

'Charlotte was abused as a kid. And I knew it was happening.'

And the distress in his eyes makes it real all over again.

FORTY-SIX

'She first told me when she was fifteen. He was Mum's second cousin once or twice or fifth removed or whatever.' I take a short sip of tea and scald my mouth. 'If only the bastard had been five thousand miles removed from us. Or from Charlotte, at least.'

Olly shakes his head at me. 'Jesus. When did it... I mean, how did it...?'

'At family functions. It had been going on for a couple of years. But the final time it happened was at Mum's fortieth.'

'The final time what exactly happened?'

'That's what I'm going to explain,' I say, putting down my tea. 'Typically, Mum wanted a big bash with a marquee. She was tweaking the house within an inch of its life. Charlotte and I were groomed like dolls. But I was spoiling it because I was furious that he'd been invited.'

'Who? The cousin?'

'Yes, but Mum was too harassed about counting the napkins to focus on why I was so upset about him coming. She just said that if they were asking Cousin Blah-blah and Uncle So-and-so, they just had to include him too. Even though he came all the way from Leeds. And then lurked about Charlotte with that leery right eye of his, which was droopy, not quite aligned to his left.'

'Eugh. He sounds revolting.'

'Thing is, on the day of the party, I overheard Mum gossiping to a friend about how talented he was and that he had once been on stage in *London*, don't you know, and I just blurted out, "Like, who cares?" And Mum was mortified in front of Lady La-di-da from the big house on the green and she sent me to my room, saying I had to learn to control my temper. But I couldn't explain because Charlotte had sworn me to secrecy.'

'That must've been hard to keep inside.'

'My God, I was boiling mad about it that day, I can't even describe it. To be honest, I wished Charlotte had never told me at all. I sometimes still wonder why she did. Perhaps to get it off her chest, guessing I was too young to understand? But I was old enough to know that it was wrong. So wrong it gave me a tummy ache. I hated how the secret had dug its way into me. I hated that I wasn't doing anything to help her. I hated her casual way of dealing with it.'

'Did she ever try to tell your parents?'

'Charlotte was more secretive than any other person I knew. She kept our parents in the dark about everything: the cousin, the clubbing, the drinking, the drug-taking, the multiple boyfriends. Everything. She was so clever about it. Meanwhile, I was always being grounded for silly crap, like the time I shared a can of cider with my best friend on the cricket green. Mum went mental, honestly. I think it was because the neighbours had spotted us and I'd embarrassed her. It was all about image.'

'She's still like that now.'

'And Charlotte was the perfect daughter on the outside. Blonde. Outgoing. Sporty.'

He rolls his eyes. 'And you were clever, beautiful and kind. But that didn't count?'

I smile. 'I can't describe it. Charlotte stole all the light in the family. I understood why my parents loved her more than me.'

'They didn't!'

'*I* loved her more than me. It's why I took a big risk that day.'

He took a slow sip of tea, which must've gone cold already. 'What did you do?'

'At first, all I did was sit on my hands at my bedroom window, hot and bothered, and watch the grown-ups drinking champagne and eating strawberries on the lawn. Then I clapped eyes on the sleazy cousin pressing his sweaty hand into the small of Charlotte's back as they ducked under the iron pergola. They disappeared down the woodchip path that led to the garage and the hairs rose on the back of my neck, hackles up.'

Olly puts his tea down at our feet as though it has suddenly turned his stomach. The surface wobbles with a grey film. 'I can't even bear to hear this.'

'But I had a plan to stop it, see? So I found my camera and stuffed it into my bag – I remember it had this cool rainbow strap. Funny the things that stick in your mind.'

Olly smiles. 'You've always believed in the pot of gold at the end.'

'Even back then, plainly!' I laugh. 'Because I just had this overwhelming feeling that I was the only one in the world who could save her from him.'

'Sounds just like you.' But he says it a little sadly.

As I go on to explain the rest, Olly doesn't interject, perhaps unable to penetrate the trance-like state I go into in the telling of it. I leave out no details.

'First I took a detour into Mum's greenhouse. There was a round basket full of garden tools there. I sifted through the implements, wondering which would be most suitable for the job. There were trowels and stubby forks of various sizes, a bent spoon, a skewer, a biro with no ink, a metal straw, and the yellow-handled screwdriver that Mum used to prise open tins of paint. I chose that, tucked it into the back of my jeans and headed across the gravel to Dad's rickety wooden garage. The padlock to the double doors was always locked to keep his old Mini safe, but the side door was left open so he could get easy access to his workbench at the back. He stored camping equipment there, dumbbells, an old pair of skis, a couple of rusty bikes and other crap, but he kept the work surface clear for odd jobs.

'I guessed the two of them would've gone in that way, which meant I needed to approach from the other end. For the element of surprise, you see.

'Cautiously, before making the next move, I took a moment to tuck myself into the leylandii hedge that buffered up against the garage side wall and surveyed the surroundings. Listening to them through the thin panels stopped my breath. I could hear the cousin, but not Charlotte. Her quietness terrified me, I remember. She'd told me that her brain shut down when it happened. Apparently, the first time, what he did had stunned her into total muteness. The second time, he had threatened her – with what, she never revealed. The third, she just went along with it. For an easier life, she said. She told me she would kill herself if anyone found out. And I believed her.

'Anyway, carefully and quietly, I loosened the screws on the lock of the double doors. The wood was spongy with damp and smelt of rot. It only took a few seconds. The padlock clunked to the ground and the door swung open with a big creak. Shaking like a leaf, I whipped out the camera and snapped a photograph of him.

'In the glare of the flash, I could make them out at the back wall.' I pause. 'I can't tell you more than that because I can't bring myself to say the words out loud. Just take it from me, it was as wrong as anything can be. And I said in a very grown-up voice, "Get off my sister or I'll show our dad the picture I just took." The boldness and innocence of my eleven-year-old self confronting a grown man like that was incredible really, when I think of it.

'He scurried out the side door, which was a useless escape route because he had to pass me again to get to his car. But it was the sight of his little smirk that pressed my buttons. Before I knew what I was doing, I was lunging at him and stabbing the screwdriver into his foot. It tore through the gauzy material of his trainer. It makes my teeth go funny when I remember the feeling of hitting his bone. Thankfully, Charlotte yanked me by the waist away from him, saving him from further harm. My attack had been enough to leave him hobbling and hopping across the gravel.

'"You freak," he said, I think, or something like that. I didn't care. I was more worried about Charlotte and whether she was cross with me. But she wasn't. She pointed at the bright yellow camera that I'd dropped at our feet and guffawed, "It doesn't have any film in it, does it?" I giggled, trembling all over – delayed shock, I guess. Then she dragged me by the hand back to the house. As we ran together, so fast I was almost tripping over, she whispered in my ear, "Thanks, sis."

'That's all. It was the last time we ever mentioned it.

'The cousin disappeared from the party and from our lives altogether after that. Aside from the odd murmur about his permanent limp, nobody cared much. He never came to another family gathering. Not even to funerals. To this day, my parents never found out why.'

Olly murmurs, 'Jesus Christ, Emily. That's horrific.'

'It was. For Charlotte. Looking back, though, I was angry all the time after that. Every day, the small stuff got to me in a way it hadn't before. I couldn't help losing my head when Charlotte nicked my stuff or told small lies to Mum about me. I had nightmares about the cousin doing to me what he'd done to Charlotte, and I slept badly. It's where my sleep issues come from, I suppose. And maybe there's part of me that understands Hayley's temper more than I want to admit.'

'Makes sense,' Olly agrees, nodding, reaching out to me. We hold hands. I feel a deep connection with him. His writer self is satisfied by the arc that explains Charlotte's behaviour, and in turn perhaps Hayley's too, dispelling the niggling unspoken notion of her original sin.

But Charlotte's death, whatever its cause, is by no means where the story ends.

What I've told Olly is the bulk of our backstory and is enough for him to be getting along with. But there is more to tell; arguably worse to tell, if you can imagine worse. Because that cousin took away far more from my sister than just her childhood.

FORTY-SEVEN

At the end of June, the girls return to St Matthew's. The first week of our morning routine is like *Little House on the Prairie*. Every day I make them healthy packed lunches, kiss them on the cheek and remind them to work hard, before leaving to catch the train at 08:02.

Adjusting to the new commute hasn't been easy. It involves a forty-minute standing-room-only journey on the overground, a forty-five-minute Tube ride across London with two changes and a twenty-minute brisk walk or bus ride. It takes almost two hours. I'm not used to it yet, but it's doable.

Our second week is less twee. On Tuesday, Hayley takes so long putting on her false eyelashes in the bathroom – now in use again – that Mia storms out of the house, forgetting her sandwiches, and walks to school alone. During a script meeting at work, my mobile flashes up with a message from the school app informing me that Hayley has received an after-school detention for skipping tutor time again. Tutor time is compulsory, and her tutor is Jamie Hanrahan. Considering the recent revelation, I forgive her for bailing out. But I am too exhausted to talk it through with her when I get home that night, deciding to cut her some slack and leave the big chats for later.

On Wednesday, Mia loses her PE kit, the bread is mouldy, and then Hayley has a full-blown panic attack about going into school, so we allow her a duvet day. Aunt Jane comes over and hangs out with her, plays cards and shows her how to crochet.

Before leaving in her Uber, Aunt Jane says to me in her throaty, brusque voice, 'I'm only a quick cab ride away, so please take advantage of me if you ever need a break. Just dump them on my doorstep.'

'Thanks. I will. Definitely.'

'Terrific. You'd be doing me a favour.'

'I doubt that somehow.'

She combs her fingers through her short grey hair, currently with a pink stripe. 'Seriously, retirement doesn't suit me. I've taken on some exam marking, which keeps me off the streets, but I miss young people. They offer a fresh perspective on life.'

'How about next time she skips school?' I guffaw, only half joking.

'I've given her a stern talking-to about doing well. And she's under strict instructions to call me on the mobile if she's having a wobble.'

Aunt Jane then gives me a solid, manly hug to go with her reassurance.

On Thursday, Hayley pretends to go in. I receive a call from an unusually formal Jamie about her unauthorised absence. We track her down. Yup, at Ayton's. It's only pride that stops me from calling Aunt Jane to beg her to take them both for ever.

The third week is no better. She goes in all of two days.

As we hurtle towards the summer holidays, Hayley's attendance record gets worse by the day.

My work-from-home days on Thursdays and Fridays are a mixed blessing. I'm here to stand at the door and wave them off, supposedly to help coax Hayley into school. In reality, I get in a flap, and she usually tells me to chill the F out and still doesn't go in.

Today, on this too-hot July morning, I've had it up to here. Today I'm on a mission. If we can end this term with an iota of optimism for our future as a functioning new family, it will be a result.

'None of the softly-softly approach today, I'm telling you,' I say to Olly. 'I'm going to make sure she goes into school if it's the last thing I do.'

Olly slides off one noise-cancelling earphone and asks me to repeat what I said. He looks dazed when I do. He has been writing at his grimly lit corner desk in the spare room since five thirty this morning.

'How do you plan on doing that?' he asks, rubbing the back of his neck.

'Not sure.' I picture dragging her by the hair along the pavement.

'Maybe one more day off then?' he suggests.

'No. No way. She can't just do whatever she likes all the time, pissing about at home thinking that's okay.'

'She does go in most of the time.'

'Only seventy-six per cent of the time, I've been told.'

'At least it's almost the summer holidays.'

'We can't tiptoe around her every time she stamps her foot. It's the principle of it more than anything.'

My shrill tone prompts him to snap his earphone back on his ear and turn back to his book. 'I have to get on.'

He's *getting on* with his book about Ellie's severed womb. Ellie is easier than me. Ellie's character is 'Emily-lite', to say the least. Olly is ignorant of the full-blooded me, of the multiple facets of my true nature. I've omitted key episodes that punctuate the well-organised linear trajectory of the life he's depicted in the book. For good reason. Those blips, those inversions, would change how he saw me. Truth is stranger than fiction.

A flash of my sister and the cousin freezes on my retinas. Until telling Olly the story the other night, I hadn't thought hard about it for years. By sharing it, I've reconnected a fine thread back to where it all began. Previously, the images of that time have only flickered weakly like ghosts of a long-gone past, appearing and disappearing almost unnoticed. Now they seem to be jangling their chains against my skull.

'Hayley?' I call, checking my phone. We're creeping closer and closer to her normal departure time. '*Hayley?*' I refuse to be a pushover.

'Yeah?' She saunters out of the bathroom in her PJs. Golden twirls of hair stick out of her topknot. Even bed-headed, she looks beautiful. I blink a few times, regroup for my tough line.

'Why haven't you got your uniform on?'

'I'm not feeling well.'

She looks peaky, but then she always does. 'In what way not well?' I ask brusquely.

'Tummy ache.'

'What sort? Here or there?' I tap my upper and then lower abdomen. Recollections of tummy aches from my own childhood pierce my firmness. Mine were as real as tummy aches could get.

Hayley rubs her lower belly. 'Period pains.'

'Well, there's some Nurofen downstairs. Take two. You'll be fine in half an hour.'

Mia appears wearing her short-sleeved shirt and uniform trousers rather than a skirt. She has gelled down her hair to the side and looks boyish. 'Good girl,' I say, hating how like my mother I sound.

'Hurry *up*, Hayley,' Mia begs her sister, before jogging downstairs.

Hayley clutches her middle and bleats, 'They're *really* bad, honestly.'

'You can't take another day off school, Hayley.' My thoughts cut straight to her consistent truancy when she starts Year 11 next term, and her failing all her GCSEs and it all being my fault.

'It doesn't make any difference.' She huffs and slams herself into her bedroom.

I stamp in after her, hand on doorknob. 'Er, excuse me, young lady, it makes all the difference,' I say, adopting my best matronly tone. 'Get your uniform on right away. It's already five to eight.'

'Can you get out, please?' she retorts.

'No, I can't get out.'

'Invasion of privacy, much?'

I'm see-sawing in my head. Is this the right approach? Or am I going in too tough too soon? Is Olly right? Should I give her another day off? Write off this term? Start afresh in September? Even as I doubt myself, I plough on, thinking of Aunt Jane.

'You don't care about doing well?'

'One day is not that big a deal.' But I can see a glimmer of concern cross her expression.

'One day becomes two days, becomes a week. It adds up. And before you know it, you've got your GCSEs.'

She laughs at me. 'You're so uptight.' It's a deliberate poke. Who am I trying to kid? I don't have a clue what I'm doing.

I throw my arms in the air. 'Laugh all you like, but you'll regret this, mark my words,' I say, deflated, blowing my cheeks out, knowing I'm wasting my breath.

I'm about to step out, take a break, rethink my strategy, when she grunts, 'Can I have that Nurofen?'

I'm momentarily surprised. 'Oh, yeah, sure.' Has she given in?

Mentally crossing my fingers, I scurry out, pop out two

painkillers for her and hurry back with a glass of water. She doesn't say thank you. Just knocks the pills back and hands me the glass, like I'm her servant. I don't say anything. I don't want to spoil the moment, desperate for this day to have the outcome I planned, able to work from home uninterrupted.

'Would you like me to put some toast on for you?' I ask.

What happened to my self-respect? What happened to standing up to her? Principles? I have others.

'No thanks,' she mumbles. I'm about to remind her that breakfast is the most important meal of the day, but stop myself. I can't push it, so I leave her to finish getting ready.

Downstairs, I'm tense, hot, hopeful, clock-watching. Nervously I wipe already wiped surfaces, chomping down the urge to fly upstairs and shout, 'For Christ's sake, hurry up!' at her. Mia's playing a game on her phone. It's now 8:16. Maintaining self-control, I calculate timings, mentally hobbled by all the crossing of fingers and toes. The walk to school takes fifteen minutes. If she doesn't come down in nine minutes, she'll be late for Jamie's register at 8:40.

In my previous life, a summer morning might include a home-made kale smoothie; a skim through the newspaper headlines; a kiss from Olly; a leisurely walk through the park with a takeaway coffee in hand; five stops southbound from Kentish Town Tube. Happy bloody days.

But I mustn't think of my life before. I must not. Things don't always pan out how you expect. *Get over it*, I tell myself.

'It's 8:23,' Mia says. She gets up and puts her rucksack on her back. 'Bye. I'm going.'

'Wait. She'll be down in a minute.' I call up the stairs, 'HAYLEY! It's time to go now!' Her leaving with Mia matters to me. Matters more than anything else right now.

I thunder upstairs and barge into her bedroom, keen to rally her, minimise how late she'll be. 'Mia's about to leave. You'd better get a shift on if you want to avoid another detention.' I stop, dig my fingers into the soft bit under my collarbone, feel the muscles of my neck at snapping point.

She's lying in the foetal position in her pyjamas.

Over her shoulder, I can see the light from her phone and her lazy scrolling.

Who am I trying to kid? She's not going into school.

The sense of failure floods me like poison.

FORTY-EIGHT

'What's going on?' I bark.

She mumbles, 'I can't go in. My cramps are too bad.'

With zero warning, and even less sympathy, the rage inside me multiplies. 'If you're that unwell, then no phone!' *No more Mrs Nice Guy.* I make a grab for her handset. It slips out of her sweaty grip and I hold it aloft.

'What the HELL!' she screeches.

'That's the rule. No devices during school hours.' I unplug her laptop and hurry out with it.

She runs after me, pulls at my sweatshirt, 'What the hell are you DOING? That's my stuff. You can't take it!'

But I push on, ignore her objections and race downstairs, frantically thinking of somewhere to hide them. My veins are pumped with adrenaline. I have tunnel vision, determined to teach her a lesson.

She chases after me, slipping in her socks. 'GIVE THOSE BACK!'

It turns out there is nowhere out of reach in the house. She follows me around.

I have an idea and snatch the car key from its hook by the

front door. Nipping out onto the driveway, I triumphantly lock her phone and laptop into the car.

Trembling and sweaty on the doorstep, I secrete the car keys deep in my jeans pocket. The sun beats down on my head.

She shoots past me and bangs on the car window, staring at her stuff on the front passenger seat. 'I NEED THOSE!' she sobs, swivelling around, tugging at my jeans pocket, unsteadying me. I manage to ward off her grabby hands, and she screams, 'YOU'RE A *HORRIBLE* PERSON! *I HATE YOU!*'

Holding the front line, I show no weakness. There's a sense that I have won, that I've outsmarted her. That she's going to have to learn the hard way now, that I've cracked it.

She will survive a day without her screens. She can read. She can watch old films with a hottie on her tummy. She can go for a walk. She can get bored. So bored she'll be dying to go to school on Monday. This is how it's going to be from now on.

But she presses on. She yells at me while I'm making a cup of tea, taking the bins out, tidying the sitting room. Worse, she's plucking at my jeans, at my T-shirt, irritating the hell out of me. Her screams are ear-splitting. She's my shadow and she's on my heels everywhere I turn, everywhere I go, like a mass shooter training his rifle on my back. She begs so hard I doubt my own thoughts.

I stand firm, refuse her the car keys for the hundredth time.

She takes her manipulations upstairs and barges in on Olly, sobs, falls to her knees and begs him, full of drama, but I implore him to stand firm. He ends up scuttling out to a local café to write.

As soon as he's gone, her attention returns to me.

I sit down at my makeshift, airless workspace in the dining room.

Her vitriol is ramped up a notch. She hovers over me and shouts in my face. I will not react. I will not give in. I can keep my cool. I'm scooped up inside, tense and wary.

Her energy is incredible. She keeps it up relentlessly. And I start flagging. I fear it will never end.

'Leave me alone,' I beg, my voice breaking for a split second. 'Please leave me alone.'

'Don't give me all that victim crap!' she spits.

'Don't speak to me like that.'

'You're such a bitch! You're such a fucking bitch!'

She yanks my chair. The hairs on my skin rise. I correct my position, clench my fist, hold back my limbs, keep my feet on the ground, open my computer.

It's impossible to concentrate while she screams directly into my earhole. *'YOU HAVE TO LISTEN TO ME! YOU HAVE TO FUCKING LISTEN TO ME!'*

Then she swipes my laptop off the table and kicks at it on the floor.

'Hayley! *Christ!*' I cry, and lunge for it, intent on saving it, specifically some complex script notes I spent days preparing for an important meeting next week. I haven't yet backed them up on a hard drive. Stupid, stupid me.

I manage to grapple my computer from her, cover it with my body, protect it. She swipes at my head, pushing my cheek, scratching me, trying to get at the key in my pocket. My skull vibrates. My skin smarts. I have fantasies of retaliation, of pinning her to the ground, of hitting her back even, but I count down from one hundred, clench my back teeth, create a hunched force field. She pummels my curved back with her fists. I cower under my folded arms, waiting for the next blow. There's one more vicious kick into my thigh before she runs screaming out of the door.

For a few minutes I stay like that, in child's pose, broken. I hate her. I hate her. I hate myself.

When I hear the front door slam and the whine of the iron gate, I know she's gone.

I unfurl, sit upright, but remain on my knees, palms flat on my laptop, shaken, wounded, thinking of my sister and what she must have gone through on the night she died.

It's clear to me that blaming Charlotte for being drunk has been a red herring, a way to cover my eyes, avoid Hayley's true nature. I recall the promise I made to Hayley on that cliff in Donegal: *If what happened that night is too much to carry alone, I can carry it with you... There'll be no consequences... You are not alone.*

Whispers on the wind. If the truth is never uttered, there's room to skirt around reality. Doubt is what I've been clinging to.

Now, I fear for my own safety and heed Jamie's warnings. An idea flits through my thoughts. It's not the first time I've had it. Before now, I've felt disloyal contemplating it. After her attack today, I no longer care about loyalty.

Still shaking, wired with adrenaline, I open my laptop and type into the search engine, *How to unlock a bathroom door from the outside.*

As I wait for the websites to load, I wonder what proof will mean for us.

FORTY-NINE

Along with a kitchen knife, I'm also armed with a credit card and some YouTube know-how. It's late. Everyone is asleep. As I kneel on the carpet outside the closed bathroom door, my thigh aches where Hayley kicked me. Earlier, when Olly squeezed it affectionately under the dinner table, I winced and he looked at me funny, but he didn't ask about it in front of Mia. Even if he had questioned me in private, I wouldn't have revealed the details. It would have made me look weak and stupid.

I wonder how Hayley's feeling about herself. Guilty? Triumphant? Scared?

I haven't seen her all day, but I know she's at Ayton's.

Since her meltdown, I've been rethinking her story so far, piecing the facts together. I do believe that she and Ayton were fooling about in bed that night; and I do believe that they caught Jamie Hanrahan coming out of the bathroom. However, after this morning's performance over a confiscated phone, it's not plausible she kept her cool in the face of her mother's affair with her form tutor. It's too out of character. She's more likely to have gone off the deep end. Obvious really, when you think about it.

Getting to the root cause of Hayley's anger drives me forward. Who is she underneath it all? What is she capable of?

The only sounds are my heavy breathing and pounding heart. I slot the tip of the knife into the small groove in the centre of the doorknob, attempting to lock it from the outside. The blade is too fat.

Abandoning that idea, I creep downstairs and search through the tools under the sink in the utility room. Finding a screwdriver that looks small enough, I take it upstairs and repeat the procedure.

Much to my amazement, the door locks. It's so easy, I can hardly believe it. I twist the knob back and forth to double-check it has worked.

First task complete.

To unlock it again, as per several more YouTube tutorials, I push my weight against the door to make a sliver of a gap and jam the credit card into it. The angle is awkward. It's too stiff at first and the card bends almost to breaking point. Before I've had a chance to try again, I hear a creak behind me.

'What are you doing?' a voice asks in a loud whisper. The landing light comes on.

I blink, drop the credit card and swivel around.

'Nothing,' I whisper back.

Olly rubs his head, leaving a tuft sticking up. 'Why not use our loo?'

'I didn't want to disturb you,' I say.

We continue speaking under our breath so as not to wake Mia.

'You go for a wee every night in ours. Why would you worry about disturbing me tonight?'

'I had a bit of a headache, wanted to get some painkillers. Go back to bed.'

'Okay,' he sighs, but then spots the screwdriver and the blue plastic at my feet. 'Is it jammed?'

'Oh, yeah. It is.' I snort nervously.

'Let me have a go for you.' He bends down to pick up the screwdriver and his eyes trail up my thigh and stop at the two flowering bruises left by Hayley. I tug down the edge of my pyjama shorts.

'How did you get those?' His fingers hover over them.

'Oh. No idea. Must have banged into something. Honestly, I'll do this. Go back to bed.'

I attempt to nab the screwdriver, but he puts it behind his back. 'You're lying to me,' he says, raising his voice.

'Olly! Shush. Jesus.'

'Tell me how you got those bruises, Em.'

'Okay, okay,' I sigh. 'After you left this morning, it got a bit out of control. But it looks much worse than it was.'

'Hayley? When she was going nuts about her phone?'

I stab the air in the direction of Mia's room. 'Yes. But keep your voice down!'

His eyes are wild. 'Oh my God, Emily. I can't believe it. I never should've left you alone with her. I just thought it was a shouting match.'

'Mostly it was.'

I push past him and jog downstairs to the kitchen. He follows. 'Tell me exactly what she did,' he insists.

I pour a glass of water and glug it down. 'There's no point. It's over now. I'm fine.'

'It's not okay that she's hurting you.'

'Don't put it like that. You sound so dramatic.'

'Look what she did to you!' He points at my thigh again. The two purple splodges are menacing under the kitchen downlighters.

'To be honest, I went pretty nuts myself, locking her things in the car like that. It's not surprising she went crazy at me. She's not used to anyone being that strict with her. It was probably my fault for winding her up.'

Olly shakes his head at me. 'You're defending her again!'

'It's the truth!'

'We have to tell someone.'

'What? No!' I laugh.

'That woman Mel from social services was nice. What about calling her?'

He's rarely looked so serious. I keep my head screwed on, wanting him to leave me alone, fixated only on the mission of unlocking the bathroom door I just locked and proving my theory. 'That's not necessary, Olly,' I say.

'You're not the only one being affected by this, you know. I can't even think straight while she's rampaging around the house. Every day since we got here, she's had a fit over something. I never know how to help you. Part of me thinks it's best to leave you two to fight it out. But when I went to the café this morning, my mind was on you all the time. I just knew you weren't safe, but I told myself I was over-worrying.'

There's something about this speech that pushes tears into the rims of my eyes.

'I *am* safe,' I whisper, hearing the crack in my voice.

'Your sister probably thought that too.'

I can't breathe for a second and turn away, blink my eyeballs dry, wash up the glass and turn it on its head. 'I can't believe you've just said that.'

'Sorry,' Olly rasps through clenched teeth. 'I didn't mean... I just meant... Look, Em, you're not her mother. You have options.'

His words smart, hurting more than any of Hayley's kicks.

In the silence, he repeats, 'You have options here. We both do. You need to have a long, hard think about all this. I really need you to do that for me.'

'For *you*,' I say drily.

'And for them. It's not too late to change direction here.'

'What are you suggesting?'

He shakes his head as though he doesn't know, but then goes on under his breath, 'There might be other families who are better equipped to take them in. Or Aunt Jane? She's got decades of experience. She told us herself she's bored, and she adores the girls.'

Charlotte's ghost is swirling between us. She is screaming into my ear, begging me not to humour him. But even as I listen to her and feel the resistance to Olly's shocking suggestion form like a rock in the centre of my chest, I know that he has planted a seed. Options. There are options. Terrifying options.

'Fuck you,' I say.

His jaw drops. I've never spoken to him like that before. I can't take it back. He storms out. I hear our bedroom door bang closed.

As though on autopilot, programmed to return to my original task, I trudge upstairs and try the bathroom door again, pushing my body harder into it to widen the crack, jiggling the card up and down at the lock.

The door pops open.

Staring into the moony glaze of the wet room, I question my motivation for unlocking this damn door. It has opened other figurative doors. This simple trick with a credit card has proved beyond a shadow of a doubt that Hayley could have been in the same room as her mother when she died.

My theory is now one hundred per cent feasible, and it goes like this: after Jamie left, Hayley lost her rag, banged on the door, demanded her mum let her in. Ayton knew a trick with a credit card and opened the door. Hayley went for her mum the way she went for me. Charlotte slipped and hit her head and Hayley left her for dead on the floor. Then she locked the door with a screwdriver like the one at my feet.

The fact that she left her there to die is the most chilling thought of all.

The more I allow my brain to calibrate this horrible

scenario, the more likely it becomes. But I've shocked myself by establishing its viability, as though the idea was unable to take shape until I had examined the logistics.

Now that I'm getting closer and closer to uncovering all the mysteries of that night, I project forward to an official confession from Hayley and again try to imagine how I'll feel.

Is it delusional to believe I can still love her when I suspect that she killed my sister?

A real mother would forgive her.

Am I capable of loving her like a real mother? Unconditionally? And for ever?

It's the ultimate test of my staying power. As I stare at the place where my sister died and picture the fear in her eyes as she slipped away, I envisage the burden of bringing up a child I hate.

FIFTY

Olly glares at Hayley when she comes in the following morning. She goes straight to the fridge, pours herself a glass of milk, doesn't say hello. She and I avoid eye contact. It takes a few goes to swallow down my mouthful of croissant. When she leaves the glass on the kitchen top, Olly says something about it. She huffs, crashes it into the dishwasher, stamps upstairs. Like we're the problem here.

'We're going to let her get away with it?' Olly asks me.

I can still taste the bitterness of his 'options' last night and his vying for equal billing in my heart. 'You sound like Beth.'

He groans. 'She's turning us into people we're not,' he rasps urgently. 'All morning you've been making me feel like I'm the shit person for speaking my mind, when she's the one being shit.'

'Maybe we are all shit people.'

Except Mia, I think. Today she has gone to the local pool for a birthday party with six school friends. I picture her yelping in delight as she shoots down the slides, escaping the tension of home.

Olly takes short, sharp sips of his coffee, scrolls aggressively through a newspaper app on his phone, and finally says, 'So you're not even going to consider what we talked about last night?'

'No. To be honest, I'm shocked you suggested it.'

Only a few minutes later, almost as if he's prepared it, he says, 'I was thinking of booking a writing retreat for later in the year. Sarah recommended this place in Cornwall.'

'Have you talked to Sarah about us?' I snap.

'Not really.' He sighs. 'Although she knows about our changed circumstances, obviously. But that's not why she suggested it. She wants to push publication to March next year. And even though it's only July now, I'm already up against it. Just knowing I've got that time blocked out would put my mind at rest.' He pulls out his phone. 'She sent me the link. Take a look. She grew up near St Mawes and says loads of her writers stay there to work on their books.'

The thought of Sarah grates on me. I've seen her thumbnail photograph on Twitter. She's blonde, young and pretty. And must be clever. A quadruple threat.

'When were you thinking of going on this little holiday?' I ask childishly.

'There's a two-week slot available from October the nineteenth to the second of November.'

I check my calendar. 'Right, great. Over the autumn half-term? Good timing.' I'm not sure why I'm being such a cow about it.

'I can leave after half-term, if you like. What about the twenty-sixth to the ninth. Is that better?'

'Slightly.'

'I'll book it in, then we can see how the next few months go.'

'Fine.'

He tugs his ear lobe. 'It will also give us a proper chance to think everything through.'

'You mean give me a proper chance to change my mind?'

'It's not that simple.'

'And if I don't give them up?'

'Don't put it like that.'

'Seriously, though, is it an ultimatum? It's you or them?'

He glances up from under his thick blond brows. 'No.' But the blue of his irises is steely with fear. *Don't make me choose between you and the baby*, they're saying all over again. My cheeks flush. My womb cramps. My body revisits the pain of five years before. After the termination, we carried on as though nothing had happened. We told nobody. Not even my parents or sister. Especially not my sister.

'Fine, book it. I'll put it in my diary as D-Day.' I press my finger into the salt dish and lick off the crusty layer, knowing he hates the habit.

He gets up, pushes the stool in. 'Let's not fight,' he says. His dishevelled sandy-haired sadness gets right under my skin. I'm so angry inside, I can't bring myself to be nice to him. What he's asking of me is too much; what I'm asking of him is too much, too.

I bustle about clearing breakfast. He says he's going up for a shower. I go outside for some air and sit down on one of the cheap sunloungers. They have seen better days. As have I. Did I ever appreciate how good it was before? I can smell the mould from the swirly fabric of the seat cushions, but the sun warms my face. There's always this simple pleasure to draw strength from. I rest my head back, close my eyes.

Visions of the day I stabbed the horrible cousin in the foot with a yellow screwdriver come to me. How my rage led me to act in a way that was shocking even to me. How my brain was devoid of sensible thought, of logic, of rationale. Nothing on earth would have been speedy or powerful enough to intercept me. The switch was flicked, the deed was done. *For my sister, I breathe.*

It seems Hayley has that same capacity to act out before

thinking through the consequences. The consequences of her rageful attack on Charlotte – if I'm right about what happened – have been much more devastating than inflicting a limp on a pervert. Luck of the draw, I guess. Had Charlotte not been there to pull me away from the cousin, God knows what I would have done to him. The idea softens me towards Hayley.

The sliding door opens behind me. I expect it to be Olly. I'm not ready to talk through our row yet.

'Auntie Emily?' It's Hayley. I keep my eyes closed, feel my lips harden.

The sunlounger next to me squeaks as she sits down on it. I open one eye. She's chewing the end of her hair. When she catches me looking at her, she drops the soggy strand and says, 'I'm sorry.' Her tone of voice is quiet, steeped in regret. It's as genuine as apologies get.

I sit up and face her properly. 'Sorry means you won't do it again.'

Her bottom lip quivers. 'I hate myself,' she cries. 'I don't know why I'm like that.'

'Shall I show you my bruises?'

'No! Don't. I can't look! I'm so sorry, I'm so sorry. I can't look.' She sobs, gaping at me, mouth open, tears cascading down her cheeks.

I can't look. Charlotte said those very same words thirty years ago. She'd bought a pregnancy test. She'd made me wait by the loo with her. *I can't look*, she said, holding out the white stick with her eyes squeezed closed. There was a little pink cross in the white plastic window. To this day, when I shut my eyes sometimes, I see that cross burned there. Scars on my eyelids. Forcing me to look at it over again.

Hayley's words echo Charlotte's. Perhaps Hayley embodies her mother's wounds.

'We're going to have to find another way for you to communicate those tough feelings.' Jesus, I sound like a therapist. Like I know how to talk about tough feelings. I can barely even think them. But I don't know what else to say.

'It'll never happen again, I swear it. I swear on my life.'

I'm less gullible than I was, want to scratch underneath her words. My bruises pulse from my thigh. The Polaroids of Charlotte's limbs come to mind. Following every incident, I imagine Hayley vowed she would never do it again. Until Charlotte was dead. I nurse the knowledge I gathered last night about the bathroom lock.

'I appreciate you saying sorry,' I say.

She flings her arms around my neck, like a much younger child, and my own arms float up and envelop her as though they have a mind of their own. In our embrace, my soul is warmed, and doubts about my search for the truth pour in. What will the cost of it be?

Strangely, as I reconcile with Hayley, my anger towards Olly ebbs away. I regret how I treated him.

It's the lingering effect of Hayley's hug, the human connection, that prompts me to go straight upstairs with my phone and scroll through my photographs of Charlotte. I begin a special folder of her, cling to the happy memories. She's holding an ice cream and smiling at me from a park bench. She's piggybacking Mia, whose feet trail on the floor. She's pulling a silly face behind Mum's back. She's resting her head on Hayley's shoulder, while Hayley sulks.

There's a loud clatter from the adjoining bathroom, as though all the bottles have tumbled out of the cabinet. I hear Olly shout, 'Shit. Shit. SHIT!' I feel bad for forcing all this on him. I'll say sorry. We'll come to a middle ground. It's going to be okay. We're both good people. All marriages have their hardships. All families have their arguments.

He emerges rubbing his head dry with a towel and stops as though shocked to see me. 'You okay?'

'Are you?' I laugh, clicking out of my camera roll.

'Yeah, the cabinet fell off the wall,' he says absently, jangling some loose screws in his hand. 'You look like you've seen a ghost.'

Maybe I have, I think. I lie back on the bed, stare at the ceiling, try to decide my next move.

He throws the screws on the duvet and exhales. 'I miss our bathroom at home. I miss our *home*.'

My heart pinches. I can't deal with this. I can't acknowledge it. I come in with a practical solution instead. 'Why don't you go up there? Have a coffee at Gail's. Mooch around the Heath.'

'Today?'

'Why not? I've got the girls covered.'

He bends to kiss me on the mouth. 'I think I might just do that.'

When he's gone, I'm relieved he's one less problem to fix, and I decide to go for a walk to clear my head and seek out caffeine. Memories are trickling into my consciousness at a steady rate, slotting into place in chronological order along that thin thread that leads all the way back to Mum's fateful fortieth. When hung together, it seems to me that Hayley's troubles are a direct continuation of Charlotte's original trauma.

Outside, I enjoy the warmth of the summer morning. My mind spools forward, leaping to the present day and what I've uncovered over the last few months: Charlotte's alcoholism; Ayton's presence in the house on the night she died; Jamie and Charlotte's love affair; Charlotte's bruising in the Polaroids; Hayley's violence towards me; and, most recently, the picked lock.

As I assemble the series of clues in order, I land upon a huge flaw in my theory about what happened that night.

I stop dead in the middle of the pavement, ignoring the

stream of people swerving around me. A light bulb switches on in my mind.

Without coffee, I loop back home through the bustling Saturday-morning streets.

What has always been a constant is how close Hayley and Mia are, just as Charlotte and I were. Sisters. Heads together. Shared secrets. Holding hands in the dark. Making sense of a confusing world together. Talking a language only sisters can understand. Yet so far, Mia has been conspicuously absent from the story of her mother's death. It doesn't add up, and logic hits home. There is no way on earth she could have slept through a Hayley meltdown. She must have been awake. She must've witnessed something.

We know she likes to play the part of the documentarian, borne out by her macabre instinct to record her mother's injuries in the Polaroids. And like any modern teen, she also takes photos on her phone all day long. There'll be digital albums stored in the cloud capturing every aspect, every minute, every day of her life.

Might there be photographs of that night?

Her laptop is on her desk. I know her password. And I'm going to log in.

FIFTY-ONE

Mia is due to be dropped home by the birthday girl's mum in roughly half an hour. And Hayley is a few minutes into one of her epic showers. Still, I don't have long, and I drag the hoover – my nemesis, but a useful ruse – into Mia's room. Nothing needs vacuuming. The room is spotless. She is the perfect child. Isn't she? She's loving, thoughtful and funny. And tidy. It's terrible to compare the two sisters, but impossible not to. So much of Hayley's behaviour we excuse. But Mia has been through hell and back too, and she's not careering around the place screaming like a banshee, leaving a trail of battered humans in her wake. But should she have been? Is it strange that she hasn't caused more trouble?

It's why I'm here in her room. To find out where she stands in the drama of that night.

At first, the password doesn't work, which is crushing. The beat from Hayley's portable speaker pulses through the bathroom wall. I debate closing the laptop, quitting while I'm ahead. The promise of information is irresistible, though. I try again, guessing I've been too hasty, made a typo. It works the second time and I let out a short, breathy sigh of relief, look over my shoulder pointlessly. The door is closed. I listen. Nothing except the permanent hum of traffic and a bird fighting to be heard in the back garden. My fingertips tremor and are sticky on the keyboard. I wipe them on my shorts.

There's a cluster of saved Word documents on her desktop with funny titles like FuzzyPeg or EllieBellyPooPoo or TheBlackHeartofCupcakes, which I leave well alone. Her photos take a while to load. The colour wheel whizzes round and round and I wait, urging it to hurry. I check the time in the corner of the screen. It's almost two o'clock, and she's due home around half past. Finally her photographs begin to appear on the screen, one by one, popping up along the rows, 5,348 of them in total. I narrow the search to one day: 13 March 2024.

Twenty-five thumbnail images form several rows.

I decide to look at them chronologically, and double-click into the one taken at the earliest point of the day, 11:02. It's of her chin. The next one a few minutes later is of her pulling a funny face, angled up her nose. To think that these were taken before her mother died, when being silly and light-hearted would not have been laced with longing and guilt.

Moving on, there are a few snaps of her and her friends goofing about in a classroom. A short video of her friends jostling each other into the Sainsbury's Local. A blurry selfie of her sticking her tongue out with a unicorn sticker on her forehead.

In all these so far, she will have been blissfully unaware of the tragedy about to unfold. The poignancy of them is hard to bear, and I forget for a few minutes why I'm sitting here in front of her computer. In another world she might have been with me now, looking over my shoulder, laughing and explaining what was going on and who her friends are.

Time is ticking on. It's 2:10. I can still hear the echoey noise of Hayley's music.

I continue clicking through her last day of innocence.

The final three videos were filmed at 19:43, 19:52 and 19:59.

Bingo. This is what I've been looking for. Three videos taken just before 8 p.m., which according to Hayley's initial account was roughly when she and Charlotte had their row about her going out on a school night.

The sound blares out from the first one. I turn the volume down a little. Muffled screams and shouts from two female voices are audible, instantly recognisable as Hayley and Charlotte. A shallow breathing noise comes from the person holding the phone, whom I'm guessing is Mia.

The screen remains an orange-brown-black smudge of nothing, as though she's holding it on her lap. Did she press record by mistake?

The second video is more of the same. A blast of ten or so seconds of audio. Enough to hear the venom in their voices. There are a number of amplified swear words here and there, but little else is decipherable. Even in this context I'm struck by how strangely discomforting it is to hear Charlotte's voice raised in anger. I'm flooded with sadness that her last few hours alive were spent arguing like this.

The third video is of Mia whispering up close into the camera, like she's confiding in a friend's ear. The din of her mum and sister's argument is background noise. 'Jeez,' she breathes, 'this is what it's like all the time. I mean, like derr, she won't let me watch an eighteen, but I'm around this every day? What the hell?' She pulls a jokey grimace and ends the filming.

I'm left in the silence that follows to consider what I've seen, whether it has any bearing on anything. My rows with Hayley are different to those captured by Mia, more one-sided. I tend to stay mute. Any remonstration I might make is uttered in a low-level mechanical voice, like a robot, unemotional and submissive. In the face of her meltdowns, I survive by shutting

myself away, slotting a barrier between me and her, clenching
every truth in my fists. I guess I always assumed Charlotte was
the same. But no, she was letting loose, going for it, unleashing
all her real feelings, and Hayley responded in kind. I wonder if
it's a more natural way to argue as mother and daughter. I have
an inappropriate pang of envy and remind myself that we don't
yet know that this volatility between them was what led to her
death. Not yet.

The sounds from Hayley's speaker get louder as she opens
the bathroom door. I freeze. The music moves with her but
recedes into the distance as she closes herself into her own
bedroom.

As I stare at the screen of viewed photographs and films, I
conclude that I've reached a dead end. I fiddle around,
wondering what next, clicking in and out of other random shots
taken the day before Charlotte's death and the day after, on
which Mia has recorded one lone film of a black cat streaking
across the garden.

My heart leaps when I hear her singing in the kitchen, but
just as I swipe the mouse across the screen to close the window,
I notice the trash icon.

I didn't think of this before. Eager to find out what she
binned, I double-click and scroll down to the relevant date.
There is only one item waiting there, ready to be permanently
deleted in two days. It was taken at 10.32 p.m. At roughly this
time, or so their story goes, Mia was fast asleep in bed, Hayley
had returned to her own room, and the night had allegedly
fallen quiet until morning. So how was Mia recording a video,
and why?

From the stairs, her voice is getting louder. There's no time
to watch the video now. Hastily I take a gamble and AirDrop it
to my phone. It makes a loud pinging sound. I shut her laptop
and Mia ambles in. I'm not sure whether I've closed the photo

window properly or sent the video successfully. It's too late to check. My cheeks burn.

'Hi, sweetheart!' I trill. Did she see or hear anything?

FIFTY-TWO

'Oh, hi,' Mia says, plainly surprised to see me in her room.

'Sorry, just taking a breather. You know me and Henry here are not friends.' I look down at the smiley face painted on the black and red hoover, imagining it winking at me in a shared conspiracy.

If Mia is suspicious, there isn't a hint of it in her grin. 'I can hoover my room if you like!' See? The perfect child.

'It's fine. All done. Tell me about the party,' I say quickly.

'It was okay.'

'You don't sound so sure.'

'Maddie and Eva kept going down the slide together, holding hands. And that is *not* allowed. It's dangerous to go two at once. There were signs everywhere,' she says, sounding cross.

'That's very naughty of them.' Little cows for excluding her. In truth, I'm being equally as naughty right now. Not only about the cyber theft of a video on Mia's computer, but for the so-called choice Olly is suggesting I make.

'Maddie doesn't even *like* Eva.' Mia's hand moves to the crown of her nearly dry tufty head and twiddles.

'People act weird on their birthdays. I'm sure Maddie will

be normal again on Monday.' But I wonder whether I will be after I've viewed the video. Normality is forever out of my reach right now and seems to exist only in the past.

'Is Hayley home from Ayton's?' Mia asks.

'Yup.'

'I'm going to say hi,' she says, leaving me alone again in her room. She'll confide in Hayley in a way she never would in me.

I drag Henry out of her room and heft him down the stairs, feeling drained by my duplicity. In the laundry room, my little confession box, I put the hoover away in the cupboard, close the door, take out my phone and check that the video sent.

I stare at it on the screen. My heartbeat hammers on my eardrums. It would be more ethical to delete it and accept there are some secrets best kept. But I owe it to Charlotte. I click play.

At first, the sound is too loud. I pause the video quickly, turn it down, freeze for a second to listen for noises outside the door. Confident there's nobody about, I play it from the beginning again.

I watch an altercation between Charlotte and Hayley through the crack of the open bathroom door. I catch my breath when I see Charlotte moving, breathing, talking, living. The essence of her comes back to me. I can smell her, feel her, love her as though her death were a bad dream. A happy montage of our lives together as siblings strobes through my mind.

But all is not right.

Hayley is shrieking at her. *'WHY WAS HE HERE, MUM? WHAT THE HELL IS GOING ON?'*

'It's... none of your biznezz,' Charlotte replies, wagging her finger, eyes hooded, slurring. Staggering to the sink, she pushes her wet hair off her face, securing her towel around her body.

'IT *IS* MY BUSINESS WHEN MY *TEACHER* IS IN OUR HOME IN THE MIDDLE OF THE NIGHT!'

'I'm... not talking t'you... when you're like this. Geddout, please.' Charlotte takes a bottle of moisturiser and starts to rub cream into her face. Smears of white are left. She looks insane. It's mortifying to see her like that. 'Gedd. OUT,' she repeats.

'NOT UNTIL YOU ADMIT YOU'RE SHAGGING *MY TEACHER!*' Hayley yells.

Out of the blue, Charlotte's face changes into a red, rageful contortion. She turns, hurls the moisturiser over Hayley's shoulder. '*I SAID GET THE FUCK OUT OF HERE!*'

'YOU'RE SUCH A *SLAG!*' Hayley screams back.

A split second before the image changes, I see Charlotte stumble at Hayley, and Hayley screams out of shot. It's not clear whether Charlotte gets to her before Mia's bare feet come into view. They're moving across the white tiles. She's carrying the phone by her thigh, so it's impossible to see what's going on, but it's clear Charlotte went for Hayley, not the other way around.

There's a blood-curdling scream from Mia – '*STOP IT!*' – followed by a kerfuffle of some kind. Frustratingly, I can't make out who or how or what. Then, with pure terror and desperation in her voice, Mia screeches again, '*STOP IT! STOP IT STOP IT!*' And the video stops abruptly.

My skin turns to ice. Goosebumps run up my arms.

What have I just seen?

FIFTY-THREE

My hands shake uncontrollably. I put my phone down on the worktop, as though it's too hot to touch. The film is incendiary. It demands action, but of what kind, I don't know.

Whatever I do, nothing changes the fact that it's cold, hard evidence that Hayley and Mia have conspired to conceal a mammoth secret about their mother's demise. Their duplicity hurts my heart, but I think I understand now.

My teeth are chattering as I emerge from the utility room. I'm stunned. I want to go back in time, erase the video, join Olly, buy some books, have a coffee, pretend that none of this is happening; think only of us and the planet, which used to be quite enough to be getting along with.

If only I could put the genie back in the bottle.

For today, I tread water, play nice with the girls. Act like the perfect auntie. Give them money to buy doughnuts and some cheap earrings from the mall. Cook them spaghetti bolognese for tea. Tell Hayley she looks beautiful in her mini-skirt that shows her knickers. Allow Mia hours on TikTok. It's strangely harmonious. Maybe this is what good parenting looks like. Letting it all go for an easier life. For fewer battles. For more smiles. Parenting revelation alert: don't sweat the small stuff and absolutely bury all the big stuff.

It was arrogant to think I could fix them by forcing a confession. I'm way too late to the party.

When Olly texts to say his train will be getting in at 21.34, I walk to the station to meet him. He's thrilled to see me. It's a balmy evening. We stroll side by side for a bit. The streets are quiet. He tells me how good it is to be home, how he needed the fix, and how much he likes Bea, the new young manager of the Town Bookshop.

All the while, my fingers toy with my phone in my pocket. I'm about to spoil his mood.

'Let's go the back way,' I say, taking the shortcut, knowing there won't be a soul around.

'This is nifty,' he remarks of the alleyway.

I stop walking, block his way. He's backlit by the orange street lamp. It reminds me of our kitchen in Kentish Town, which was filled with the same strange glow.

'I've got something to show you before we go inside,' I say.

My thumb hovers over the play button. I can't bring myself to watch it again. I thrust the phone at him before plugging my fingers in my ears.

Three minutes and twenty-two seconds later, he'll know as much as I know, and I'm eager to gauge his reaction. I watch his face, see his brow furrow, his lips part, his chest expand. I drop my hands to my sides.

'What the hell?' He searches my face as though I have been hiding this from him.

'It's awful, isn't it?' I say.

'It's unbelievable,' he rasps.

'I think they picked the lock to get in and then locked it again after Charlotte fell. Scared shitless, I'm guessing.'

'They saw her dead and just left her there?'

'Hmm. I doubt they knew she was dead. They were used to her passing out drunk all the time, remember.'

'I never thought they'd hide something that big from us. And lie over and over again.'

'But you see why they did, right?'

All he can say is 'I can't believe it.' He repeats this a few times.

'I know they've done a terrible thing. But it's obvious it was an accident, right?' I need him to agree with me.

He shakes his head vigorously. 'It's grim seeing Charlotte like that.'

'It's clear it wasn't one-sided, isn't it?'

'It's hard to make out what's going on. But Mia's definitely screaming at Hayley to stop it.'

'I think she's saying it to both of them,' I correct him.

'Hayley's lost the plot though, that's obvious.'

'She's understandably upset. I would be too if I caught my mum having sex with my teacher.'

'She didn't actually catch them.'

'As good as.'

He hands back my phone. 'I wish I hadn't seen this.'

'Do you? Why? I know it's distressing viewing, but I think it clears it up, doesn't it?'

'What does it clear up?'

'That Charlotte slipped in a tussle, not because of a targeted attack from Hayley, and definitely not because Hayley is some evil Chucky-style kid. I mean, Charlotte was being totally horrible in that clip. It's hard to accept that about my own sister, but' – I drop my voice – 'after seeing this, I can't deny she was in part responsible for her accident.'

He glances over his shoulder and breathes, 'What we can't deny is that we now have proof that they've lied to us about being there, and that Hayley's got anger issues, and that the two of them might have caused the death of their *own mother*.'

I frown at him. 'Like the thought has never occurred to you? All along I've been telling you something wasn't right. And then there were Charlotte's bruises in those Polaroids. And what Jamie said.'

He shakes his head. 'The reality of it is different. Maybe I never truly believed it was possible. Or I couldn't imagine it. It's so dark. I definitely never thought Mia was involved.'

'It's surprising to me that you're reacting like this. Because when I saw it, I had the opposite reaction. I felt for them, you know? I finally understood what it must have been like for them to live with her. What it must've been like to see her like that all the time. It was eye-opening. Can't you understand that?'

'I don't know how I feel about it.'

His inability to see it from my point of view is shattering. 'But it's clear that whatever happened was an accident in a volatile situation,' I urge. 'That's all that matters, right?'

'What about your parents? Are you going to tell them?'

'No. Of course not!' I cross my arms over my chest. 'What the hell is going on here, Olly? I really thought you'd feel the same as me about it.'

'To be honest, I'm finding your positive spin on it really hard to get my head around.'

Positive spin? 'I regret showing you now. I didn't have to.'

'I wish you hadn't,' he breathes, and squeezes past me and strides to the gate that leads to the back of the house.

'Where are you going?' I hurry after him. 'Please don't say anything to the girls about this!'

He stops, turns briefly. 'I'd never say anything to anyone. I wouldn't do that to them. What good would it do?' He drops his voice even lower. 'But... I don't know... I'm really shaken by it...'

'Me too. Of course.'

'It's different for me. I thought Mia and I were close. I feel like a total mug for believing her. And I trusted Hayley would sort herself out in the end. But not now. Not after seeing what happened.' He points at my phone. 'I don't know...' He visibly shudders. 'It kind of confirms all my doubts about this whole thing working.' He stares at me for a second. His eyes are watery, glistening in the reflection of the light above him. I can't speak. He turns away. The gate slams behind him.

I don't hurry after him. I'm rooted to the spot. Clutching my phone, I press play on the video again. On second viewing, I see it through Olly's eyes, and my first instincts falter. His strong reaction leaves me wavering about what to do.

Had our interpretations been in sync, I might have deleted it and moved on, in agreement about Hayley and Mia's innocence. Shockingly, though, we are poles apart. Which leaves the girls where?

And me where?

In an impossible situation.

FIFTY-FOUR

'Sorry for storming off,' Olly says in bed that night.

I turn around to face him and whisper. 'Sorry too.' It's true, I'm sorry for so much. Too much to qualify probably. Have I lost perspective? Am I blinded by my feelings for the girls? Am I being unfair to Olly? Or is he using the video to see what he wants to see so that he can wriggle out of a bind? But I say, 'It's an impossible situation.'

'Not completely impossible. I think Jane is an amazing woman and she might be the answer to all this. A middle ground for us.'

'She is great,' I say neutrally, eager to agree with him to keep the peace and hold onto this closeness between us. But I can't help feeling that it's less of a middle ground and more that I'm losing ground altogether. 'There's a lot to weigh up.'

'Uh huh.' He's non-committal.

I admit, it's not impossible to imagine Aunt Jane agreeing to take them in. Maybe it doesn't have to be permanent. Maybe the problem is that we're rushing everything. Maybe her caring for them in the interim is a temporary solution while we work things out. It'll give Olly time to adapt, to forgive them. Give me time to think it through. Rolling this idea through my mind is allowed. And it can roll right back out again any time, no harm done. But, like the tide, it comes back in repeatedly, relentlessly.

My thoughts and feelings are tangled. My head and heart clash.

I need to talk to someone on the outside, a third party with a fresh eye. Jamie is the obvious answer. He's the only one with a secret about that night that's as big as ours, who risks losing everything if it came out. He's also someone I once considered a friend and whose opinion I valued. Moreover, he'll provide the two-against-one argument: either he'll come down on Olly's side or he'll reinforce my initial instincts. I'll go with consensus.

In the morning, I call him and we arrange to meet in the supermarket car park nearby.

I park up next to him. There are only a handful of other cars here. It's Sunday, before opening hours, and nobody is about. I get into his estate. The brown leather seats are cracked in places. There are baby wipes in the footwell. He tugs at his goatee. The last time we saw each other was unpleasant. We lock eyes. Forgiveness is suspended between us.

There isn't any preamble. I hand him the phone and tell him to press play.

He watches the video. The smiling bee air-freshener bobs and twirls as he shifts in his seat, emitting wafts of synthetic honey.

This time, I listen, make sure I remind myself of what we're dealing with. Considering Jamie has levelled the abuse accusation at Hayley, he might not be able to rewrite the story of Charlotte's victim status. It's likely that he will feel the same as Olly and condemn the children for their deceit.

The leaves of the plane trees behind the fence that borders the asphalt dance and bob. A snake of trolleys is jangled across the car park by a Sainsbury's employee, who looks at us briefly. Nothing to see here.

The film comes to a stop. I wait.

Jamie plays it again. Again is an agony.

Afterwards, his eyes are hangdog. He shakes his head very slightly, as though any other movement is too much for him. 'I'd never seen her like that before.'

'Hayley?'

'Charlotte. That night. She was already out of it when I arrived, which was why I thought she should have a shower, to sober up. I literally had to undress her myself and put her under the water. And that's where I left her. Standing there grinning at me, pouring shampoo on her head, waving goodbye all goofily. Nothing more happened between us that night. I never would have... I didn't...'

'Yeah, yeah, okay, I get the picture.' I shake my head.

'But she wasn't being aggressive at all. She was giggling a lot, being all loopy and sweet.' He leans on the steering wheel and puts his face into the crook of his elbow. His breathing is long and slow. 'Honestly, I never thought she had a problem...' he murmurs.

'She was a complicated person.'

He jerks his head up and scowls. 'I was too blinded by my feelings for her. That's why I didn't see it. We were so selfish. We didn't think about who we'd hurt. Not enough, anyway.'

'Charlotte was one of those people. Even I didn't see it, and could get pulled along into all sorts of schemes.' I break off, breathe deeply, feel the memory of one particular scheme of hers hurtling at me at a hundred miles an hour. 'I knew her better than anyone. Or thought I did.'

His voice takes on a shy edge. 'Tell me some more about her.'

I hesitate, wonder where to start and what he wants to know. Then I decide I don't care. I want to talk about her in positive terms and I tell him about the steady stream of boys queuing around the village green to take her out; how she went through a phase of wearing everything blue – blue bandanas on her wrist, blue sneakers, blue bangles, blue streaks in her blonde hair; how much she loved to eat strawberries straight from the fridge but never in a bowl, saying they tasted better standing up. How she'd leave the chewed stems on the worktop for me to clear up before Mum spotted them. And how I would get told off for her crimes. I tell him that Mum worried about her more than she did about me.

'Sounds like she gave her more to worry about.' He chuckles.

The cousin's horrible hands come to mind. 'Mum never worried about the right things, though.'

'What do you mean?'

I feel compelled to explain to him that Charlotte was a victim. A real victim of a heinous crime at a very young age. The need to qualify it feels overwhelming.

'Something happened to her. When she was in her teens. Mum never knew.'

He straightens up and turns to face me.

While I speak, I stare absently at the Sainsbury's guy grappling with the trolleys. My voice comes out flat, monotone, as though this might strip out the horror of what I'm saying. 'There was this relation of ours. A cousin of Mum's who used to come to family parties. He'd persuade her into doing things.'

I stop there, glance at Jamie sideways to see if he understands. It's clear he does.

A cluster of three trolleys escape the train and slide towards the car. A disaster waiting to happen. 'But I don't think she saw it like that,' I continue. 'She said he didn't hold her down or anything and that she could've said no and that she was never sure why she did it.'

'How old was this fucking arsehole?' Jamie blurts.

'About forty.'

He twists away, '*Jesus Christ*,' he hisses.

We sit in silence for a few moments.

'The good memories fade,' he says vaguely, 'but trauma never does.'

'I don't think her trauma ever did, no.'

'Neither has mine. It's impossible to get rid of it in here, and it comes back to visit you when you least expect it.' He rubs his fingers on the centre of his forehead, up and down.

'I'm sorry,' I say uselessly.

'It's definitely not your fault.' He smiles sadly.

'Charlotte and I never once talked about it as adults. I never dared bring it up. I guess I didn't want to upset her.'

'Sometimes things are best left alone,' he says.

'I believe that. I really do.'

I focus on my phone, stare at its home screen. It's of Hayley and Mia grinning from a shallow bubble bath with green frog shower caps on their heads. They are six and three respectively. It feels like yesterday.

'Do you worry about taking Hayley on?' he asks me.

Every minute of every day, I think. 'It's a big commitment, obviously.'

'How does Olly feel about it?'

'Honestly? After seeing this? Not good.'

'Has it changed how you feel too?'

'I don't know. That's why I need you...'

'To be frank?'

'Yes. That's exactly what I need. Frankness.'

'Charlotte's accounts of Hayley's violence live in here.' He stabs his temple. 'And with that as the backdrop, as the *context* for that snippet' – he points at my phone – 'I think it's likely that Hayley was responsible for what happened to her. How I feel about that? Fuck knows. She's a kid. It was an accident. She never would've imagined her mum could die. Mums don't die. They're immortal. Go figure.'

'So what do I do now?'

'If it was Tiger and Fleur,' Jamie says, 'I'd delete it and forget about it and try and live a normal life. They could commit the most heinous act and I'd still love them as much as I ever have. It's primal.' He stretches his lips back. 'Not sure what kind of person that makes me, though.'

'It makes you a very good dad.'

'Emily, remember that nobody would expect the same of you.' He breaks off, starts again. 'Hayley and Mia are not yours. What I mean is, however much I love my own two nephews, it's a totally different feeling.'

'Believe me, I know all about the difference.'

His head tilts to the side. He looks puzzled for a second. But I realise I've got my answer. 'Two against one,' I say.

'Eh?'

'Olly also thinks Hayley was to blame for Charlotte's fall, which leaves me outnumbered.'

When I think of the conversation Olly and I face, terror squeezes my heart. If I accept his interpretation of what happened, will he expect me to give up on the girls? If I disagree with him, what does it mean for us?

Losing him is unacceptable. Losing the girls is unthinkable.

FIFTY-FIVE

That afternoon, Olly suggests that we leave Mia and Hayley to their own devices. Their Sunday routine consists of homework and room tidying and rarely involves us, so I agree, feeling scared about what he'll have to say.

We take the bus to Richmond Park. Just the two of us.

Despite my nerves jangling throughout the rather stinky, noisy journey, it's pleasant when we get to the park. Deer mooch around. Men whoosh past on bikes. Dogs potter at their owners' feet or sniff deep in the undergrowth. It's like the countryside, and I imagine it is the right environment to hear what I suspect will be a definitive decision from him.

We hold hands. I love the feel of his big hand around mine.

'This is nice,' I say.

'Beautiful.'

Our interlocked fingers are a tense weight between us. The light is golden on his worn face. I love his face.

'I should have given you some warning before I showed you the video,' I say under my breath, getting that in quickly.

'To be honest, you have been trying to tell me what went on

that night since the very beginning. But I haven't been listening properly.'

'And I wasn't listening to your side of it either.'

His steps slow right down. 'Oh?'

'Cards on the table, I saw Jamie this morning.'

'What? When?' He releases my hand.

'You were still asleep.'

'Right.' He frowns.

'I showed him the video. Wanted his take on it.'

'What? What the hell did he think of it? Jesus Christ!'

'He was shocked, obviously. Deeply disturbed by Charlotte's anger. Hadn't seen that side of her.'

'Did he have a problem with what the girls did, though?'

'He thought Hayley's temper was at the root of it, yes,' I concede, stopping abruptly, out of breath on the slight incline.

He switches back on himself, stands in front of me, puts one hand on my upper arm and grips it a little too tightly. 'You see? I told you. It's not safe, Emily. What went on that night wasn't right. What Hayley did to you the other week wasn't right either. I don't trust her. And now I don't trust Mia either. This morning I could barely look her in the eye. I'm so sorry, but I can't pretend to want to take them in as my own. I'm not sure I have what it takes to do that. I really don't.' He drops his hand by his side, palm facing out.

Tears fill my eyes until Olly's familiar, comfortable face is blurred, rubbed out. Frantically, I try to think, blinking, blinking, blinking, until I can see him clearly again.

'Please don't make any decisions yet, Olly. Please,' I beg. 'I haven't decided myself yet. While that video is so raw in our heads, everything is skewed. Let's allow it to sink in a bit more before we make up our minds. Please, Olly. For me. For them.'

His mood turns slightly. 'It's unfair to emotionally blackmail me like that.'

I'm aghast. 'That's not what I'm doing here. I'm just saying this is a huge decision for both of us. One we have to live with for the rest of our lives.'

'The thing is, if I decide I don't want to take them, are you going to leave me?' Anger and upset saturate his words. 'You can't make me choose between you and them. You can't do that to me.'

An emotion surges at me from the past and I shock myself with my sharp, low, hurtful comeback. 'Now you know how it feels.'

He passes a finger over one eyebrow and looks to the side. 'Don't rake that up again.'

My hand is on my stomach when I say, 'Would you have left me if I'd decided to have our baby? Like Jim wanted to in your book?'

He jumps down my throat. 'For Christ's sake, it's a work of fiction! His internal dialogue is made up. When will you get that into your head?'

A dog-walker overtakes us on the path, looking at the ground, embarrassed for us. Her black Labrador lingers, stares up at us. Its soulful face seems to understand there is something profoundly wrong here, something to be concerned about, before it bounds ahead to its owner.

I drop my voice. 'Don't give me that crap! I know you too well. Jim's character is too well drawn to be made up.'

'Oh right, thanks a bunch. You don't think I'm talented enough to make it up?'

'I'm not saying that. It's just I know. Underneath it all, I sensed it at the time. You were just waiting for me to do what *you* wanted me to do, because *you* wanted to be a famous writer and *you* didn't want to burden the planet with more children. For *your* principles, for your ambition! To hell with my feelings! So when I read it in your book, it just confirmed everything I already suspected.'

He storms on ahead, muttering. 'I can't believe this. I actually don't understand you sometimes. You always said you didn't want children. You always said that.'

'Shit happens, Olly. I felt that little life inside me. Jesus. Then more shit happened. My sister *died*!'

He rounds on me. 'And you jumped at the chance at taking her kids, desperate to be their mother from the second she died!'

I reel back from him. A shudder rolls up my spine, as though it's shaking off what he just said. I don't trust myself to speak.

His mouth opens and shuts. 'I didn't mean that.'

'But you said it,' I breathe.

'Seriously, I didn't mean it.'

I can't look at him. I don't even want to be near him. I hurry ahead. 'We'd better get home,' I murmur.

He spends the rest of the evening trying to convince me that he didn't mean I was a maternal version of an ambulance chaser, some barren desperado who leapt into my dead sister's role with glee.

He makes biscuits with Mia. Laughs at Hayley's joke about me eating her cookie dough ice cream. Suggests we watch a family movie.

In bed that night, I say coldly, 'You're right, your trip to Cornwall will be a good opportunity for us to spend some time apart. We both need to make a decision.'

FIFTY-SIX

Before we know it, Olly's trip to Cornwall is upon us. At the front door, with his holdall at his feet, he whispers into my ear, 'Love you.'

The lack of 'I' says it all. But I'll take it. It's more than I've had from him in months, probably since before our shouting match in Richmond Park.

The weeks over summer have disappeared in a monotonous way, gobbled up by routine. Olly and I have been like ships in the night. While he writes all hours, my days go from computer screen to moody kids and back again: a sloppy script editor at work and a disengaged automaton at home. Here and there, I take Hayley and Mia up to see my parents, who remain oblivious to the crumbling state of my marriage and to the doubts that dog me about the girls' futures.

Hayley's moods have been less volatile. There've been a couple of hissy fits over this or that. One minor panic attack over a top she'd ordered online that didn't arrive on time. One major one about the campsite we'd booked for a few days in August – it hadn't been in the right part of Poole, where some of her friends were going to be.

Harmless stuff. Nothing I couldn't handle.

I haven't breathed a word of the video to either child. It has become symbolic of my indecision. If it's never brought up again, it's like it never happened and nothing has to change. I've locked down so much and dissociated to such an extent, I do nothing more than go through the motions in all areas of my life.

'I love you too,' I say now, putting in the 'I'. Then I blurt out what I haven't been able to admit before. 'Everything has moved so fast, but your feelings have equal billing in my heart. You do know that, don't you?'

'Thanks, I appreciate you saying that, Em. I get that it's harder for you. They're your flesh and blood, and you're a much kinder person than I am. Stubborn as hell, but kind.'

I grin at him, smooth an errant tuft of hair in one of his thatched blond eyebrows. 'True.' His anxiety shines back at me.

As we part ways, I realise how much we have taken each other for granted; how stealthily resentment can set in. We kiss longingly, drag out hugs, say our goodbyes a million times over. He seems genuinely affectionate when Hayley and Mia mooch down from their rooms to say their own farewells.

'I'm going to be so lonely without you guys,' he says, stretching the corners of his mouth down cartoonishly, pinching Mia's ear lobe. They share more embraces.

When I close the front door, I sink gingerly into the sofa with a cup of tea and contemplate what the next two weeks will bring. Not only will it be a test for Olly, it'll be a test for me.

Can I do this on my own? Can I cope with Hayley alone?

I tell myself I can. Of course I can.

But am I scared of her, just a little bit?

Of course I am.

FIFTY-SEVEN

A week after Olly's departure, I'm hauled in for another chat with Jamie at St Matthew's. There have been many already this term. It's the same old discussion about the ongoing flare-ups between Hayley and Jennifer Conway and it's beginning to bore me. Today, Hayley is forced to sign a 'behaviour contract' before we leave.

As she and I stamp home in the dark, I endure her non-stop rant about Jen. My ears and fingertips sting in the bitter November cold. I'm struggling to muster any sympathy. This time perhaps I should, considering Ayton has been cheating on her with Jen. I do feel sorry for her. Or I know I must. Maybe I can't allow my heart to be wrenched by her on any level until I know what Olly's decision is going to be. Until then, I'm anaesthetising all emotional investment.

'Ugh. That was such a waste of time,' she says, dumping her coat and bag on the kitchen table and on top of the fruit bowl, probably bruising the bananas. 'And now I've hardly got any time to do my English.'

I tidy away her bag and coat. 'Oh dear,' I reply. It's half-hearted, but I know what's coming next.

She glugs a glass of water, pants as she asks, 'Can you help me with it?' which really means, *Can you write it for me?*

'I'm just going to lie down for a second. I've got a bit of a headache.' I want complete separation from her for at least an hour.

'You're not going to help me? Even though you know that I need to do good on this, specially after today.'

'Do *well* on this,' I correct, holding onto the banister as I plod upstairs, feeling a headache seed itself in my skull and begin its deathly pulse.

She follows me up. 'Why won't you help me?'

'Of course I'll help you. But not now.' I sigh, losing my footing briefly, finding the next step down to rebalance myself. My tiredness is causing delirium. 'Tomorrow we can sit down together. Today has been a lot.'

'But it needs to be in by tomorrow!' she whines.

'Why have you left it to the last minute?'

'I forgot!'

'What's it about?'

'*Inspector Calls.*'

'But I've never even seen or read that play. I'll be of no help at all. Can't you say you're unwell?'

'It was supposed to be done over half-term!'

'So why are you only telling me now?'

'I *forgot!*' she screams.

My heart rate runs at double speed. Cautiously I move a comfortable distance away from the top of the stairs and stand in the frame of my bedroom door.

'I'm sorry, Hayley, I can't face it tonight.' I grip the doorknob. 'You're going to have to do it on your own or face the consequences, I'm afraid.'

'Like I haven't got enough going on in my life with a dead mother or anything!' Her voice cracks.

I have a moment of weakness and almost relent, but then

remind myself she's manipulating me. I'm wiser to that now and decide not to back down.

'You can't use that excuse for ever,' I say firmly.

While battling my guilt for saying it, I'm also astonished that at first it seems to work. She loses steam for a minute, as though she knows I mean business. But it doesn't last. As she saunters into her room, she mutters under her breath, 'Mum always said you could be a fucking bitch sometimes.'

The numbness of many months wears off as quickly as it might take for a surgeon's knife to be plunged into my flesh. In what can only be described as an out-of-body experience, I feel myself flying after her, batting her bedroom door back so hard it slams against the wall.

'*HOW DARE YOU SPEAK TO ME LIKE THAT?*' I explode, making her jump, going on to expel what has been trapped inside me since the first sulky backchat comment of hers in March when we moved in. The rage that I have carried towards her and Charlotte surges up from my gut. 'I'm sick to death of it! I'm sick of tiptoeing around you, terrified of what you'll do next! You're not the only one who's lost someone. You don't own all the grief in this house, you know? I literally can't take any more of your moods, can't be the fall guy for your shit any more. I can't take it. I just can't *TAKE IT*!'

'Don't then,' she mumbles.

'Is that what you want? You want me to do what Uncle Olly's done? He couldn't take it either! It's why he left. Do you want me to leave too? Do you want to push me and push me and push me until I break? Is that what you want? If it is, then it's working! I'VE GOT *NOTHING LEFT*!'

As I'm yelling, I'm not sure who I'm yelling at. Charlotte or Hayley? Decades of self-control splinter into pieces. My chest is heaving. Hayley has jammed her body into the angle of the wall, slid down it, pulled her knees up to her chest, and is peering up at me wide-eyed, flinching with every word I screech.

It mortifies me to realise she is cowering. She puts her arms over her head as though expecting a blow. Our roles are reversed. I'm her and she is me. As soon as I recognise it, my rage shrivels and dies. I falter, stop shouting. I retreat, and bump straight into Mia, whom I hadn't noticed was behind me.

'Sorry,' I whisper. 'Sorry.'

I flee to my own room and close the door, trembling all over, clammy and terrified. Not of Hayley, but of myself and what I might have been capable of in that small window of rage. I remember the yellow screwdriver. How the urge had come over me, how out of my mind I had been. If Charlotte hadn't stopped me, I might have stabbed him to death. We know he deserved to feel pain. But Hayley doesn't, oh God, Hayley does not.

With my fingers still quivering, I call Olly, even though we promised we wouldn't speak to each other for the two weeks he was away. I hear the ringtone, pray he'll pick up. When he doesn't, I fling my handset onto the bed like a bratty child. Then I retrieve it and try again. And again. And a fourth time. I don't feel bad about disturbing his writing. This is urgent.

Guessing his phone is on silent while he's working, I send a text: *I need you. Please call me back asap.*

It takes him ten long minutes.

'Hello. Is everything okay?' He sounds panicked.

'No, it's not okay!' I gasp, barely able to breathe through my sobs. 'It's not okay at all. I can't do this, Olly, I can't do it. She's a nightmare. You were right, she's horrible and she's turning me into a horrible person. I never used to be like this!'

'Shush, shush, what's happened? Tell me what's happened.'

I begin the sorry tale, starting with the fight at school. But halfway through my hoarsely whispered account, I hear a female voice from his end.

'Everything okay, Olly?' she says.

I stop dead. 'Who's that?'

'Oh. It's Sarah.' He sounds so matter-of-fact.

My back teeth grind into one another. 'What the hell?' I breathe.

'I'm working in the pub today. She just came in with the dogs. She's down here with her family.'

Goosebumps crawl over my skin. 'It sounds very quiet for a pub.'

'I'm in a little booth at the back. Go on, tell me what happened.'

'Has she gone?'

'Sarah? Um. I think so. Oh, she's sitting at the bar with some people.'

'Will you join her?' I say coldly.

'Emily!'

'What?'

'Don't make this into something it's not. Tell me what happened with Hayley. Why were you so upset?'

'No, no,' I murmur. 'It's okay. We had a fight. It's nothing. I was just tired, you know. We both were.'

'It didn't sound like nothing.'

'Honestly, it was. Just hearing your voice has calmed me down. I'll text you later.'

'Don't be like that. You sound weird, please don't—'

I don't hear the rest of his sentence because I hang up on him.

After some time lying on my bed staring at the ceiling, I drag myself up and go knock on Hayley's door. I don't know what to expect. Probably that she won't talk to me.

'Come in,' she says, quiet as a mouse.

She's at her computer, fingers on the keyboard. She offers me a hesitant smile.

'I'm so sorry,' I say, biting my quivering lip and looking up to the ceiling, blinking once and then returning bravely to her face.

'I should never have said any of that. It's not true that I can't give you any more of what I have, or whatever it was I said like some crazy drama queen. I certainly can give you everything you need.'

And everything I have? It appears my fate is to be wrung dry by this child. The fantasy was believing I had agency, that I could choose to have her or to not have her, like Olly can. I mean, let's face it, who would willingly choose to enter a psychological torture chamber every day? But neither can I stomach leaving her inside such a place alone. She's my fate and I must resign myself to it.

'That's okay,' she says, sniffing, grinning shyly. 'I'm the one who should be sorry. I'm so horrible to you all the time.'

I wipe the tear away from her cheek. 'We're peas in a pod,' I say. She looks at me funny and I regret saying it.

The next day I wake up with a start. For as soon as my eyes blink open, I experience the hallucination of Sarah's voice at the other end of a phone line.

The sense that I might have lost Olly to her is a hair-cloth tunic that I wear next to my skin for the whole day ahead, and throughout all the other days leading up to his return. The nasty itch of it is my deserved punishment. I've asked too much of him. What did I expect?

What is he going to tell me when he walks through the door? Will he walk through it ever again?

FIFTY-EIGHT

Olly's decision will be as absolute as mine will be default. I won't actively be choosing to keep the girls, but neither will I be able to give them up.

It's almost astonishing when he returns home. I'd convinced myself he wouldn't. He's fresh-faced, bright-eyed, windswept. The break is evident in his appearance. He looks younger, more relaxed. It confirms what I already know. He's happier without us. He'll choose to be happy. Who wouldn't?

Living here with Hayley and me is hell. He was right when he said that she would make me ill. Ill in the head. As time wears on, I feel less judgemental of Charlotte for drinking too much. I myself have become reliant on a glass of wine at the end of the day, and I'm less and less tolerant of Hayley's meltdowns as a result.

Why would Olly want to put himself through all that night after night if he didn't have to?

The kiss that lands on my mouth is unexpected. He lingers there. I pull away. I can't sink into that yet. Don't trust it.

I make tea. We make small talk. About his journey. About

the cold weather. About his book. All the while I'm thinking, *I'm so frightened of being alone with this.*

'The last round of edits are done,' he says hesitantly, peering over the rim of his mug. 'I really never thought I'd get through it.'

'That's great, Olly, well done.'

His blue eyes dance with their trademark anxiety. 'Thanks. It feels pretty good, I have to admit.'

He holds my gaze, must know that I'm waiting, fretting.

'I know we've got to talk,' he says.

My mouth is dry. I manage to croak in a falsely jokey way, 'What's the verdict, then?'

He shakes his head and my heart sinks. Then he says words I can't believe I'm hearing. 'We can't give up on us, Em.'

I'm astounded, wonder if I've misunderstood. 'What do you mean?'

'I want to make this work.'

I let out a small cry of 'Oh!' and press my fingers into my eye sockets, hold my breath, shake my head. 'What made you change your mind?'

'It was something Sarah said in Cornwall when we were having an impromptu meeting about the book. She said her stepdad didn't love her in the way her mother loved her, and sometimes he and Sarah didn't like each other much, but he was kind to her mum, and he provided for them. And it was enough. They became friends in the end...'

My mouth goes dry as he tells me a little more about Sarah's relationship with her stepdad. Annoyingly, her backstory plays into my hands. Revealing any jealousy would cut my nose off to spite my face and unravel this wonderful decision of his, so I stay quiet as he continues, even though I loathe that he came to this understanding with her help.

'... I never wanted to be a parent, and I just don't know if I'll ever be able to love them quite as much as you do. Not like a real dad. But I think that's okay. I do think they're great kids.'

His eyes are bloodshot, full of guilt. He's being honest. I can't blame him for that. I can't think too hard about Sarah. For now, I'm able to accept this compromise with enough of my heart to say, 'Yes. That's okay. You might feel more like a real dad in time.'

'Fake it till I make it?'

It's glib, almost too much, but I let it go. He's trying. He loves me enough to stay.

Later, Mia makes Olly welcome-home blueberry pancakes, and we sit down around the kitchen table. The girls have no idea how close they came to losing him.

Hayley fills him in on the gory details of her split with Ayton. When he offers some typical dad-like advice about there being plenty of fish in the sea, she laughs. It's clear she has missed him. As they chat, my mind drifts off and returns to our conversation earlier about him faking it until he makes it. Because there's fakery in me too.

'... at the Town Bookshop.' I hear the tail end of what he has just said. He adds, 'What do you think, Em?'

'Of the bookshop?'

He pauses before answering. 'I was just telling the girls that I'm thinking of holding my book launch there next year. Sarah thought an independent would be more personal than one of the bigger shops.'

Sarah thought. Eye-roll, seriously.

'It's a lovely bookshop, yes,' I say. Far be it from me to disagree with Sarah.

'You always say it's fusty in there, though.'

'Oh God. Don't listen to *me*.'

There's a pause before he says, 'But that's what I do best.'

'Awww,' Mia says.

I eye him, doubting he's serious. 'It's really nice in there,' I say, 'and super boho, and they're passionate about books. And it's our local – or was.'

'It's good to support local,' Hayley says.

His eyes light up. 'I think you're right.'

'We're always right, aren't we, girls?'

The four of us chortle. It feels so good to share a laugh, almost tearfully good.

I wonder if this is where Olly can learn to become a real dad, around this table, over plates of home-cooked food. In this moment, we're like a real family. Even more wonderful than a real one perhaps. Because of what it has taken to get here.

And then I think of Sarah again, which messes up the pretty picture I've just painted.

FIFTY-NINE

Three weeks before Christmas, I get a call from David on my mobile. I watch his name flash up and let it ring out. He calls again the following day. He doesn't leave a message. The third time, Olly insists I answer it.

I pick up, skip the hello and say, 'Yes?'

'Hi, Emily.'

I purse my lips and wait for him to tell me why he's calling.

'I really miss them, you know? And I want to find a way to mend bridges.'

I leave the silence hanging. He goes on. 'Beth and I, we were kind of hoping that they might consider coming over for Christmas.'

I guffaw down the phone, unable to hold back my blast of outraged laughter.

'Oh my God, David,' I splutter. 'Sorry. Whoa. Let me catch my breath here. Wow. You really don't get it, do you?'

His voice is steely when he speaks again. 'They are my daughters.'

'Oh right, yeah! Golly, sorry, forgive me for forgetting for a second there!'

'Would you at least ask them for me?'

I bite down on my fist to control my temper. It's in both our interests to keep our heads. Rage tremors through my voice when I respond. 'No, David. No, I will not ask them. They've just started to settle finally.'

'I don't need your permission. I could contact them directly.'

'So why didn't you already?'

'I wanted your support.'

'You don't have it.'

'I'll text them then.'

'Yeah, you do that. See how it goes.' I'm calling his bluff, not sure how it will go if he does.

'Thanks a lot, Emily,' he says sarcastically, hanging up on me.

Either he doesn't text them or the girls never mention it to me, for they do not go to Ireland for Christmas, and never will again if I have anything to do with it.

Instead, we visit Mum and Dad in Shropshire and manage to convince them that our new family unit is working out just fine. We return home with full bellies and wallets stuffed with gift cards.

As soon as the holiday season is over, Olly returns to his laptop in the dark corner of the spare room and works on a treatment for his second book. I hoped he'd give himself a breather between now and when *A Severed Womb* comes out in March, but he can't seem to go a day without writing. It feels to me there's an unspoken pact between us: Olly agrees to stay with me – but not as a real dad – while I shoulder the day-to-day demands of the girls alone, without complaint or expectation.

Regardless, I battle on through a rainy January.

And it's a bloody battle.

Before Hayley, I prided myself on my self-restraint and self-control. Shouting and over-emoting were Charlotte's thing.

After Hayley, it's like I'm topped up with so much anger, the smallest provocation sends me over the edge. Too easily I flip to the dark side and go down with her. Or up, depending on how you look at it. Imagine a hurricane of *The Wizard of Oz* sort. Picture me and Hayley whizzing around along with Dorothy, Toto and various pieces of furniture. We can be at it for hours and make no headway, just going in circles.

At times I've physically pinned my arms to my sides when she calls me a bitch. The willpower it takes for me to hold back a clip around the ear is the stuff of Marvel films. I want super-hero status.

After these storms have passed, she and I are not immediately skipping along a yellow brick road holding hands. First, we're emotionally flattened in a dark room coursing with hatred. I've never felt stress like it, like I can see my hair turning grey before my very eyes. Then, after some hours of stewing, we let it go.

Surprisingly, the mutual love that floods in after these rows can be intense, heady almost. We snuggle up on her bed chatting for hours, putting the world to rights. I probably share more of my real feelings with her than I do with either Olly or Mia. I guess that's almost like skipping down a yellow brick road.

Why we need to have the blow-ups first before we can like each other again is anyone's guess. Parenting Hayley is about extremes, and it's relentless. Made harder by how alone I feel.

After this evening's row, I'm boiling over with excess anger and storm in on Olly in the telly room.

'Why the *hell* did you just sit here and let her treat me like that? Why couldn't you step in and help me out for once?' I'm near tears, baffled by how he can justify his disconnection. It's not the first time I've pointed the finger at him for this.

He rubs his face. 'I don't know, Emily. You both spiral together, and to be honest, I'm not even sure what you're arguing about or how I'd help if I got involved. You even sound alike when you're shouting at each other. It's freaky.'

We *sound* alike? Hearing this, I step back, feel my skin prickle with fear. This last remark is why I drop it, even though I have so much more to say.

SIXTY

'Will you two come to my book launch?' Olly asks the girls over breakfast one morning in February.

Mia yelps, 'Yeah! Of course!'

Hayley is guarded. 'When is it?'

'Next month. Thursday the twenty-seventh of March,' he announces proudly.

March. On 13 March we plan to visit Charlotte's grave with my parents to mark the anniversary of her death. The prospect of it is a kick in the gut.

'Where is it going to be?' Hayley asks.

'The Town Bookshop on Kentish Town high street. Remember we talked about it?'

'Oh yeah. Cool,' she says.

'You can buy something new to wear if you like,' he says.

'What are you saying? That you don't like what we wear now?' Hayley fires back.

I glance at Olly, who looks unsure of himself, and hold in a sigh, but then Hayley's face cracks into a smile. 'Just kidding. Hell yeah, I might even buy a dress.'

Olly laughs. 'Great. I'll transfer fifty squids to your GoHenry accounts today.'

'*Fifty?*' Mia cries.

'Yup. I feel flush. It won't last, so spend it wisely.'

After they've ambled off, I say to Olly, 'Fifty is a lot. Can we spare it?'

'Rachel called earlier and told me I might bag a German rights deal. It's good money if I get it.'

'Oh my God! That's amazing.' I hug him, thrilled that it's coming together, feeling overwhelmed by his success, appreciating the injection of cash.

'Sarah said she's getting loads of amazing quotes from famous authors who've read the proof copy. It looks like we're going to get one from Sadie West.' His smile shows on his lips, but I can tell it's mostly an inside one. 'Sarah says she's manifesting it on the *Sunday Times* bestseller list.' He chuckles.

Sarah. Sarah. Sarah. Her name spoils everything.

I pull away, turn to clear the plates. 'That's great. You really deserve it.'

'Don't go all weird on me.'

'I'm not!' A plate almost slips from my hand as I slot it into the dishwasher.

'You do it every time I bring Sarah up.'

I snort. 'No, I don't.'

'You'd like her if you met her.'

'Uh huh.' Internally my eyes are rolling up to the sky and round to the back of my head.

'And she's on our side.'

I turn to him and shoot back, 'We don't need anyone on our side.'

'We might. I know things are better, but Hayley's like an unexploded bomb.' He bunches one side of his mouth. I have an urge to throttle him for criticising her. Logically I know this is unfair, but a word springs to mind: *primal*. Jamie used it to describe his love for his children. The word strikes a chord now, and then unexpectedly catapults me back in time to the panelled bathroom of our childhood home. My fifteen-year-old sister is writhing on the floor. Her groaning is animalistic. Her sense of loss is primal.

Her pain will last her whole lifetime.

This bad air from the past is rushing out of its locked room. With all my might I'm leaning into the door to keep it closed, but my muscles are sore and I'm worn out and I'm not sure how long I can last.

Trying to stay with the present, I make a point. 'The problems we're having with Hayley aren't any of Sarah's business.'

'They are if they're affecting my writing.'

'And Sarah is only concerned with your writing, is she?'

'What do you mean by that?'

'You seem to confide in each other a lot.'

'Talking about books always pulls up a lot of personal stuff, that's all.'

'You wouldn't tell her about the video, though, would you?'

He screws up his face. 'I would never do that, and you know it,' he breathes.

I leave a pause, then say breezily and ever so cruelly, 'If you ever want to run off with her, just give me some warning, yeah?'

He reels back. 'What?'

I exhale, feeling tired of holding everything in all the time. 'I wouldn't blame you. She's pretty and smart. And I'm in a permanently foul mood.' It might sound like I don't care.

He shakes his head at me, sighs and walks out.

SIXTY-ONE

Olly's fears about a bad turnout at his launch are unfounded – the bookshop is buzzing – whereas mine about Sarah are founded. She's much prettier than her photograph online. Her creamy complexion, super-straight flyaway bangs and ridiculously long eyelashes lend her a flush of youth.

'Hi, lovely to meet you finally,' she says very poshly, blowing her fringe out of her eyes, holding out her hand. Her grip is loose, her eye contact brief, her full cheeks catch fire before my eyes. 'I've just got to...' and she doesn't finish her sentence, just legs it off into the bustle of the shop.

Olly glances at me, as though embarrassed for her, for us, for him, but before we can comment on her, he's collared by someone in marketing at Hodgson Press. I'm standing like a lemon next to them, nodding and smiling.

As the evening progresses, Olly and I are separated. Mostly I cling to Hayley and Mia, intimidated by the literary lot in a way I'm not by TV people.

The girls are good company, especially Hayley, who seems to be enjoying herself, while Mia makes gallant runs for more crisps from the drinks table. I'm so proud of them both. Hayley's even wearing a dress, shock horror. Her fair, wispy locks have kinks in them from the rain and her cheeks have colour, perhaps from how muggy it is in here, but it suits her. She has painted delicate black liner in the rims of her eyes, which brings out the watery blue of her irises. Mia wears her new dungarees and a black T-shirt and hair so short it's almost shaved. She looks cool in the way I wished I'd been at her age.

Before we left this evening, they presented Olly with a good-luck card with a message inside saying they believed in him and couldn't wait to buy loads more outfits with cash from his book sales. Olly's eyes were damp. He hugged them, and we shared a look over Hayley's shoulder that I hope confirmed why we were doing what we were doing.

Now Mia whispers in my ear. 'Look, there's a queue for Uncle Olly's books!'

Most of the guests here tonight, Olly promised, won't have read *A Severed Womb* yet, which is comforting for a split second until I see the line of potential readers. Every time one of them flips the front cover open, my heart skips a beat. I remember his gratis copies arriving in a brown cardboard box. I filmed him unboxing them for a reel on social media. Inside the front cover, there's a dedication: *To Emily, my love.*

I hope he still feels that way. Over the last few months, he has been good-natured about my mood swings and my grubby tracksuits and my lack of affection. I've become a hot mess of irascibility, anxiety and existential crises. What Hayley accuses me of when she screams at me is getting right under my skin and implanting as fact. And I've been turning to Olly for reassurance and white lies, needing him to tell me that I'm not those things, that I'm still lovable. Since Cornwall, he has been more patient with me and takes Hayley's vitriol with a pinch of salt. Maybe his admission that he couldn't be a real dad took the pressure right off. Or maybe he's just nice and I am horrible.

Now, in this cosy bookshop, I'm full of love and brimming

with pride, and trying to act like a normal woman and a
supportive wife and repay the favour.

An ex-police-officer-turned-thriller-author is telling me she
wants to branch into scriptwriting. She's impressive. I like her
and give her my email address. She probably likes me, which
feels unfamiliar these days.

I spot Olly on the other side of the room. He's got his head
thrust forward with a listening side-tilt, nodding at an older
woman draped in amber beads who's chucking her arms about
to emphasise a point. The furrows in her forehead suggest she's
cross. About the book?

'This is going well for Uncle Olly, right?' I whisper to
Hayley, nudging her.

'You know,' she says, 'without you, he never would have
been able to write it, yeah?'

Her generosity knocks me sideways. 'No, I didn't do
anything.'

'You do so much. I don't know what the three of us would
do without you.'

My heart soars. You see what I mean about extremes?

'I don't know what I'd do without you either.' I pull a strand
of her hair forward. 'You look absolutely beautiful tonight.'

She does too. But am I biased? Like a mother would be?

I spot Sarah coming our way. She introduces the girls to a
children's author they might have heard of, and I move away to
get another drink. To be fair to Sarah, she has made them feel
welcome. I've also noticed that her outfit is a little frumpy,
almost twinset and pearls, which cheers me a little. I know. I'm
horrible.

Or can we say insecure?

The chatty thriller author by my side is dragged off by her
agent to talk to someone else. I'm left shuffling about alone for a
few minutes looking for the girls and for Olly. I sip at my Prosecco, which has gone flat, and try not to look awkward.

I'm rescued by a tall, lanky man who taps my arm and introduces himself. 'Hi. You're Olly's wife, Emily, aren't you?' He stoops to shake my hand. 'I'm Paul. Olly and I share an agent.'

'Oh, Rachel's brilliant, isn't she? Such a shame she couldn't make it tonight.'

'I have to admit I loved Olly's book,' he says, crossing his arms, tucking his empty flute into the crook of his elbow, glancing over my shoulder.

'I'm so glad you enjoyed it.' I scan the room for Olly, wishing he'd appear.

'What do *you* do?' he asks, but before I get the chance to reply, he jumps in with 'No, wait, let me guess, you're a landscape gardener.' He chortles. Ellie in the book is a landscape gardener. I flush to my hair roots.

'Ha.' I laugh at his joke, certain he meant well. 'I'm a script editor, actually.'

His brow rises, 'Right. Wow. Okay.' He seems to reassess me and asks me some polite questions about it before saying, 'I've just seen... I'd better...' and he's off.

I'm feeling tired. Olly's still not about. Even seeing Sarah might be welcome. Neither of them springs out. Mia is in an armchair in the corner reading a hardback with a red cloth cover. Outside, the light is dusky. The street lamps have been switched on. Rain spatters the shop window.

I weave through to Mia. 'Hi, sweetheart. How's it going? Where's Hayley?'

She peers up from her book and shrugs. 'No clue.'

'I think we'll be able to disappear soon,' I whisper, yawning behind my hand. 'You've done brilliantly.'

'I heard this guy asking Uncle Olly if his book was about you. Is that true?'

'What did Uncle Olly say to that?'

'He said it was fiction. Like doh. But why did the man think it was about you?'

'Its main character is called Ellie. Which sounds like Emily. That's probably why he got confused. People can be very stupid.'

'He thought he was verrrry clever, I can tell you.'

'Ha. Yes, there's a lot of that about.' I glance at Paul, who has his elbow on a bookshelf as he talks at a young woman with multiple piercings.

From my crouched position, I look for a door to another room where Olly might be hiding. I'm guessing there's a toilet somewhere. Perhaps there's a private room or a kitchenette at the back. As I creak up to standing, planning to snoop about, the front door to the shop flies open. The little bell almost falls off. A few heads turn briefly. My heart stops when I see Hayley in the doorway. She's drenched. Her eyeliner has run down her cheeks. What's happened? Where has she been? Why was she outside in the rain? My breathing becomes shallow. If she makes a scene and ruins this for Olly, he'll never forgive her.

Trying not to push anyone out of the way, I edge and shimmy impatiently through the chattering guests to reach her. She sees me and her eyes widen, then she turns on her heel.

SIXTY-TWO

I follow Hayley out onto the street, pulling my jacket around me to protect my satiny dress from the wet weather.

'Hayley!' I call out to her. 'Wait! Where are you going?' It takes me physically pulling her arm to stop her. 'What's up?'

'Nothing.' She wipes her cheek, smearing her make-up towards her ear.

'What's happened?' I'm baffled by this turnaround. 'Have you and Mia quarrelled?'

'It's nothing like that.' She sniffs.

'You've been crying. Tell me what's wrong.'

'I can't.'

'Of course you can.'

'You'll hate me if I tell you.'

'Why would I hate you?' Thinking with a sigh, *What have you done this time?* 'Did you have an argument with Uncle Olly or something?'

She shoves her hands into her jacket pockets and scuffs her DMs on the pavement. I feel the rain flatten my hair as I wait.

'I can't. I just can't,' she whispers.

'Better out than in,' I coax.

She starts walking away again, but I keep up. We end up sitting on a bus stop bench, sheltered at least.

'I saw something,' she says finally. 'And I'm only going to tell you because it's right you know.'

I wait for her to go on. In the pause, I experience a small shiver. Someone crossing my grave. 'I can handle it,' I say.

'I saw Uncle Olly with that editor woman.'

The shiver becomes a seismic tremor in my heart. 'Sarah? Where?'

'They were out the back in the courtyard bit.'

'I didn't know there was a courtyard.'

She side-eyes me. 'Did you hear what I said?'

'She's his editor, Hayley. They are allowed to talk, you know.' I laugh at her. Mean.

She scowls and looks in the other direction. 'Is kissing him part of her job too?'

I shoot up and glare down at her. 'Stop that!'

Her eyes are unreadable as she holds my gaze. I recognise too much in them.

'Take that back,' I hiss.

She shrugs. 'Sure. I take it back.' Then adds, almost under her breath, 'I guess it was dark. I couldn't see clearly.'

'Why would you even say it then?'

'You know what I'm like. I just love winding you up for laughs.' Her voice is deadpan.

'This is funny to you?'

'Yeah, hilarious.'

'Am *I* laughing?'

She doesn't respond.

My voice breaks. 'Am I laughing, Hayley?'

'No,' she whispers. Her eyes fill and her chin is dimpling.

'I can't believe you sometimes.' I shake my head at her. 'You're out of control. It's like your lying is pathological. It never stops. You're impossible to love.'

Her eyes seem to freeze open. I feel the drop in temperature inside me.

The regret is instant and terrifying. I'm horrified by what I've said, can't imagine looking her in the eye ever again. Somewhere in the depths of me, a tiny voice presses me to believe her, but I cannot – *will* not – accept it. I clamp my mouth shut and stumble away, stopping briefly in a cobbled alleyway a few yards from the bookshop to hurl bile into the drain.

Leaving Hayley at the bus stop alone, especially after what I said, feels both utterly wrong and yet totally justifiable. Wrong because she's young. Right because she'll stop at nothing to destroy my happiness. What happens to her will be her problem, not mine. I've tried. I've tried with everything I have. What more can I do?

When I go back inside the bookshop, the faces in the crowds melt into a clump. Except Sarah's.

SIXTY-THREE

Sarah is tittering at something someone is saying to her, blowing her fringe. On reflection, she isn't as pretty as all that. Her cheeks and lips are plump, and her eyes are too small. She isn't Olly's type. *Don't make this into something it's not,* he said on the phone from Cornwall.

It can't be true. I won't let it be true; can't bear that it might be.

The crowd has thinned out. I avoid people's eyes, worrying that if I look at them they'll recoil from me. I'm a wreck, feel clammy and quivery. I believed there weren't any buttons left for Hayley to push. What a cruel joke. It seems she was saving the best until last. Now I know what it feels like to be tested. And to fail.

When I think about her eyes, red-rimmed and intense and burning underneath her strawberry-blonde frown, I see my own rage reflected back at me. My failures. My past. Our past. Her beginnings. My lies. My love for her.

No. It's impossible to love someone who hates me this much.

When I see Mia's little face topped by her tufty hair, I steel myself, straining a smile. As ever, she'll become the victim of her big sister's actions. As I was of Charlotte's. I once supposed I had agency in our sisterhood, equality even, sometimes even superiority. I'm doubting now that I had any of those things.

The book's a lie! I want to shout at the soon-to-be readers of *A Severed Womb*, and swipe the two remaining copies off the table. When these strangers eventually read it, I imagine they'll be intrigued about Ellie/Emily's so-called severed womb, try to be clever, sort fact from fiction, speculate about our marriage. I admit, much of it is true. All of it, perhaps. It's what's missing that's the problem. The irony of it will be lost on them. They'll want their money back when they know. You might too. Because Hayley is the missing piece.

Now that Charlotte's gone, I'm one of two people in the world who would know how to write the prequel to Olly's book. In that story, Hayley would get her first proper mention.

'Hi,' Olly says, coming up to me. 'Where did you get to?'

I notice his hair is damp, like mine. I say, 'Outside. Same as you by the looks of it.'

'We've been everywhere trying to find you.'

'We?'

'Oh, phew. You found her,' Sarah says, appearing behind him. Her fringe is stuck to her forehead now.

'None of us seem to have had umbrellas,' I say, trying to laugh.

'Are you okay?' he asks. 'Why were you out in the rain?'

'I was looking for Hayley.'

He surveys the room. 'Did you find her?'

'I did. She was upset.'

His micro-glance at Sarah is so quick, it could've been missed. But not by me. It's obvious he has confided in Sarah about Hayley. Could he have told her about the video? Is she the reason for his honesty after Cornwall? Did she tell him he didn't have to feel guilty?

'What is it this time?' he asks.

'We can talk about it when we get home,' I say, trying not to picture Hayley's dimpling chin when I seethed at her.

'Can't wait.' Wryly he wrinkles one corner of his mouth.

Sarah claps. 'Let's focus on the success of tonight, shall we? It has been a triumph.'

She's upbeat for him, like I used to be. Ha! She thinks she can control the narrative! Ha ha! A trick of the trade, perhaps, but not so easy to pull off in real life.

'You think it went well?' Olly says. His eyebrows twitch at her, seeking out her reassurance. That used to be my job.

'Honestly, it's unheard of to sell that many hardbacks on launch day,' she replies.

I can't stand it. I grab his hand, snuggle into his neck – so very unlike me – wrap my arm around him, say, 'Everyone I spoke to who's read it' – one person – 'absolutely raved about it.'

He responds by putting an arm around my shoulder and patting it. 'That's nice to hear.'

When I look at Sarah, I try to detect jealousy. She's looking away, pushing her fringe back from her shiny forehead. Has she even noticed us canoodling?

Hayley is a liar, right? I tell myself that, and that Olly still loves me as much as he ever did. He'd never betray me. Not after everything we've been through this year. He's not capable of this level of deceit, standing here playing the good husband, especially not after judging Hayley and Mia so harshly for their lying. On that front, Hayley has form. Olly does not.

When it's time to go, I execute an insincere goodbye to Sarah. I'm tempted to suggest to Olly that we make our way home without Hayley. A small part of me dares myself to leave her in north London to sink or swim. Actions have consequences, Hayley.

I wouldn't. But the appetite is there for a millisecond, believe me.

'I think I know where to find her,' I say, hoping she's at the same bus stop. 'I'll go. You stay here with Mia.'

He agrees that might be best and asks Mia to help him and Bea clear the champagne glasses from the shelves and return the furniture to its original arrangement.

Under the street lamp, I can make out a hooded figure at the bus stop. Then I remember that for once Hayley isn't wearing a hoodie. She's in a lovely dress. She must be freezing. It's the first worry I've had about her since I strode away. I could take it as a sign that all will be well between us again, that I still care, can forgive her, but that would be a fib. I care because she's a fifteen-year-old kid alone in the dark in London on a wet, cold spring evening. I'm not a monster.

To find that she's not at the bus stop is a shock. I was picturing her there. Where else would she go? I swivel around, hoping she'll be tucked into the newsagent's doorway, or under the awning of the closed-up café on her phone, or leaning into the corrugated-iron kiosk under the street lamp.

She isn't in any of those places. I begin to jog further up the road, passing a few scary-looking crazies I would not like her to encounter alone.

I feel helpless. London is huge and frightening and I don't want her to be traipsing along these streets. A trickle of rainwater runs down the back of my neck. My toes are damp. My arms are gooseflesh. It's cold in my heart. If anything happened to her, it would be my fault. If those words of mine were the last we exchanged, I would never recover. If I lost her, I'd want to die. It doesn't mean I've forgiven her or that I love her.

But I know I need to tell her who she really is.

I continue heading towards the Heath. Like a homing pigeon, I'm getting closer to my flat. Something tells me she might have gravitated there, having visited often and loved the heathland as a younger child. Olly and I often reminisce with her about it.

After fifteen minutes of walking, I eventually pass Dartmouth Secondary and see a figure by the railings leading into the park. Her hair looks almost white in the dark and shines conspicuously in this deserted spot. I run towards her. The relief is replaced by another feeling, that isn't love in a recognisable form and certainly isn't hate; is more powerful, more compelling, more frightening than that.

It's the urge to tell her the truth.

She sees me before I can call out to her.

'I found another pound!' she yells over to me. Not 'I hate you' or 'Fuck off.' Both of which I deserve.

I slow down, trot the rest of the way, realise my chest is heaving.

She goes on excitedly. 'I've found eight pound coins so far, can you believe it?' She turns to the railings again and exclaims, 'Oh my God, I've found another one!'

Despite the confusion of everything that has happened this evening, I'm now equally dumbfounded, for completely different reasons. '*Really?*'

'Yeah! Look! Someone must have left them here by mistake!'

'How extraordinary,' I breathe. The last time I left money here was last year. There's no way on earth they're the coins I left. Hundreds of kids would have trailed past and pocketed them. Has someone else taken over from me? Did someone see me do it?

'It's like my guardian angel left them. How else would I have got home?'

I'm speechless for a second, but finally stutter, 'I never would have left you.'

'Yes, you would have,' she hisses, picking up another two

coins. 'Eleven pounds. It's exactly how much it costs to get home on the train.' The accusation swells inside every word.

She stamps off in the direction of Kentish Town high street. Her hands are in her pockets, her head is down, a frown is locked into her expression. She passes me as though I'm a stranger she has no concern about, like I needn't have bothered searching for her, like she doesn't need me at all for anything ever again.

'Okay, yes!' I yell after her. 'I wanted to leave you here to fend for yourself! What do you expect?'

'Nothing, I expect nothing from anyone!' she screeches without turning.

'Good! That's a bloody relief then!'

I pull her shoulder, but she tugs it away. 'Let go!'

'Hayley, stop a minute!'

'No!'

'You have to stop.'

'No! I don't need you!'

I snap. 'I'm telling you right now, stop or there'll be trouble!'

She comes to a halt so abruptly I almost bump into her, then turns and screams into my face. 'YOU CAN'T TELL ME WHAT TO DO. YOU'RE NOT MY MOTHER AND *YOU NEVER WILL BE!*'

Every pent-up emotion I've ever suppressed is rising to the surface. It almost feels like acute nerve pain. I grab her by her shoulders, and with a wanton lack of constraint, I drop the guard I've had in place for over sixteen years and unveil our secret, Charlotte's secret. 'But I am! That's the point!'

She tries to escape my clutches, but I squeeze tighter, saying slowly and clearly, 'I. Am. Your. Mother. Okay?' Then I repeat it, needing to hear it again myself. 'I am your mother. Always have been, always will be. And I wish to God that I wasn't.'

She whimpers at me, shaking her head, confusion darting across her eyes. 'No. You're not.' I let go of her, wishing I could release her from what I've said. 'You're not,' she repeats, but although liberated from me, she doesn't run.

I could backtrack, bluff my way out of it, pretend I only meant I *wanted* to be her mother, that I was her *new* mother. I could say this. But I can't bring myself to go through with the colossal lie. After sixteen years of lying, I don't have the strength to keep it up for a day longer.

'I'm your biological mother, Hayley,' I say, adding, 'For what that's worth.'

SIXTY-FOUR

Switching back on myself, I drag my feet away from Hayley's horror towards my old flat, if only to be near the place where once I was happy and safe.

Hayley's breathing is ragged at my shoulder as she fires out her legitimate questions. None of my answers are sinking in. I trudge on, pained by her pain. My urge to cry is sucked back inside me. I'm dry. The rambling medical facts I'm spouting go over her head. She is becoming increasingly confused and distressed by my inability to cut to the chase.

At the last minute, I divert our route and take a detour to Marty's bench. Marty isn't there, which usually means he's found a bed for the night. The thought of his resilience gives me courage. Here in his spot, I sit with my head in my hands, detecting the faint smell of vomit on my fingers, and start again from the beginning.

'When your mum was fifteen, she got pregnant.' Okay, not quite from the beginning. She doesn't need to know about the limping cousin.

'Are you serious? She got pregnant at my age?'

'Yes, your age,' I say, scanning her youthful face. It is unbelievable to think that Charlotte was the same age as Hayley is now when she hunched over the instructions of the pregnancy test. Back then, she was my big sister and seemed so grown up to me.

'But the pregnancy was ectopic, and afterwards she got an infection in both her fallopian tubes, and very sadly she was told it would affect her ability to have babies in the future.'

I stop to make sure Hayley can keep up. Her expression is expectant, eager almost, waiting to hear what this has to do with my status as her biological mother.

'She was infertile?' she asks.

'Well, it wasn't as simple as that. When she and your dad got married, they had problems conceiving, and she was told her chances were so slim she shouldn't hold out any hope. It was why she asked me to be her egg donor.'

Hayley recoils from me. Her stomach is concave, as though I've punched her in the guts. Her mouth is twisted in dismay. She slides away to the end of the bench, clings to the metal arm, glowers at me.

'It seemed like the perfect solution at the time. She and your dad were desperate to have children, and I was only twenty-five, busy climbing the ladder in the TV world and nowhere near settling down. I kind of saw it like I was giving her a clump of my hair. A no-brainer. It made me feel better about never wanting my own children, like I was putting all those healthy eggs to good use.' I add more honestly, 'And you know I would've given your mum everything I had.'

'Why didn't you want kids?'

'I think I saw my own parents' life and thought, that's not for me. Mum didn't enjoy being a mother much, and I was hyperaware of that growing up. I didn't want to feel that way, to resent my child, and I wanted more freedom, less convention, I guess.'

'Did Dad know?'

'About the egg donation?' I bite my lip. 'Yes, he was an inte-
gral part of it. He loved your mum so much, he would have done
anything for her, and they wanted to be a family. After I agreed,
it was all pretty plain sailing. A few weeks later, the three of us
jumped on a plane to the Czech Republic, and your mum and I
had the procedures done, which was uncomfortable but not the
worst. After that there was lots of nervous waiting, but within
two months she was pregnant.'

'With me?' Hayley rasps.

'Yes, with you, sweetheart.'

'But what about Mia?' she cries, remembering her little
sister's existence as though it might disprove my whole crazy
theory.

'She was conceived naturally, which was a massive shock.
We now know it happens all the time – women being told
they're infertile and then they conceive – but it knocked us sideways, I have to admit.'

'I bet Mum wished she'd never had me like that after she got
Mia,' she shoots back.

'No! Not at all. You and Mia were both miracle babies, for
different reasons.'

'But I've always been different, haven't I?'

I pause, perturbed by this. 'There's nothing wrong with
different.'

'Seems like I got the bad genes from you and Mia got the
good ones from Mum.'

Her words sting, and perhaps echo Charlotte's unconscious
thoughts. The short video of Charlotte losing her temper before
she died re-emerges as a reminder of why it isn't as simple as
good and bad. 'I'm sorry you feel that way.'

'Do Granny and Grampy know?'

I sigh. 'No, your mum didn't want them to know. She told
them the doctors had got the infertility diagnosis wrong, and
they didn't question it. I guess they didn't really think beyond

their joy at becoming grandparents. And it's plain just by looking at you that you're related to each other.'

'I think I look more like my dad.'

'You have his colouring, sure. But your eyes are... I mean, look at the shape of your eyes and face, they're like...' I reach out into the space between us, stopping short of touching her, letting my hand rest on the bench between us. 'They're just like mine.'

She jumps up, startling me, and glares down at me.

'NO! They're not! You're *nothing* like me! We'll *never* be alike. I *hate* you. I hate you. I hate you more than I've ever hated anyone in my whole life!'

And there I am loving her more than I have ever loved anyone. The bunch of cells I gave to my sister. The embryo I signed away. The child I never had, never wanted, never needed. Until now.

SIXTY-FIVE

Hayley's rejection of me is absolute. She refuses to talk to me or walk back to the bookshop with me. She's catatonic, glued to this lonesome spot on the bench in the dark. I call Olly in a state.

'She won't come home.'

'Why? I just don't understand. Why is she doing this to you?'

'I guess she hates me,' I say distantly, staring at her a few feet away.

'We're already in Oxford Street.'

'Oh. You left?'

'Mia was getting tired and we didn't know where you were. Sarah ordered us a cab.'

Sarah, Sarah, Sarah. 'Thank you. No worries. It'll be fine,' I say automatically.

As I take the phone away from my ear, I hear him asking me how we plan to get home. I hang up.

I know who to call.

While we wait, Hayley lays her head on my lap and sleeps.

. . .

An hour and a half later, Aunt Jane rescues us in an Uber and coaxes Hayley into the back seat with her. I ask the driver to ramp up the heating to warm us up. Aunt Jane asks how the launch went and I tell her about the evening as though nothing has happened since then. For the rest of the journey, we listen to ballads on Heart FM.

It is a relief to arrive at Charlotte's. But Hayley will not budge from her seat.

Ignoring my pleas, she turns to Aunt Jane. 'Can I stay with you tonight?'

Aunt Jane being Aunt Jane doesn't ask for an explanation and takes Hayley home with her.

I go in alone, and I'm shocked by that. Olly is still up. I'm soaked through. My teeth are chattering. I see the Mexican peppermill painted with the blue dancers. Fertility symbols, taunting me. A wry, silly emblem of our secret, for all to see but none to understand. I remember how we laughed together about it, co-conspirators, ever so clever.

I lunge at it and throw it across the room. It hits the wall, making a loud crack, but remains stubbornly intact.

Olly gapes at it and then at me. 'What the...?' he begins, before he sees that I'm crying.

He runs me a bath, sits on the loo to talk.

'What happened between you two?' he asks.

'Does anything need to have happened for there to be irrational behaviour from her?' I reply dishonestly, sitting forward to hug my knees, one cheek turned to rest on them.

'I guess not. But recently I really thought we were making progress.'

'Four steps forward, two steps back?'

'This is about ten steps back.'

I can't disagree, don't know what to say, have no energy to explain how our row started or how it ended. Bringing it up risks a confession from him, which would break me. I can't lose both of them in one night.

SIXTY-SIX

For a few days, then weeks, we pretend that life can go on like this.

The gap between my exterior and interior selves is like the gazillion miles between the earth's outer crust and its core of molten fire. Needless to say, my outer layer is fortified by a renewed sleeping pill prescription.

I live for Aunt Jane's insights. She comes over every few days to report on Hayley, who rarely leaves her room, refuses to go to school and won't eat anything but cereal, day and night. Apparently Ayton visits and brings weed, to which Aunt Jane turns a blind eye. Jamie drops round work sheets for her. 'Such a dedicated teacher,' Aunt Jane says admiringly.

Mia takes the bus to visit her after school and comes home with a similar story. Hayley hasn't told a soul about what I revealed to her, which doesn't make me feel any better. Part of me would welcome her coming clean, saving me from shaping my mouth into those impossible words again.

Meanwhile, Olly has been enjoying accolades from reviewers. *The Observer* describes his book as 'a masterstroke' – not quite a masterpiece, but close. The *Daily Mail* writes it up as 'a modern tale about a man and his feelings. Searingly honest. Not to be missed.' Foreign language rights are sold in six different territories. Waterstones make it their 'Book of the Month', catapulting it into the *Sunday Times* bestseller list, where it has remained for six weeks in a row.

A TikToker with over a million followers films herself reading it with a sparkling tear rolling down her cheek and text bubbles saying she's fallen in love with men again: '@ollytaylorauthor takes the toxic out of masculinity and gifts us an intoxicating read,' quote, unquote.

We have our fingers crossed for a summer number one on Amazon. When I say we, I mean Sarah.

In short, he's the hottest writer on the block. He has brought man back from the brink of extinction. I might add, at my expense, but that would be churlish. Apparently, despite changing my mind a few times before having the termination, I am a hero too. If only I'd known sooner.

I guess I should take my hat off to him for being brave enough to write a male character who risks losing the love of his life to save the planet, which is testament to Olly's skilled characterisation. Oh, the male character is called Jim, by the way. A name that sounds nothing like Olly.

Sometimes, when it goes to Olly's head, when he's acting as though he has saved the world already, I want to remind him that he'll need a few more people in India and China to jump on board first. But hey, I'm a fine one to talk. I burdened the planet by facilitating Hayley's conception. If the press got wind of his wife's stealthy procreation, Olly would be discontinued, cancelled, a social media pariah.

The vultures of social media are not his only enemies. I'm the one to watch. If I blabbed to him in a weak moment, he'd cancel me and our marriage.

Sarah has sadly not been cancelled. I suppose we have her to thank for believing in Olly and his book. Yes, I'm bitter. Bitter and twisted, that's me. Hard shells have downsides. But they are one hundred per cent necessary when times are this tough. My protective layer is as thick as the earth's crust.

Because. I'm. Fine. I'm so bloody fine I could conquer the world.

Then Aunt Jane suggests we have a little chat.

She brings over a bottle, pours three glasses of wine and makes a request, and an earthquake rips a zigzag of terror through my chest.

SIXTY-SEVEN

Aunt Jane still has the poised, intimidating aura of the head teacher, with her arms crossed over her stout chest and remnants of sternness even when she's smiling.

Her thickset liver-spotted arm jerks out to reach for her wine. Before she takes a sip, she ruffles her hand through her short hair and says, 'This isn't working, is it?'

I'm assuming she means that Hayley living with her isn't working. 'I understand,' I say. 'I guess I hoped she'd snap out of it sooner, but it doesn't seem like it's going to happen before Easter.'

The thought of Easter sends a shot of panic through me. It's my parents' favourite weekend. They like to parade their grand-children at church. Currently they think Hayley's temporary rebellion has been caused by a potent mix of grief and teenage hormones. We've underplayed it, made light of it. Dad respects Jane and trusts she's caring for his granddaughter well. But if Hayley refuses to visit over Easter, he and Mum will take it up with her, and Jane, being Jane, is likely to be upfront with them.

'Let me phrase that better,' she says. 'Do either of you actually want to be Mia and Hayley's guardians?'

The question is so offensive, I want to leap up and tell her to get the hell out of my house. Charlotte's house. I look to Olly, then wonder why I thought I would find outrage there. His expression is oozing with what can only be described as sheepishness.

'Yes, of course we do,' I say to make my position as clear as a bell. 'Do you think we would've gone through all this if we didn't?'

'Olly?' Jane's like a teacher mediating between two fighting students. A bully and a victim?

'It's been tough, I can't lie,' he admits.

I leap in. 'But we're getting through it. It was never going to be easy, was it? Parenting isn't.'

Jane ignores me, focuses on Olly. 'Olly, tell me why you want to take on the responsibility of being their nominated guardians.'

'You're asking me *why*?' He shakes his head, as though the 'why' has never occurred to him before. 'Because they need us?' The question in his response doesn't make a strong case.

'They need guardians, yes,' Jane says, 'but that doesn't have to be you two.'

'But they're my nieces and we love them, don't we?' I look at him pleadingly. *Lie*, Olly, *lie*. For me, please lie. You can have Sarah, you can have your brilliant career, you can have everything you want, just give me this one thing.

He nods. 'Obviously we love them.' Oh, I want to hug him!

'Loving someone can come in all sorts of different forms,' Jane says.

I pull out my trump card. 'Charlotte made it clear to me when she was alive that she'd want me to take them if anything happened to her.'

'I'm sorry to sound harsh here,' Jane says, 'but Charlotte isn't with us any more. We need to find the best solution for the girls. Not for Charlotte, who won't know either way.'

I can't hold back my outrage. 'Are you saying we're not the best solution for them?'

'I'm not saying that at all.'

'Then what are you saying?'

'I'm saying that kids are smart and pick up on everything, and if they sense that you don't really want them, that they're a burden to you, they'll react badly.'

'That's definitely not the problem here,' I scoff, taking a sip of wine, hoping it will knock the fear out of me.

'I think it is.'

Olly is sitting so still, I have an urge to pinch him.

'You don't know the whole story,' I say cautiously. 'Hayley and Charlotte had a very difficult relationship. Charlotte, for whatever reason, hid that from us. Hayley has violent tendencies and a capacity to lie that might stagger you. Honestly, what we're dealing with here is a very damaged child. I think you need to know that.'

There is a twitch in her cheek that confirms I have shocked her. 'In what way violent?'

'She lashes out when she's angry. Loses her temper. I've been injured by her. As was Charlotte.'

'What kind of injuries?'

'Bruises. Burns. Scratches.'

'Burns? How?'

'To be fair, that one was mostly an accident. She pushed me and I lost my footing and put my hand on the hob.'

She combs her fingers through her hair again. 'I see. I didn't know about any of this.'

I feel triumphant. 'That's what I mean. It's more complicated than Hayley makes out.' Imagine if Aunt Jane knew about the video.

She sighs. 'Yes, okay, that's good to know.'

'It's not your problem, though.'

She looks to me, then to Olly, and then back to me. 'I want it to be my problem.'

I laugh, trilling, 'Believe me, you don't!'

'I want to be their guardian. I want to foster them first with a view to adopting them long-term. Obviously we'll have to consult with David, but I—'

Gobsmacked, I stand up, unbalancing the chair behind me. 'No fucking way.'

Olly intervenes. 'Emily, please.' And then says sorry to Aunt Jane for me.

'I'm not sorry,' I say.

'Emily, think about it. I have the experience and the time. I've fostered teenagers in the past. You've never wanted kids and you're plainly not happy to have been landed with them. It's etched on both your faces. You think it's only short-term, that you'll be shot of them at eighteen, but then there's college and the years they move back in because they're saving for a mortgage, then they'll move out and move back in again with their own kids as they save for an even bigger mortgage. You have kids for life, not just for Christmas.'

'We do know that,' I say with steely politeness, thinking, *you patronising cow*.

'Before Charlotte passed away, you two had a good life. One that made sense to you. One you'd chosen. I read your book, Olly. It's really good, but it's also revealing.'

'With all due respect, Jane, it's fiction,' I say.

'My love, I've known you since you were two hours old. You were born with a stubborn little frown. Stubborn and kind, that's our Emily. But stubbornness isn't working for you here. For either of you. It's time to let go.'

I tighten my jaw. 'No, I'm not going to take this. I think you need to leave before we both say things we regret.'

'Sit down, Emily,' she barks at me.

And for some reason, I do.

'Listen,' she says, 'I didn't want to have to break it to you, thought that maybe you'd bite my hand off at this opportunity to unburden yourselves, but since you haven't' – and she sighs – 'I have to tell you that this is Hayley's wish.'

'What? No.' I shake my head. The chair is a little way away from the table. I've weakened my position but am too stunned to move.

'She asked me to take her.'

'Hayley actually asked you to be their guardian?'

'Yes.' She nods.

'Mia wants this too?' Olly asks.

'Hayley thinks she'll want them to stay together. Apparently Mia said to her that she misses you guys being their auntie and uncle, like it was before, when you were happy.' Her pause is measured, professional, giving us time to take it in. Olly and I share a look of astonishment.

'Mia always goes along with everything Hayley says,' I say.

'Obviously there is a lot to work out.' Aunt Jane nods. 'But separating them would be a mistake. We'll have to sit down as a family and talk it through. Including David, obviously, who'll have the final say. Though I honestly doubt he'll have any objection, given that he's washed his hands of them good and proper.'

'He might object,' I say. *I object*, I think.

She tsks. 'We'll cross that bridge when it comes to it. But once he okays it, I'm going to suggest we bring in someone from outside to help us through the transition.'

'To be honest, I can't get my head around what you're saying,' I say. 'I don't think this feels right.'

'It's what Hayley wants,' she concludes simply.

'No.' The tears cascade down my cheeks. My palms are flopped up in my lap. I shake my head. 'No, it's not. She doesn't know what she's saying. It can't be true.'

It seems that motherhood is more than the physical act of giving life. It is more than DNA sequences. It is about being good enough. And it's plain that I am not.

Because she doesn't want me.

SIXTY-EIGHT

The following day, Olly, Mia and I drive to Aunt Jane's.

'This is going to be hard going,' Olly whispers to me as we watch Mia being hugged by Aunt Jane on her doorstep.

I make a *hmm* noise that suggests I agree, because forming any kind of proper response is beyond me right now. He doesn't understand. None of them can comprehend what this is like for me.

Inside, we're led into the dining room. The mahogany table is cleared of administrative rubble at one end, where we sit. Next to me is a pile of maths exam papers that Aunt Jane is marking. The lace curtains in the high, small 1930s windows let in a subdued light. Aunt Jane serves tea in cups with saucers and loose tea leaves. Everything is done properly here.

I feel cold and clammy, panicky inside, and yet I am outwardly calm. In order for Hayley and Mia to communicate their true feelings, I will keep mine at bay. I do not harbour any hope of changing Hayley's mind; I simply want to allow her to speak freely and find her way through this without any guilt.

Last night, Olly admitted that he felt released from a huge burden, and that Aunt Jane was brave for calling us out. I didn't shout or scream at him. The shutdown inside me had taken place earlier. Aunt Jane's words, *It's what Hayley wants*, had closed the door on my own views and wishes, rendering them pointless and unimportant.

I'm transported to the abortion clinic five years ago, lying on the gurney like a zombie. For Olly, I scooped out my desires with an ice pick. It was a logical, practical decision made for everyone else, for the planet no less.

It's no different now. *It's what Hayley wants*. The four words that cut a thousand wounds into my heart are now deeply embedded as I sit opposite her at this formal table.

I am gripped by her face. Her eyes, deep-set and intense, in which my maternal genes are there for everyone to see and nobody to notice.

'She's got that determined look in her eye, just like her Auntie Em!' I remember Jane saying once. A natural observation under ordinary circumstances. Oblivious to its double meaning, she carried on slicing a loaf of bread for our lunch. Charlotte then overcompensated by going on about the traits she and Hayley shared as mother and daughter. I felt like an impostor, guilty for being Hayley's donor. The fact of me made Charlotte feel insecure.

Aunt Jane pours tea and starts talking.

'Mia, we wanted to know what you thought about the idea of coming to live here with Hayley for a bit.' There's a certainty to her voice that winds me up. I worry it presents as a decision already made and might inhibit Mia. 'We know you miss each other terribly at the moment. And if you both like being here, maybe it could be a permanent arrangement.'

She has made it sound easy and sensible. Perhaps there was a time in my life when I'd accept a solid practical solution like this. But all I care about now is hearing how everyone feels inside. Forget boundaries and parameters and sensible solutions. I want all the feels, right now. I want the mess of self-expression and authenticity, making connections, sharing contradictions, doubts and truths.

Whatever they want, I will grant it, even if that means giving them up, but I need to know where they're at first. Deep down.

'Um... Umm. I'm not sure.' Mia is trying to respond to Aunt Jane's suggestion.

The politeness is typical of her. I say gently, 'Mia, it's okay. It's really important you say how you feel. I can take it, I promise.'

'Yes, that's right,' Aunt Jane agrees.

Everything about Aunt Jane is pragmatic and sensible, everything about her speaks of responsibility and stability, professionalism and experience. But I can't fathom how she can love the girls even half as much as I do. Her emotions would never get that soppy and messy, that illogical.

I look at the two of them. Mia is easy to love. Hayley is different. She is the ultimate test of unconditional love. I know everything there is to know about her, all her flaws, all her darkness, all her secrets, and I realise that I still want her. *Actively* want her.

To describe the process of losing them as 'hard going', as Olly suggested, does not get close to it. It is not possible, even for an empath like my husband, to understand what it feels like for me. A part of me is literally dying inside as I watch in slow motion how Hayley and Mia are slipping away from me.

Aunt Jane cannot claim that. She'll never see the video of the night Charlotte died. Has yet to hear the truth about how Hayley was conceived, and has not been on the receiving end of her bad temper. I wonder if this is why Hayley is taking cover here, shut in a creaky spare room, numbing her feelings with cereal and Netflix and weed. She's hiding from herself. Looking at me is perhaps like staring into a mirror. She's scared to see the whole Hayley. But I'm looking at the whole Hayley and I love her with all my heart.

If I try to prise out her innermost feelings, or Mia's, I'll appear coercive, as though I'm putting words in their mouths that aren't perhaps even consciously there yet. So I remain silent, and try to listen.

'I don't know,' Mia says, wringing her hands, looking at her sister.

Hayley refuses to look anywhere but down at her feet, which intermittently kick at the dumbbell that acts as a doorstop. It clangs against the wood like a thudding on my brain.

'Go on, sweetheart, you can tell us,' Olly coaxes.

Mia speaks directly to him. 'Is this like it was with Dad and Beth? Because you can't cope with us?'

I cut in, remonstrate as passionately as I can. 'No, no! Absolutely not! It couldn't be less like that!'

Olly's muted 'It's not exactly like that' is lost in my enthusiasm.

'We're basically fighting over you!' I add for good measure.

Mia lets out a small 'That's silly,' with a twitch of a smile.

Aunt Jane clears her throat, frowns at me, and I realise how stupid it was to put it like that, leaving their loyalties torn.

'That wouldn't be my way of characterising it,' she says, correcting my mistake. 'We just want the best for you, which means looking at the bigger picture. It's about where you'd be most settled and happy in the long term.'

'With Auntie Emily and Uncle Olly!' Mia cries. 'I want to stay with you at home in my own bedroom!' Then adds formally, 'Sorry, Great-Aunt Jane. No offence.'

Finally Hayley speaks up, firmly and succinctly. 'And I'd rather slit my wrists than live with Emily.' Her dropping of 'Auntie' slices through me almost more than the gory suicide threat. She folds her arms over her chest. Her scowl fills the room.

'But *why?*' Mia asks.

'Because they don't want us?' Hayley retorts sarcastically.

I interject, 'But we *do* want you.'

She studiously avoids my eye and focuses on her little sister. 'No, she doesn't. She's lying, Mia. She's never wanted to be a mum, and Uncle Olly has never wanted to be a dad either. Just read his book, then you'll know.'

She read it? I shoot Olly a filthy look and have fantasies of incinerating every copy. I hope he can feel the silent burning of my hatred for him.

'But Auntie Emily is the best ever!' Mia cries, tears flowing now. 'She listens to all your shit and hardly ever shouts, unless you really deserve it, and even when she does shout, she always gives you a big hug afterwards and says sorry, even when you know you've been in the wrong. And don't tell me you don't love your long chats in bed. I hear you laughing together, and sometimes I'm jealous, because I know you're never grateful for it. You shout and scream and get all the attention, and now you're being so unbelievably stupid and ungrateful. So ungrateful and so mean. *So, so* mean for saying you don't want her to be our... our... *second* mum. I hate you for it. I'll hate you for ever for it!'

I'm knocked sideways. Dumbfounded. Second mum? Although she is talking about me, and they were possibly the most heart-rending words ever uttered, I hold my breath, don't interrupt, fearing it will break the intensity of their communication.

Hayley responds to her sister with quiet vitriol. 'Imagine what Mum would say if she was listening to you. She'd think you've moved on and found another mum, one you prefer, just like that, easy-peasy, like the years she was our mum don't count. It's like you've already forgotten about her, as though she never existed.'

I hold my breath in horror, try not to disturb the air, wonder if the two of them remember we're in the room.

'Mum's not listening to us, you idiot! And she never will again!' Mia yells. Then, through a sudden, violent sob, she cries out, 'And who cares if she does? You know what she was like! You and me are the only ones who know!'

There is alarm in the air. Aunt Jane steps in. 'What was she really like, Mia?'

Through heaving splutters, Mia continues wildly, 'She slapped and kicked Hayley so badly she'd bruise her. When she was drunk, she was scary, like she turned into a monster or something.'

'*Mia!*' Hayley shouts. 'Stop it!'

'No!' Mia remonstrates. 'Mum was horrible to Hayley when she was drunk. She snapped at the smallest thing, and her eyes would become weird and different and she'd go nuts throwing things around, yelling her head off. She'd hold Hayley down, like when she was trying to stop her going out or something, and she'd get bruises around her wrists...' She breaks off to look at me.

'The photos were of Hayley?' I croak. 'The Polaroids I found?' Like she could be referring to any others, but it's impossible to recalibrate everything I thought I knew.

Olly finally finds his voice. 'Why did you both lie to us about all this?' he rasps, and I guess he's also talking about the bigger lie caught on video.

'I'm sorry, Uncle Olly, I'm so sorry.' Mia looks at Hayley. 'But Mum doesn't deserve to be protected any more. She slapped Hayley so hard she lost her balance. That's how she hit her head. That's why she's dead!'

'*Stop it*,' Hayley growls, but she doesn't deny it.

Mia bites her lip. Her juddering breaths, sniffing and quiet weeping continue into the stunned silence.

Aunt Jane's cheeks are inflamed. 'Is that why you haven't told us the truth, Hayley? To protect your mother?'

Hayley doesn't answer. Her expression is one I recognise. There's something she can't keep inside, there's something coming, there's a tussle underneath her brow in those eyes we share. I know it. I know her. And I now speak to her as though we're alone, evoking the fraught intimacy that has grown between us, wanting to remind her that I'm on her side, no matter what. 'Why, Hayley?' I ask, feeling jittery and frightened, aware that by cracking her open, I risk her revealing everything we've been keeping close. 'Why didn't you feel you could tell us? We would've understood.'

And then it happens. Hayley shoots out of her chair and screeches right in my face. 'BECAUSE IT'S MY FAULT THAT MUM WAS LIKE THAT, THAT'S WHY! SHE DIED BECAUSE SHE HATED ME SO MUCH!'

I don't flinch, not scared of her any longer. 'How could it be your fault?' I breathe.

'Because I made her life a misery! Because deep down she hated me! She hated me so much and I felt it every day! But at least I know why now! Because I wasn't really hers! I was YOURS!' She hits the exam papers off the dining room table and flies out of the room.

SIXTY-NINE

Olly is packing a suitcase. I'm paralysed with shock and fear as I watch him gather his things to leave me. Silently I go over everything that was revealed at Aunt Jane's. Not only my own confession, but Mia's too. In the dining room, as I held her small hands in mine, she talked me through exactly what it had been like on the night Charlotte died, filling in the gaps, answering my questions with terror-stricken honesty. All the while, Olly and Aunt Jane were upstairs, trying to coax Hayley out of her room.

'You're leaving because I'm not as principled as you thought?' I ask him, clutching at ways to make him look worse than me.

'Don't make me sound like some bloody militant,' he retorts tightly. 'I'm not thinking about the planet right now. Or the book. And you damn well know it.' He glares at me for a second. 'You lied to me, that's the problem here.'

'I didn't lie.'

'You're right. It was worse than a lie.'

'It wasn't my secret to tell. It was Charlotte's. And I had Hayley to think about.'

'I'm not just anyone, though, am I? You should have trusted me.'

'Trusted you? Oh, right. Am I really able to trust you, Olly?'

He pushes his trainers into one corner of his case and doesn't respond.

'Olly?' I say again.

He looks up at me from under his thick blond eyebrows. His eyes are a weak blue beneath them. I suddenly want to take back the question and silently urge him to lie to me. He has never been able to lie to me.

'I never meant for anything to happen,' he says.

My knees almost buckle underneath me. There is a big difference between suspecting and knowing. Knowing is a heartache I'm not sure I can bear. I want to reach for my sleeping pills, just over there in the bedside drawer. How can I block this feeling? How can I move through this pain in my chest?

As I try to take it in, I hiss, 'But I told Hayley she was a liar when she said she saw you two together. I told her that she was impossible to love. I did that because I couldn't believe what she was telling me. Because I... because I trusted you.'

'Did you, though? Trust me?' he says, an echo of my question to him.

'Yes,' I say, gritting my teeth.

'When I was in Cornwall,' he fires back, '*nothing* was going on with Sarah. Bloody nothing. But you thought something was because she happened to come into the same pub as me. Then when I came home, everything was a struggle, and you were in a permanent mood, and every time I mentioned Sarah, you were suspicious. And then the night of the launch, when you were more focused on the girls and what they were saying or doing, I just thought, what the hell am I doing here? This is the most important night of my life and she's not even seeing me, not even engaged with how huge it is for me, more worried about whether Hayley kicks off. And there was Sarah. Putting me first. I want to be loved like that, I want someone to put me first.'

My heart feels cold. 'Do you love her?'

He sidesteps my question. 'Don't pretend you haven't been unhappy.'

'Would it be easier for you if I admitted I'd been unhappy?'

'I don't know, I just don't know what's in your head any more. And after this morning, I'm not even sure I've ever really known you at all.'

'You're questioning everything about me because of one thing I kept from you?'

'That one thing is Hayley.'

I try to picture Hayley and Mia in the spare room at Aunt Jane's, where we left them, imagining they'll feel ravaged by their outpourings and bereft of the shiny memory of their mum. Aunt Jane will no doubt have cajoled them downstairs at some point and papered over their distress with some wholesome distraction. Perhaps they'll be playing Uno or watching *Blue Planet*. I want to rampage through the image, scribble over it with angry red pen.

'I was Charlotte's donor, that's all,' I say.

'That's all?' Olly splutters with an incredulous 'Ha!' and then, 'But you weren't anonymous, Emily. You've been there watching her grow up, been part of her life every step of the way. Don't you see how that changes everything?'

'But it doesn't define me.'

'Motherhood defines every woman, whether they like it or not.'

His use of the word 'motherhood' leaves me clawing inside for a denial, unable to accept it, viewing it as both an overstatement and a reduction. The best I can do is 'And dull, sweet Sarah doesn't want kids, I presume?'

His jaw slackens and he looks at me pityingly. 'We're not even close to being at that stage,' he says. 'But either way, she can't have them. She had a hysterectomy when she was twenty-one after they found a tumour. I guess it's why she related to my book and wanted to publish it. She felt that her child-free life was being validated at last.'

I feel for Sarah, but I can't block what's coming, what Olly has triggered inside me. The fury is galloping up from the depths, and my voice is arch and nasty as I fire out the words. 'That figures. Now I get it. You're safe with Sarah, because you'll always be the most important person in her life. At least we've arrived at the truth finally. So let me get this straight. You wanted me to terminate my pregnancy because you were worried I'd love our baby more than you? It's less valiant than I thought, but hey, it's more human.'

He frowns. 'What? No.'

'Is that why you made me do it?'

'I didn't make you do anything.'

It provokes an eruption from the deepest parts of me. '*You made me abort our baby*,' I growl monstrously, electrified by fresh loathing. It must flash from my eyes.

He stops packing and says in a small, frightened rasp, 'You think I made you do it?'

'Don't act dumb.'

He recoils. 'Is that really how you see it?'

'It's how it was!'

'I don't know how many times I have to tell you, but Jim's thoughts in the book are not my own. For the story to go a certain way, I needed him to have extreme views. I swear it, Emily. You have to believe me.'

The doubt begins to rush at me, but I blunder on. 'I would have done anything to hold onto you.'

'But that's too much to put on me.'

A lump forms in my throat. 'You basically gave me an ulti-matum.' I can't let go of the story in my own head.

'No, that's not true. I didn't. That's not how it was for me. I would have had hundreds of babies if I'd known I'd lose you.' He sounds bemused. 'How can you even think...? No, you're rewriting history. You made the decision yourself. It was *your* body, your choice. We discussed it, I made it clear how I felt about it, but I would have accepted it if you'd chosen to have it. I never made you... No, that's not fair.'

His response takes the wind out of me. I am, for a second, frozen. His truth, which he communicates with sincerity and bewilderment, dispels anything I read in his book, and the sudden clarity becomes what I know to be my truth too. I wasn't coerced. I wasn't bullied. I wasn't forced to have an abortion. I made the decision myself.

The torment of the procedure comes back to me as though it were happening all over again. I wrap my arms around my stomach and bend double. 'But... but... when I was lying there...' I splutter, 'I didn't want them to do it... I didn't want it...' I heave, covering my face, shaking my head, as though I might shake away the horror, 'but I couldn't find my voice, I couldn't speak... I couldn't move... Oh God... I couldn't, I just... I just thought I had to do the right thing.'

Then Olly is there, holding me. 'I didn't know you were so torn. I swear I had no idea. I'm sorry. I'm so sorry. I thought when you went through with it that we were on the same page, honestly, that's what I thought. I'm sorry, Emily. I'm so sorry.'

With nobody to blame any longer, my anger is replaced by terrifying regret and sadness; emotions I put away on the day I walked out of the abortion clinic five years ago.

A racking sob shudders through me, almost like a current, and finally the barrier falls and the feelings flood out, and I mourn the baby I let go of that day.

But as I'm left empty and exhausted in Olly's arms, confronting the visceral pain of one loss, I'm filled with the prospect of another. Yet I know I will not let it happen a second time. This time I will not bow under pressure. This time I'm going to fight for my baby.

SEVENTY

Olly left for Sarah's place late. I wasn't sure if he was leaving me for good. No, I was unable to say with confidence that it was the end. It was why I let him go without a fight, perhaps didn't have the energy. Our argument had brought clarity too, swept out years of cobwebs inside me.

This morning, I'm equivalent to an emptied shed. Damp and cold and unloved, but ready for a fresh beginning, prepped for my new purpose. I don't know yet how that will look or whether Olly will ever join me in this new space, nor do I know how I'd feel about it if he did.

One thing is clear: he doesn't come first. I'm done holding his hand.

I want to hold Hayley's. And Mia's. I want to be their second mum.

The bunch of cells I provided the clinic with doesn't qualify me for that job. Neither does my auntie status. Neither does love on its own. Proving it is what counts.

Nevertheless, for all my fighting thoughts, I have no idea how I'll go about doing that, who I must become to be worthy of them. Do I need to give up work? Sell the house to fund it? Do I need to beg Olly to come back to me? Do I need to throw away all my weed? Stop worrying so much? Quit the sleeping pill habit? Become titanium in every single respect so that nobody can pick holes in me and question my ability to take the girls? What do I need to do to prove I'm good enough?

Probably all the above.

As I wander through the house, in and out of rooms, following in my big sister's footsteps, I clock how it has been left: exactly how she would have wanted it. Olly and I have made tweaks here and there – more books on the shelves and fewer black silk cushions – but before any changes, I've always sought permission from the spirit of Charlotte.

When I think about what went on in this house, what she did, I feel like ripping the place apart. Her path is not mine. She gave up that privileged position the moment she laid an angry hand on Hayley's young limbs. Every mark on that precious skin undermined Charlotte's rights as her mother. She struck not only at Hayley's body, but at her well-being and her self-esteem, her sense of self and her resilience. She struck at her soul. If she were here to atone, make amends, build bridges, I would be open to that. But she is not. That task is left to me.

I stand at the bathroom door.

What Mia told me about that night is a strobe of images on fast-forward through my mind.

Hayley discovering her form teacher on the landing, putting two and two together and going nuts.

Jamie backing off, running through the alley and into the night.

Charlotte singing too merrily, perhaps belligerently, in the shower.

Ayton showing off his street know-how by using his credit card to pick the lock.

A furious Hayley shouting right up in her mum's face.

A regretful Ayton popping up his hood, wanting no part in their rowing, hurrying out via the back garden gate.

Mia filming Hayley and Charlotte, zooming in on her mum in order to show her the next day what she's like in this state.

Charlotte slapping Hayley before losing her balance and slipping over onto her back.

The girls staring down at their mum's body at their feet, telling themselves she's passed out, knowing from bitter experience not to approach her in this state, fearing she'll come round and go for their ankles.

Mia shaking in terror as she locks the door with the screwdriver, erasing their presence at the scene.

Flash, flash, flash, imprinted on my retinas.

When I think back to Mia admitting that they'd known deep down that their mummy lay dead on the cold tiled floor, I shudder. How they'd both tossed and turned all night, huddled in Hayley's bed, tortured by nightmares, too petrified to look behind the door again.

Personally, though, knowing these facts from Mia amounts to nothing. I have no clue – as Hayley herself would say – about what to do about any of it now. The only other person with unprivileged access to the darkness at the heart of our family is Jamie, and I feel compelled to talk it through with him. He will be a listening ear at least.

A while later, Jamie is sitting quietly on the kitchen stool as I spill my guts. I begin by relaying exactly what happened at Aunt Jane's, and reveal the story of Hayley's beginnings.

When I've finished, he murmurs, 'My God, Emily. You've all been through so much.'

'It has been a lot. For them mostly.' I sigh deeply, wondering how we'll heal their wounds.

'It was an incredible thing you did for Charlotte.'

This comment stands out in my mind. It is the first acknowledgement of the act I took in my stride as a headstrong twenty-five-year-old woman with high ideals and no idea.

'For all the good it did her. Considering she spent the rest of her life resenting Hayley.'

'Weird, when you think about the lengths she went to to get pregnant in the first place.'

'I've been thinking about this very thing all night,' I say, which is true. Literally all night. 'I don't think she wanted a baby for the so-called normal reasons. I think I've always known it went deeper than that for her, that her motivations weren't totally healthy. Even when she asked me to be a donor, she was weird, almost frantic, so impatient and snappy. There was this life-and-death kind of feel to it, like she didn't think she'd survive it if we couldn't make it happen right this minute.'

'Sounds like she put pressure on you.'

'Not exactly. It was just so obvious how badly she wanted it, and she put forward a bloody good case, I guess. But when she did eventually get pregnant, she said the strangest thing: "This'll make up for it." I thought she was talking about the years she and David had been trying to conceive, but honestly, now that I think about it, she must've been talking about what the cousin did to her. I think she believed he'd taken away her fertility and that this was her way of proving to herself he hadn't ruined her life.'

'Hmm,' Jamie says thoughtfully. 'Ironically, Hayley was like a walking, talking trigger or something. It must've been why she couldn't handle her.'

'It makes sense. I wish I could talk to her about it now. So much of her behaviour was about the abuse she suffered and our parents' detachment from it. If we'd had the courage to unpick it when she was alive, maybe the outcome for the girls would have been different.'

'And would it have been different for you?'

'In what way?'

'I read between the lines of Olly's book.'

My cheeks flush. 'Ellie wasn't me. Or... okay, she *was* me. But she was what Olly *thought* was me. Does that make sense?'

'Not at all.'

I exhale. 'He wasn't the reason I had an abortion.'

'What was the reason?'

But I can't say it. My throat is plugged.

'You can tell me,' he says, as though he knows the answer already.

'I can't,' I whisper.

'It was because of Hayley somehow? You thought you'd be betraying her?'

'No, not that.' I stand up, walk to the window, and decide to come clean. 'It might sound silly to you.'

'I teach teenagers. Nothing fazes me, believe me.'

'You see, if I'd had the baby, the child would've had a half-sister. And I would have wanted them to know that. I could lie to the whole world about everything, but the thought of lying to my own child was somehow intolerable to me. Especially having watched Charlotte lie to Hayley. But if I'd been honest about it, it would've meant telling Hayley the truth. And I just couldn't break her heart like that.'

'So you broke your own.'

I shrug. We smile sadly and sit with it for a while. Eventually we move away from it to discuss the changes in his life, finding some light relief in his marital situation. He and Kristin are seeing a counsellor, they're reconnecting. He's happier now.

Soon enough, however, our conversation returns to the business at hand.

I lean forward. 'How do I get them back, Jamie?'

'That's definitely what you want? I mean, your aunt sounds like a good person.'

'She *is* a good person, and because she's a good person, she'll be an excellent caretaker. And I guess I've been the opposite of a good person since I've had them. I've been awful to Olly, I've been crap at work, my friends are probably wondering if I'm still alive, I hate living in that house, and I've become a seriously good liar – even to my own parents. It has been a mess. And it's hellish knowing I'm not the centre of my universe any more, that they're the centre of it... But it is also the most amazing journey I've ever been on. I don't want them because I think I can be the perfect carer – like Aunt Jane might be on paper. On paper, I'm all over the place: I smoke too much pot, need pills to sleep, work long hours, and I'm now probably going to be a single mum. And I shout all the time these days. But I want them because I know I can love them better than anyone else in the world can ever love them. And while Hayley hates me with every bone in her body right now, I can take that on the chin and still love her with my whole heart. And when hopefully she hates me that little bit less, I'll still be here like a mug. Basically, I know now that they can do anything, throw anything at me, and I'll be here like a fool waiting for them to be ready, taking the punches with open arms. That's what they need. They need *me*.'

He holds my gaze and says, 'Okay then. That's bloody awesome.'

'And another thing...' I click into my phone, hold it between us so that he can witness what I'm going to do. I swipe up. We're confronted by the frozen image of Charlotte at the start of the video. Jamie stares at her contorted face. Fresh dismay and horror are etched on his features.

'This is Hayley and Mia's trauma,' I say. The night plays out through my mind one last time. The police concluded – albeit with fewer facts – that it had been a tragic accident, and they were right. 'And I'm going to erase it for them.' My thumb presses delete on the video.

He nods. 'Primal,' he says.

'Primal,' I agree.

'You'd better go tell well-meaning, bossy Aunt Jane that she can't have them. Right?'

'Simple. Ha,' I reply, snorting, covering my excitement.

'Yes. Simple.'

I'm unable to stop the grin from spreading across my face. 'Can I really do that? Without asking the girls first?'

'It's for their sake that you're doing it.'

SEVENTY-ONE

I deliver my speech to Aunt Jane, burning with passion, fists clenched, stubborn as hell. I'm ready for a fight. Will take her down.

'... and I'm ready to fight you in the courts if that's what it takes,' I conclude, and wait for her to argue with me, take me by the arm and march me out of her house. I'm ready. Wow, I'm so ready.

But she does something unexpected. She smiles. A big, wholesome smile with twinkly eyes. 'Okay then. If you say so.'

'What?'

'No need for court, dear.'

'Are you serious? But you were saying... you said that... you—'

She interrupts. 'Spit it out. What exactly was I saying?'

In a small voice, I mutter, 'That Hayley didn't want me.'

'Ha!' she scoffs. 'I didn't believe that any more than you did!'

'Even so, I thought you were saying I wasn't good enough for them?' Even as I speak the words, I doubt my recollection.

'I never said that,' she confirms. 'That's what you decided to hear. What I said was that I wanted them to feel wanted. And I needed you to face up to the fact that you did want them. I needed you to fight for them. Because I know you are more than good enough.'

I'm flabbergasted, and stumble over my words. 'But... but what if I hadn't?'

'Then we would have had our answer. And I would have gallantly taken them under my very capable bingo wings. But I have a little inkling that you've been on a steep learning curve with them and understand that you can't control Hayley, that none of us can control anything in this life, and that sometimes kids have more to show us about ourselves than any book or expert can. That is, if you're willing to listen. And you definitely listened to Hayley. Whatever it is that you've been through together, or in your life – and reading between the lines of Olly's book, that'll be quite a lot we didn't know about...' I blush deeply, am about to explain, but she stops me. 'You don't need to say anything now. I just wish you'd felt you could talk to me at the time.' I nod, can't speak, can't see through the tears. She takes both my hands in hers and says, 'It's so bleeding obvious to me, my love, that you've learned that doing the right thing isn't always the right thing. Life's messier than that. Love is messier.'

She envelops me in her strong arms and pats my head, 'Your mum – and my dear useless brother – have never fully appreciated your qualities, Emily.'

As I fight back the tears, I hear the door creak open. Hayley is standing there. Mia is behind her. Both with blotchy skin and swollen eyes. Without hesitation, I unravel myself from Aunt Jane and gather them into what I hope in turn offers them the sense of security I found in my aunt's arms.

Hayley's shoulders silently judder in my embrace. I kiss her head, which she nestles deeper into my chest. I brush a hand over Mia's soft bristly hair. She looks up at me and says in that open way of hers, 'I'm glad you came back.'

'Me too,' I reply.

'Me three,' I hear mumbled into my sweater. The warmth of Hayley's breath meets my skin and spreads through my whole being.

I say firmly, 'I think it's time I took you both home, don't you?'

Hayley unfurls from me. Her pale hair is damp and sticks to one cheek. With a smile forming on her face, she says, 'Jeez. You're such a control freak.'

I laugh through my tears. Mia thumps her on the arm. And I say, 'Takes one to know one, missus.'

We hug as though we're standing together in the eye of the storm, where everything around us is mayhem but everything within is calm and still and safe.

And this is where I find motherhood. In the arms of two children who love me. In a world that will never make any sense. In a family of three.

EPILOGUE

EIGHT MONTHS LATER

The three of us carry four hot drinks. Hayley has two, and Mia and I hold the others.

'Is that him?' Mia asks, pointing over to the bench with her mittened hand.

I spot Olly's jacket. A splinter of regret spikes my heart. 'Yup, that's him.'

Our breath comes out in white puffs as we hurry eagerly into the park.

Flanked by the girls, I stand in front of the bench, grinning from ear to ear, not at Olly, but at Marty. He still wears the down parka that Olly gave him on Christmas Eve two years ago. 'Marty! You've had your hair cut!'

'Hello there.' His oily skin and watery eyes are the same, but there's a shined-up, clipped-beard, cared-for quality to him that I've never seen before.

'This is Hayley. And this is Mia,' I say proudly. They're wrapped up in colourful wool scarves. Their hair is tangled and damp from the frosty walk here. There's cheeriness in their smiles.

'Nice to meet you,' he says in his Eeyore-like tone.

Hayley hands him his coffee. 'Two sugars, extra hot,' she says.

'Put it down there for me, thank you.' He uses his elbow to gesture at his feet and keeps his hands around his belly, which looks distended under his coat. I'm scared about what a swollen stomach means, remember how cold it gets at night; experience a brief flashback of Olly's melodramatic shivering and his sullen mood after handing over the parka he knew we could afford to replace. A red flag I should have heeded, perhaps.

'Please do sit down.' Marty shuffles along the bench, allowing us space.

Last time I saw him was a month ago, on the day we got the keys to our new flat. I'd nipped out to get a coffee to fortify myself for unpacking – aka taking a break from the girls' bickering – and swung by his bench. But I didn't notice anything wrong with his stomach then.

'So how's it going, Marty? Everything okay?' I ask tentatively, bracing myself.

'Oh, you know, not too bad.' He offers up a beardy smile. 'Got to keep myself going for this little guy in here.' He unzips his jacket to reveal a scruffy black puppy curled up on his tummy.

I press my fingers to my mouth and gulp back a wave of relief. 'Oh look!'

'Oh my goodness! So cute!' the girls squeal.

The furball opens its sleepy eyes, raises its head, wriggles out of Marty's arms and bunny-hops onto Mia's lap.

'He's called Sonny,' Marty says. 'They found him in the dustbins with the rest of his litter. Owen, the park manager, said I could keep one. He knows how good I am with dogs. And since I've got my new place now, I thought, why not. But he's not just for Christmas, you know.'

I glance at Hayley and Mia and smile inside. *Hell yeah, I know.*

'You have a new place?' I ask.

'Just moved in.'

'Congrats,' I say. 'To new starts!' I tilt my cup at him, adding, 'Speaking of which...' I point in the direction of the school. 'These two have just started at Dartmouth Secondary. You can keep an eye on them for me at chucking-out time.'

He nods mysteriously and says to them, 'I hear gold coins line the walkways there.'

The girls laugh uneasily.

'You think I'm joking,' he says. 'When one fairy godmother was away, another one took over the job.' He pats the side of his nose conspiratorially. I pull my scarf up to hide my burning cheeks. It was him?

'Oh, I see,' Mia says politely, plainly not seeing at all.

Hayley has a faraway look. 'A fairy godmother. That's cool.' And I wonder if she recalls the night of the book launch, when she found the exact amount she needed to get her home. We've come a long way since then. The calm periods can stretch out for many weeks. Sometimes I forget how it was before.

'A fairy god*father*, perhaps?' I ask Marty wryly, arching an eyebrow, wondering what he went without to carry on the tradition.

With a twinkle in his eye, he shrugs. 'I couldn't say.' He winks at me as he scratches behind Sonny's ears. 'You never know what's around the corner, right?'

'No, you really, really don't, Marty.'

I drink in Mia and Hayley's beautiful, baffled faces and count my blessings. Reflexively I reach for my mobile to send Charlotte a photograph of them. It causes me a searing pain when I remember I can't. It happens a lot. I ache for a gossip with her about them and about the move to our lovely new flat, and about so many other things. Mum and Dad, for instance. My sister was the only one who listened to my whingeing and understood that our parents' disinterest in me and everything I do is renewable and toxic, like nuclear energy; and only Charlotte would rant as enthusiastically as I do about David, who FaceTimes his daughters sporadically, and threatens to visit but never does.

Charlotte is the something missing of my every day. She's irreplaceable.

Presently, before the three of us get up from the bench to say our farewells, I nudge Hayley and pass her the twenty-pound note. In turn, she elbows Mia, who takes the money and slips it into Marty's pocket like a pro. He's none the wiser, or so I always thought.

As we amble back home, chatting about plans for the Christmas holidays, I notice a fancy black saloon car slow down on the other side of the road. I inhale sharply. Olly stares at me through the driver's-side window. He has grown stubble. He wears a black rollneck. A blonde woman – Sarah, I think – is by his side. It has been eight months since he left me. The hurt comes rushing back. He'd been cold about it, severing ties cleanly, collecting his stuff from Charlotte's while I was at work. I was robbed of the satisfaction of kicking him to the kerb.

Through the grapevine, I heard he'd bagged a six-figure book deal with one of the big six publishers and was moving to Highgate with Sarah. I take my hat off to him. He has gone up in the world, achieved success by sticking to the masterplan, fusing himself to one lofty ambition, gently stepping on heads, mildly flicking off any irritants that got in his way. He's living proof that selfishness pays off. A round of applause for Olly. A more generous person would be happy for him. I'm definitely not there yet.

The car glides by. I smile, guessing he'll be glued to his rear-view mirror, assessing us, trying to gauge how much damage he caused. I link arms with the girls, smile, pull out all the stops to radiate peace and love. Then realise it takes very little effort. Much of it comes from within. Although I have found myself in a life I never intended, never dreamed of planning – in my right mind, anyway – I am happy. I sleep better at night.

Losing Charlotte was catastrophic, like a bomb going off. Her death left a crater of sorrow. Yet her mistakes and her passions have marked my life profoundly and for ever. She gave me Hayley and Mia. She's alive in them. They are her legacy. They are my everything.

And in my book – and this literally is my book – I'm the one who got the million-dollar deal.

A LETTER FROM CLARE

Dear reader,

Thank you for reading *After I'm Gone*. Every single one of my readers holds a special place in my heart. If you want to learn more about my books and hear up-to-date news of upcoming releases, please sign up below:

www.bookouture.com/clare-boyd

Writing this book in the first person and in the present tense was great fun and quite liberating. Out of all the main characters I've written, I wonder if Emily's voice is closest to my own?

More than anything, I love writing about parenthood. It's such an emotionally knotty job, and it comes in so many different forms. Emily learns that it isn't about being the perfect mother figure to Hayley and Mia; it's about loving them with everything she has. By confronting her own flawed behaviour, she's able to accept the girls for who they truly are, unconditionally, warts and all. The goal isn't perfection. The goal is love.

Lastly, I wanted to say that I'm a bit of a shy social media user, but I do use it to spread the word about the books that inspire me, and always post news about my own. So please do follow me if you like.

Again, thank you for reading.

Clare

KEEP IN TOUCH WITH CLARE

facebook.com/clare.boyd.14

x.com/ClareBoydClark

instagram.com/claresboyd

ACKNOWLEDGEMENTS

Thank you to Jayne Osborne, whose sensitivity and intelligence will continue to feed my writing long after this book is out.

Always my thanks go to the brilliant Broo Doherty at DHH and to Jessie Botterill, who'll be back in the Bookouture fold very soon.

Huge thanks to Flossie Clark, at the Children's Social Care Academy, who spared time to talk me through the ins and outs of a social worker's home visit and other protocols, and unwittingly lent insight into the incredible work she does in keeping our children safe.

I'm so grateful to Karen and Marcus Panchaud, who went above and beyond to help me, which is exactly what they do for all of us every single day at the NHS.

Thank you, Maria. Will I ever write a book without you? And many thanks go to Kirsty for her nuggets of information about school processes.

Last but not least, I want to thank Alistair Southby, a retired coroner's officer, who was kind and patient with me and unbelievably generous with his time. Another extraordinarily dedicated person to add to the list.

Any mistakes I've made are mine and mine alone.

PUBLISHING TEAM

Turning a manuscript into a book requires the efforts of many people. The publishing team at Bookouture would like to acknowledge everyone who contributed to this publication.

Audio
Alba Proko
Sinead O'Connor
Melissa Tran

Commercial
Lauren Morrissette
Jil Thielen
Imogen Allport

Contracts
Peta Nightingale

Cover design
The Brewster Project

Data and analysis
Mark Alder
Mohamed Bussuri

Made in the USA
Las Vegas, NV
12 August 2024

93740057R00215